"Full of passion, action, and memorable characters."
— Whatchamacallit Reviews

Undone

"Fast-paced . . . plenty of excitement. . . . A cliff-hanger ending will keep fans eager for the next installment."
— *Publishers Weekly*

"This is a good read, full of nail-biting action, some really creepy kids, and a final chilling revelation." — *Locus*

"A lot of action and a fast-paced plot. The cliff-hanger ending will make you want to find out what happens next."
— SFRevu

"Ms. Caine takes readers on a fabulous new journey and introduces us to a powerful new heroine who's been forced into a reality she's not equipped to handle. . . . *Undone* well exceeded my expectations, and I'm really looking forward to seeing where the series will go from here."
— Darque Reviews

"A fantastic start to another auto-buy series. Whether a newbie to the world of the Wardens and Djinn or a veteran of the series, *Undone* will capture and thrill you."
— The Book Smugglers

"Superb." — Genre Go Round Reviews

The Weather Warden Series

"You'll never watch the Weather Channel the same way again. . . . The forecast calls for . . . a fun read."
— #1 *New York Times* bestselling author Jim Butcher

"[As] swift, sassy, and sexy as Laurell K. Hamilton . . . Rachel Caine takes the Weather Wardens to places the Weather Channel never imagined!" — Mary Jo Putney

"A fast-paced thrill ride [that] brings new meaning to stormy weather." — *Locus*

"An appealing heroine with a wry sense of humor that enlivens even the darkest encounters." —SF Site

"Fans of Laurell K. Hamilton and the Dresden Files by Jim Butcher are going to love this fast-paced, action-packed romantic urban fantasy." —*Midwest Book Review*

"A kick-butt heroine who will appeal strongly to fans of Tanya Huff, Kelley Armstrong, and Charlaine Harris." —*Romantic Times*

"A neat, stylish, and very witty addition to the genre, all wrapped up in a narrative voice to die for. Hugely entertaining." —SF Crowsnest

"Chaos has never been so intriguing as when Rachel Caine shapes it into the setting of a story. Each book in this series has built-in intensity and fascination. Secondary characters blossom as Joanne meets them anew, and twists are revealed that will leave you gasping." —Huntress Book Reviews

"The Weather Warden series is fun reading . . . more engaging than most TV." —*Booklist*

"If for some absurd reason you haven't tucked into this series, now's a good time. Get cracking." —Purple Pens

"I dare you to put this book down." —*University City Review* (Philadelphia)

"Overall, the fast pace, intense emotion, cool magics, and a sense of hurtling momentum toward some planet-sized conclusion to the overarching story are keeping me a fan of the Weather Warden series. I continue to enjoy Joanne's girly-girl yet kick-ass nature." —Romantic SF & Fantasy Novels

Books by Rachel Caine

Weather Warden

Ill Wind
Heat Stroke
Chill Factor
Windfall
Firestorm
Thin Air
Gale Force
Cape Storm
Total Eclipse

Outcast Season

Undone
Unknown
Unseen
Unbroken

Revivalist

Working Stiff

The Morganville Vampires

Glass Houses
The Dead Girls' Dance
Midnight Alley
Feast of Fools
Lord of Misrule
Carpe Corpus
Fade Out
Kiss of Death
Ghost Town
Bite Club
Last Breath

ine

UNBROKEN

OUTCAST SEASON, BOOK FOUR

A ROC BOOK

ROC
Published by New American Library, a division of
Penguin Group (USA) Inc., 375 Hudson Street,
New York, New York 10014, USA
Penguin Group (Canada), 90 Eglinton Avenue East, Suite 700, Toronto,
Ontario M4P 2Y3, Canada (a division of Pearson Penguin Canada Inc.)
Penguin Books Ltd., 80 Strand, London WC2R 0RL, England
Penguin Ireland, 25 St. Stephen's Green, Dublin 2,
Ireland (a division of Penguin Books Ltd.)
Penguin Group (Australia), 250 Camberwell Road, Camberwell, Victoria 3124,
Australia (a division of Pearson Australia Group Pty. Ltd.)
Penguin Books India Pvt. Ltd., 11 Community Centre, Panchsheel Park,
New Delhi - 110 017, India
Penguin Group (NZ), 67 Apollo Drive, Rosedale, Auckland 0632,
New Zealand (a division of Pearson New Zealand Ltd.)
Penguin Books (South Africa) (Pty.) Ltd., 24 Sturdee Avenue,
Rosebank, Johannesburg 2196, South Africa

Penguin Books Ltd., Registered Offices:
80 Strand, London WC2R 0RL, England

First published by Roc, an imprint of New American Library,
a division of Penguin Group (USA) Inc.

First Printing, February 2012
10 9 8 7 6 5 4 3 2 1

To the amazing professionals who risk their lives every day to bring those devastated by angry nature to a safe place and helping hands . . .

To volunteers who sacrifice their time, their money, their energy, and their safety to pull survivors from the rubble, serve up food, hand out clothes, deliver comfort, and do a thousand other things that we take for granted in our normal lives . . .

To all those who donate to rescue organizations and give so constantly and generously to improve the lives of those stricken . . .

You are my heroes.

ACKNOWLEDGMENTS

The last book of the Outcast Season was an emotional and exhausting one, and I want to thank all of those who have loved and supported me during this amazing eight-year ride with the Weather Wardens. May your skies always be fair, my friends.

Special thanks to my husband, Cat, who bore all my hours locked in solitude with cheer, delivered caffeine at regular intervals, and never made me feel as if I was neglecting him, even when it was true. Love you, sweetie.

I also have to thank Claire, Griffin, and Nicola in New Zealand, and Felicity in Australia, all of whom made my journey down under so amazingly fun. THANK YOU!

WHAT HAS GONE BEFORE

MY NAME IS CASSIEL, and I was once a Djinn—a being as old as the Earth herself, rooted in her power. I cared little for the scurrying human creatures who busied themselves with their small lives.

Things have changed. Now I *am* a scurrying human creature. Thanks to a disagreement with Ashan, the leader of the True Djinn, I can sustain my life only through the charity of the Wardens—humans who control aspects of the powers that surround us, such as wind and fire. The Warden I'm partnered with, Luis Rocha, commands the powers of the living Earth.

I find myself caring too much about Luis, and his niece, Isabel, and others who never would have mattered before. The leader of the Old Djinn tells me that I must destroy humanity to save the Djinn, and all other life on Earth. I do not believe that. I cannot.

I have become too . . . human.

Before, that would have seemed like a curse.

Now I believe it may be a blessing.

But it will take all I have, all I have *ever* had, to stop what is to come, because the Earth has awoken, and in her madness she may kill us all.

Chapter 1

ON THE MORNING of the end of the world, I woke up curled beneath the cover of fallen leaves. It was extraordinarily quiet that morning, a hush like nothing I'd ever heard before . . . the calm that falls before the storm, but this storm, when it came, would never pass.

Not for us.

For most of a million years, the planet beneath me, the pulsing, living Earth herself, had been silent—not dead, but dormant, like a long-sleeping volcano. The past few years had seen warning signs . . . explosions of violence, as if she had been restless in her dreams. But just yesterday, something wondrous and terrible happened: She awoke in pain.

The quiet around me now was not peace. It was the indrawn breath before the scream.

I lay still for a few moments, savoring the silence. A bird's wings flapped somewhere in the distance, and condensation tapped on leaves as it slipped from tree branches overhead. The sun was rising, tinting the low-lying mist a soft orange.

I was cold, wet, and afraid, but I felt a precious moment of peace. I could almost believe it was the beginning of the world, the beginning of hope, the beginning of everything. . . .

Except that I knew, as we all did, that it was the end.

Next to me, buried in the leaves and sharing my warmth, Luis Rocha stirred, groaned, and opened his eyes. His heavy sigh said everything about how he felt about the dawning of the day, and no wonder—of the two of us, Luis had taken the most abuse in the battle of the night before. *"Chica,"* he said, "if you tell me there's no coffee, I'm going to die. I mean that. It's not a metaphor or anything."

I turned my head in his direction and smiled. It was not a nice smile. "There's no coffee," I said. "Nor is there likely to be any for some time."

"You are one cold bitch. It's a good thing I love you." He sounded miserable, but at least he was talking. Breathing. Living.

I brushed the mess of leaf litter away from my leather jacket and jeans, and stood up to stretch my arms high, toward heaven. My muscles were cold and tight and bruised, and I winced with the hot red twinges that the movements woke. My hair was damp and tangled. I looked, I thought, like some strange madwoman, like an ancient Greek maenad who'd spent the night running the hills with the beasts . . . only perhaps a great deal more frightening. I'd seen it in the stares of others, how odd I could seem—tall, pale, sharply angled, with the unnaturally green eyes of a Djinn.

Luis tried to sit up, failed, and flopped back onto the leaves. He closed his eyes, and his dark caramel skin seemed to pale almost to gold. "Okay, that was a freaking bad idea. A little help, Cassiel?"

I silently extended a hand, and when he took it,

hauled him up to his feet and held him there while he swayed. He was still favoring his leg—injured, inexpertly patched—and I was concerned about the continued pallor of his skin. His breathing came in short, pained gasps, then slowly evened out.

I was worried about him, but I didn't dare say it. Luis wouldn't thank me for it, and there was little help I could offer now. I could draw power out of the earth around us and speed the healing process, but drawing attention to myself today with the use of my gifts was dangerous. Wardens were going to die today, many of them. Too many, most likely.

I did not want us to be among those unfortunates.

"How's your leg?" I asked, knowing he'd lie. As he did.

"Fine," Luis said, and put his weight on it. I felt the wave of pain that cascaded through him in a hot red ripple, but apart from the tightening of his lips, he didn't show any sign of it on the outside. I was never sure whether he knew how much I felt through our link; my Earth power was channeled by and rooted through his, and it gave me access to emotions and physical sensations I knew he'd sometimes rather keep private. "Where's Ibby?"

Stupid of me not to have immediately thought of her, and I cursed my own lack of maternal instinct, of human connection. Ibby was a child, and she ought to have been foremost in my mind from the moment of waking. That she wasn't would be unforgivable to Luis.

I turned toward the spot where I'd left her safely tucked in a few feet away. "Isabel?" My breath steamed in the chill, quiet air. "Ibby?" I'd left her next to us last night, carefully concealed from the elements and wrapped in a thin silvery blanket to hold in her body heat. She had been safe, as safe as we could make her.

But now she wasn't answering.

Luis scrambled to the piled leaves and brushed them aside. He looked up at me. "Not here," he said. The tension and suppressed panic in his voice was unmistakable, even without any connection between us. "She's not *here*!"

I had hesitated to use power before, but I reached for it now, horrified by the thought that she might have slipped away in the night . . . or been taken. She'd been taken from us before, violently, and the thought it might have happened again while I slept only a few feet away . . .

I heard a rustle in the tree above us, and looked up to see Isabel a dizzying height up. She lay belly-down on a thick limb, and she looked delighted with the trauma she was causing—that smile was pure mischief, and her dark eyes were alight with amusement.

She was six years old, and climbing trees to make her loved ones suffer was likely perfectly normal. I wondered if my anger was equally natural. "Ibby!" I snapped. "Get down. Now!"

Luis was also staring up at her, and if I was angry, he was *furious*. He let loose a storm of Spanish, concluding with an emphatic gesture that clearly indicated she should waste no time making her way to the ground.

"Oh, chill out; she's fine," said another voice, and I heard a slight rustle in the branches—the only warning before a massive snake's coils slithered into sight about twenty feet above me. The coils twisted, and the human half of Esmeralda's body—the upper half—came into view. She was a pretty young woman, with a bitter cast to her smile, which was also more than a little cruel. "I brought her up here for safety. Don't worry, she stayed warmer than you did. I'm only *half* cold-blooded."

I tended to think of Esmeralda as a girl—a teenager—

but she was, in fact, a failed Warden, a dangerous psychopath, and an expert killer of Djinn. From the waist down, her body had twisted and smoothed into the scaled, powerful shape of a snake—a rattlesnake, grown to nightmare size. It was the punishment of the first Djinn she'd killed, that she live out her life in that monstrous form, locked and unable to shift from it.

It did not seem to me to have chastised her as much as it ought. And it greatly worried me that little Isabel had come to hero-worship the bitter soul within that warped body so much. Still, Esmeralda *did* seem to care for the girl. That was something.

"Bring her down," Luis said. He still sounded tense, but at least he'd switched back to a calmer voice, and his English. "Carefully."

"I'm fine, Tío," Isabel protested, but neither of us were in much of a mood to take her word for it. The two girls exchanged a silent, eye-rolling look that clearly said, *Adults—what idiots*, and then Esmeralda grabbed Isabel in a hug and expertly slithered her way down to the leaf-littered floor of the forest.

"See? She's fine," Esmeralda said, as Ibby's feet touched ground. Luis opened his arms to give her a hug, but Ibby stayed where she was and folded her arms. "You need to stop treating her like a little kid, man. She's not."

Isabel was, indeed, not a typical six-year-old. When I'd met her, only a short time ago, she'd been an innocent child, sunny and sweet, but then her parents had been killed, and she'd been abducted by a twisted, powerful evil who'd once been a Djinn. Isabel had been . . . altered. Powers had awakened inside her that were not meant for a small girl's form, and she had seen and done things that I didn't fully comprehend.

But she was still, physically, the same innocent little girl I'd loved from the moment I had met her, and it was a difficult adjustment for me to make. How much worse was it for Luis, who was not only human, but her uncle?

"They're never going to get it," Ibby said to Esmeralda, and flopped down in a dejected pile of sharp elbows and knees. Like all of us, she looked dirty and rumpled and tired. "I wish I was older."

"Well, you're not," Luis said, "and you need to do what we tell you, Ib. You know that. Don't be giving us grief now, not now. It's too dangerous."

"I know that," she shot back, and kicked leaves. "I know better than you."

She likely did, but it was difficult to hear, especially with the militant, pouting edge to the words. Luis shook his head and limped away, facing the woods; I joined him as he took some deep breaths. "I know we kind of need Snake Chick," he said, "but I *do not* like her. And I don't like how Ibby is around her."

"I can hear you!" Isabel yelled. Luis squeezed his eyes shut, then limped off into the woods. I hesitated, but Isabel seemed safe enough; Esmeralda had coiled herself into a pile nearby, and she was combing her fingers through her long dark hair, trying to pick out the leaf litter and cursing under her breath. It was possible that Esmeralda wouldn't defend *us*, but she wouldn't allow harm to Isabel.

I went after Luis.

I found him about twenty yards away, sitting against the bole of a tree with his legs stretched out straight; he was hugging himself against the chill and shivering a little. He seemed thoroughly miserable. "I wasn't kidding. I need coffee," he said. "Water?"

I had a canteen, and I offered it to him. He unstoppered it, closed his eyes, and concentrated for a moment. I felt a hot pulse of power, and then smoke began wisping from the mouth of the container. I touched it. Hot.

"One thing that's good about being an Earth and Fire Warden," Luis said, "I can change water into delicious moka java, and I can heat it up, too." He took a sip and passed it over. Black coffee, smooth and bracing. We drank in silence, watching the growing sunrise. "We've got to rethink what we're doing, you know. Isabel's a *kid*. I know she's got powers. I know she wants to fight—maybe *has* to fight. But we shouldn't intentionally put her in the thick of things. I want to take her someplace safe, Cass."

"Where would that be?" I asked. "I'm sorry, but the Earth herself is awake. There *is* no safe place; you know that. Anything built by man can be destroyed. She's safest with us."

"But we're going to be in the fight, and it's no place for a kid, dammit. What about the Wardens? They've got to be taking those children they were looking after someplace safer than—well, than wherever the hell we're heading. I want her with them."

It was Luis's choice, as her only living relative, but I couldn't help thinking it was a wrong one. Isabel had a possibly dangerous faith in her own abilities and she *did* have a great deal of power ... and leaving her with those unprepared to deal with her very strong will might be a recipe for disaster. Then again, he was correct about our situation. We were definitely going to enter into fighting that would be extremely dangerous, and having Isabel with us would cripple us, and put her even more at risk.

I had no answers for it, so I drank the coffee in silence. There was something primitively comforting in its bitter warmth.

Luis was pouring out the dregs and starting to talk about finding a water source when we both felt a sudden, shockingly deep wave of power cascade through the forest, the ground, the sky—through us. It was as if energy drained from every living thing for just an instant—a split second of death, followed by a terrific flood of adrenaline and panic. Luis blurted, "What the *hell* was that?" His eyes had gone wide, pupils narrowed to pinpoints, and I knew I looked just as startled and pale. I shook my head.

"Isabel," we both said, and I bolted upright, then hesitated as Luis struggled up as well. I was torn between a need to run to her and a need to ensure he was all right, but he waved me urgently on as he slung the canteen's strap around his neck.

I ran the twenty yards back to the girls in a blur and skidded to a stop in the clearing. Nothing was out of place. Esmeralda still sat coiled, though she'd gone quite still. And Isabel . . .

Ibby wasn't there.

No, she *was* there, but for a disorienting moment I couldn't process what I was seeing as she turned to face me. *That is not Isabel,* I thought, but it was. I could see the ghost of the child in the shape of her face, the fine dark eyes . . . but that child had been six years old, going on seven, and this girl was at least *twelve*. She'd grown more than a foot, and her body had developed and rounded with it; she looked strong and lovely, and *wrong*. So very wrong.

I stood there frozen for a long moment. I heard the crunch of leaves as Luis limped rapidly up behind me, and went still and quiet as well.

Then I turned on Esmeralda. "What have you done?" I said it in a whisper, but my voice was trembling with outrage. "What have you *done*?"

Esmeralda faced me squarely, with a haughty, imperious tilt to her chin. "You've been out there arguing about what to do with her," she said. "You couldn't deal with a six-year-old, right? Well, she's not six now. And she can take care of herself."

"How . . ." Luis shifted uneasily, unable to take his gaze away from his niece's suddenly altered face. "How did you do this?"

Esmeralda shrugged. "I can't do it now, but I did it to myself when I was younger," she said. "Part of what got me in trouble. But I told the kid how. It was her choice to actually do it—and she's got the skills. Look, she was bound to do it sooner or later. Better she age herself out of it now, so she won't be as vulnerable."

It was a cold assessment, one that I might have made myself once. There was an eminently logical component to it that I couldn't really deny.

But Luis looked as if he might throw up. "Ibby," he said. "Jesus, how could you?" He knew, as I did, that she couldn't reverse the process; a Djinn might be able to manipulate the structure of a body at will, but the changes a human Warden made in aging one were utterly beyond fixing. She had lost six years of her life, at least physically; the cost to her lifespan would be much, much greater, because the power it took to do this was toxic.

"I had to." Ibby gave him an apologetic look, but focused her reply to me. "I can't be a little kid anymore, Cassiel. And I can't have you guys worrying about me all the time. You need me to be strong, and I'm going to be. I have to be able to take care of myself." She seemed calm and more certain than I felt at this moment. "Esmeralda showed me how to do it, and it didn't hurt as much as you'd think."

I had nothing to say, because it was useless to debate the issue now. They had been careful to invoke such power out of my sight, out of my control; there could be no going back for Ibby now. She had lost her childhood, instantly; there would be consequences for such a flagrant use of power, things I could not yet imagine except that her life would be harsher and shorter. Aging a body so quickly ensured pain, accelerated aging, and deadly mutations. Isabel was no longer looking at a normal human lifespan; hers would be brief, like a candle lit with a blowtorch.

Not only that, the *risk*—using Earth powers at such violent rates, when the Earth herself was awake and aware ... that had been a hideously dangerous thing to do. It could have ended all of our lives, abruptly and very painfully.

And yet I couldn't find it in my heart to disagree with her choice, either. Today was the beginning of the end of mankind, unless a mighty miracle occurred. She'd lost her childhood, but perhaps all childhoods were over, everywhere, starting on this cool, silent morning.

But I mourned the sweet child Ibby had been. The girl who stood before me now, fragile in her newfound power, was not the same at all.

Esmeralda was still staring at me in defiance, dirty chin raised. At the end of her serpentine tail, a rattle hissed softly.

I broke the tension by turning back to Isabel, who stood tense and defensive. "We'll have to discuss this later; there's no time for it now. The power you used lit up the aetheric like a flare. We must move fast."

"Hang on," Luis said. His voice was soft and even, but very definitely dangerous. "I'm not even going to pretend to be okay with this. I am *not* okay. Ibby, what you did—you're an Earth Warden; you can't use power this way. It's perverted. It's dangerous. In different times you'd end up on an operating table getting your powers removed for gross misuse. Understand? Just because the Wardens are a little too panicked right now to enforce the rules doesn't mean there aren't any; it just means we have to try harder to stay on the right side of the line. And you crossed it."

She had gone steadily paler and more still as he talked,

but she didn't look away, and she didn't try to defend herself, either. She just looked at him for a moment in silence, and then said, "I'm sorry. I'm doing my best. But I was going to hold you back, and I couldn't do that. I just couldn't."

He sighed, swiped a hand over his forehead in a gesture of utter frustration, and then limped over and hugged her. Hard. She came almost up to his chin now. "Okay, here's the deal. You're going to feel sick, and you're going to hurt, a lot. Your bones are still forming. I'm going to see about finding you some calcium pills, vitamins, that kind of stuff; you're going to need it, a lot of it. You start feeling bad, you *say so*—none of this silent heroics crap. This shit is risky." He kissed the top of her head, and then looked up at Esmeralda, who was smirking at the two of them with an entirely inappropriate amount of satisfaction. Luis's eyes turned dark and dangerous. "*You* keep an eye on her, too. And don't think we aren't going to talk about this again, Es."

"That'll be fun," she said. "I'll bring cookies."

I cleared my throat. "You were scouting last night," I said. "Did you find out if the Warden party and the children made it safely out?" Last night, we'd narrowly escaped a trap meant to kill or capture dozens of gifted Warden children; we'd gotten separated from them, as Ibby and her friend Gillian had gone after those who had tried to kill us. I'd taken Gillian back to the others, but Isabel had refused to turn away, and it had been late enough that neither Luis nor I could force the issue. Luis had been too badly hurt to make the run back, and I couldn't leave him behind.

Hence, our uncomfortably chilly beds of leaves in the forest for the night.

Esmeralda seemed happy to change the subject, too. She said, "All of them from the school got picked up by a

Warden convoy. They're heading for Seattle, I think. Safe, as far as I know. We'll need them soon, though. All of them."

"Not yet," I said. "Let them be children for as long as they can." I was looking at Isabel as I said it, and she raised her chin with a jerk. It was bravado, not self-confidence, and I could see that she'd learned that, too, from Esmeralda. The idea of the two of them forming this instant and dangerous connection made me deeply uneasy, but there was nothing I could do to stop it; Esmeralda was an undoubted asset to us, and she had no reason to love those we'd be fighting. As allies went, she was more than acceptable.

Just not for Isabel.

"You're living in a fantasy, you know; you guys think these kids are some kind of innocents. They're not," Esmeralda replied calmly, staring directly into my eyes. "They never have been. They're Wardens, down to the core. You're trying to pretend they're all pure at heart. I know. I was one."

"You were a killer," I said bluntly. "A psychopath. And, I observe, you still are."

The girl smiled, but not all her teeth were human; she had a viper's fangs hidden inside her, and now she lazily showed them to me as her pupils contracted to shining, blind vertical slits. "Got that right, bitch. Want me to prove it?"

"Hey!" Isabel said sharply. She put herself between the two of us and glared—I was relieved to see that Esmeralda got the same level of outrage that I did. "Enough! We've got real enemies, don't we? The Lady out there, she wants to kill us, and so does Mother Earth, and probably the Djinn now. We've got plenty of trouble without this."

I, who had existed since before the human race had descended from trees, was being chastised by a child, and it rankled, because the child was right. Esmeralda was not my favorite choice of companion, or even a safe one, but she was Isabel's friend, and any allies at all would soon be welcome.

I bowed from the waist, spreading my hands to show I was releasing the moment. Esmeralda took an insultingly long moment to fold her fangs away, clear her eyes back to entirely human, and shrug. "Whatever," she said, and slithered off through the hissing forest debris. "I need breakfast."

"Do I even want to know what that means?" Luis asked, as he limped over to me. He'd held back, I realized, because he'd hoped that Esmeralda might overlook him as a threat if she and I came to a fight. Smart, but then, that was Luis; he was a great deal more capable than I sometimes gave him credit for. And capable of more subtlety than me.

Isabel snorted. "She doesn't run on granola, Uncle Luis." Already, it seems, she'd perfected the irritated teenage roll of the eyes. "Relax. She doesn't eat *people*."

"That you know of," Luis said. "*Mija*, that girl's dangerous. She's killed before, and she'll kill again. I don't think you understand what you're getting into with her."

"I'm not a baby," Isabel snapped back, and her dark eyes flashed with a hint of the power I knew she possessed. "Don't treat me like one. I know what she is, what she's done. She told me."

I doubted that what Esmeralda told her was the truth, either in its breadth or depth, but there was no point in arguing with the girl. She'd not be convinced now, not by the very adults to whom she wanted to prove herself.

Luis started to speak again, but I met his eyes and shook my head. Like a sensible man, he subsided, but the frown remained grooved on his forehead.

I kept watching him as Isabel busied herself with

other things, because Luis did not look well. There were dark circles beneath his eyes, and lines of pain tight around his mouth. I moved to him, and he put his arm around me. "Hell of a night," he said. His weight shifted just a bit, and settled more on me than his wounded leg. "You doing okay?"

"Fine," I said. "You're still in pain."

"It's good." It wasn't, and I gave him a long look in reply until he said, eyebrows raising, "Okay, well, maybe *good* isn't the right word. It'll be all right until it heals on its own."

"Let me be the judge of that," I said, and before he could protest, I crouched down and put my hand on his thigh, just at the level where the injury had occurred. He'd been very lucky not to have bled out; the tear in the artery had been grave indeed. I closed my eyes and invoked Oversight, an overlay to the real world that imbued it with the rich, shifting colors and images from the other layers of reality, the *real* worlds that were the natural home to the Djinn.

Luis, painted with those colors, seemed pallid and gray, and his leg pulsed with red and black energy. I could sense the sickness taking hold inside, the rot and ruin waiting to consume his feverish, dimming light.

No. I would not lose him now. Not after all this. I *could not.* It was no longer a selfish need, that of a Djinn depending on the skill and power of a human to provide her with energy for survival. . . . No, this was something else altogether, a burning and desperate need to have *him* alive. To preserve the beauty of what I knew was within him.

Our eyes locked, and Luis's lips curved a little in a tired smile. "You'd better get up before someone takes a picture and we're both porn stars," he said, but the smile faded after a second, and a look of alarm came into his face. "You're not going to—"

I didn't look away from his face as I opened the connection between us, and a golden wave of Earth power flowed from him into me, drowning me in deep, soft, rich energy. I couldn't stop the sigh that escaped; feeling that incredible sensation, so close to pain and pleasure, made me remember what it had been like to exist in that flow, that state of being. It was not so much that I missed it as when I touched it, I was a starving woman remembering the taste of food.

It was addictive, that power. And dangerous.

Especially now.

Luis tried to cut the connection as his eyes widened in surprise. "No, you can't. . . ." He knew how dangerous it was to use power now, and he also knew I had not done it lightly. "Cassiel, stop—"

I poured the power out again, through my fingertips, bathing his wound in a flood of healing energy.

It hurt. And it was glorious.

Luis collapsed against the tree trunk behind him and slid down, eyes closing as a moan escaped his suddenly pallid lips. I helped cushion some of the shock, but I couldn't stop the pain; the infection had crept deep into him overnight, unusually fast and deadly, and it took concentration to seek it and burn it out of him. That didn't stop the sensations that continued to squeeze him in their grip, though—complex waves of heat, cold, orgasm, agony. The tissues of his damaged artery knitted together in strong, rubbery layers over the thin patch that had held him through the night, and then the muscles and outer layers of skin bonded over it.

I didn't stop until he was healed.

As the last cells absorbed the healing energy, I let the connection whisper closed between us; I'd consumed much of Luis's reserves, and my own as well, but it had to be done. I couldn't bear to think of him suffering any longer.

Odd, how that had taken over from concern for myself—the only concern I'd had for so many millennia.

Now, in the wake of that urgency, I found myself swaying on my knees, falling, and caught in Luis's strong hands. It felt good. Safe. The pleasure I'd felt in channeling all that effusion of power was gone now, and in its place was an aching emptiness, a weariness that descended like nightfall and make me feel weak, lost, alone.

Luis gathered me against his chest, and I let my head fall against his chest. "Shhh," he whispered to me, and smoothed my leaf-littered hair. "Thank you, Cass. But you shouldn't have done that. You know you shouldn't have."

"No choice," I whispered back. I felt as bloodless and ill as he'd been before. "Infection. It would have killed you."

"I know." The calm with which he said it surprised me, and he smiled a little. "Death ain't no new thing for me, *chica*. It's kind of what we were born for, humans. Never expected to live long, as a Warden. Not expecting to survive these next few days, for damn sure. None of us should."

The words were sober, the tone kind. I felt a chill, listening to him; he had a calm conviction that was difficult to comprehend. We were not so given to the inevitable, we Djinn. We liked to *be* the inevitable, not its victims. Humans had a kind of courage I'd never truly understood: the courage to face their own doom.

I didn't know if Djinn had that same bravery; we'd never been called on to use it, if so. Suffering, we understood, but obliteration was something else again. We could neither fully comprehend it, nor accept it.

"We've had some differences lately," Luis continued. "Said things, done things . . . but, Cassiel, I want you to know that it doesn't matter now. None of that. All that matters is that I love you. Understand?"

He meant it. I could feel the warm, steady pressure of his stare, and the surge of emotion inside him. He did love me, with all the fragile power of his human soul.

I smiled slowly and said, "I understand." I did not tell him I loved him, but I did not need to do so; he could feel it, flowing between us like the golden-hot energy of the Earth. The Djinn love intensely, and rarely, and I was still shy of admitting what I felt aloud . . . but he knew.

He leaned forward and kissed me, a warm, damp brush of his lips that turned serious and deep as I leaned forward into it. It was not the time, or the place, for such things, but I felt frantic with the need to tell him, without words, how valuable his life was to me.

"Easy," Luis whispered, and put his warm hands on either side of my head. "Peace, Cass. This isn't the time for any good-byes."

I took in a deep breath and nodded. Here, in the calm before the storm that was to come, was the *only* time to say our good-byes, but I understood that once we did, once we let go of each other on some fundamental level, it would rob us of energy we might need to survive. As long as we fought for each other, for Isabel, we had a chance.

"Then we should be moving," I said, and got to my feet. I offered him a hand, but he rose easily, testing his leg and nodding approval. "No pain?"

"Eh, a little. Not enough to matter. Good job. So . . . where are we going, exactly?"

It was a dangerous tactic, but I decided to forego Oversight and rise up directly into the aetheric; it took a frightening lot of effort to do so. I'd spent most of my reserves of power in healing Luis, and detaching myself from physical form and drifting into the next realm seemed a huge accomplishment. I drifted there, recovering, and then propelled myself up, higher, deeper into the aetheric plane.

The forest in which we were physically located was unchanged . . . a deep well of living green, shot through with vertical splashes of brown and gold, an impressionist's view of trees and grass. Living things glittered and shimmered as they moved through the protection of the branches. I saw Luis's aetheric form there below, glowing in blues and whites. Next to him was my own physical form, but gone gray without my inhabiting spirit. Isabel was an opal-brilliant swirl of colors a few feet away, and there, streaking smoothly through the trees, was a poisonously green figure that could only be Esmeralda.

We were alone here.

I turned my gaze outward, over a confusing jumble of colors and shapes, ever changing, driven by human events as much as nature. Change is the fundamental principle of all living things, but humanity makes it an obsession, a religion. Today, however . . . Today it was dwarfed by the explosion of bloodred, bruise black energy cascading up from all sides. Mother Earth's rage and pain glittered in the heavens like cutting-hard rain. It turned in angles in the air, held high and ready to fall.

I felt cold and small, seeing that. When that storm fell, the world would end for mankind, in blood and slaughter.

I saw the roil of colors on the horizon that marked a Warden battling back the powers of the Mother—a useless victory in an entirely foregone war, but the Wardens, like all humans, simply never gave up. They couldn't. Djinn could, and did, withdraw to other realms. Humans had only this one. They were committed, until death.

And some were dying, right now, as I watched. I could see the vicious snaps of Djinn responses to the Wardens' attempts to control the fire that was blazing its way relentless toward a helpless population center. With the fuel of Mother Earth's anger behind it, the flames couldn't be contained by normal human firefighting methods; it would burn things that ought not to burn, and spread like oil on water.

The Wardens were few, and brave. And they were dying.

As I watched, more Fire Wardens joined in, though their powers were limited by distance. It would not be enough, and surely they all knew it. Any effective defense would be smashed by the shock troops of the Djinn, now fighting not for themselves and their own agenda, but in defense of, and at the command of, Mother Earth.

I had felt it before, that ecstatic possession, the loss of self and identity. It was, for the Djinn, euphoric and beautiful—for most of them, at any rate. Those with a fondness for the human race, of specific individuals ... those would be trapped in a miserable horror, forced to feel pleasure at their own actions against humanity, yet still retaining some core of self deep inside that fought. I thought of David, reluctant leader of the Djinn descended from humans, and shuddered. His ties to the human world were deep and constant. He loved a Warden, a woman whom he would inevitably face in a battle to the death now.

All stories eventually end in tragedy, but that was more tragic than most.

Luis's touch on my shoulder drew me back down, and I fell into my body with a snap of sudden sensation as nerves and muscles woke and complained of my absence. "How bad?" he asked quietly.

"A wildfire in the forest. The city's already lost,

though they'll fight to the last." My voice was soft, and a little sad. Some part of me, some Djinn part, craved that experience, the wild and furious power, the lack of responsibility for my own actions. Glorious destruction.

"What city?" Luis was already digging out his map from the pack he'd somehow managed to carry strapped on his shoulders during our mad run through the forest last night. The map was waterproofed in plastic, which was a lucky thing, as rain was starting to fall now from the gently gray sky in a soft, steady mist. Luis spread it out on a log and looked at me questioningly.

My knowledge of human geography was sketchy, at best, and I studied the flat lines and names uncertainly.

Isabel appeared at my shoulder and pointed decisively. "Portland," she said. When we both glanced her way, she shrugged. "Fire Warden," she said. "I can feel it." She frowned a little, at the dot on the page, and her fingertip touching it. "I've been sending them power, but I don't think it'll be enough. Do you?"

I silently shook my head.

"Any Earth Wardens working it? Weather?" Luis asked.

"Five Earth Wardens," I said. "And Lewis Orwell is working from a distance. I could see his aura from here." Lewis was the most powerful Warden alive today, but even he couldn't stop what was coming. Not by brute force. "He's managing the evacuation, such as may be possible. But there will be loss of life."

It was a still, quiet morning, and it was the beginning of the end of the human world.

The three of us stood in silence for a moment, considering that, and then Luis cleared his throat and said, "We need a plan, and I got nothing."

"I do," Ibby said. "You won't like it, but—"

"Hush," I said, but I didn't even know why, in that

moment, except that a feeling had crawled over my skin, an instinct as primitive as fear of the dark. *Predator,* something whispered to me. *Danger.*

The forest had gone quiet. Luis started to speak, but I held out my hand to silence him and listened, head down.

When the attack came, it came with the suddenness and ferocity of a bolt of lightning. There was no gradual gathering of power, no sense of a warning—only a sudden, shocking, overwhelming blast of fury, power, and hatred.

I had no time to prepare, but something in me, some vestige of Djinn, had gathered up such power as I still had, and flung it outward in defense. It wasn't much, and it didn't stop the Djinn that rushed at me, but it did slow her, just enough to allow me to grab Luis and Ibby and drag them down, straight down, into the living earth. I didn't have enough power left to sustain us, and unlike a Weather Warden, I couldn't draw air to us once we were buried in the smothering, softened ground.

But I didn't need to. Isabel and Luis, after a shocked second of adjustment, both added power to our flight through the ground, and the three of us swam around rocks, through the gnarled traps of tree roots, diving down and then up through the black gritty soil. I hardened the ground behind us as we rolled up into the open air, gasping and coughing, and sealed it behind us.

It wouldn't save us for long. The Djinn had senses we couldn't imagine, and powers we couldn't match. We needed help, powerful help.

"Ground yourselves!" I shouted, and grabbed both Luis's hand and Isabel's, as the two of them drew power out of the thick taproot of the world's energy. It should have come as a thick flow, like honey, but instead it was a geyser of power, blasting into Luis, into Isabel, channeling through me into a blinding, crippling burst. A shield burst out around us, a thick pearlescent shell that crackled and sizzled. . . .

And on the other side, I saw a form striding out of the mist, heading for us with relentless, steady speed. It was indistinct for a moment, and then took on shape and color. He was tall, lean, and with skin an unsettling indigo color, and silver eyes.

The Djinn Rashid had not developed an appreciation for human clothing since last I'd seen him, but his nakedness did not seem to me to make him vulnerable, or weak; instead, it made him seem eerily invincible.

As he was.

"Rashid!" I called, but even as I did, I knew it was useless. That was the shell of the Djinn I had known, but not the essence of him; his uniqueness had been displaced, overridden by the madness and need of our mutual mother.

He held out both hands toward us as he continued that steady advance, and an intense white-hot fire poured out of his hands toward us. It met the shell we'd thrown up, and the thin protection hissed, sizzled, went opaque beneath the incredible power of the onslaught. Around us, trees were burning, bursting as their sap boiled within. We'd be dead in seconds once the shield failed.

Inside the bubble, things were not good either . . . of the three of us, none had Weather talents, and the temperature and quality of the air trapped within rapidly degraded into a molten, sour mess. It would be a close race to see which would destroy us first: fire, seared lungs, or simple asphyxiation. But fighting Rashid, or any Djinn, was a desperate gamble now; he had infinite resources and few vulnerabilities. Attacking him was our only real option, but we'd be cruelly exposed for a few seconds, and it wouldn't take him that long to finish us.

I didn't count Rashid as a friend, exactly, but he'd been an ally, a strong (if sometimes treacherous) one. If I could reach that part of him, perhaps, just perhaps, there was a chance we might survive this.

I had to try. Dying inside our own shield had no glory at all.

I didn't tell Luis or Isabel what I was doing; there was no time for the inevitable debate. I took in a hot, searing breath, sent out a silent prayer to whatever power watched over wayward, fallen Djinn, and yanked my hands free of theirs to break the circuit.

The bubble around us shattered, and I put my hands flat on the backs of my lover and his niece and shoved them facedown into the leaf litter of the forest, then sprang up out of my crouch and straight for Rashid. I had no facility with fire, but one of the two Wardens I'd left behind me managed to counter his attack for a split second, just enough to put me close enough to grab him.

It was a suicidal tactic, but all I had left. I wouldn't allow him to kill those I loved in front of me, not as long as I had breath in me.

The silent, peaceful forest was now a vision of hell. I could feel the fury and pain of the Earth vibrating through the ground, pouring out of the burning, mutilated trees. The fire cast a ruddy glow over the mist, turning it bloody even as the heat burned it away, and in the unnatural flames Rashid's skin looked blue-black, his eyes as hot as molten metal.

I held his hands apart and out from his body, and fire poured from his fingertips to ignite the fallen leaves piled around us.

"Rashid!" I shouted, and pulled myself closer to him, body-close, feeling the feverish intensity of the Mother through his skin. "Rashid, *stop*! You must *stop*!" I was using physical contact, trying to waken his individuality, his memories, his conscience. I saw a flicker in those unnatural eyes, just a bare second, and I knew he was still there. Trapped, fighting, but there.

He couldn't win the battle any more than I could, though. We were still allies, but helpless to reach each other.

I was going to die. So would Luis and Isabel.

No. Not that. Not now, *now*, after all the fight and pain and blood. I would not allow that.

I pulled power from the Earth beneath me—not the sentient power of the Mother herself, but the silent, pulsing well of her blood, her energy, her life. I could reach it only through my connection to Luis, but he'd locked it fully open now, and although it was direly dangerous I consumed as much as I could pull, fast and painfully dragging it through Luis's fragile human form as he lay on the smoldering leaves.

I used myself as a lens and blasted it on through Rashid's body, sweeping away the influence of the Mother, just for a single fierce moment.

The fire stuttered and stopped its rush from his hands, leaving only floating cinders, and Rashid's eyes cleared, blinked, and focused directly on mine.

"I can't," he whispered. He sounded shaken, more vulnerable than I'd ever heard a Djinn to be. "I'm sorry, Cassiel. I can't do it. I'm going to kill you. All of you. And I don't want that."

I sensed a presence behind him, twisted and dark, slithering up in the confusion of burning vegetation. He didn't; he was focused on me, on the distraction I had inadvertently provided.

I held his gaze. "I'm sorry, too," I said, very sadly, and then looked over his shoulder. "Do it now."

Esmeralda rose up behind him, a terrifying specter of twisted nature. Her eyes were slits of gold and black, and her fangs had appeared, cruelly sharp and curved, jeweled with venom.

She struck so rapidly I never saw her move; suddenly her fangs were buried in the hollow of Rashid's neck, her reptilian eyes burning into mine from the distance of mere inches, and I saw her jaws work, forcing in the venom.

Rashid screamed and tried to turn, but I held him still. Those silver eyes rolled up, turned pure white, and I felt him grow limp in my grip, dragging me down with him. He collapsed into the burning leaves, and I rolled free.

Isabel climbed to her feet, extended her hands, and began extinguishing the flames. Fire is a living thing itself, growing and consuming, and like any creature it will fight for its existence; Isabel needed help, but I lingered where I was, looking down at Rashid. He lay silent and limp, eyes open and white.

There was a rustle in the leaves, and Esmeralda rose up next to me, swaying on her snakelike body. She wiped silvery blood from her pretty mouth, staring down at her victim with an avid hunter's gleam in her now-human eyes. "He tastes like the Mother," she said, and licked her lips. "Like life and death and power. I could get used to that."

"No," I said softly. "You couldn't. Is he dead?" He looked dead, and although I had reconciled myself to the idea that many, many worthy souls would perish today, it hurt like raw open wounds, seeing him so still and . . . *broken*.

Esmeralda shrugged, as if she couldn't care less. "Don't know," she said. "My venom has killed Djinn before, but he's pretty strong. Probably not. He'll just be out of the fight for a while." She slithered off to check Isabel and Luis.

I crouched down and put my hand on Rashid's forehead. Djinn didn't have pulses, not unless they were manifesting a completely human form; Rashid didn't bother with such minute details. But I could feel a tiny, whispering thread of power still inside him, like an echo. He was there—injured, frail, on the verge of falling into darkness, but *there*.

I bent closer, put my lips close to his pointed indigo blue ear, and whispered, "Don't come after us again, Rashid. I don't wish to kill you, but I will. You know I'm capable of doing that, even to you."

"Cass?" Luis's voice, from behind me. I sat back on my heels and looked over my shoulder at him. The flickering firelight was almost extinguished now, but the trees were still popping and smoldering, dropping cinders, not flaming leaves. Heavy gray smoke had replaced the earlier mist, and it rolled sullenly around our feet and hazed the air. "Cass, we've got to get the hell out of here. If there's one Djinn, she'll send others."

"Maybe not," Isabel said in a distracted tone as she focused on controlling the last still-burning tree that ringed us. "The battle with the Wardens outside of Portland is really fierce. I don't know if she'll care enough about us."

"Better we don't find that out, Iz. Let's get these out and move." Now, Luis linked hands with her, and together they snuffed out the flames.

Isabel looked at him oddly. *"Iz?"* she said. "You've never called me that before."

He stomped out a few remaining embers that were trying to take root in the half-burnt leaves. "I called you Ibby," he said. "But Ibby's gone. You're different. So now you're Iz."

She'd aged her body overnight, and matured in many ways over the past few months, but that was still the hurt of a child on her face, swiftly hidden. "Iz," she repeated, and forced a smile. "Okay, Tío. Iz it is."

"Iz it is," Esmeralda repeated, and laughed. She held out her hand, and Isabel slapped it. "Awesome. I like it better. Ibby was a baby's name. Now you're fierce."

She was. There was something sharp and angry in Isabel now, something forged out of hardship and pain. I didn't like it, but I was practical enough to know that we needed it now. All of us needed to be sharp, angry, and *strong.*

This world was no longer any place for a child.

I cast a last look at Rashid, lying almost-dead in the leaves, and nodded to Luis. "Let's go."

Chapter 2

OUR REAL ENEMY was not Mother Earth, but she was a formidable obstacle to overcome in finding our true fight; she was awake, though not fully *aware*. In the entire history of the Djinn, I could remember only a handful of times she had stirred in her long, ancient sleep, and those had been catastrophic events that had obliterated entire species, simply wiped them from the geologic record.

I'd never seen her so close to actual living *thought*. If she came fully to life, was able to direct the Djinn as a real army instead of an instinctive team of antibodies fighting infection, the battle would be short, devastating, and there wouldn't be even bones to mark the end of the human race, which seemed to be where she had focused her rage. Animals, plants, insects — those were collateral damage, as they so often were. But humans ... Humans were the target. Their homes would be gone, their illusions of safety shattered. There was nowhere to hide when nature herself hunted you.

By contrast, the enemy we sought — my former sister,

Pearl—had wrapped herself in layers of protection, hiding herself so thoroughly that it would be hard indeed to dig her out now. She *hoped* that most of humanity died; it would be easier for her to rule in the aftermath, I suspected.

"We need to join the Wardens," Luis said when we stopped for water and to consume a piece of energy bar that he'd split among us (except for Esmeralda, who smiled and told us she'd eaten her fill before; I think none of us wanted to know exactly what she'd consumed). "They're getting hammered out there. They need every possible pair of hands."

I wanted to argue that we should continue against Pearl, but my heart wasn't in it. There was no point in winning that fight, should the Wardens lose their own; one way or another, humanity would perish. "All right," I said. "For now we will join them. Where is the need greatest?"

"Hang on," Esmeralda said. "I didn't slither my ass all the way up from New Mexico to come fight on the side of the fucking *Wardens*. I thought we were going after the bitch who did things to Iz and the other kids."

"We will," I said. "But this is more pressing. You know what's at stake. Is your grudge more important?"

Esmeralda tossed her hair back over her shoulders, crossed her arms, and swayed on the thick, muscular column of her snake's body. "Pretty much, yeah," she said. "I don't forgive, and I don't forget. I thought you knew that, freak."

I smiled. It felt sinister on my lips. *"Freak,"* I repeated. "Interesting, coming from you."

"Hey!" Isabel said sharply, and put herself between us. "Es, I need you with me, and if Cassiel and Luis say we need to help the Wardens, then that's what we should do. Are you with me?"

Esmeralda didn't look away from me and my smile. "Sure," she said. "But I'm not with *them*. I'm never with *them*, and they don't get to give me any fucking orders."

"We'll see," I whispered. Her dark pupils began to contract into reptilian slits.

"Enough!" Isabel shouted, and pointed at me. "Cassiel, *stop it*. You, too, Es. This is the last thing we need!"

She was right in that, although I thought it wouldn't be long before Esmeralda and I chose to finish our dance. I nodded and stepped back. The mutant girl nodded, too, and showed just a *little* of her snaky fangs as she grinned, like a swordsman baring the first inch of blade.

Luis was staring at me with worried focus. "We going to have a problem?" he asked. "Because Iz is right—we don't need it right now. And she saved our lives. Rashid was going to roast us like marshmallows."

"I know," I said. "And I also know that she can't be trusted. Not completely." I didn't bother to keep my voice down.

"And you can?" Esmeralda took a swig from a water bottle and passed it on to Isabel, who drank as well. "Because I heard you were all about Djinn first, humans second."

"I used to be," I said. "Not so long ago. Yes. But I've changed."

I hoped I had, at any rate. At this moment, with my instincts and hackles raised against Esmeralda's perceived threat, I wasn't so certain . . . until Luis took my hand, and I glanced at him. The concern in his dark eyes warmed me and made the darkness slip away in shame. Yes, I'd changed. We'd all changed.

Even Esmeralda, because before she'd become friends with Isabel, she'd never have bothered to act to save a life except her own. Not that Esmeralda would ever acknowledge it.

Around us, the forest was coming alive again—birds calling, the soft whisper of animals moving through the underbrush. The oppressive sense of danger had passed, and below us the trees stretched down into a soft winter-brown valley still streaked with mist even now that the sun was high. It was chilly, but not cold, and the clear blue sky promised no chance of snow, which was good news for our progress.

"We need to get to the road," Luis said. "Commandeer some transport—the bigger and stronger, the better. We can't walk all the way to Portland."

"We need a van," Isabel put in. "Maybe a moving van, something Es can be comfortable in."

That made the snake girl look at her oddly, as if no one had ever really considered Esmeralda's comfort before. That might have actually been true, or at least since she'd changed into that form and been locked there by vengeful Djinn; she was dangerous, and quite possibly as sociopathic as I had been before being trapped in human form.

Yet Isabel managed to reach some hidden depth in her that wanted the emotional connection of friends. That was Ibby's gift, perhaps . . . and Iz's, now, even if this new, questionably improved girl was different in many ways.

When Isabel smiled at me, unguarded, it melted my heart and made me love her all over again, as she had been, and as she was. As she would be, in days when she was fully adult.

Should we survive so long.

"Yes," I said aloud. "A van. I'll see to it."

I had no interest in wider human affairs, but as I watched the road below for a suitable vehicle, Luis sat on a rock outcropping, ankles crossed before him, and played with his cell phone. "Weather looks pretty stable here," he announced, not that it meant anything much; human forecasters couldn't anticipate what was coming, now more than ever. "Giant gas main explosion in San Diego, took out the convention center, lots dead. Guess Comic-Con is off for next year. Tornado storm in the Midwest, at least ten F4 events, a couple they think were F5. Grass fires on the prairies. That's just the United States. There are tsunami warnings out in Asia, and earthquake damage on just about every fault line."

I couldn't imagine the chaos of Warden Headquarters, caught in the jaws of all these things....They were already fighting a desperate war against an enemy of their own, and now the Earth was turning herself against them....

"There," I said aloud, as a long, silvery truck edged around the curve below and onto the straight descent. "That will do."

Luis nodded. "You need me?"

"Not for this," I said, and stood up. "Stay with the girls."

"I *know* you didn't just mean that the way it sounded, *chica.*"

I flashed him a smile, raised an eyebrow, and stepped onto the steep slope of the hill on which we had paused. It would have been risky for anyone except an Earth Warden, or a crippled Djinn channeling such power; I broke off a large piece of rock and rode it in a rushing, hissing curve down the slope. It was a bit as I imagined surfing to be, only with more dust and bumps; still, when I kicked free of the rock and landed on my feet on the road, I was smiling with the adrenaline rush of it.

The truck was just coming up on me.

Locking a vehicle's brakes is easy, since almost all of the mechanical components of a truck fall within the control of Earth Wardens; this truck was just below the size of one needing air brakes, and I pressed abrasive pads to drums and brought it smoothly to a halt as the baffled driver pressed his gas pedal, which roared the engine and caused the truck to shake uselessly.

I opened the passenger side, climbed into the cab, and said, "Perhaps you should stop that."

He stared at me, openmouthed, and pressed the gas harder. I sighed, put the truck in park, and turned off the engine.

"Hey!" he said, voice shaking. "What the hell is this, lady? What are you—"

I reached into the vehicle's glove compartment—in which gloves were rarely found—and pulled out a rental agreement, maps, and, finally, a holstered handgun. I unholstered it and pointed it at him. "I'm taking the truck," I said. "I apologize. We'll try not to damage it, but I can't promise much."

"But I—you can't—!" He was babbling now, and quite pale beneath his straggly beard. He smelled of unwashed sweat, stale clothes, and fear. "I got stuff in the back!"

Stuff that was utterly unimportant, but he hadn't yet realized it. "We'll be careful with it. Now get out."

"Here?"

"There is a ranger outpost two miles in that direction." I pointed with my free hand, then used power to unlock his door and crack it open with the latch release. "Out. Now."

He blinked, but he must have seen in my face how very serious I'd become, because he didn't try to argue, or take the gun from my hand. He simply slid off the seat and ran.

Satisfactory.

I closed the door, strapped in, and started the truck as I heard the back door sliding up. The truck shifted a little with the addition of more weight in the cargo area. Esmeralda was on board, and I heard the flexible metal rattle down again.

Luis slipped into the passenger seat beside me, strapped in, and nodded. "Good to go," he said.

"Isabel?"

"In the back with Es." He shrugged. "Couldn't see any reason to insist."

He was right, of course, but it did sting a little that she preferred the musty interior of the cargo area to sitting in the front with us. I rolled down the windows to clear the stench of the former driver out as the truck started its roll down the long decline. I'd never driven something this large, but it wasn't difficult, other than adjusting to the increased mass and wind surface. I still missed my motorcycle, abandoned somewhere behind on the trail; there was so much freedom in that kind of travel, in being one with the machine, the free and open air.

I disliked enclosed cabins.

The icy blast of the winter air was bracing, or so I told myself; my breath steamed in the chill, and Luis was shivering. "Seriously?" he asked, staring at me steadily until I sighed and grudgingly rolled up the window to a compromise halfway position. Luis shook his head and looked behind the seats, which search yielded an ancient, untrustworthy-looking blanket that he settled around his shoulders with a sigh of satisfaction.

"You could make yourself warmer," I pointed out. "You *are* an Earth Warden."

"Try it sometime," he said. "Takes a lot of energy conversion, and we're supposed to be keeping it on the downlow right now, so I'll take the blanket. Besides, first rule of having Warden powers: Don't default to them without checking for a nonmagic solution first. Blankets work."

"I was a Djinn," I said. "Mundane solutions don't

come naturally to me." Like many things, the simplest possible things humans adjusted to from birth. The overwhelming power of their senses, for one. Someone in this truck had eaten far too much cabbage, and quite recently. I inched the window down just a touch more. Luis had a blanket, after all. "Luis . . . you understand that what we're doing will likely end in disaster. We're fighting the Djinn and the Mother herself. This can't end well for the Wardens, or for humanity."

"Well, if it goes bad, your Pearl problem is solved," Luis said. "Since we'll all be dead, she'll lose her power supply. End of game for her. She'll *want* to keep us alive."

"For now, but only until she finds the right moment to strike at the Mother. If she's able to do what she intends, she won't need us. She'll be able to tap directly into the lifeblood of the planet. Her consciousness would replace the Mother's."

"And that would be bad," Luis said in a bland tone that reeked of understatement. In essence, a mad, violently selfish Djinn would *become* the consciousness of the Earth—a vast, sentient creature carrying us all on her skin. One thing I knew about Pearl: She enjoyed the suffering of others.

Humanity wouldn't be cleanly destroyed, as the Mother so clearly intended; under Pearl's control, there would be horrible plagues, slow destruction, deaths that might make the worst sadists flinch.

I shifted gears as we reached a long, straight curve; dark green pines brushed the dull sky, and far overhead, a thin silver shard of a plane scratched the sky. That, too, would stop soon; airplanes were far too vulnerable to the Mother's anger. But then, so were all manmade things: Trains would be twisted off the tracks. Cars would be swallowed up by roads. Houses would be crushed. Cities would burn.

All starting . . . today.

"Cass," Luis said. "What are you thinking?"

I reached over and took his hand in mine. Warm, strong, *human.* Fragile and temporary as a breath, yet strong and resilient as a river.

There was hope. Always hope. And it was those like Luis who would be the bearers of that hope, and the victims of it; heroes they were, and heroes died so that others might live.

I took a deep breath and said, "I wish we had more time, Luis."

He misunderstood me. "Yeah, things are happening fast. Can't travel much faster, though. Not unless you intend on hijacking a plane, which I'm pretty sure would not be a good idea, either."

I'd meant something far different. Far more personal. When he touched me, my mind flashed to sensations . . . the stroke of his fingers along my eager flesh, the indrawn breaths, the taste of sweat on his skin. The quiet, hushed, beautiful moment at the top of the pleasure curve, when the universe expanded before me with the beauty of a Djinn's dreams.

I wished we had more time *together.* Not like this, not tired and dirty and exhausted, speeding to another confrontation. *Together.*

I started to speak, but then I caught the sad, gentle look in his eyes, and realized that he hadn't misunderstood me at all. The echo came through the link between us, soft and subtle, a sense of loss. Of letting go.

"Survival tactics," Luis said aloud. "It's what humans do. We either cling to things so desperately we can't let go, or we let go before we get hurt. It's not that I don't want . . . us. It's that we can't afford to put *us* ahead of *them,* Cass. We can't."

He was right, but it was because he was, in his deepest

heart and soul, a hero. I was not. I wanted to cling to him with all my strength and not allow anything to come between us, not even the fate of the world and humanity.

But instead, I smiled. "I know," I lied. I'd become very good at the lies, I realized. "We should focus on the mission at hand."

"No distractions," he said.

I nodded as if I truly believed it, and focused on driving. The less I thought about him, about me, about us, the better it was.

But God above, it hurt.

The weather worsened as we drove toward Seattle; rain at first, a slow mist that turned to drops, and then to curtains of near-freezing downpour. The tank had run low, and I pulled the truck in at last at a small roadside gas vendor. His lights cast a welcome red-and-white glow into the chilly sameness of the rain-washed road, and I pulled in and stopped at the fuel pump.

"Cash only," Luis read on the sign, and sighed. He dug out his wallet and handed it over. "Make it fast. Get us some food and water for the road, too. Extra blankets and pillows if they have them."

I nodded and slipped out into the rain. The shock of it was breathtaking, and I quickly uncapped the gas tank and inserted the pumping nozzle before dashing into the small store.

There was a dead man behind the counter, sitting on a stool like some ghoulish prop for a cheap horror movie. He had fallen back against the wall, but was delicately balanced so that he hadn't quite tipped off his seat and to the floor. The details of him surfaced in my mind slowly, from the shock: older, with graying hair; no obvious wounds, but there was a thick, dried crust of vomit streaking the front of his shirt and chin. His eyes had filmed over, but I could see the broken blood vessels underneath the glaze.

Dried blood had gathered at the corners of his eyelids, and cherry-black threads of it ran from his nose to his mouth.

I stopped where I was, and slowly, carefully extended my senses toward him on the aetheric. What I saw there, on that plane, was far worse than this—a rotted, horribly ripe *thing* throbbing with living sickness.

He was dead, but the infection inside him was alive, and violently hungry.

I slowly backed up, touching nothing. Little details began to surface, now that the initial shock had passed. Disordered shelves. An open cash register a few feet away, its drawers lolling empty.

I look at the scene through Oversight and found a confusion of colors, shapes, hints, and images. Others had been in the store before us, and at least some of them had taken items. But glowing brightly, *very* brightly, was the ghostly image of a Djinn, stretching out a hand and touching the proprietor's head with a fingertip.

I knew her, or the *her* she'd been before Mother Earth had awakened. Priya—like me, one of the original Djinn, formed out of fire and primal instincts. But Priya had always been kindly disposed toward humans, and this . . . this was none of her doing. Not of her own choice.

In that image burned upon the aetheric plane, Priya's face was cold and set, her eyes blazing with power. She had simply walked into this place, touched the man on the forehead, and left.

And he'd sickened and died, within minutes.

Luis saw me, wiped fog from the window of the truck cab, and frowned in concern. He rolled the window down and said, "What's wrong?"

"Look at me in Oversight," I said. "Check me for infection. Do it quickly."

He didn't waste time asking; I saw his eyes lose focus as he used another kind of vision to inspect me. It didn't take long.

He shook his head. "Nothing. What the hell?"

"The man inside is dead," I said. "Infected with . . . something. Something very nasty. We can't take the risk of touching anything in there. It must be burned, all of it." I felt shaken, I realized. No, more than that: I was *actually* shaking. My muscles were loose and trembling. "Others have been here. We have to find them. This will spread quickly."

Luis froze for a few seconds, then nodded. "We need the gas for the truck," he pointed out, ever practical. "There's a button inside, behind the counter. Somebody has to press it."

"No," I said. "No one goes inside."

I heard the door slide up at the back, and the sound of someone jumping down . . . then the whispering slither of Esmeralda's descent. Isabel looked around at me, then at the store. "What are you doing standing in the rain?"

I didn't feel like explaining again. "Can you trip the switch to get gas from here?"

"Yeah, but there should be someone in there who—"

"Just do it, Isabel!" My voice sounded unlike my usual self—to raw, too sharp, too shrill.

She gave me a dark look. "Tell me why."

Esmeralda slithered toward the door, and before I could tell her not to proceed, she recoiled—literally, pulling her snakelike body into tight, defensive coils. I heard a faint rattle. "Dead guy," she said. "Damn. He looks sick."

"He was," I said. "And is. Going in is not an option."

"Then what?"

"There is a switch under his hand. It must be flipped from *out here.*"

Isabel looked toward Esmeralda, who nodded decisively. "I wouldn't be eating no Ho Hos out of this place—that's for sure. Flip the switch and let's get the hell out before we're puking all over ourselves and bleeding from the eyeballs. *Vámanos.*"

Ibby was stronger by far in Fire Warden powers than her uncle; for her it was a mere shrug to trigger the connection that powered the pump. As I set it in action, the counters rolled on a price that would never be paid now. I filled the truck to the brim, then replaced the nozzle and climbed back inside to drive the vehicle off away from the building, slowly.

Esmeralda and Ibby stayed behind, and Luis watched them in the rearview mirror. It took only a moment for the fire to begin, consuming the little store. The two girls made it to the truck and slammed the door down just as the gas pumps blew in a spectacular orange-and-red mushroom of power. What was left of the station store collapsed in on itself, burning even more fiercely.

Ibby thumped on the wall behind my seat. "Go!" she yelled.

"First of many," Luis said quietly. "Don't know his name, but I've got to think he wouldn't want to infect anyone else. Best we can do for him now is purify him."

Purify. That was, I thought, a good word, a hopeful word. The dead man was purified.

I, on the other hand, felt sick and filthy within. There would be no honor today, no *purification* for those of us charged with defending life. I could feel that, as surely as I felt the cold wind pouring through the open window of the truck. "We need to find the others," I said. "And stop Priya."

"Priya?"

"Djinn." I rubbed my face with both hands, wishing I could rub all of this misery away as easily. "She was here, carrying a plague. It kills fast and lingers long. He won't be her only victim. We need to find those who came to this store before we did and try to heal them."

Luis looked as grim as I felt. "Even if you were a full Djinn, that'd be a hat trick," he said. "You said it kills fast. They wouldn't get far. What we need to do is find their bodies and burn them—but *you* need to go after Priya while we do that. Only way this works is if we split up. Me and the girls, you after the Djinn."

It made sense, and I took a deep breath and nodded. "I need transportation."

He gave me an unexpected grin, but there was little humor in it. "Yeah, well, I checked the nav system. Turns out there's a biker bar about two miles ahead. I'm pretty sure someone will be happy to give up their chopper for the cause."

A motorcycle. Freedom, and the wind in my face, and the exultance of the chase.

I smiled back, with just as much of the predator in my smile as I'd seen in his. "I'm sure," I agreed, and pressed the accelerator hard.

As I parked the truck at Busty's Roadhouse, I admired the selection of two-wheeled vehicles neatly lined up outside. Gleaming, well-maintained machines, with the addition of a few muddied, hard-ridden trail bikes. I immediately focused on a Victory; the sleek shape drew me to it like a magnet. This particular model was different from my cherished Vision; it was more aggressive, muscular, heavily chromed, and a steel-hard blue.

I loved it.

"Cass." Luis had gotten out of the truck, and was now

quietly standing beside me. When I looked up at him, he jerked his chin toward the roadhouse. "Too quiet in there for this many guys."

He was right. I'd been caught up in my fascination with the machine, but now as I looked in that direction, I realized that I heard music playing inside, but nothing else. No laughs, shouts, conversation. I turned and saw the grim set of Luis's face. We didn't need to speak about it. I nodded and led the way into the building.

They were all dead. All of them. The bodies lay everywhere, fallen and limp and silent; the jukebox still banged out a loud tune from the corner, but it was playing to an unhearing audience. I crouched next to the first one nearest the door—a barmaid, dressed in shorts and a tight red top, young and fit—and looked at her face.

"It's the same," I said. Her eyes had the same redness, and the smell of vomit was overwhelming in this abattoir, mixed with other rancid odors that made my stomach clench hard in reaction. "Look in Oversight."

I did it at the same time Luis did, and heard him murmur, *"Dios."* The room was a rolling boil of black and red, infection and disease and agony. The bodies crawled with it. I saw the stuff trying to jump from the bodies around me to my own, and edged backward. "Spread by contact, looks like," Luis said. "These boys must have grabbed stuff at the store back there and come straight here, just as they started dying. Anybody they touched got it, too."

"Then someone should have lived to make it to the motorcycles, or to a vehicle," I said. "Humans are masters of self-preservation. Someone must have tried to exercise it, and run."

"We don't know how long the symptoms take to set in. Could be seconds, could be minutes." Luis shook his head. "Got to be thirty people in here, Cass. And they haven't been dead long."

"I'm more concerned with any that might have gotten away. If they make it to a point where they can infect larger groups that disperse . . ." As fast-burning as this illness was, it would be devastating in the context of a town, or a city. Priya might already have appeared there, beautiful as a burning star, to deliver that deathly touch. She could have gone *anywhere*, far beyond my reach, far beyond the capacity of humans to fight her unless an Earth Warden was standing right in front of her.

This was what the Earth would become: fields of the dead, cities of silence, where lonely music played unheeded. It took my breath for a moment, and for the first time, I felt fear. Real, bone-deep *fear*. We were butterflies in an avalanche, and what could we do, really do, to stop it?

"Steady," Luis murmured. His hand gripped mine, strong and warm. "Bright side: This stuff isn't airborne, or we'd already be dead. It's contact only, which means it's containable. . . ."

"Not if she spreads it in a city," I said. "Or an airport. Or—"

I caught a flash of movement from the corner of my eye, and spun around . . . to find a pale, glowing hand outstretched toward me, a single finger pointing at my forehead. Behind the hand, the face of Priya, her Djinn-fired eyes burning into me with unseeing intensity.

I stumbled back, and Luis grabbed her forearm.

"No!" I screamed, but he ignored me. His whole focus was on Priya, who turned her gaze on him, as emotionless as a machine. She didn't attempt to break free of his hold, or move at all. I reached out for him, but Luis shook his head sharply.

"Don't," he said. "I'm already infected." He sounded so *calm.* So sure. "I can do this, Cass. Just stay back."

He couldn't. A human, even a Warden as powerful as Luis, couldn't defeat a Djinn one-on-one in that kind of single combat ... not when she was pouring infection into him, rotting him from within. He needed me, he needed someone to amplify and direct that power with fine control, like a laser. I could do that. I could help him hit her where she was most vulnerable.

But instinct told me to back away. Stupid, ingrained human instinct that demanded I preserve my life at all costs, even the cost of the ones I loved ...

I am not a human. I am a Djinn. Djinn!

I gasped in a breath and lunged forward, adding my grip to his where it wrapped around her arm. "Together," I said. "We're stronger together, Luis. Let me help you!"

He let out a strange, wild little laugh, and closed his eyes. Priya wasn't trying to pull away from us; she simply stood like a hot, burning statue, not quite flesh, not quite spirit. Exalted by her mission, and hardly noticing us at all, any more than a star might notice the ants crawling far below.

The sickness was already eating its way inside Luis, and the most difficult thing for Earth Wardens to do was to heal themselves; I channeled his energy out, and back in, burning the infection away, and then helping him drive back against the source. Priya was a teeming, seething incubator of the plague; she had been hollowed out, filled with this blackness, and set in motion. The Priya I had known was gone, as surely as those who'd inhabited the dead around us were no more. And that struck me hard, the grief of it; Priya had been an immortal, and she had been thrown away to become a vessel for destruction.

She had been my sister once.

I closed my eyes and threw myself into the fight, rising into the aetheric to more clearly see the struggle. Priya's body was no longer the beautiful, harmonious form it had been; it was distorted, rotted, cancerous with the poison she carried inside. Luis glowed bright as a star, tinted with a fire's edge of glittering orange from his rage and fear, and as I watched, his fire burned clean the portion of Priya's arm he held. I poured my own strength into him, careless of the cost, and guided his Earth Warden instincts into the pathways inside her body, carrying his purifying fire deeper. Each second was a bloody, costly struggle for supremacy between the infection trying to kill, and Luis—with my focus magnifying his power—trying to heal. Priya's body went a milky pale white where his healing touched it; the flesh was only a shell now, and as he destroyed what filled it, all that was left of her was the diamond-hard casing that was not quite living tissue.

And even so, even with spending so much power, so much strength, so much courage . . . we began to lose.

Priya did not fight us, because she didn't need to; the infection roared back, boiled up within Luis and began to choke off his strong, steady pulse of life—and through him, mine as well. Death was stronger than our temporary passions, and it was patient as the tide.

Just when I felt him struggling, though, and knew we were going to fail, another power joined us—strong, burning-hot, and wild and uncontrolled. It fell to me to channel and focus that power as well, and it was like trying to direct a raging river down a narrow pipe, when the power threatened to rip the pipe itself to shreds. *Isabel,* I realized, in the single second of awareness I had to spare. It was Isabel's power, raw and new and stunningly powerful, and added to Luis's, lensed through mine, it was more than Priya—or the infection that had overtaken the Djinn—could fight.

Even so, it took a long time. Longer than I thought any of us could endure. Luis chased the infection, burned it, boiled it down to a pure hard core in the very center of her ... and then focused a beam of power on it so bright that even in the aetheric it seared my vision. It resonated across the aetheric in a rippling wave ... and then Priya was empty. A glittering glass shell that began to crack and collapse under its own pressure into sharp, fragile edges.

I felt a strange burning in my eyes, and for a moment I thought it came from the violence of Luis's final assault that had broken the spine of the disease ... but then I realized that the ache was in my flesh, a heat that had nothing to do with the fight we'd been waging.

I was infected.

I was dying.

And as I watched, Priya's human-shaped form collapsed into fine, gray dust, and Luis staggered and went down in utter exhaustion.

I collapsed, too, sprawled in the open doorway. Weak winter sun hurt my eyes, and I couldn't seem to get my breath.

I can't die this way, I thought. *Others will sicken. Others will be infected from me. Ibby ...*

Even as I thought her name, I saw her face. She looked older, taller, a confusing and alien version that didn't match to the sweet, chubby girl I still held in my heart. The eyes were the same, though, a child's wide eyes, full of concern.

Her lips shaped my name, and she started to lean down toward me.

"No," I whispered. I felt hot now, feverish, burning up with it. Something twisted violently inside me. It would not be an easy death. "Don't."

But Isabel reached down and took my hand, and I couldn't stop her.

I felt the infection's surge through my body toward hers. "No," I said again, more strongly. *"No!"*

But it met an impenetrable wall where Isabel's flesh touched mine, and I felt the infection recoil, as if it were intelligent, alive, *afraid.*

And then Isabel reached into me and crushed it.

This was not the smooth, clean destruction that Luis had managed on Priya; this was, instead, a brutal display of absolute power, uncontrolled by anyone, even Isabel herself. She mashed the infection, ripped it apart, destroyed it in a child's vicious rage.

It hurt. I think I screamed, though I struggled to hold the agony inside; the infection died hard, but it died, and Isabel sank down on her knees next to me and smiled. It was a pure smile of triumph, but it was not sweet. Not the expression of a child, any child. "There," she said. "It's better now, right?"

I couldn't speak, but I nodded, or tried; my head jerked unevenly as the muscles seized in protest.

Together, the three of us had just *killed a Djinn.* And not any Djinn . . . one fueled with the direct, angry power of the Mother. I could understand what Luis had done, but *Isabel* . . . At her age, with her experience, she should never have been able to try it, much less succeed in saving me. Not from a disease that had never been seen before on this world, something clever and aware on its own.

Isabel was still smiling as she said quietly, "It was a weak one."

"What?" I concentrated on breathing in slow, steady rhythm as the waves of pain began to recede.

"The disease the Djinn was carrying. It wasn't as bad as it could have been. There'll be more. Worse. You know that."

I did, but I'd tried to avoid thinking of it. Priya had

appeared out here in the woods, not in the center of a populated city. *Why*? My only answer was that some last vestige of the old Priya still fought, however inadequately. She'd managed to avoid catastrophic loss of life.

But others might not have fought so hard. Even now, it could be happening.

As if she'd read my mind, Isabel said, "It's happening all over. There's one like her in Boston right now. Four more that I can see on the aetheric around the world— two in Europe, two in China. I don't think Crazy Bad Mommy Earth can make too many at once, though. She can't afford to; it destroys the Djinn, and she needs them for other things." Isabel sounded utterly certain of this, unnaturally so, as if she were a Djinn herself. She blinked, and some of that eerie gleam left her eyes as she extended her hand to me. "Come on. We need to get Uncle Luis and get out of here. They need us in Seattle."

I was hardly capable of helping anyone at the moment, and to my humiliation I *did* need her assistance in finding my feet. When we found Luis, he was groggily scrambling up, avoiding the area of dust that had once been a Djinn's physical manifestation. When he saw me, he lunged for me and wrapped his arms around me. "Damn," he whispered, and his warm breath caressed my neck and ear like an intimate touch. "What were you thinking, *chica*? Could have gotten yourself killed!"

"As could you," I said. "If I hadn't stepped in."

Isabel snorted. "Yeah, and I had to save both of your butts," she said, and then, oddly, giggled. "I don't think you ever let me get away with saying that. Butts!"

She broke into gales of laughter, in a room full of the dead, in the ashes of a destroyed Djinn, and a chill came over me. The sound was so like the old Ibby, the innocent child, but I couldn't shake off the feeling that there was nothing innocent about this now. She was a child, still, in the body of a teen, and a power almost equivalent to a Djinn—some of that had been her inheritance, a genetic code that would have made her an extremely powerful Warden in the fullness of time, but it had been wildly enhanced by Djinn intervention—by Pearl's *treatments* that Ibby had endured while her prisoner. It was such a dangerously volatile combination that I could not see, could not *imagine*, how it would not blow up in all our faces.

Luis still had his arm around me, and I felt his shudder through my skin.

Yes.

We had a lot to fear today.

Chapter 3

THE DEAD DID NOT need their vehicles, at least. Isabel took an unsettling amount of satisfaction in burning the roadhouse, and as the flames billowed high into the air, waving flags of black, acrid smoke, I checked out the Victory I'd coveted before. Over the past few weeks Luis had developed his latent power as a Fire Warden; as we were partners, linked at the aetheric level, it was simple enough to tap into his power, and a stroke of my fingers on the ignition fired it to rumbling life under me. The familiar throbbing purr of the engine made something tense in me relax, made me remember that mankind had survived on this powerful and dangerous earth for a long time ... and not only survived, but thrived. They had taken steps no other species had done—they had refined nature, rivaled it, harnessed it, and conquered it in small ways. The motorcycle I had mounted was an incredibly strong yet precise piece of engineering—as much of a miracle as the workings of a cell, or the vast and ceaseless wandering of the wind.

Humans simply couldn't see it.

"You don't need that," Luis said. He was leaning against the truck, watching me with his head cocked to the side. "You can ride with us."

I shook my head and revved the engine, just a little. "I prefer to be more . . . mobile. You can use a scout driving ahead, spotting for trouble." That, and I wanted my freedom. Being walled up in the cabin of a truck, *especially* if I was not driving—it was not how I cared to spend what would likely be my last day alive.

Luis smiled. "You never look as happy as when you're on one of those," he said, and then gave it another second's thought. "Okay, I can think of one other time you're happy, but the position is kind of similar."

That woke memories that merged pleasantly with the steady, low vibration of the motor between my legs, and I raised my eyebrows and challenged him with a stare. He gave me a small nod and climbed up into the cab. Isabel was sitting beside him now, with Esmeralda still coiled up in the cargo area.

I eased the Victory out behind the truck, then thought better of it and leaned into a wide arc as I accelerated, whipping smoothly past and out in front before the first broad, sloping turn of the road came about. The day was still bright, the wind cool and fresh, the air scented pleasantly with winter pine . . . but I could smell the smoke of the pyre left burning behind us, and I knew that the death we'd just witnessed was happening now, on a devastating scale, in places far distant from this.

The end of the world would not happen all at once, and that made it all the more appalling.

The weather turned on us within an hour; the clear, cold skies were covered fast by a rising curtain of bruise black, punched with brilliant stabs of lightning. I did not like the look of that, and even without a true Weather Warden sense to guide me, I could tell that it was full of anger, violence, and power. The first drops began falling in an ice-cold rush. I was without much to protect me, and was almost instantly chilled, first to shivering muscles and then to aching bones. My flyaway pale hair was plastered flat to my face, and I could not feel the fingers of my real, flesh hand where they gripped the throttles. Curiously, I *could* feel my other hand, the false one I'd fashioned with the last of my Djinn power to replace one corrupted by my sister's black powers. *If thy hand offend thee, cut it off.* Most humans treated that as a metaphoric saying from the Bible. I had taken it quite literally, and it should have crippled me.

Sometimes the odd metallic gleam of that arm and hand startled me, but just now, I was grateful for it; in a hostile world of cold, it felt . . . warm. Soothing, somehow, powered by a tiny spark of what I'd once been.

But the rest of me was suffering badly, and over the next hour I was so concentrated on staying on the bike that my vision had tunneled to an intense focus on the blurred road ahead. I failed to hear the horn honking behind me over the roar of the engine and the rain until Luis flashed his lights, illuminating the black, shadowed rain in glowing strobes. I forced my clenched fingers to respond, and slowed the bike as I pulled it over to the side. The truck eased in behind me, and Luis got out and ran to my side. He'd found a jacket in the truck, a thin blue windbreaker, which he tossed over my shoulders. "Let's get your bike in the truck!" he yelled. "You can't stay out in this!"

I felt immense, stupid relief at this; it hadn't occurred to me, in my focus, to give up and seek shelter. I almost fell in getting off the bike, and Luis had to catch and stabilize me. "You're ice cold," he said. "Go on, get in the cab. I'll get the bike loaded."

I stumbled to the truck and opened the door as he

jogged by with the rolling Victory to the back of the truck. I supposed that there was a ramp of some sort, but the mechanics of it fled my mind as soon as I crawled into the warm, dry cab and slammed the door. I was shuddering with cold, and the blast of warm air from the vents felt like a lost, tropical paradise. Only gradually did I become aware that Isabel was sitting next to me, her hand tucked in my metallic one.

"Do you want me to help?" she asked. "I can."

"No," I said through chattering teeth. "You've used enough power today. Rest. It isn't necessary."

She immediately pulled her hand free and crossed her arms. I recognized the line that formed between her brows, and the harder jut of her chin. She'd inherited that from her father, Manny, and for just a flash, I felt the loss of him all over again. He'd been my first partner, my first human friend. My ally. And I'd let him down. "Fine," Isabel said coldly. "Then freeze. I don't care."

She did, I knew that; it was a child's anger, a child's acting out, but it still stung deep. As she meant it to do. I said nothing, just closed my eyes and drank in the warm, hot-metal scented breeze that was slowly beginning to ease the chill. Isabel, not getting the reaction she'd wished, busied herself with twisting the radio dial. Bursts of static flared in time with lightning as it laddered overhead, but she finally landed on a relatively clear signal.

It was not good news.

The radio announcer was shaken; that was clear even through the grainy, static-hissed connection. "—Desperate situation right now as the area has been hit with both extremely violent, wind-whipped fires and a damaging earthquake that seismologists report measured at least an eight point five. Surrounding states are sending assistance, as is the federal government, but there is news pouring in of flooding and extreme tornado activity in other areas, and frankly, there's a limit to what rescue and volunteer efforts can accomplish at this point. The focus has turned to evacuations and saving those in the path of the destruction. In other news, in Boston, a spokesman for the CDC has confirmed the outbreak of a dangerous new virus, and the city government has called for an immediate, citywide quarantine. While there has been speculation that this illness, which has claimed an unknown number of victims over the past twenty-four hours, was some type of bioterrorism, the spokesman stressed that they are conducting a thorough and speedy investigation to determine the point of origin of the virus."

Isabel said nothing. She just turned the radio off as Luis opened the door and threw himself into the driver's seat. He was soaked as well, despite his jacket and the oily trucker's hat he'd thrown on, but he still flashed me a concerned look. "You okay?" he asked.

"She's fine," Isabel answered before I could speak. "There are lots of fires and earthquakes. What do you want me to do?"

"Nothing," he said. "Rest. You're going to need your strength, Iz."

"I'm not tired!"

"Yes, you are; you just don't know it. You can't burn through power like that and not have consequences—not even you. Just relax and let yourself heal inside."

"But—"

"Iz. I said *no.*"

She slumped down in the seat, glaring at nothing, and Luis exchanged a look with me over her head as he started the truck again. He didn't need to speak; I could understand his thoughts well enough.

It was going to be difficult with her from here on out. Luis sighed and said, "We're going to need beer."

*   *   *

Esmeralda had been quiet—dangerously so—in the back of the truck, but as we drew nearer to Seattle, I heard her rustling and banging in the back. Finally, there was a sharp, annoyed rapping against the wall behind our seats, and Luis pulled the truck in at a closed, but covered, gas station. "Need a fill-up anyway," he said. "Thank God for credit cards at pumps. You check on Reptile Girl back there, Iz."

She had been steaming and glowering the entire drive, and now she gave him a frosty stare. "Say please," she said.

"I thought you wanted to be treated like an adult, not a little kid," he shot back. "Get your ass out and check on Esmeralda. Please."

It clearly didn't improve her mood, but she wiggled across the seat and darted toward the back. The rain was still pounding down, and the sound it made on the tin shield above us was a continuous, metallic din. Still, we were dry, and I couldn't really say I was displeased with the trade. I stood outside with Luis, enjoying the smell of the rain, as he filled the gas tank. Isabel reappeared and said crankily, "She had to pee. So do I."

"Open the store and go to the bathroom."

Isabel rolled her eyes. "She's a *snake*, Tío; she doesn't use a toilet. She's out there in the rain. She's pretty angry about it, too."

"Just go do your business and get back here," Luis said. "Lock it back up when you're done, okay?"

She didn't answer. I had to smile at the thought that Luis had felt a need to lock a store during what would be, most likely, a time of chaos; Earth Wardens did tend to be more responsible with their powers than others. Most Fire Wardens would have melted the lock in their quest to get relief, and I didn't like to think what a Weather Warden might have done.

Isabel vanished inside the store.

"How about you?" Luis asked me. "Need to go?" When I shook my head, he said, "Okay, then watch the pump. I'm hitting the head."

He moved in that direction. I concentrated on the boring task of watching the numbers spin meaninglessly on the pump; Luis had—probably uselessly—given his credit card for the payment, but economies across the world would stumble today, shatter tomorrow. Soon, it wouldn't be how many imaginary dollars, or pounds, or yen, were in an imaginary account. . . . It would be about survival, and survival required tools. Things to barter, things to use. I began making a list of what would be good to acquire.

The pump stopped with a thud and click, and I replaced the nozzle where it was meant to go . . . and then realized how alone I was. Esmeralda was still missing, somewhere out in the rain; Luis and Isabel were in the store itself. It was just me, and the constant, punishing rain.

But there was someone watching me.

I stayed very still, facing out toward the downpour-obscured road. I saw nothing, but I sensed . . . something. A presence. The damp hair on the back of my neck prickled, and I felt the need to back up, but I stood my ground.

There was a sigh of wind, and the curtain of rain parted in a clear, square corridor. Water sluiced off the invisible top and down the sides. It was a precise, dangerously controlled use of power, and at the other end of the opening stood a child. Small, delicate; girl or boy, I couldn't tell, and it didn't matter greatly at that age.

"Sister," the child said, and that voice echoed out, too large and powerful for that frail form. "I need to speak with you."

I didn't know the child herself, but she was only a vessel. The power that loomed larger around her was familiar, and dangerous indeed. Pearl had come to see me—not in the flesh, but occupying it, piloting it from afar.

The open, rain-free corridor was an invitation, an obvious one that lured me toward the child. It was stupid of me to consider going toward the danger, but I was in a blackly strange place, and danger was all around me now.

So I went.

The sound of the rain drumming against the child's shield was punishingly loud, until I stopped a few feet away. Then, the roar cut off cleanly, leaving a silence so charged with tension that I could feel the hair on my arms stir and shiver.

The child had dark eyes, short-cropped silky hair, and a secretive little smile too old for her years. I thought of Ibby, of the destruction of her childhood, and forced the anger away. "Sister," I said. "Too weak to form your own flesh now?"

"Too careful," she said, in that lazily amused tone. "What a judgmental thing you've become, Cassiel. Humanity has corrupted you quite to the core. Did you like your taste of the Mother's love? She'd have killed you, you know. Supped on your blood and gnawed the power from your broken bones. She's a cannibal. And all your human friends will be food for her feast."

"Hers or yours," I said, and shrugged. "Death is death, Pearl. You offer nothing better."

"I offer a stay of execution. A partnership to keep humanity alive. You need me, sister. You know that you do."

"For what? You're only seeking to save your own existence. If the Mother destroys the human race, you go with it; you've hidden yourself very well, I have to admit, and you did what all the Djinn thought impossible—you hid yourself away and drew power from humans, growing in power as they did. I'd applaud, but I doubt you can successfully root yourself so well in the power of the cockroaches who survive after them, although that would certainly be apt."

The child's eyes sparked with a sudden red glow, and power crackled around me in blue-white zaps along the edges of the corridor. "Softly," she said. "I may not love you so much as all that, Cassiel."

We fought like humans, I realized then . . . like siblings. Bitter and acrimonious, too sensitive to each other's moods and vulnerabilities. The most violent hatreds came from families.

I took a step back and forced myself to stay silent. The glow faded slowly, and the crackling power hissed and fell silent, although a burnt-ozone smell filled the space around me.

"I came in peace," Pearl said. "I came to save you."

"We don't need you," I told her. I said it firmly, but without anger, and I even gave her a small nod of respect. "If you wish to fight, do so. But the Wardens fight alone, as they always have."

"You speak for them."

"They'd say the same."

The child's smile was, this time, truly unsettling. "You think so? Really? We'll see, my sister. But the truth is, I don't need you. You are an annoyance with which I no longer wish to contend. I gave you a chance. Now I hope you enjoy the consequences. Good-bye, my sister. Say hello to our mother."

I had a second's warning this time, purely because Pearl couldn't help but gloat; it was just enough time to drop to one knee on the muddy ground and punch

power down into the water-drenched soil. I had no dominion over the water, but the soil responded to me,
sluggish but powerful. It rose up in a thick, slippery wave
under the child's feet, throwing her—him?—off balance
with a high, surprised cry. The attack that was blasting
toward me missed, but only just; I felt the incredible
heat of it blister my skin and sizzle my hair, and completed my forward motion to fall flat on the mud. My
shirt was blazing, and I rolled over to kill the flames. As
I did so, I kept moving the ground under the child's feet,
and riding the thick, shifting sludge kept the Fire Warden from launching another effective assault.

The rain shield overhead collapsed, and ice-cold water hit my burned skin in a punishing, breathtaking slap.
I felt power shifting on the aetheric, and desperately
kept pushing the earth around, trying to buy time. This
child's power was enormous, and extremely well controlled; if I gave a second's pause, she would respond
with a blistering assault that would burn the skin right
off my body and leave me dying in the mud, or worse. I
was fortunate that the child was strong in fire; earth was
a good defense against that, if I could stay ahead of her
and anticipate her moves.

It was hard to do, but while rocking her off balance
yet again, I simultaneously pulled the mud up in a coun-
terwave that buried me but left a tiny hole through
which I could catch a breath. I sucked in a deep one, and
rolled even as I sank deeper into the muck, reaching,
reaching. . . .

I felt the mud suddenly harden around me, and the
heat against my back was sudden and stunning, as if I'd
been shoved beneath a giant broiler. She was trying to
bake me, if not burn me. I sank deeper to avoid it, then
twisted up, hands outstretched.

My fingers closed on the stick-thin legs of the child,

and I sent a massive burst of power up through her nerves to force an overload and shutdown.

The child toppled over in a sudden, helpless heap.

I clawed up from the mud and flopped next to her, gasping and letting the rain pound me as it sluiced the grit from my face and eyes. Then I checked the child for signs of life. She was breathing, but unmoving. Her heart was speeding too fast, trying to fight me as I held her in that state. I put my palm flat on her forehead, closed my eyes, and eased her into a deeper state of calm and then, finally, unconsciousness.

"Cass?" Luis lunged out of the rain. He looked frantic as he dropped to his knees beside the two of us. "What happened?"

"One of Pearl's," I said wearily, and almost pitched forward as I lost my balance. Luis's warm hands grabbed my shoulders, and he pulled me back against him, arms wrapping me in safety. "She's going to the Wardens to offer her help to them against the Mother. And they'll accept; they're bound to. They don't understand what she is. What she wants."

"Then we have to tell them," he said. "She tried to shut you up, right?" He looked down at the small form of the girl. "Cass, did you—"

"She's alive," I said, and coughed up a mouthful of dirty water, retching mud up from my stomach in a sudden rush. I didn't feel better for the purge.

"Well, we can't just leave her here. She'll freeze."

"We can't take her, either. She's dangerous."

But now Isabel was there, too, and she reached out with a cry for the little girl. "What did you do?" she shouted at me, glaring, and I didn't have the energy or the heart to explain. "You're always hurting people! Always!"

"Iz, stop, hang on a minute—"

But she avoided Luis's outstretched hand, picked up

the little girl, and carried her off toward shelter. The look she shot me was full of dark fury and distrust.

"Iz!" Luis yelled, but if Isabel could hear him, she didn't care. He turned his anger on me, instead. "Cassiel, do you have some kind of death wish? You can't just walk off and have a chat with that evil bitch without backup—you *know that*! What were you *thinking*?"

It was as if his frightened, protective anger was contagious, because suddenly irritation inside me sparked into rage, and I shoved free of him and stumbled up to my feet. The rain no longer felt cold; it seemed soothing as it slapped down on my face and hair, soaked into my clothes. I was still shaking, but the chemicals in my body driving it were from a far different source.

"I was *thinking* that there's no point!" I shouted back at him, and shook my head so forcefully that spray flew in a mist. "It's the *end*, Luis! And there's no point in being careful now. It's all risk, and loss, and I can't—" I ran out of breath, and the anger wasn't enough to cushion me against the sudden, horrible reality of the losses, and the ones that were to come. "I can't *live* through this. There's no point."

He felt sorry for me; I could see it. Fool. He didn't understand, didn't see what I saw, didn't understand the gulf that yawned black and hungry beneath our feet. We were rolling down a steep hill into a chasm, and there was no stopping it now. The Mother would destroy us, or we could cling to the false comfort held out by Pearl, and die later, and more horribly.

Ashan had exiled me from the Djinn because I'd refused to kill humanity—a clean masterstroke of strategy that would have destroyed Pearl along with them. His response had been to cast me down into human form, but I had grown to realize, over this time with them, that it hadn't been punishment so much as another, long-game strategy. I was the miserable hope that Ashan had placed in the center of this, placed to bring about the end of the game if I had the courage . . . a useless, fragile, broken *human*. I couldn't save anyone. I couldn't even save myself.

Ashan had thought far too much of me. It was all useless, and shattered, and wrong, and the hope and love in Luis's eyes were tragic now.

I pushed past him and slogged through the clinging mud toward the truck.

Esmeralda was coiled up in a loose tangle of scales and limbs near the back door, looking as drowned and annoyed as I felt. Her tail rattled as I passed her. "Saw you out there," she said. "Have fun with your *hermana*?"

"Shut up," I snapped.

"You can't let Isabel keep doing that, you know," she said. "Picking up strays."

"Like you?"

Esmeralda smiled, but there was a hint of the snake in that smile. "Some strays bite. This one will. You can't save them all. Got to make sure Iz understands that."

Esmeralda wasn't saying anything that I didn't feel myself, gut-deep, but it offended me that she was echoing my own thoughts. I didn't want this Djinn-killing sociopath on my side, or in my head.

"Saving children may not be your priority," I said coolly, "but perhaps it should be ours. Keep away from the girl. She may yet be salvageable."

"Keep telling yourself that!" she yelled back, as I climbed into the truck's cab. "She's going to melt your faces off, and don't say I didn't warn you!"

Isabel was already inside, sitting stiffly in the center of the bench seat with the little girl in her arms. She'd wrapped her in the blanket I'd used before, and asleep, the child seemed innocent and heartbreakingly vulnerable. I slammed the door. Isabel edged away from me, putting clear space between us, as Luis got in the driver's side. I heard the back door slam as Esmeralda took her place.

Nobody spoke at all as we drove away, into the storm.

Luis still had a working cell phone, and charged it using the plug-in port in the truck. His first call, once we were safely out of the heart of the storm and into something more like normal rain, was to the Wardens.

"Crisis Center," said a sharp male voice on the other end of the line. "Name?"

"Luis Rocha, Earth. Checking in," he said.

"You mobile and able to take work?"

"Yes," he said, and gave me a quelling look when I started to speak. "Are they back?"

"They who?"

"The ones who went off on the cruise," he said. The cruise in question had not actually been a vacation; a large number of the most powerful Wardens had boarded an ocean liner and sailed away from the coast of Florida, trying to prevent a major disaster. So far, there had been no word of their return . . . but then, we'd been preoccupied.

"Not yet," the voice said. "They should be docking in a few days, though. We've made contact and told them how dire the situation is here. They're making best possible speed, but it's up to us to hold until they get here."

From the stress in the man's voice, he didn't think that was very likely. I didn't hold out much hope, either. Mother Earth, conscious and angry, could destroy much of human civilization in a day, never mind a week. The Wardens remaining wouldn't be able to stop it, especially with the Djinn co-opted against them.

"I need to speak with Lewis Orwell," I said. "Now."

"Who's this?"

"Cassiel, who was once a Djinn. Put me through." I had, I thought, learned my humility lessons well; I had at least thought to give some context to my name, instead of presuming that it still held a resonance of power on its own.

"Can't do that, lady."

My voice went lower and colder. "Put me through."

"Warden Rocha, please tell her that—"

"He tells me nothing," I interrupted. "Put me through to Lewis Orwell *now*."

A heavy sigh rattled through the phone, and the unfortunate in the Crisis Center said, "I'll try. Hold."

Luis said, "You really think you're going to get the fucking Lord High Master of the Wardens to chat with you right now? Jesus, Cass, get a grip."

"If Pearl wants to form an alliance with the Wardens, it will have to be stopped, and he's the one to stop it," I said. "He needs to know. Now."

"Sometimes I think you just don't get the concept of *boss*. He's not going to—"

These was a click, and a different voice, scratchy with distance and a fragile connection, came on. "Orwell," he said. "And it had better be breaking news, Cassiel."

"It is," I said. "You remember why I was cast down."

"Well, I don't know if *down* is very flattering to the rest of us. Cast *out* might be a better term. But yes, I remember. Ashan wanted you to kill the human race, and you said you wouldn't. I hope you're not calling to ask for a thank-you, because we're just a little busy." He sounded *very* grim, far more so than I'd expected. Orwell was one of those perpetually confident men, and yet now . . . "The Djinn who came with us are dying. Cut off. We're in a black corner."

A *black corner* was a Warden term for one of the

burned-out areas of the world, where such an explosion of power had taken place that it destroyed the aetheric, and prevented Djinn from accessing their power. Djinn stranded in one of those areas would starve to death, slowly or quickly. Most black corners were small, isolated areas; even an injured Djinn could crawl out before permanent damage was done. But out on the ocean, when the aetheric was so ripped and bloodied . . . they might not survive. Any of them. They were New Djinn, most of them, but there was one. . . . "Venna," I said aloud, and felt a surge of dread. "Is Venna—?"

"She's sick," he said. "Very sick."

"No." I said it softly, and almost involuntarily. Venna was a True Djinn, like me; she was ancient and incredibly powerful. I'd been puzzled by her recent affiliation with humans, but then, she'd always been intrigued by the strangest things. "Not Venna." The loss of someone such as she would bring down the heavens, I thought.

What hurt more was the realization that I hadn't felt her distress. Venna and I had links that went back farther than the human race, and yet . . . yet I felt nothing of her danger, or pain.

Lewis sighed. "Get to the point, Cassiel."

I gulped back my pain, my shock, and focused hard to say, "Pearl. The enemy I've been fighting. She's become very powerful, and now she will approach the Wardens, offer to fight by their side. You must *not* take her offer, Lewis."

"Is it a trap? Is she going to *not* fight on our side?"

"No—she will. She must. She needs humanity to live, for now, until she achieves her ultimate goal . . . but then she'll turn on the Wardens, destroy you all. When she no longer needs them, she'll kill the rest of humanity as well."

He was silent a long time, long enough that I feared

the connection lost, but then Lewis said, "Good to know. Thanks, Cass. We should make landfall in a few days, but meanwhile, I need every Warden out there to *fight*, understand? Don't give up. Shield all that you can."

"You must promise me that you won't accept any help from her!"

"How can I?" Lewis sounded—not himself. That was a cry of bleak despair, and the words that followed were just as dark. "I had twenty-five thousand Wardens when I started, to protect almost seven billion people. Know how many I have now? It's tough to get a real count, but I was down to about ten thousand, and now—now it's maybe half that. The Djinn are either dying or puppets for Mother Earth. We've got *nothing*. You expect me to throw back the only possible ally we have?"

"She'll kill you," I said softly. "She'll kill you *all*."

"Listen to yourself," he replied. "Even after all this time, you can't think of yourself as one of us."

He hung up the call, and I sank back in the seat, feeling weary and utterly defeated. Luis silently put the phone away and concentrated on driving for a while.

"Well," he finally said, "at least you warned him. But I've got to be honest: He's right. He's got to pick the lesser of two evils right now."

"Pearl isn't the lesser. She only appears to be, from the Wardens' perspective right now."

"Yeah, well, you can argue it when we see him." He yawned, shook himself out of it, and said, "We can't keep this up. We're burning power every time we turn around, and it's going to wear us down, Cass. We haven't even made it to an actual fight yet, and already I'm drained. So are you." He checked his watch and the fuel gauge. "We've got at least another eight to ten hours before we get to Seattle, and that's if the roads hold out and we don't run into trouble, which we damn sure will."

"And your point . . . ?"

"We need rest. We need to figure out what to do with Pearl Junior there, because you can't keep her unconscious from now until this all shakes out, and having her at our backs is the definition of a bad idea."

"What are you saying?" I half turned in the seat now, staring at him.

"I'm saying that we've got the hell beat out of us more than we can handle already, and we're going to have to handle a lot more. We need to refuel, recharge, get ready. Going in drained means we ain't helping anybody."

"They'll bring the fight to us!"

"Maybe," Luis said. "But out here, away from the cities, it's still quiet. And we're stopping to rest before we do something stupid, because we're too tired to think straight."

He took his foot off the gas.

I flooded power through the metal, and the engine growled deep. The truck lunged forward, inciting a chorus of yelped protests from the others. I held Luis's stare with mine, and then said quietly, "Watch the road. We're not stopping. We cannot stop. There's no more rest, no more time. Do you understand?"

"You're crazy. We're *human*, not Djinn. We can't just— Let go of the pedal, Cass."

I said nothing. There was something in my stare that made him go quiet in the end, and he faced forward.

We kept driving.

Thirty minutes later, we slowed for the first signs of trouble—a tangle of wreckage in the middle of the road. Luis stopped the truck, and we both went to examine the damage. It had been a car once, but there was nothing left of it now to identify it as such, save one mangled tire still visible. From the fluids leaking from the crushed object, there had been occupants. They were beyond saving.

"Any idea what did that?" Luis asked me. I shook my head, but that was a lie. There was no damage to the close-crowding trees on either side of the road, which argued against an attack by weather; I could visualize a Djinn easily compacting the vehicle with careless blows, driving the metal in on the occupants. But why *this* car? Why . . .

I found a severed hand by the side of the road, a perfectly undamaged specimen sheared cleanly by some incredible force. It was a woman's hand, with manicured fingernails that had seen better days, and a great deal of recent abuse.

In the palm, when I checked it in Oversight, there shimmered the ghost of a stylized sun—the identification of a Warden. I looked at the crushed car, startled, and the agony and violence that bloomed on the aetheric made me shudder. A Djinn had done this. A powerful, furious, mad Djinn.

Because they were Wardens, headed—as we were—to battle.

"Luis," I said softly.

"I know," he said.

"Wardens."

"I *know*. Get in the damn truck, *now*."

We ran for it, but I slowed as I felt the aetheric bending around us. Something had just arrived. The hot, intangible rush of power blasted through me, and left me scorched and trembling inside.

I stopped and turned to face it. Luis made it to the door of the truck, but turned as well. I heard him whisper, softly, *"Madre de Dios."*

A Djinn was standing in the road, blocking our path. He was the size of a man, but he was not anything like one, really; the form was correct, but his skin was a deep violet-indigo, his eyes blazed silver, and there was an aura around him that was visible even in the human world—power, madness, *rage.*

Rashid. He'd recovered far faster from Esmeralda's bite than any of us really had expected, and he was still under the control of the Mother. At least I believed he was.

Like Priya, he had no choice in what he'd been sent to do.

"Cass?" Luis said. "What do you want to do?"

"Get in," I said. "I'll keep him busy."

"Cassiel—"

"Do it!"

Luis yanked open the door and slid in, and I saw Rashid lower his chin. The glow in his eyes brightened, sparked with fury that was beyond even my experience.

I reached deep into Luis, into the deepest reserves of his power, and pulled all I could without damaging him beyond repair. I heard him cry out, but there was no time, no time at all, not if any of us were to survive the moment, the *second.*

I hit Rashid with a blast of pure white fire.

It was hardly enough to sting him, but it pushed him off the road and into the dirt, where he hit, rolled, and came to his feet with his skin dripping fire.

"Go!" I screamed, and heard Luis hit the gas. The truck rocketed past me, tires screaming; I felt the bumper brush me out of the way, but I had no time for pain because Rashid was rushing at me, and I knew, without even a hesitation, that I was about to die.

And that was, oddly, all right.

The world went quiet, still, pure, calm. Rashid was an indigo smear against it. I searched for the fear and rage that I needed to sustain me in this fight, but it was gone. Nothing left but a vast acceptance and readiness.

I'd felt this before, the detachment, the lack of fear, the *power*. Only once, since I'd been cast out from the Djinn, but the single bright spark of *that* Cassiel had never died, never surrendered.

Some part of me, some normally unreachable core, was yet a Djinn—trapped, limited, maybe even mutilated by what Ashan had done to me, but he couldn't destroy it, not utterly. And in this moment, when I shed all my human faults, fears, hopes . . .

The Djinn emerged, and flowed into me again, unnatural, inhuman, *perfect*. My body glowed with a pure white light, and I caught Rashid's arms and forced them wide as he rushed upon me. We were locked together, bodies pressed, eyes focused on each other.

And I was not afraid, any more than I'd been afraid when I'd seen an infection crawling up my arm and taken a weapon and brought it down to sever the flesh and bone. I'd known what had to be done, and I'd done it without hesitation. It had been a glorious madness, just like this.

I could hold Rashid here, trapped with me. I *would* hold him, for as long as necessary to ensure that Luis and the girls got safely away. For eternity, if I must.

No. *No.* I could do more. *Must* do more.

I tightened my hold on him. He was brutally strong, powered by the Mother's rage, but there was something in me, too, something that I'd carried with me. A core that wouldn't break, wouldn't yield.

His rage flowed over me, through me, out of me, and back into the Earth from which it sprang.

Rashid, I whispered, my lips kissing close to his. *Rashid.*

He was there. Unlike Priya, he was not yet gone, not

yet burned away. He'd hidden himself deep within, and I could feel him there, his terror and pain, his anguish and rebellion.

He needed help.

He needed . . .

It came to me with a stunning shock what he needed, and without thinking I released him and stepped back. I couldn't save him like this, or stop him from going after those I was sworn to protect.

But I *could* stop him. And save him.

The instant I released him, Rashid flashed away, chasing the truck. I dove into the underbrush and found the thing I'd glimpsed, a single flare of brightness in the dark.

A glass bottle.

It was a beer bottle, still smelling of hops and malt.

Seconds left.

Rashid was in front of the truck now.

Summoning his power.

"Be thou bound to my service," I said, and concentrated every ounce of the power inside me on his distant spark. "Be thou bound to my service. Be thou bound to my service, *Rashid*!"

There was a scream on the aetheric, a ripping of the fabric, and power flowed like blood toward me, through me, into the bottle.

I slapped my hand down on the top, trapping him within, and collapsed to my knees on the fallen leaves. A chilly blast of wind made me shake, but it wasn't only that—the fear came back, and the emptiness, and the fragility of flesh. The Djinn Cassiel had visited me and gone, and left me a human shell full of weakness.

But I had Rashid. I *had* him.

There was mud caked at the bottom of the leaves, and I slammed the bottle down into it, sealing it tightly. It looked empty, but on the aetheric the glass container swirled and glowed with trapped energy.

I didn't know if the binding would keep him controlled by my will, or if it had only bound him into a prison; the only way to test it would be to release him, and that was a dangerous risk. Too dangerous, for now. Later, perhaps, it would be worth taking the chance.

The truck was still moving, already out of sight. Safe, for now.

And I was once again on foot.

Chapter 4

TWO MILES DOWN THE ROAD, I found the Victory motorcycle sitting neatly parked on the edge. The tire marks told me that the truck had stopped, unloaded it, and driven on. *Good.* I leaned against the bike for a few moments, head down. The rain continued, but it was fitful now, and light; no other traffic had passed in either direction.

I mounted the bike and started it with a spark of power, then patted the sleek side with absent fondness. "Let's find them," I said. I opened the saddlebag strapped to the side and found men's clothing, rolled up tightly; the beer bottle with Rashid's spirit fit nicely inside the curl of a pair of soft blue jeans, and I cushioned it further with a fleece shirt.

Then I eased the Victory out onto the black ribbon of road, and started the ride.

The punishing vibration of the engine felt magically soothing to me, pounding the kinks from knotted muscles and clearing my mind. The wind and rain in my face woke something primal in me, something that thought clearly and coldly about our chances. They were, of course, poor at best. Lewis Orwell himself had admitted that; until the bulk of the Wardens docked from their mission at sea, those of us stranded here were the thinnest possible line of defense. There was no chance we wouldn't be shattered.

But we had an unexpected, even shocking advantage, if we could actually trap and bottle the Djinn. I'd always loathed that loophole in the freedom and power of my kind, but now I felt grateful for it; without it, the humans wouldn't stand a chance, and ultimately neither would the Djinn themselves *or* the Mother. We had to maintain a fragile balance to fight for reason, for peace, and for the defeat of our real enemy: Pearl.

The Mother was experiencing agony and the temporary madness that came of it. If we could soothe her, it would pass. But Pearl . . . Pearl was a cancer at the very heart of the world, and she had to be burned away.

The bottle in my saddlebags represented a step toward all of that. Perhaps. At the very least, it symbolized a chance we hadn't had an hour ago.

I saw the white flash of paint ahead on the road, and accelerated around a curve. The truck was just ahead now, climbing a rise. I could catch it in only a moment.

I was still half a mile back when the vehicle made the top of the hill . . .

. . . And exploded in a fireball, raining metal and debris into the trees.

"No!" I screamed. It burst out of me in a fury, ripping a blood path down my nerves and flesh, and I pushed the throttle hard over, heedless of the slick road, the dangers, *everything* except the burning wreck that was overturned there at the top of the hill.

No one could have survived that.

No one.

* * *

I found the first body lying in a burning heap on the side of the road. The pine trees were aflame, and the sound of trees snapping as the sap boiled was like war.

It was very still.

I leaped off the Victory while it was still in motion, letting it slide to a stop as I ran to the body's side. I turned it over.

Luis.

His eyes were tightly shut, his hands fisted, but as I touched him the flames snuffed out into surly little curls of smoke, and he drew in a deep breath.

His clothes were burned, but as I frantically checked him I realized that the skin beneath was unharmed. Reddened, but not seared. He had a broken ulna and two cracked ribs, but nothing that couldn't be fixed.

"Did my best," he whispered. "Christ. That hurt."

I smoothed his wet hair back. He smelled acridly of burned plastic and metal, but he was *alive*. Improbably, alive.

"Iz," he said. "Over there. She jumped, with the girl." He pointed with his unbroken arm. I kissed him quickly and rose to move in that direction.

The trees there were *broken*, snapped off at the base and laid out in an eerily neat circular pattern, like wheat stalks bent flat by the wind. And in the center of it was Isabel, curled up like an infant.

No sign of the girl at all.

I turned Isabel over. Her eyes were tightly shut, her skin pale, but she was breathing. Improbably, she wasn't even scorched—not a single mark on her.

She was whispering under her breath. I pulled her into my arms and bent my head closer to make it out.

"—Couldn't stop her, couldn't stop her . . ."

"Isabel," I said. "Ibby. *Ibby!*"

Her dark eyes flew open, but they were shockingly ringed by red now, as if every blood vessel in them had exploded with effort. She didn't seem to see me at all. "Couldn't stop her," she whispered. "Mama, I couldn't—"

"Shhh, Ibby, hush, it's all right; you're all right." It appalled me that she was, in this extreme, calling on her mother, on a mother she'd seen gunned down. "It's Cassiel. I'm here."

"Mama," she wailed, just as she had on that terrible day, and then her arms went around my neck. "Mama, I couldn't stop her. I tried but she just—"

Me. She wasn't calling on Angela, on the ghost of her mother who was gone. She was calling *me* by that name. *Me.*

My breath left me in a rush, and I held her tightly against me. Breathed in the smell of her hair, kissed her forehead, and felt a sunburst of feeling so large, so overwhelming that I could not even properly call it love. It was more than that. Much more.

"The girl," Ibby said, whispering now with her head against my shoulder. "It was the girl. I thought she was sleeping, but she woke up and I couldn't stop her. She was so *strong.* . . . It's my fault. . . ."

I carried her over to her uncle. "Luis is all right, my love, you see? He's all right." I sat her down next to him as he struggled up, and he hugged her with his good arm. "You couldn't have done more. You saved him, Ibby."

"Es," Ibby whispered, and turned her tear-streaked, eerily red-eyed face toward me. "Where's Es?"

The truck was a blazing inferno, belching black smoke and radiating an intense, crippling heat. I couldn't see anything within it except the stark bones of steel pillars. If Esmeralda was inside, there was little left of her.

"I'm right here," Esmeralda said, and I confess, I jumped; she was wrapped around a pine tree, dangling her human half upside down. Her fangs flashed as she laughed. "I'm no fool, Iz. You wanted to pretend that little bitch was safe, so I bailed out on the road and got in the trees to follow. I'm just surprised it took so long for her to try to blow you up, that's all. I'd have done it way sooner." She slithered down the trunk of the tree and righted herself to face me. "Hey, why aren't *you* dead, anyway? No way you could take down that Djinn."

"You—you left me?" Isabel said slowly, sitting up. "You just *left*?"

Esmeralda shrugged and crossed her arms, leaning her upper body against a tree trunk for support while her coils stacked around her. "Yeah, so? You act like a dumbass, you get left. First rule of survival, Iz. So don't do it again. This ain't no rescue mission, and you can't save anybody. Right, Albino Barbie?"

I supposed that was meant for me, but I was watching the disillusionment on Isabel's face, and it hurt. She'd trusted Esmeralda, formed a partly imaginary bond with the older girl. She hadn't realized what I'd always known— that Esmeralda's capacity for devotion, and for love, was severely blunted.

"Indeed," I said, raising my eyebrows. "Not everyone can be saved. But the difference between you and Isabel is that Isabel will *try*. And that is a virtue, not a vice."

Esmeralda shot me a murderous look, a rude gesture, and sank sullenly into her coils. "Fine, let her Pollyanna along all you want, but the time's coming, Djinn bitch. Time's coming she has to make a choice, and if you get in the way, you'll get hurt. You know I'm right."

"You *left* me," Isabel said. "You knew it was going to go wrong, and you didn't even try to help!"

"Girl, look at me. I've got no freaky powers now; your Warden friends saw to that." Esmeralda shrugged. "You wouldn't have listened to me anyway. Right?"

Isabel turned her face away. Her uncle hugged her closer, but she pulled free and walked toward the burning truck. She extended her hand, and I felt the stirring not just of the air as the fire slowly died, but also on the aetheric. The girl was a massive flare of power. A beacon of light in the dark.

She snuffed out the flames and left a smoking, frighteningly charred wreck in its place. "We have to move it off the road," she said. "Somebody could crash into it."

Luis looked at me, and I saw the exhaustion in his face. "Esmeralda," I said. "Help her."

"I told you, I ain't got no—"

"You have strength in your body," I said. "Use it."

She glowered, but sullenly shifted her coils, wrapped around the wreck, and began dragging it with a metallic screech off to the side. "It's still hot," she complained. "Ow."

"Big baby," Isabel observed. "It's not *that* hot."

Esmeralda rattled her tail warningly, and Isabel kicked it and walked back to Luis. "Give me your arm," she said. When he hesitated, she sighed theatrically. "Tío, you can't run around with it broken, and it'll take days for you to heal it yourself. Just let me do it."

Over her shoulder, I nodded at him. He let her take his hand in hers, and even though I looked away, I felt the astonishing power as it swept through him. Ibby's gifts were not natural, and she did not yet have the fine and delicate control that Luis possessed, but for sheer force, it rivaled the most powerful Wardens in existence . . . and, I thought, might even rival a Djinn.

The fact that she'd been forced into that power still woke a sickened feeling within me. Her body would never develop along a natural path, or survive as it should. Pearl was to blame for that—Pearl, and the circumstances we now faced. *If you love her, stop her,* a whisper inside me said. *Take her out of the fight. Protect her.*

But I couldn't. There was no safety in this world, and no protection.

If you were her mother, you'd protect her.

Somehow, that whisper hurt more than anything else. I wanted to fill that aching void in Isabel's life, but I was as crippled as Esmeralda. As untrustworthy.

I could not disappoint her so badly.

Luis's bone knitted together cleanly, though he'd have to be careful in lifting for a few days. If only all our troubles could be so easily fixed. "We've got a transportation issue," I said. "I can only carry one on the motorcycle. Esmeralda can go on her own, but—"

"Take Ibby," Luis said. "I can hike it."

He couldn't. He was drained, and it took time for an Earth Warden to fully recover from such profligate efforts as he'd shown the past week. Physically, mentally, and psychically.

"It's twenty more miles," I said. "I'll take Isabel, and we'll find something suitable. We'll come back for you both. Until then, rest yourself. You know you need it."

"So do you," he said, and lowered his voice as he took my hand. "Cass, you're not a Djinn. You're flesh and blood, like me. And you've done too much already."

He was right, of course; my reserves of power were faint and shallow, but they had to come from him, through him. Resting would not help me as much as forcing *him* to rest.

"Isabel will protect me," I said, and smiled a little. "I'm just the driver. Promise me you'll rest. *Promise.*" Because now that I looked at him, in the cold afternoon light, he seemed so pale, and the dark rings around his eyes more pronounced.

But the smile was still as radiant as ever. "*Chica*, I get

it. I promise." He pulled me closer, and just for a moment, our lips met in a soft, sweet echo of that promise. No passion in it, not now, not here, but something even deeper than that.

Trust.

I drew in my breath slowly as I pulled back, and the wind stirred my pale hair and caressed his cheek with it. I didn't want to let him go, but I knew that I had to do it. The longer I delayed, the worse our situation might be.

"Look after him," I told Esmeralda. "If anything happens to him—"

"Yeah, yeah, you'll make me into a coat, a pair of boots, and an awesome hat, I get it," she said. "Just go. I'm sick of looking at your pale, bony ass." She flicked a hand at me dismissively. I gave her a hard five-second stare before walking to my Victory. I'd laid it flat, but on the side *not* holding the precious bottle; I levered it upright, checked it—save for minor cosmetic damage, intact—and swung my leg over.

"Isabel," I said. "Let's go."

She hopped on without a hesitation and put her arms around my waist. For a second I was reminded of her as a smaller child, in this same position on a different bike, on a different day. A more hopeful one, perhaps.

Then I shook my head, started the engine, and we left Esmeralda and Luis behind, with the dull smoke still staining the air above them.

I was worried about Isabel still; her use of power had lit up the aetheric again, like a lightning strike on an inky night . . . and it would draw attention. Right now, she might be the most powerful Warden not shrouded by that black corner, far out to sea, and that meant she would be a target.

But all the vigilance seemed to be in vain. We rode fast,

but smoothly. The road was empty of traffic or threats. No wrecks littered the highway. The sun had slipped beneath the line of trees now, casting cool velvet shadows across the asphalt. I drove with part of my awareness on the aetheric. If the Djinn—or Pearl's forces—decided to attack, they wouldn't give much warning. A split second might mean the difference between life and death.

Less than fifteen minutes later, we topped a steep hill, and below us in a soft, mist-shrouded valley lay a small town. The billboard-large sign proclaimed it HEMMING-TON, A NICE PLACE TO LIVE, and proved it with an utterly artificial photo of a smiling family.

It was very quiet below.

I slowed the bike and stopped, idling. Isabel rose to look over my shoulder. "Why are we waiting?" she asked. "Come on—let's go!"

"A moment," I said. There was nothing unusual, either in my field of vision or on the aetheric, yet something gave me pause.

"Look, there's a parking lot," she said, and pointed. "Right there. We can get a van or something. We don't even have to go that far."

"We need food and water," I said.

"Toilet paper," she added. "For sure. Maybe that pre-moistened kind. There's a store right there. C'mon, it's fine. There's nothing in there. The whole town's empty."

She was right—the place was ghostly silent. Lights burned, but I sensed no human habitation at all.

"In and out. Quickly," I said. "You see to the van. I'll drop you there and go on to the store. If there's any trouble at all, take the wheels and go. You can drive, can't you?"

She laughed. "I was *a kid* yesterday, but I can learn fast, Cassie. Don't worry about me."

There was no point in hesitating; the danger would be

there, or not, and waiting wouldn't improve our chances. I pressed the throttle and sent the Victory gliding down the long hill. I kept the rumbling to a minimum, out of instinct as much as caution.

Too many predators out, and none of them in clear view. Staying quiet and small was as good a defense as any.

The parking lot wasn't large, but it had several choices of vehicles that would do; the largest was the work truck of some sort of contractor, and stocked with tools, from what I could make out of the interior. Not clean, but useful. I pointed to it as I rolled to a stop, and Isabel nodded as she slid off the bike. "Ibby. Be careful," I said. She waved impatiently, and I felt a spark of power as she unlocked the door to climb inside. I felt a primitive impulse to stay with her, watch over her, but that would only increase our risks. Better to divide the job.

I drove the bike onto the sidewalk in front of the store. It was called Mike's EZ Stop, and there were three cars out in front, all silent and deserted. When I killed the engine on the Victory, I could hear sounds—music, applause, talking voices, all of it softened by distance.

Televisions and radios. Not living souls.

The thick glass windows showed nothing—a brightly lit interior of shelves, groceries, coolers at the back fully stocked with cold drinks and packs of beer. I pushed open the door and heard a soft electronic tone, but no one appeared. The registers were open and bare, as if someone had methodically stripped them of cash, but there was no vandalism here.

I took two cloth bags from the environmentally friendly pile—ironic, now—and went shopping.

I checked the aisles methodically for anyone hiding as I grabbed two loaves of bread, peanut butter, jam, dried jerky, energy bars—anything that would keep without refrigeration. I avoided the canned goods, only because the water would be heavy enough; if this proved safe, we could always come back for more.

I was putting the last of the water into the bag when I rounded the corner and faced the last wall of coolers.

They did not contain beer.

The dead stared back at me, frosted and ice-eyed— employees still in aprons, a man in a tan jumpsuit who might have gone with the van Isabel was taking, a small boy crumpled into a fetal ball, a fat old woman in a flowered dress, more; they were stacked in the cooler in a horrifying mess.

Not all were intact.

It couldn't be all of the town, as overwhelming as it seemed.

I backed up into a row of shelves, and jars of spaghetti sauce clinked together. One popped free and shattered in a mess of red and broken, jagged glass.

Out. Get out. Something screamed inside me, some instinct more human than Djinn, though there was alarm within my Djinn soul as well. I tightened my grip on the bags, whirled, and ran for the doors.

The glass suddenly went opaque with cracks.

I threw myself forward into a facedown slide on the linoleum floor just as all the windows shattered inward, shredding the interior of the store like a bomb. *Wind.* Not just any wind. No, this was traveling at insane force, blowing over shelves, ripping up counters, and flinging them into the air. I saw a register fly by overhead before it hit a sliding metal shelf and blew apart into sharp fragments of metal and plastic. The electrical power cord hissed wildly in the air like a living thing and slapped the floor only a few inches from my hand.

I had no defense against weather. Not in here.

The initial burst of air had destroyed things, but now

it sucked out again, then turned, and turned, warm and cool colliding in an insane battle for supremacy. The debris swirled and sped up into a blur, and the roof of the little store ripped away with a shriek of cracking steel and timber.

Gone.

The walls went next, unraveling into bricks and beams. I curled up tight on the floor and felt the wind sucking at me, ripping me with teeth made of steel and glass, wood and sharp plastic. It would flay me alive, or pull me into the storm of deadly, grinding debris. The linoleum floor, which was being ripped away around me, was at least under my control; made of largely organic materials, it was something within reach of my Earth powers, and I first rolled and wrapped the thick, flexible coating around my body. It protected me to some extent—enough that I began grabbing and dissolving the other organic debris in the air, especially the cutting and stabbing surfaces, into dust. The wind could still throw me at fatal speed, but at least it couldn't rip me to pieces quite so easily.

But it had other tricks, this tornado formed—I felt it now—of sheer, volcanic hatred . . . and as it shredded the coolers at the sides of the store, bodies joined the debris. The wind scoured them apart in seconds, into wet flesh and sharp, flaying bone. It was all organic, all under the domain of my Earth power, but it was too much, too fast, especially now that the storm was mixing so many different kinds of weapons together.

The dead attacked me in the second wave, and I'd already spent what power I had to stop the first assault. The bones stabbed at me like flying knives, and skulls pummeled me with the force of thrown bowling balls. The thick flooring couldn't protect me completely, or forever, and the tornado seemed to be growing in fury now, focused solely on ripping me to pieces. . . .

And then something entered the fight, on my side. A brilliant rush of power that threw up walls around me, solid earth and concrete, rigid metal, a berm of safety that gave me relief from the pummeling.

And then, quite suddenly, I felt the back of the tornado snap as the power fueling it withdrew. The wind faltered, scattered in all directions, and bones and ripped flesh and debris rained down on the shelter that covered me.

I couldn't breathe. The linoleum had wrapped tightly to my body, and the air within the shelter had been exhausted in only a few gasps.

I'd suffocate here, in my safe haven. . . .

But then the top peeled away with the ease of a can opening, and a face looked down on me. Two faces, actually. One, veiled with a fall of dark hair, was Isabel's, looking pale and frightened.

The other was indigo blue, silver-eyed, and I felt a surge of frantic panic as I realized that it was *Rashid*. Rashid, whom I'd imprisoned in a bottle . . .

. . . That was now held tightly in Isabel's hand.

"Get her out," Isabel ordered. Rashid ripped the shelter further open, took hold of the linoleum, and unrolled me from its stifling embrace. I gagged in dusty breaths and stared at his extended hand for a few seconds before grabbing it.

He lifted me effortlessly out and into a wasteland. A very limited and specific one, covering only the building that had once been Mike's EZ Stop; there was nothing left but scattered bricks, rubble, and the pulped remains of the dead. Not something I wanted Isabel to witness, but not something I could easily shield her from, either.

Isabel grabbed on to me and hugged me, wordless and shaking. I hugged her back and looked over at Rashid, who inclined his head just a tiny bit.

"You're sane," I said.

"Well," he replied, with a sharp-toothed smile, "that is not a *common* opinion. But I am no longer a puppet of the Mother's will. Only of *hers*." He cast a dark look at Isabel, and my arms tightened around her in reaction. "You are well aware how I feel about such things."

"Don't," I warned him. "She's a child."

"Old enough to hold my bottle," he said. "Though that was your doing, my sweet dear cousin, sticking me in one. For the *second* time. There will come a reckoning. Soon."

"Then reckon with me. Not her. She took possession only to save my life." I hesitated a moment, then said, "What happened here, in this place?"

He didn't have to answer me; a captive Djinn could easily use the rules of his confinement to throw endless obstacles in the ways of humans with whom he had issues. I counted it a fairly good sign that he said, "Djinn. Of course. There is an *anima* here. They waked it and moved on, and it did the rest. And will continue to do so."

An *anima* was the spirit of a place, a kind of tiny splinter of the Mother's consciousness, though it was difficult to tell how linked it was to her, or whether it was its own creature, like the Djinn. *Anima* were generally benign, though some darker ones gave rise to legends of hauntings.

This one, though, was mad and angry, left to stalk through a dead town and rip apart anything that intruded on its fury. There would be many of these, I realized now . . . pockets of seeming calm that would lure in the unsuspecting, only to trigger a boundless rage. The Djinn had set traps, knowing that humans would seek safety in places that looked safe, comfortable, *normal*.

I couldn't help a shudder. The *anima* wasn't dead here, only hurt and waiting. It wouldn't wish to fight a

Djinn, so Rashid's presence alone saved us . . . but the next to stop here wouldn't be as lucky.

Rashid stared with those unsettling eyes and an expression I couldn't read, then said, "If you're done with using me, child, you can put your toys away."

"Oh," Isabel said softly. "Oh, uh, I don't know how—"

"I'm hardly likely to *tell* you." For all his menacing talk, Rashid was, I thought, showing remarkable restraint. Djinn were naturally inclined to take every advantage to trick their masters, but he was deliberately refraining.

Isabel looked frankly panicked. This was well outside the narrow bounds of her experience, and her hand was shaking. Any Djinn with half an impulse toward freedom could have startled her enough to drop the bottle, shattering it on the rubble and setting its captive free.

But Rashid did not move.

"Find something to put in the opening," I told Isabel softly. "A cork would be best. Something that fits tightly." She looked around frantically, while Rashid crossed his arms, rocked back and forth on his heels, and shook his head. She finally held up a triangular cosmetic sponge to me, and I nodded. "Now tell him to go back in the bottle."

"Go back in the bottle," she said in a rush, and then her cheeks turned red. "Please?"

"For the Mother's sake, school her if you want to keep her alive," Rashid told me, but he disappeared, and I gave the girl another nod.

"Push the sponge in tightly," I said. She did, and let out a sudden gust of breath. She held the bottle out to me, and I took it. "Good job, Iz. Never forget, a captive Djinn is not your friend, only your tool, and tools can turn in your hand. Don't use him unless you have no choice." I gave her an odd look then, and voiced the question that had suddenly come to my mind. "How did you know about the bottle?"

The hot red blush in her cheeks grew stronger, and she looked down. "I thought I'd better get your bike," she said. "I was putting it in the truck when all this started. I was kind of—looking around."

"And how did you know what it was?"

She frowned and stared at the bottle in my hand—an ordinary empty beer bottle, somewhat ridiculously sealed with a flare of cosmetic sponge. "Can't you see it?"

I saw nothing beyond the obvious. "What do *you* see?"

"Him," she said. "It's like a sun inside there. It burns."

That was . . . impossible. I stared from the bottle to her, thoughtfully, and then became aware of a sharp ache in my right side. The first of many complaints from a body that had sustained much abuse; it was the first voice of a mob's roar, all clamoring for attention. I had many cuts, some deep, and more than a few cracked bones and torn muscles.

And no time for any of it. "My bike is in the van?" I asked. "And where is the van?"

"In the parking lot," she said. "I'm sorry, Cassie, I was going to go, but—"

"But then you saw what was happening," I finished for her. "And you decided to stay and help. Iz, you can't do that. You *must* follow orders. Do you understand? I told you to take the van and go. You might have gotten yourself killed along with me."

"I didn't," she said. "And you needed me. You did."

It was difficult to argue the truth of that, especially when I had to use her stabilizing arm to limp my way out of the wreckage of the store.

The contrasts were eerie. The store was a pile of wreckage and shredded human remains, but just beyond it the street lay quiet and calm, only a few scattered bricks to show any disorder. The parking lot where Iz had left the van still sat unmolested, all the cars shrouded now with a faint coating of dust that still hung in the twilight air.

"What was that?" Iz asked me, as we got into the van. I took the driver's side.

"I don't know," I said, and looked out on the still, picturesque little town. "But I don't think we'll find anything else we can use here."

Or, I added silently, any survivors. A few lights burned in the windows, but there was an emptiness to this place that went deep, all the way to the unsettled core of the earth.

We would, I thought as I jump-started the van and got it rolling toward the exit, go around this place. Well and far around. For all its peaceful appearance, there was a curse hanging on this place, and a powerful one. I wondered what Rashid would tell me if I removed him from the bottle and asked what had happened here to madden the *anima* so horribly.

I wondered whether he would lie to me.

Probably.

Transportation acquired, we chose a different route at a crossroads rather than visiting the silent town of Hemmington; this one led to an even smaller hamlet, but thankfully there were people on the streets and cars passing through. The people were scared and nervous, and the cars seemed to be loaded with possessions, but it was better than our last stop.

Luis, always cautious, gassed the van up and did the grocery shopping himself (as if it had been *my* fault!). . . . He returned with much the same choices I would have made, but had thrown in some candy bars and soft drinks. "Comfort food," he said. "Ain't like we're going to have a whole lot of comfort, overall. Here, I also picked up camping gear. We're going to need it, one way or another. Not likely to be a lot of four-star accommodations in our future."

He'd also, without pointing it out, added some interesting survival tools to our supplies, including a rifle, ammunition, some wickedly lovely knives, and other things whose purposes weren't quite as clear to me. Esmeralda understood their purpose, however. "Water disinfection tabs, portable chemical heating pads . . . You're getting serious about this survivalist stuff. Good for you. This shit's going to get real, fast."

"You didn't see that town," Isabel said from where she sat on the dirty floor of the van, knees pulled up to her chest. She wasn't looking up as we inventoried the contents of the bags that Luis had brought, and I worried about the stillness of her posture. It seemed more traumatized than I had expected—but then, I had dragged a child, only six years old in real years, if not in body, into a place full of danger and very real horror. What had I expected, that she would easily adapt? Simply accept what she'd seen?

I sank down beside her and put my arm around her. "We won't go back," I said.

"We should," Iz whispered. "All those people. They all needed help, and nobody was there for them. Now they're just . . . waiting. All alone."

It was, I realized, the neglect that bothered her; we'd left that town without burying a single body, recognizing a single lost life.

I took her hand in mine and squeezed, just a little. "I know," I said. "But, Isabel, you know we cannot go back there. We just can't. It's too dangerous, and all that we can offer them is a pyre or a grave. There are people who need our help to stay alive, and that is where we must turn our efforts."

"We could use him," she said.

I knew who she was talking about, but it was something I didn't want to bring up—not here, not in front of Esmeralda, who was tightly coiled in the corner, watching us with her bright, odd eyes. She was, I thought, jealous. Jealous of the two of us, together, sharing this small grace. Perhaps she'd even been jealous of the fact that I'd taken her with me on the trip to Hemmington. I had no way of knowing; she'd never admit it, if so.

But I didn't trust her, and couldn't help that fact. Telling her there was a Djinn captive in a bottle was something far too dangerous. The temptation would be irresistible for her—either to torment the Djinn, or to use him for her own benefit. She had a bad history of that kind of behavior, after all.

No, far better I keep Rashid as a secret, for now. I might have need of him—or Isabel might, though I couldn't trust his forbearance with her for long. He wasn't a creature of patience.

"Hey," Luis said, and I glanced up at him. Iz did not. "Let's talk outside a minute, Cass." I nodded, hugged Iz once more, and stood to follow him out of the van. He slammed the grimy back door and turned the handle to secure it, then walked away. Not far, but far enough that it was clear he didn't want to be overheard.

Then he turned on me and said, "You almost got her killed."

"I know," I said. "I'm sorry. I never intended—"

"You may not intend it, but you can't say you couldn't anticipate it. I'm not letting her out of my sight again. Or you. No more splitting up, no matter what."

"You needed time to—"

"To heal? Yeah. And you're covered in cuts and

bruises and from the way you're leaning, you've got a cracked rib going on there, too. So you tell me, how are we protecting each other, exactly? How can we?" He swallowed hard and put his heavy, warm hands on my shoulders. "We have to look out for each other, because we need each other more than ever. So don't try to protect me by putting me in the rear, okay? And I won't do it for you. We look after the girls, and we watch each other's backs." He paused, and smiled a little. "God, you're beautiful."

I laughed out loud, because it was blackly comical—I was dirty, covered in bruises. My hair still had the shredded remains of leaves from the night in the woods. I'd been coated in dust in Hemmington, which at least had served to mask the nightmarish remains of blood and other less identifiable substances from the abattoir of that destroyed market. "No," I said. "Not now, and perhaps not ever. But I think you are just surprised to see me standing."

"Hell, girl, I'm surprised either of us is breathing. And you are beautiful. Always." He kissed me so tenderly that it stilled everything for a moment, all the pain and fear and worry and time ticking away. And then he made me smile by saying, "Okay, I'm not saying you couldn't get an upgrade with a shower and shampoo, maybe a change of clothes. I would personally love to see you in a towel right now."

"You're insane," I said.

"Yeah, well, some people cope with certain death by getting a little bit horny. Why, are you saying you wouldn't like that right now?" Oddly enough, even after everything—or, perhaps because of it—the idea had a certain bizarre appeal. I was overwhelmingly aware of time passing, of the situation worsening around us, but the fantasy that somehow this could stop just for an hour, perhaps two—that we could find some beautiful, quiet space for the two of us and live that fantasy out, in private—seemed breathtakingly lovely.

And impossible, of course. But I was starting to realize that today, and every day after, would be a study in the impossible. Each minute we both still lived was an improbable gift.

"If you can find a motel," I said softly, with my lips close to his ear, "and find a way to keep the girls safe and elsewhere, then I will be happy to show you how I feel about your suggestions. Though I fear now is not the time."

"I know," Luis said, and pressed his lips to the sensitive skin beneath my ear, waking shivers. "But I figured the thought might keep us both focused for a while."

It was certainly having a focusing effect upon me, but just then a sharp, shrill tune came from Luis's pocket, and he pulled back and fumbled for it with evident surprise. "Thought all the grids were down," he said as he checked the screen of his phone. "Back up, I guess. For now."

"Who is it?"

He shook his head and pressed the button to accept the call. "Rocha," he said. "Who is this?" I couldn't hear the response, but I could see his face—still and frozen halfway to a frown. "What?"

I mouthed the obvious question again, but he looked away from me, frown slowly deepening. When I started to speak aloud, he held up his hand, palm out, to stop me.

"Yeah, I hear you," he said. "You can't be serious. It's me, Cassiel, my niece—we aren't exactly the infantry. You want an extraction, you're going to have to send in reinforcements. Lots of them."

Another pause. He turned completely away from

me and lowered his voice. I picked out words that were disturbing, in or out of context—suicide, dangerous, impossible—but then he ended the conversation as suddenly as he'd started it, and shoved the phone back into his pocket. He stayed turned away from me for a few more seconds, hands fisted, and then slowly faced me.

"So," he said. "I guess you heard something about that."

"A suicide mission," I said calmly. "Impossible. You used the word *dangerous*, but clearly that was superfluous, given the rest of it."

He grinned, but it was a small, tightly controlled expression, and above it his eyes remained serious. "They've got a small group of Wardens trapped, and they need an Earth Warden to go get them. They're Fire and Weather, can't do it on their own. So I guess we're drafted."

"Where are they?"

He pointed down. "They're trapped in a collapsed mine shaft," he said. "And it's deep. But since there are six of them, and we're losing manpower all the time, I guess HQ doesn't feel like writing them off quite yet. They want our—and I'm quoting here—best efforts at rescue."

I raised my eyebrows. "How far down?"

"Honestly? Nobody's sure. You know those miners in Chile they rescued a couple of years ago? Not quite that far, but farther than any sane person should have ended up. I'm guessing a Djinn shoved them in there and slammed the door."

"And could still be guarding it," I said. "Perhaps."

"Yeah, maybe so. Which is why I don't want Iz and Esmeralda along for the ride on this one. We take them all the way to Seattle, get them settled and safe, and then we go on to the rescue."

"We just agreed we wouldn't split up."

"You want to drag two kids down hundreds of feet into gas-filled tunnels where any little spark could blow us all up? I'm pretty sure Esmeralda wouldn't go anyway, which would split us up to begin with. And I don't want Iz down there. Call me crazy, but I think we've done enough to her for one day." By *we* he meant, of course, me. I'd done enough to her for the day. And he was entirely right. "We're going to need help, especially if there's a Djinn involved."

I cocked an eyebrow. "Will you trust me in this?"

"Don't I always?" he asked. "What am I trusting you about, specifically?"

"I'd rather not say right now."

His head tilted a little to the side as he regarded me, and although the trust I'd requested was there, so was a healthy dose of doubt. I didn't blame him. I'd have felt the same, really. "But you're going to say before we're half a mile underground and getting hammered by a pissed-off insane Djinn, right? And it'd be real handy if you had, say, a Weather Warden in your back pocket who could manufacture breathable air, because I'm thinking the lack of that will be a little challenging."

"Trust me," I said again.

He dragged a gentle finger down the side of my face. "Oh," he said. "Cassiel, if I trust anybody today, it's you. I got no choice, do I?"

In truth, I wasn't sure that made me feel very much better.

"Excuse me," said a new, and very tentative, voice. I turned, and there was a woman standing a few feet away, with her hand clasping that of a small boy of about six years old. She was pretty, and the uncertain voice seemed to match her hesitant body language. "Did you come from out of town?" That was a polite way, I thought, of saying that we weren't from around here. The boy ogled

Luis with fascination, especially the flame tattoos that licked the skin around the rolled-up sleeves of his shirt.

"Yes, ma'am," Luis replied. He sounded extremely polite suddenly. "We're just getting a few supplies, then we're heading out."

"Oh, I wasn't— No, of course you're welcome here. I'm sorry if it sounded like you weren't, sir. That wasn't what I meant, not at all. . . ." She was flustered now, and solved it by extending her free hand to him. "I'm Lucy. Lucy McKee."

"Hello, Mrs. McKee."

"I only asked because the phones are down, and there's a lot of rumors—the TV reports look just awful. Is it terrorists? Do you know? A lot of people are saying it's terrorists." She had large blue eyes that her son had inherited, and they both looked at us with grave, hopeful intensity.

"No, ma'am, I don't think it's terrorists," Luis said. He said it gently, but firmly. "Right now, there are a lot of things going on, but none of them are man-made as far as I'm aware. You should tell your family to stay together. You have a disaster plan, don't you? How to contact each other? You've got food and water supplies?"

"Well, a few, but—"

"Get more," he said. "Mrs. McKee, I don't want to scare anybody, but I'm not telling you anything that they won't be saying on the radio and TV soon. Keep in contact with your people, and get yourself supplied with food and water. Don't try to go to a bigger city right now. That's where the trouble will be worse. Understand?"

She nodded silently. I saw a glimmer of tears in her eyes, and fear, but she blinked and forced a smile for her son. "We'll do that, won't we, sweetie? We'll go to the store right now."

"Can I get Pop Rocks?"

"If you want to, of course you can." She looked up at us, oddly embarrassed. "I don't usually let him, but—"

"Let him have what he wants," Luis said. "Today. Stay safe, ma'am."

She gave him another smile, fainter this time, and hurried her son along. We watched them go down the block, to the same grocery store Luis had already visited.

"Do you think they'll live?" I asked him softly. He didn't look at me.

"Do you think any of us will?"

Without another word, or waiting for my answer, he walked back to the van.

Chapter 5

OUR GIRLS WERE QUIET for the most part, although Esmeralda was grumpy and restless; this was not, I found, shocking. Iz seemed too quiet, too withdrawn, and I tried to engage her in conversation for a while before abandoning the attempt and letting her ride in silence, staring out the window.

"Couple of hours more," Luis said. "It's going to get more dangerous the closer we get to Seattle, so stay alert. Cass, I need you up on the aetheric if you can manage it. Keep a lookout for any trouble."

I nodded and took his hand; physical contact between the two of us made access to the aetheric realm easier for me. A small burst of power sent me soaring up, out of my body, and the world took on the nacreous shimmer of mother of pearl, then dissolved into lines, light, whispers, fog. My native environment, as a Djinn, but I was no longer at home in it, and I felt the steady, though small, drain of power required to sustain me here. It was a risk, doing this; Luis was still weak, and his reserves of power were less than either of us might have wished.

Mine were still shallow, too, but I was more concerned about him; I could only channel power through him, and draining him past safety put us both at risk.

For now, though, it was only a minimal exposure.

The forest around us was very much the same on the aetheric as it was in the human world; more impressionistic, perhaps, suggestions of trees and shadows of animals moving through them in streaks of subtle color. Life was bright, even plant life; the trees pulsed with slow whispers of golden energy. Beautiful, and calming.

But there was trouble everywhere around us.

The road on which the van traveled was a thick dead slice through all that life, a thing of man's making, too recent to have any real history and place on the aetheric, where time was as much a visible dimension as the others. Not everything mankind created looked so awkward here, but new construction did. The town we'd left behind had more weight and natural ease to it, because its history gave it reality as much as the wood and glass and metal of which it was built. Time had given it life of its own, and the memories and events that had taken place there, good or bad, had created its own aura. It was, I thought, a good place to live, full of small joys and long peaces. No human place was free of sadness, madness, death, but in their town, at least, that was outweighed by something I could only call . . . happiness.

I didn't wish to, but I found my aethereal body turning slowly, facing another direction . . . toward Hemmington.

The town was a blackened scar. For all its apparent peace and silence in the human plane, here it was a shriek, a vibrating well of agony, an open wound in the world. Something had happened there, something great and terrible, and the death that had followed hadn't left only human corpses; it had rendered that entire town, and everything in it, poisonous.

It was a trap, but instead of something that would blow up intruders, it would lure them in, lull them, and then destroy. My own trauma there had added to the scarring, I realized; so had Isabel's.

I looked at the girl, sitting silently in the van below me, and saw the taint of that place inside her. It had infected her in subtle, awful ways. She'd heal, I thought, but for now, the germs of it continued to fester. I mourned that, and the blackening of the roots of her power that she'd done to herself. Isabel was still beautiful, a shining star on the aetheric, but she glittered more darkly than she ought.

I turned away from Hemmington, extending my vision farther out. Not far away, Portland burned. The Wardens had withdrawn their forces, fallen back to Seattle. By the standards of human cities, Portland was a young place—only a little over a hundred years of buildings and settlements, and little that had lasted for any length of time. It had held a significant population, though most had scattered now, in bright groups that fled in all directions. The forces pummeling Portland were full of bright, bloodred fury . . . flames that seared away what humans had built and returned it to ashes.

The death toll must have been significant, but the suffering was done now; what was left in that city belonged to the Djinn and to the Mother. Humans had no place there now.

Not so far away—and too close for comfort—the Wardens had regrouped and gathered their forces near Seattle. They'd kept the destruction confined to Portland so far; I could see that their efforts were focused on evacuating the people and finding them safety, not on trying to douse the unnaturally bright flames that continued to devour what had once been one of America's great cities. It was, I knew, far from the only disaster they were facing; there was a great, dark energy rising from the midwest of the continent, where floods raced out of control and Weather Wardens struggled to divert storms and tame rivers. It would not end well, from the raw, bleeding colors of the aetheric. There was more—the harsh stabbing oranges and stark ripping greens of earthquakes were flashing along long-dormant rifts, toppling houses and rocking the tall towers of distant cities. The ocean's tides were rising under the whipping winds of forming hurricanes far out to sea.

There was death coming, and it would not stop.

I already knew it, but staring at it here, in this way, it shook me how fragile the Wardens were, how utterly useless their defenses. I'd heard the grim despair in Lewis Orwell's voice, and now I felt it, as well; this was a fight to the death, but the winner was a foregone conclusion. All we could do was bind up wounds and defend for as long as we could. Without more Wardens, without the supporting power of Djinn, humanity had very little time left as masters of the world.

If they'd ever truly held that title, other than in their own minds.

We had avoided truly being attacked thus far, mainly because nature was directing its hatred toward the largest concentrations of what it perceived as threats . . . toward cities, and the Wardens who clumped to defend them. As we came closer to Seattle, we'd start drawing unwelcome attention; Isabel's bright power would ensure that we couldn't pass completely unnoticed. Even Luis had an impressive presence on the aetheric, though Iz's light effectively hid his, and I presumed mine as well.

I was watching the ongoing battle of the Wardens when I felt the first stirring of . . . awareness. It was not so much something seen as felt . . . the power that was consuming Portland, that mindless beast seemed to pause and look. I felt the impact of its stare, like clouds over the face of the sun. All of the aetheric seemed to dim and go quiet.

It was looking at us.

I did not dare to move, not even to drift down into my body. There was a sense of a vast, predatory interest focused on us, and any tiny mistake could bring disaster.

The flames in Portland faltered and began to fall silent, but the energy behind them did not fall away; no, it gathered itself, a beast tensing to spring.

We were too close.

Freezing like prey wouldn't save us, I realized. I dropped back into my body with a breathless, icy rush, lunged forward to brace myself against the dashboard of the van, and gasped out, "Turn! Get off this road!"

"What?" Luis asked. "Jesus, Cass, what is it?"

"Get off the road. Do it now!"

"*Chica*, there's nowhere to go!"

"Turn around!" My shout must have conveyed the true depths of my alarm, because he didn't hesitate anymore. Luis hit the brakes, brought the van into a shuddering, tire-burning slide. Momentum threatened to tip us, but he controlled it somehow and accelerated into the drift. The tires caught traction, and suddenly we jerked forward, heading back the way we'd come.

"Faster!" I yelled. "Get us off this road!"

Luis didn't ask any more questions, just pressed the accelerator to the floor. When the van responded sluggishly, I felt him working the engine with Earth power, opening up clogged valves to pull more power out of the churning metal parts.

It wasn't going to be enough.

I could see it now, through the back window—a blazing arrow of power coming behind us, like liquid sunlight flowing down the road. The trees on either side were igniting into brilliant orange. Everything it touched died.

And it was going to catch us.

"Stop," Isabel said.

"Can't do that," Luis said. "Cass is right. We can't fight this."

"You can't run fast enough," she said. She sounded scared, but certain. "Cassie, we need him."

She was talking about Rashid, but Rashid would be of no real help to us; he might possibly be able to preserve our lives, but this power would simply drown us, consume us, and even a Djinn's power was limited by his master's endurance. Sooner or later, he would lose that battle, and we would be dissolved, digested, gone.

The benefit for Rashid would be that the glass of his bottle wouldn't last, either; he'd be free again, free to join the crusade against the hunted remains of humanity. Though I wondered whether he would take quite so much joy in it as others.

"Cassie!" she shouted. We had seconds, if that. She was right. There was nothing else we could do, not against this vast force of nature that rolled toward us.

I lunged over the seat, into the back of the van, thumping down next to Esmeralda, who was staring out the window with a grim, silent concentration that was not quite fear and not quite delight. An uneasy mix of the two. "Beautiful," she said. "Death's really beautiful, you know."

"Shut up," I said, and ripped open the saddlebag of the Victory, parked beside her coils. Her rattle stirred with a dry hiss, but I kicked it out of the way and grabbed Rashid's bottle. I ripped the foam stopper out. "Rashid! You're called!"

He could have dawdled; any enterprising Djinn could have used delay to his advantage, especially one with a grudge, but instead he was instantaneously crouched in front of me, silver eyes gleaming, naked indigo body coiled almost as sinuously as Esmeralda's reptilian form. His teeth glittered as his lips cut in a smile. "What will you?" he asked me.

"Take us safely to the Wardens in Seattle," I said. "Now."

"You forgot to say painlessly," he said.

Too late.

Rashid wasn't one of the Djinn capable of transporting humans cleanly through the aetheric. . . . That was a skill only a very few possessed, and those who did hardly ever bothered to use it. What he could do, however, was pick up the entire van and move it at speed the mechanical beast was never meant to achieve—speed that flattened me back against the van's wall, drove the scream back into my chest. Bones creaked under the strain, and my cuts reopened, sending red trickles rippling not down, but up and back, driven by the incredible force of our passage.

It took seconds, but it felt like an eternity, trapped and terrified. When it passed, it did so suddenly, a deceleration that sent me slamming with stunning force against the metal van doors at the end, with a hail of unsecured metal tools around me. Rashid was kind enough to ensure that I wasn't killed by them, but he didn't bother with minor injuries—more cuts and bruises to add to my collection.

Esmeralda fared better, but only because she'd coiled herself tightly and wedged herself between the van's driver's seat and the bolted racks of tools. Even then, as my vision cleared, I saw that her nose was bleeding, and so were her ears. Even her eyes had turned ruddy in the whites.

I fumbled for the van's door and tumbled out onto a cold, hard surface—and almost off the edge of a roof twenty stories high. I caught myself in time, just barely, and slowly edged backward.

The van was precariously on the edge, well off the center of a yellow painted circle that was, I suddenly realized, meant for helicopters. The paint on the van had blistered and peeled away in places, and as I watched, it settled slowly down as all four tires deflated.

The driver's side door opened, and Luis fell out. Luckily, he was not so close to the edge of the roof as I'd been. He flopped over on his back, staring up at the sky, gasping hoarsely. Like Esmeralda, his face was gory with blood from ruptured blood vessels, and he coughed and spat up more red, then groaned.

"Ibby," I whispered. I managed to scramble upright, clinging a moment to the van's open back door, and then felt my way around to the passenger side.

Isabel lay across the seat, eyes tightly shut. Her face was paper white, and her nose was still bleeding. I fumbled in the glove compartment and found a box of tissues; I grabbed a handful and used them to mop the blood from her face. Her eyes fluttered open, and she took the tissues and pressed them to her nose herself.

We didn't speak. I smoothed her hair with one trembling hand and realized that I was still holding Rashid's bottle in the other, uncorked.

Rashid was standing just at the edge of the roof, balanced on his bare toes, staring down. He still hadn't bothered with clothing, and now he turned and faced me, hands on his hips. "No gratitude?" he asked. "I suppose I deserve that. But you're safe, and the Wardens are on the floors below. On their way to you now." In a sudden rush, he was standing at the van's door, leaning in on me. His eyes had gone from silver to an even more unsettling steel color. "A word of advice, Cassiel: You've woken a devil, and it will come for you. The Wardens won't welcome you."

"In the bottle," I said. "Now."

He grinned at me in a way that made me think of the

amusement of cannibals, and vanished in a puff of soft blue smoke. Theatrical now. But not a liar, I thought.

I'd lost the foam sponge, but Esmeralda held it up as she leaned over the seat to look at Isabel. I nodded thanks and squeezed it into the neck of the bottle as Esmeralda asked, "How is she?"

I didn't need to answer. Isabel gave us a thumbs-up gesture, took the tissues from her nose, and sniffled cautiously.

"I think it's stopped," she said, and sat up. "Yeah, it's stopped. Es? Are you okay?"

"Five by five," Esmeralda said. "Your uncle don't look so good."

Luis was still lying on his back, staring at the cloudy sky. I took more tissues from the box and went to sit next to him. As he wiped the blood from his face, he said, "Next time, tell me about the goddamn Djinn in the goddamn bottle before you pull that shit." He sounded tired, but oddly calm. "Good call, though. We weren't going to make it. If ever there was a time for a panic button, that was it. How'd you get him?"

I shrugged. Every muscle in my body ached now, as if it had been stretched on a rack. "Luck," I said. "And I think he let me, in a way. Rashid isn't one who's been longing for the end of the human race. In a strange sort of way, I think he likes you humans."

"You're one of us," Luis pointed out. "Which you keep forgetting, by the way. Doesn't make me feel better about our future."

"We don't have one," I said. "Any of us."

"Ouch." He rolled over on his side, then up to his feet, with an assist from me. "Damn, that feels about as good as I expected it would. What the hell did he do?"

"I think it's best we don't ask in detail. The Wardens are on the way—"

I was wrong, I realized, as the door on the other side of the roof banged open, and a stream of people poured out. Some were regular humans dressed in military uniforms and carrying weapons; some were unarmed, but far from regular. Power glimmered around them, even to the human eye. There were five Wardens, by the time they'd all arranged themselves around us, and an equal number of armed military personnel.

One of the Wardens stepped forward: male, older than Luis, with short black hair graying at the temples and a whippet-thin build. He had an unusual face, I thought—handsome, but with a strangely ironic twist, and very dark eyes. There was something very strong about him, and very dangerous. "Luis Rocha," he said, and turned that stare on me for a second. "Cassiel."

"Pleased to meet you," Luis said. He was leaning on me, but now he straightened and centered himself. "That's my niece Isabel in the van. And her friend Esmeralda."

The Warden inclined his head just a touch, not so much agreement as acknowledgment. "I'm Brennan," he said. "Nice parking job. Want to tell me exactly how you managed that? Because I'm pretty sure that only a Djinn could have blasted through our defenses and landed you so neat and pretty on our roof. Twenty-two floors up."

"I'm a Djinn," I said.

"Was," he corrected, and extended his hand. "Hand it over."

"What?"

"The bottle you used to get here," he said. "Hand it over, or you're going to get to street level without the benefit of the elevator." Brennan was, I realized, a Weather Warden, and a powerful one. I felt a sudden, damp gust of air slam against me—a bully's warning shove.

"I'm disappointed," Luis said. "Considering you've got all those shiny guns."

Brennan snorted. "Yes, Bre'r Rabbit, I'm going to walk you into the briar patch," he said. "Threatening Earth Wardens with guns. That's a winning strategy." He sounded genuinely amused, but in the next snap of a second, that was utterly gone. "Hand it over, or I'll hand you over to gravity, and I assure you, she isn't as kind as I am."

I smiled thinly. "No."

He cocked an eyebrow. "Excuse me, I think I heard you say no. I must have been wrong about that because—" Suddenly, the wind's shove turned into a persistent, strong push that, despite my efforts to stabilize, moved both Luis and me back over the roof toward the edge; not quite over, but the distance was halved before he finished his sentence. "Because that would really be very sad. I'd have a moment."

"So would I," Isabel said. I hadn't seen her get out of the van, but she was now standing on the other side and facing Brennan from that angle. "And you wouldn't like that, Mr. Brennan."

"Oh, it's just Brennan," he said. "You're a cutie, aren't you? Don't." Once again, his voice went from warm and oddly gentle to utterly cold in the whiplash space of an instant. "If you think you're going to whip up a little fiery surprise for me, I wouldn't. See Miss Walinsky, there?" He nodded to a slight young woman in a violently purple hoodie, with blue streaks in her hair and a ring through her nose. "Miss Walinsky makes your normal firestarters look like wet rags. I don't think either one of you wants to be getting into it. Portland already burned. We're trying to keep that kind of behavior to a minimum here, so put a cork in it. So to speak."

He returned his attention to me and held out his hand again. He didn't need to speak.

And neither did I. I was an arm's length from the

edge, and now I took a giant step toward it, and held the bottle out, dangling it carelessly from two fingers over the drop. "I think we have room for negotiation," I said. "Don't we, Brennan? And the next time you threaten that child, I'll take it out of you in flesh."

His face went still and his eyes went empty, and for a second I couldn't tell what he was doing or thinking. Then it was as if he flipped a switch, and he was all smiles. The hand lowered back to his side. "That would be interesting," he said. "But let's put a pin in that for now, shall we? Why don't we get in out of the cold and have a nice, comfortable discussion? Always nice to see more Wardens. We damn well need the help. Okay, everybody stand down. Down. We're all friends here."

I sincerely doubted that, but he made gestures, and the armed military were the first to head back through the roof door. Then one by one the other Wardens followed. Miss Walinsky, I noticed, went next to last, and Brennan slowly backed up toward the exit while still carefully watching us. The pressure of wind against my body faltered, and stopped; I hadn't even realized how much there had been until he released it. For a Weather Warden, he had an impressive amount of power and control.

"Come on down," he said. "We've got coffee. And I promise, no more strong-arm tactics."

This wasn't because he had a moral aversion to them, I thought; it was because he was smart, and flexible, and he knew they wouldn't work. Not with me.

I exchanged a look with my partner, and Luis shrugged, then winced from the twinges in his strained muscles. "Unless we want to live up here, no point in hanging around," he said. "You realize he's going to try to commandeer that bottle for the cause, right?"

"Of course," I said. "I'd do the same in his place. But it's not going to happen. The Wardens don't do well with

Djinn. They never have. And I'm not betraying Rashid to their tender mercies."

"Well, there's one good thing," Luis said, and put his arm around Isabel as she came to join us. The van shifted on its flat tires, groaning, as Esmeralda slithered her way out as well. "We're not on our own anymore. And there's coffee. I don't know about you, but I could use some of that."

I agreed about the coffee, at least.

In fact, the coffee was excellent, but as Luis murmured to me, it was Seattle; hardly extraordinary, given their obsession with caffeinated drinks, that they knew how to properly make it. I sipped a cup and let the warmth soak into my abused body; I was Warden enough to ensure that there were no subtle chemicals included to, say, put me to sleep in order to liberate Rashid's bottle. And Brennan, at least, wasn't stupid enough to try that.

Instead, he was trying persuasion. And logic.

"Look, we're happy you're here," he said as we took seats in what had once been some sort of corporate conference room; the chairs were opulent leather, the table large enough to seat thirty in comfort, and the lights were controlled from a remote that he operated with apparent expertise. On the far wall, a flat-screen television was tuned to a twenty-four-hour news channel. Both the chaotic footage and the scrawling text below reported mounting death tolls from the ongoing disasters around the country and the world. "As you can see, we need all the Warden power we can get."

I remembered the still, breathless morning, and my conviction that it was the last peace the human race would know.

It was a pity I'd been right.

Esmeralda had declined to come with us; she'd ignored the shocked looks of the Wardens, and the out-right white-knuckled fear of the military, and slithered into an office. She ordered food, a lot of it, and water, and slammed the door. I wasn't expecting her to join the conversation anytime soon.

Isabel was with us, and the look she gave Brennan was unsettling. She didn't like him much, and I supposed that was Brennan's own fault, really—nevertheless, it was a pity. We needed to work together, and his actions had made that more difficult.

"Yeah, we were heading to join up with you," Luis said. "I got a call from Warden HQ. They wanted to divert us to the mine problem."

"Ah," Brennan said. He sounded more subdued than he had before. "They got split off from us heading out of Portland. Going into the tunnels was the only way they could get away, but once they were in, there was no getting out. Their Earth Warden was killed, and without him, they're stuck. They're alive, but they need help, and we need them."

"So you won't mind if we go on and do that, then."

"Not at all, but before you do, let's talk about—"

"We're not talking about the bottle," I interrupted. "Because it stays with me. There's no point in discussing it."

Brennan settled back in his chair, dark eyes fixed on me. "You want to explain to me exactly how you managed to get a Djinn in a bottle? Because that trick stopped working some time ago, as far as I was aware. Not that I'd test it out."

I stared at him, expressionless, until I knew I'd made him uncomfortable (though he was better at most in hiding it), then said, "All you need do is wait for a Djinn to try to kill you, have a bottle ready, and be able to hold him off long enough to repeat the ritual three times. Of course, your chances are somewhat slim."

Brennan shook his head. "Slim," he repeated. "I don't think that's the word I'd choose. Thanks. I'll keep that in mind."

"Yes," I said. "Do."

Luis, sensing the tension between the two of us—oh, and it was thick, for reasons even I did not completely understand—leaned forward, sipped his coffee, and said, "Okay, so, we need to make sure that the girls will be safe here with you while we're gone."

"And how do you propose I guarantee that, Mr. Rocha?" Brennan asked. "I can't guarantee anything to anyone, as of yesterday, and you should know that better than anyone."

Isabel was frowning now, and she looked at Luis with her arms folded. "I don't want to stay here," she said. "I can go with you."

"No, you can't, *mija*," he said. "Where we're going is very dangerous, and I want you here, where you can do the most good, okay? The Wardens need your strength. We won't be long, I promise."

Her frown stayed, but she didn't say anything more. Giving in so easily wasn't like Isabel, and I wondered what she was plotting under the cover of that silence. Nothing I'd like, almost certainly.

"She'll be just fine here," Brennan said. "I just can't give you any absolutes, of course, but we've got other young Wardens here as well. They're being very helpful. I suppose you know about Portland . . . ?"

"Of course," I said.

"They came here to help defend Seattle after what happened there. Just arrived a few hours ago, but already they've been tremendously helpful. I'm sure your girl will do very well with them."

I felt a sudden surge of alarm, and looked over at my partner. He had put down his coffee cup and pressed both palms flat against the conference room table. "Warden kids," he said. "How many?"

"Four," Brennan replied. "Pretty damn gifted, too. They came with their guardian."

I held out no hope that it was Marion Bearheart, or another truly qualified Warden, but I forced a smile. "I see," I said. "That's very fortunate. Perhaps we could meet them so Isabel could get to know them . . . ?"

Brennan shrugged. "Sure, I've got nothing better to do than to make you two feel comfortable." His sarcasm was thick enough to score steel. "Come on, I'll introduce you. Maybe you can all huddle up and sing 'Kumbaya.'"

"I'll go," I said to Luis and Isabel. "You stay here."

He understood, and nodded. "You be careful."

Brennan gave us an odd, impatient look, but shrugged and led the way out into the hallway to the bank of elevators. It was evident no one had been concerned with cleaning for a few days; the steel surfaces were smudged with fingerprints and—in one case—spattered with what looked like dried blood.

"Were these Warden offices?" I asked. They were generic enough to have housed anything from consultants to bankers, with neutral reproduction paintings and sturdy mock-antique desks. The receptionist's desk opposite the elevators was manned by a burly tattooed man with a shaved head who picked up the ringing phone and ordered whoever was on the line to hold before stabbing a thick finger at another flashing button. He didn't look like the clerical type.

"No, they were my cousin's," Brennan said. "Well, not his, but he ran the office for his company."

"And they don't mind you taking them over?"

"Their headquarters were in Portland," he said. "I don't think they're going to mind much anymore, at least for a while. My cousin sent everybody home and handed over the place. It was easier than commandeering a motel, and it's got better infrastructure, for as long as the phones and computers last."

He was right—they wouldn't work forever; as more of the world fell apart, those delicate systems would be among the first to shatter, isolating people more, giving rise to ever-increasing panic and paranoia. Humans clung to the illusion of normality, even in the face of evidence to the contrary, but communication was what fed the illusion; starved of that, they would begin to band together in protective small groups, and those affiliations would create discord, even where none existed.

Society didn't take long to break down, once the trappings of it were taken away. For now, it was merely smudges on the surface of an elevator, but once the electricity failed, once there were no more news announcers to urge calm and give some kind of perspective, however skewed, it would rapidly grow worse. We were days from anarchy, and Brennan knew that. I could see it in the tight lines around his mouth and eyes. He seemed sardonic and uninvolved, but that wasn't true.

We were all involved now.

The elevator dinged its pleasant, civilized chime, and the doors slid open, revealing a windowless, airless box framed in wood. It was as small as a coffin, and I hesitated, then took a step back. "Are there stairs?" I asked him.

"Problem, Warden?"

"Yes. I don't wish to leave my survival suspended on a mechanical cable and a whim," I said. "Stairs?"

He shrugged and led the way off to the side, where an EXIT sign glowed red. "They're fire doors," he said. "It'll be locked in the stairwell, no reentry. You're an Earth warden, so I don't expect you'll need any key card to finesse the locks around here. Just bang on the door if you get stuck."

The stairwell was clear and cold, and we walked down five floors before Brennan used his key card on a swipe pad at another door and clicked it open. "After you," he said, and held it for me. "Down the hall and on the left. We put them in the smaller conference room."

I opened the door he indicated, and found a room half the size of the one above us where Isabel and Luis waited. In it, two small forms lay still in sleeping bags in the corners, and three people sat at the table, talking. They immediately fell silent when we entered.

Two of those at the table were children, no older than nine years old—a boy and a girl, neither of whom registered strongly with me at the moment. No, I focused on the woman sitting in the middle.

The guardian.

She rose and bowed to me, graceful and unhurried. She was of Japanese descent, lovely and fragile, with the calm precision of one who'd been trained from birth to be beautiful, and she was, oh yes, she was. I didn't know her, but it didn't matter what the history of the flesh might be, because flesh was all it was.

The power that resonated out of her was utterly inhuman, and utterly unmistakable to someone who'd fought her to the death once before.

"Hello, sister," I said. Next to me, Brennan gave me a sharp look.

"My dear Cassiel," she said, and inclined her head as she folded her hands together.

The flesh didn't matter.

What was inside her, glowing and feverish with power and madness, was my sister. My enemy.

Pearl.

Chapter 6

THE SILENCE HELD BETWEEN US, deep and thick as polar ice, and neither of us moved. Brennan finally cleared his throat and entered the room; he was no fool, in that he took up a point out of the line of fire, and equidistant from us both. "So you two know each other."

"After a fashion," Pearl said. "Many years ago. But we have been . . . out of touch. Isn't that right?"

I didn't answer her. I was considering options, and none of them were good; Luis was getting stronger again as he rested, but it would take time for him to be up to full strength and, even then, taking on Pearl meant taking on her four child-followers. She wouldn't be here, in flesh, unless they were her best possible bodyguards, which meant they would be hideously strong and—no doubt—impossible to persuade of her real motivations. True believers were always the most dangerous, and children were more dangerous than most.

I finally said, "Yes, we've been out of touch. I confess, I preferred it that way, Pearl."

"Shinju," she said, and pressed a delicate hand to her chest. "My name is Shinju now."

"Still Pearl, just translated into a different language," I said. "Don't play games."

"I'm not. We have common foes, my sister. I'm here to help, with my children."

"They're not yours," I shot back. "They have families, and they were taken from them."

"These? No. These children came willingly. Their parents wanted them safe and protected, trained and nurtured. And I have done this, as you have with Isabel." Her eyes were dark, and so was what dwelled in them. "This is Pamela. At the age of four, she was able to start fires with her mind, but she didn't understand what she was doing; there were accidents, tragedies. Her family gave her up so that she might learn how to protect herself and those around her." The girl looked up from the plate of unnaturally golden macaroni and cheese in front of her, and gave me a look that was eerily identical to Pearl's; there was no real feeling in it, only assessment.

Pearl put her hand on the other girl's shoulder now, and she straightened in evident pride. "Edie was medicated to stop her from tantrums," she said. "But she didn't need medication; she needed only reassurance and training in her craft. Weather, you see. Like Mr. Brennan. She can create a drop of water or a storm with equal ease. I'm sure you appreciate how valuable that skill can be to us now, in these dangerous times."

"The kids are amazingly powerful," Brennan said. "Let's face it—we need every hand at the wheel right now. It's not like we've got a snowball's chance in hell as it stands without them." He couldn't mean it, not entirely; there was something about Pearl—Shinju—that radiated darkness, and he *had* to feel that, no matter how desperate the need . . . didn't he? "The good thing is that they've committed to guarding our position here. As defenses go, they're about as good as we can possibly have."

"But they're not being sent to rescue your Wardens trapped in the tunnels," I said. "I find it curious that they're so powerful yet unable to do such a simple thing."

"You can't expect me to risk these children," Pearl said, raising her delicate eyebrows. "I must protect them at all costs, mustn't I? Isn't that what any responsible adult would do? What *you* would do?"

Protect. The hypocrisy of the word coming from her lips made me so angry that for a moment all I could see was the red sheer curtain of blood, and her face smiling through it; I felt power surging inside me, hungry for release. She was mocking me, mocking us all. Pearl had no interest in the welfare of her children; they were tools, to be honed, used, broken, and replaced. She'd treated Isabel no better, and she'd gladly take possession of her again just to use and break her again.

It occurred to me, with an unpleasant shock, that Pearl could have gone anywhere, shown up in any Warden encampment, and been welcomed with open arms . . . but she'd come here. To Seattle. She'd tracked me and anticipated where I would go.

She wanted Isabel back.

"No," I said aloud.

Her eyebrow slanted up in elegant mockery. "I should not protect them? Is that what you mean, sister? Shall I leave these poor children to the mercy of the world, to those who fear and hate them? Do you imagine their lives would be better? Their families were terrified of them. The human world had no answer for it. The Wardens turned their backs, saying they were too young. Only I could step in and keep them safe. How could I have done otherwise?"

The utter self-serving mockery turned my stomach. The children might believe it — I was certain they *did* believe that she cared for them; they'd hardly have that manic glow in their eyes, that love, if they thought otherwise. But Pearl had no love in her, no concern, no honor. It was all just flash and theater to her, the people in this world no more real to her than paper dolls.

"You've come for Isabel," I said. "You won't have her. Not again."

"Isabel? Isabel — oh, yes, I remember her. A cute little thing, but a bit underpowered for what I needed." Pearl shrugged. "I don't want her. Besides, sister, she has you now to care for her. Why would I wish to intrude on that loving relationship? Why, you're almost a mother to the poor thing." Her smile was as swift and cruel as a hawk's strike. She knew what it was like between the girl and me; she knew how complicated and difficult and dangerous it was for me to love a child of such power. To care, really care, in ways that Pearl herself did not.

And I hated her for knowing it.

Brennan cleared his throat. "Ladies," he said. "Problem?"

Before Pearl could offer up the platitudes that were surely ready, I said, "Yes. If you keep her here, you're accepting your own doom. She'll destroy you. You need to get her out of here, *now*."

Brennan thought I was joking, at least for a split second, but he must have quickly realized I was in deadly earnest. "What are you talking about? She's — "

"Not a Warden," I said. "Not in any way. The fact that she wields these children like weapons does not mean she is in any way sympathetic to your cause, or your challenges. She's radioactive, Mr. Brennan. Use her, and you may win a short-term victory, but a slow, long-term death. It's not even vaguely a possibility that she will allow any Warden on Earth to live once she has what she wants."

He didn't answer for a long moment. Shinju continued to smile faintly, untroubled, watching me with those unsettling, lovely eyes. Her hands remained gently on the shoulders of her two followers, who were likewise fixed on me with the intensity of hunting wolves.

"My sister is mistaken," she said. Shinju's voice was a weapon, too—full of music, gentle regret, false comfort. "I am heartbroken to be the cause of such strife, Mr. Brennan. You have given me shelter and safety here, and in return, I and the children have promised to protect this home you have offered us. We mean you no harm, I promise you. I am sorry for Cassiel's bitterness, and her rage, but I do not share it. What may I do to offer you reassurance?"

He had to know, I thought. He was no fool. He had instincts. He had to *know* she was a danger to us all. The feeling she radiated was like razor blades on my skin, absolutely and unbelievably menacing.

"Back off," Brennan said—not to her, but to *me*. "Shinju and the kids came here and contributed; that's all I ask. How about you, Cassiel? You going to pitch in? Or you going to start a war right here, with a bunch of children?"

He didn't see it. Couldn't, of course; Shinju was a perfect flesh disguise for Pearl. Her frail beauty roused protective instincts, especially in male humans; her courage and quiet power raised other instincts in them that made them wish to believe her, trust her, want her. She was clever, my sister.

And insane, in ways the humans could not possibly guess.

"Our mother is ill," she told me. "It is up to us to protect each other from her wrath until sanity comes again.

That is the job of the Wardens, is it not? And anyone gifted with power and the will to use it."

"Don't," I said. "Don't think that I'll ever believe you, or fall for what you've promised these people. I know you, Pearl. I know what you want, and what you intend. And I will stop you."

"No matter the cost?" she asked, and put her arms around the two children. They leaned against her. It was a pretty, and damning, picture. "If you attack me, you attack them, Cassiel. You make war on children. How can you do that?"

"Stop hiding behind them, then." I was angry enough to gather power around me, and I felt it crackling inside me like a storm.

Pearl's eyes widened, and I saw the dark joy in her.

The child on her left extended his hand, and I saw the hissing power of lightning forming around it.

I lowered my chin and readied myself for a fight that would level the building.

"Enough!" Brennan said. He came to my side, grabbed my arm, and pulled me violently off balance. "Enough, all of you. If you can't play nice, you don't have to share the playground. Cassiel, come with me. Shinju—just do what you were doing. As far as I'm concerned, you're all on notice—no trouble here, or everybody goes. Clear?"

He had no power here, no power at all. Brennan's authority was entirely mistaken. If she wished, my sister could have blown him apart with a snap of her fingers . . . if she was ready to make that move.

Clearly, she wasn't. Not quite. Instead, Shinju bowed toward him. "Very clear, Mr. Brennan. I apologize for this awkwardness. My sister has always been—difficult."

I laughed wildly. "She's a killer," I said. "You're a fool. You're putting your trust in a wild animal, and she'll turn on you. Soon."

"You're not acting too damn house-trained yourself," he said, and shoved me out into the hall as he banged the conference room door closed. "What the hell was that?"

"You have no idea," I said. "No idea what you're doing. What you're risking."

"You'd be real damn wrong about that," Brennan said grimly. "Follow me. Let me show you what we're risking."

The hallway opened into a large open workspace filled with desks. The smell of the place was sharp and familiar—sweat, desperation, old trash, humans who'd gone without rest or comfort for days. A few were asleep where they sat, with their heads down on their arms; a heavily pregnant woman was asleep on a black leather couch pushed against the far wall, near the bathrooms. It was a chaos of ripped paper, overflowing trash cans, and haphazardly placed shiny boards on which were scribbled all manner of things—calculations, crudely drawn maps, notes. . . .

And on one wall was tacked a giant, oversized map of the United States. There were pins stuck in it, a confusion of colors.

Brennan led me over to it. "Yellow pins are for reports of earthquakes and other Earth events," he said. "You can see that they follow a lot of the natural faults and seams, but we've got a few brand-new ones that don't have any historical basis we can find. Red are wildfires; the larger the pin, the bigger the problem. We ran out of sizes, so we started just drawing the boundaries in marker for the biggest. Blue is weather-related events—tornadoes, storms, lightning, and the like. Black pins are Djinn incidents."

I took a deep breath as I looked at the map, because taking each color individually painted a clear picture of a world in crisis . . . deep crisis. But combining them showed something quite different, and horrifyingly obvious.

There was no way to stop it. Even had the entire ship full of Wardens stranded out at sea and helpless docked today, even had every high-powered Warden alive come racing to the rescue, it would not be enough . . . and this was one country. Just one, in a world full of upheaval. And likely not even the worst, in terms of loss of life and impact. It was too much, too fast, and too vast in scope.

"How many dead?" I asked.

Brennan was silent for a moment, as if he couldn't really bring himself to speak, and then he cleared his throat and said, "In this country, right at this moment, we're looking at about ten million in casualties. That could be low. We've lost touch with some major population centers, so we could be off by several million by now."

Millions. *Millions.*

Weakness took me, suddenly, and I closed my eyes. Brennan's arm went around my shoulders, a comfort that I should not have wanted, or accepted, but I leaned gratefully against him. Like the others here, he smelled of sweat, desperation, simple unwashed skin . . . but that no longer repelled me.

He had not given up. He'd watched this map of despair form, and he'd still kept his team focused, working, hopeful.

Somehow, hopeful.

"We need her," he said softly. "Do you see it now? We need every goddamn one of us. I'm not saying it will be enough, but it can never be too much. Not now. Not if we expect to hold even one more day against this tide, and Orwell told me personally that I *have* to hold it. Have to. Understand? This isn't about your personal spats or future dangers or any of that crap. This is about the next half hour, and whether or not more millions of people live to see it."

"Shinju isn't the answer," I said. "She's taking advantage of your panic, your fear. If you turn to her, you're only running to the wolf pack to escape the dogs."

"Which one's going to eat us slower?" he asked. "Because that's the choice I have to make, Cassiel. And if you can't deal with that, get the fuck out of my sight, because I not only don't have the time, I damn sure don't have the energy."

Harsh as that might have seemed, it helped. I steadied myself, breathed in, out, and nodded. "I will help you," I said. "But you need to clearly understand, Brennan, she will turn on you, and soon. You can't trust her for even a moment."

"Hell, I already knew that," he said. "I don't trust her. I don't trust you, either, lady. You just got here, and frankly, you scare the shit out of me. If I didn't need every damn spark of talent on the planet, I'd kick both of you out the door. But the fact is that I don't have that luxury anymore. If the devil himself shows up trailing ashes and holding a pitchfork, I'm putting him to work on fire duty."

I put my hand on his and gripped it, hard. "It would be better to trust the devil," I said. "He at least needs souls. Pearl doesn't."

Then I pulled free, walked back to the conference room, and opened the door.

Shinju was sitting calmly, hands folded. The two children had their eyes closed, but they were not asleep. They were working.

"Well?" she asked me. There was no real doubt in her as to what my answer would be, and I didn't trouble to hesitate.

"I won't work with you," I said. "Not now, and not

ever. But I will not fight you here. If you choose to help them, then help, but if I see you even think of turning on them, I'll fight you to the ashes of the world."

Pearl smiled, very slowly, with terrible beauty and emptiness in those eyes. "Oh, I will save them," she said. "All those people. And you will help me, my sister, because that is who you are. You were never a murderer. Not as I was. Not as I am. Ashan was a fool to believe it, even for a moment."

The leader of the True Djinn, Ashan, had asked me to kill the human race, and I had said no, and now—just as he'd foreseen, somehow—this was the reward I had reaped. The end of humanity being forced upon us, and Pearl the savior of it.

For now. Until she had all she wanted.

The enemy of my enemy . . . would never be my friend. Never.

"I'll still destroy you," I told her. "This is just a small breathing space. Enjoy it while it lasts, Pearl."

Her smile widened, lost its formal grace and became a thing of true, horrific amusement. "Charming," she said. "And now you can go explain to Isabel why you're allowing me to help these people. You made her promises, didn't you, that you'd fight me at every turn? And now you must break them."

She was right.

I said nothing, and I left the conference room door open as I walked away to the stairs. Five flights went too quickly, but I was glad of the slight distraction of the activity. I wanted to run now. Run until my body was full and my mind was empty.

Run from everything.

Upstairs, Luis rose from his chair and said, "Cass? Are you okay?" Isabel came slowly around the table, tentative and worried. I don't know what they saw in me, but whatever it might have been, it must have mirrored the blackness inside me.

"Pearl's here," I said. "And we need her. We can't fight her now. I'm sorry."

Isabel's eyes widened. "The Lady's here?"

"Yes." It hurt me that there was only a little fear in Iz's eyes, mixed with a larger portion of excitement. It wasn't her fault. Pearl had taken her from us, and she'd twisted Isabel in so many ways—not just waking her powers prematurely, but convincing the girl that it was for her own good. She'd convinced Iz that her uncle hadn't loved her, that I had betrayed her, that Isabel could only trust herself, in the end.

Pearl had destroyed Iz's childhood, but she'd made her strong, and the Isabel that existed now valued that more than anything else. More: Pearl had made the child love her, in a way that I never could.

I tried not to feel a rush of hatred for that, and despair, but I was honest enough now to admit that I deeply wanted that love from Isabel, that unconditional devotion; I wanted to give it in return. But Pearl had precedence, and Iz couldn't trust me, not completely.

I was not born to be a mother, it seemed.

"Where is she?" Iz breathed.

"Doesn't matter," Luis said. "We're not going anywhere near her. Cass, have you lost your fucking mind? You can't let her near Isabel!"

He hadn't seen the map, hadn't felt the gut-wrenching power of the true scope of what we faced. I knew that, but still, the disbelieving betrayal in his face made me hurt. "Talk to Brennan," I said. "I promise you, this is what must happen. Not what I want, but what we need. Just talk to him, and decide for yourself. I won't interfere."

"You let him mess with your head," Luis said. He was

tense and angry now, fists clenched. "You were the one who called Orwell and laid down the law, damn you. You said—"

"I know what I said," I interrupted him, just as tightly furious. "But we won't live to see the dawn unless we work with her. We won't, Luis. There are no angels to rescue us. Only devils, and we must take whatever hand is offered now."

He shook his head and stalked out—no doubt, in search of Brennan. Isabel gave me a last, silent look and followed, and I sank down in a chair and put my aching head in my hands. I had never felt so trapped, or so human.

I had sworn I would never accept a peace with Pearl, but now . . . now I'd not only done it, I'd promised cooperation.

The enemy of my enemy . . .

"Mother," I whispered, close to tears. "How could you desert us? How could you bring us to this?"

But the Mother had never spoken to me, not directly, and she did not do so now. There was only darkness, and silence.

I wasn't sure how much time passed, but it seemed like only moments before someone was shaking me by the shoulder. I hadn't meant to sleep, and wasn't sure that I had, really, but the momentary shame and confusion was burned away by the sight of Luis's face, and the urgency of his voice.

"Come on," he said. "We need you. Now."

I followed him at a run down the hall. We slammed through the fire door and onto the concrete steps, which he took two at a time, running at a careless speed that held no concern for his own safety. Five floors down, we came on the locked door. He had no card, but before I could find the one I'd been given, he extended a hand and simply melted the lock of the door. "Stupid anyway," he muttered. "What the fuck is there to steal now? Money? No damn use at all."

The hallway was busy with people coming and going, but they parted for Luis as he shoved through; we passed the small room that Pearl had been in, but both she and the four children were gone, leaving sleeping bags, plates, and glasses scattered carelessly around.

They were all in the main room, all the Wardens. Pearl and her four followers were there, too, standing slightly apart. She looked calm and detached, but unsmiling—at least until she caught sight of me.

"What is it?" I asked Luis. He ignored the question as he pushed through the standing crowd of Wardens. Isabel was at the front, standing with Brennan. Even Esmeralda had come out, I saw; she was coiled up ·in the back corner of the room, and had lifted her human torso up to see over those in the way. Her eyes had gone slitted and reptilian.

I didn't need an answer, because my eyes fell on the board, and the Warden who was pulling out pins from an area of the map in the middle of the country. It had been filled with yellow and red, blue and black . . . but all the pins were being removed and dumped in boxes.

There were tears on the Warden's pale face, and she paused to wipe them with the back of a hand before she continued.

Then she took a black marker and drew a thick diagonal line through the open space. Then another, crossing it.

"We've lost control of most of the Midwest," Luis said. "St. Louis is gone; it's a goddamn heap of junk after the last earthquake. Kansas City is badly damaged, too many dead to count; everything's in chaos now, people fighting for food, cars, gas. . . . It's all coming apart. Still some communities holding together, mostly smaller towns, but tornadoes are targeting them specifically, ripping them up one by one. Too much, too fast. Brennan had to pull the surviving Wardens out when the Djinn began coming after them directly."

I looked around at the others. There were more tears, and silence so deep and aching that it made me tremble.

Brennan finally said, "We don't have time to grieve. I'm sorry. I know everyone knows someone who's been affected by this—the losses are enormous, and shocking, and I'm sorry we can't give it the attention it deserves. I'm sorry that the dead can't be honored now. But there are living people we need to save, and we still can save them, if we stay focused. You're doing it, people. You're making a difference. We knew this would happen, so don't let it stop you."

There were a few nods, and some gulped back their tears and wiped their faces. The Warden who'd drawn the X through a tri-state area of the nation put down the marker and stepped back, head bowed. I saw her lips moving in silent prayer.

I wondered how many bodies lay dead and unburied there. How many millions of lives had just been lost, or were being lost, right now. We were abandoning them to their fates.

It seemed heartless, but I could see that it was a choice the Wardens had to make. We couldn't grieve. We couldn't count costs. We couldn't worry about enemies, and the future, and what might happen tomorrow.

Surviving this eternal, exhausting day would be achievement enough.

Pearl said, in a soft but carrying voice, "I have followers near the borders of Missouri. They will take up stations at the borders."

"Can they fight off a hundred Djinn?" Brennan snapped. "Don't throw away lives. Those Djinn will do anything they want, and we can't stop them."

"I can," Pearl said with perfect calm. "I have a weapon that will destroy any Djinn who touches it."

There was silence again, but in the silence I felt the electric surge of hope that raced around the room, leaping from human to human like a wildfire. "What kind of weapon?" Brennan asked. He didn't want to commit, I realized, but even so, he was seduced.

As she'd intended.

"Me," Pearl said, and bowed slightly. "I can destroy the Djinn. And you must help me accomplish it."

Pearl had won, and I knew it. In the face of such disaster, such enormous losses of life as were piling up now, there was nothing that the Wardens could do but accept her, regardless of any later consequences or costs. Even I acknowledged it.

But not Luis.

"Are you kidding me?" he whispered furiously. "This is nuts! They're just going to roll over for her, just like that! Kill the Djinn—are they insane? The Djinn are the only thing that have a hope in hell of stopping *her*!"

We were standing off to ourselves in a corner of the large room; the Wardens had drifted back to their desks, not so much to work as to process all the overwhelming flood of information in solitude. As for Pearl, she had settled in the opposite corner of the room, looking calm and smug; her children had gathered around her, sitting in a semicircle on the floor. They didn't speak. Neither did she. I supposed that it would have been unnecessary, as thoroughly as she owned them now.

Isabel hadn't joined them, but neither had she joined us. She was standing against the wall near Esmeralda, watching all of this with uncertain intensity. I wanted to give her some kind of surety, but I had none myself to share.

"They're not so insane," I said. "Think of all the Wardens have suffered these past years, and often at the hands of the Djinn; from the moment that the Djinn were released from their bonds, they've been dangerous to mortals, and especially to the ones who'd once held them captive. After all, my people have a very long memory. That distrust and hate might have gone on for millennia, even without any other problems to complicate it. Humans hate, but they forgive. Djinn . . . cannot forget, and don't often forgive."

"So what are you telling me, that you agree with her? That you want the Djinn dead?"

"Of course not!" I snapped, and controlled my raw temper with an effort. "But the Djinn are a deadly threat now, and they are not acting on their own. In a war there are casualties, and unless you want them all to be on the side of the humans . . ."

"She's not talking about killing one or two, Cass, which is bad enough. She's talking about slaughtering all of them. The Djinn exist for a reason. They're the balancing force. Without them—"

"I know," I said. "Believe me, I know. But we must find a way to make use of her—the Wardens won't do otherwise. The best we can do is to try to minimize the damage that is done. Yes?"

He didn't like it, and he gave me a tired, angry frown to show it. "Yes," he finally said, but not as if he in any way agreed in the details. "I can't believe it's come to this, that all of a sudden we're on the same side with *her*. God, Cass—"

I put my hand on his cheek. It felt rough and gritty; he'd been without bathing or shaving, and the dark stubble on his face grated my fingertips. Oddly, I found it soothing. "She's in flesh," I whispered. "In flesh, Luis. Always before, she's stayed on the aetheric, made herself impossible to wound in any real way. But now . . ."

"Now she's vulnerable," he finished. Light sparked in his eyes, and he kissed the palm of my hand. "Why didn't I see that?"

"You're tired. We're all tired. She had to take flesh at some point to channel the power given her by her acolytes, but she waited until she was certain it was necessary, and we were vulnerable ourselves."

"She could shed that form, though. Anytime."

"Not easily," I said. "Not quickly. And if we can seal her inside it, cut her off from the sources of her power, then she'll die along with the shell."

"You mean cut her off from the children."

I didn't answer, because that was not what I meant at all. The children were her well-trained minions, yes, but that wasn't where Pearl's power was truly founded. . . . Like me, she had no direct connection to the aetheric, and therefore to stay alive had to draw power through others. I was joined to a Warden, whose connection was broad and deep, and not only sustained me but gave me access to considerable power.

Pearl was different in ways that I couldn't, still, comprehend, but her power was aggregated not from one person, but from millions. Not Wardens, but regular, unmagical humans, whose life force connected only weakly to the aetheric . . . but the connection existed, and could be exploited. Had Pearl tried to source herself through one of them, she'd have killed him instantly; spreading that access across a million lives or more gave her a constant, vast draw of energy. Renewable energy. She could tap anyone she liked, anytime she liked.

No wonder Ashan had seen that the only solution

was the death of the human race; nothing else could possibly destroy her.

And she *had* to be destroyed before she gained enough power, and killed enough Djinn, to attack the Mother at her most vulnerable.

"So what's the plan?" Luis asked me. He looked past me to the corner where Pearl sat. I followed his gaze. My sister smiled at us and inclined her head. No doubt she knew we'd be scheming; she'd be a fool to assume otherwise. She also knew, no doubt, that we had few choices ahead of us, and none of them were good.

"Trust me," I said, and walked across the room toward Pearl. Luis, after a few seconds, pushed away from the wall to follow. So did Isabel, although Esmeralda merely stirred uneasily, then settled back to stay where she was, arms folded.

Pearl's children watched me with blank intensity as I approached. I could sense the vibration of power around them. Earth, Fire, Weather . . . and the boy sitting closest to Pearl, the one whose power was a negative energy that was the most like what I sensed in Pearl. He was a Void, the power of unmaking and consuming other energy. Of all of them, I calculated him the most dangerous, only because there were few effective counters for him in a fight.

"Sister," Pearl said. "Come to join us?"

I sat down on the floor only a few feet from her children, comfortable and cross-legged. Luis hesitated, then joined me, although he didn't look nearly as at ease at it as I did. But he hadn't had all the thousands of years of deception to practice. "Of course," I said. "Your logic is flawless. For humans to survive this conflict, they need a champion, one of power. You are the only one disposed to help them. What do you propose?"

"First, we gather all the Wardens together," she said. "You know of the ones trapped in the mine?"

"I've been told."

"I'll send one of my children to help you. She'll be the most useful—her name is Edie; she's the strongest Weather power I've ever seen." Pearl reached out to place her hand on the shoulder of the tall blond girl, who straightened with pride. "She can help you sweeten the air while you work toward them."

"There may be Djinn," I said. Pearl nodded.

"And I will also send Alvin," she said, and now the Void boy stirred, turning his gaze toward her. "Alvin will deal with any Djinn very effectively."

"But you said I'd stay with you!" he said, and reached out to put his fingertips on her knee. "Lady, I want to stay with you. . . ."

"You'll go where you're needed, Alvin. And I believe that you're needed to protect my sister." Her smile was faint, but malevolent for all that. "I'm among friends here. Or at least, I'm among those without the power to harm me in any significant way. I'm sure that your brother and sister can keep me safe until you return."

She was keeping Earth and Fire with her—two powers that could be used destructively in the confines of this building, should it come to a pitched battle. I wasn't surprised that she'd thought strategically, but she might have made an error with the boy; Alvin seemed mutinous about being sent away, as if this was a personal slight to be dismissed from her presence. The girl, by contrast, seemed proud to have a special mission from the hands of the Lady.

The boy would bear closer watching.

"When do you wish to leave?" Pearl asked me.

"Now," I said. "If that's convenient."

"Of course." She reached out and took the hand of the boy, and then that of the Weather girl. "Children, my sister will look after your safety. One thing I know about

Cassiel, she does take her responsibilities seriously. She won't allow any harm to come to you."

The two looked at me with identical cool expressions of mistrust; Pearl had done an excellent job of poisoning them against anyone else. This wouldn't be an easy partnership.

"I'll take care of them," I agreed. In my heart, I was thinking that I would take far better care of them than she ever had, but it didn't bear speaking aloud. The children had been twisted to her point of view; they'd never understand how much she'd taken advantage of them. I'd seen the ones she'd used and abandoned, the damage and wreckage she'd left written in small bodies. They hadn't, and couldn't, understand. "It'll take an hour to reach the mine. I'm not certain how long it'll take to reach the Wardens. It depends on how deep they are, and whether the Djinn have left any surprises for us."

"I'm sure they have," Pearl said. "I would."

I nodded and rose. The girl came to me immediately, held out her hand, and said, "I'm Edie."

"Edie," I said, and shook hands. "Cassiel. This is Luis, my partner."

She nodded, every bit as professional as any Warden I had ever met. The boy rose, too, but he didn't bother to introduce himself. Edie nudged him, frowning. "And this is Alvin," she said. "He's kind of an ass. Don't mind him."

Alvin sent her a dark, scorching look. Edie topped him by at least six inches, but it wasn't that they were dissimilar in age; both seemed to be about nine years old, perhaps close to ten. Edie was developing faster, though Alvin had a stocky weight to him. They didn't seem to particularly care for each other. It was their mutual devotion to Pearl that had forged them together.

"Where are your families?" I asked them. Both would

have come from Warden parents; that was a common theme for the children that Pearl recruited.

Edie said calmly, "They're dead. My mother died five years ago. A Djinn killed her. My dad committed suicide." She sounded as if she were reciting something learned in class, not something that had affected her personally. "Alvin's mom had cancer. His dad got killed fighting another Warden. The Lady's our mother now. We don't need any other family."

I wondered if any of that was true. When Iz had been in training with Pearl, they'd convinced her that I'd killed her uncle, simply to ensure that all her ties to the mortal world were cut. . . . These children might have living mothers and fathers, or the losses might be real.

Or Pearl might have arranged for the deaths and then lied about how they occurred. Anything was possible with her.

But it wasn't the time to sort out the lies, not now. There were six Wardens trapped, and the world's clock was ticking down.

"Too bad," I told the children. "You're stuck with us as family now. We stick together. We work together. We defend each other, always. If we don't watch out for each other, we'll die on this mission. Do you understand? So think of us as . . . your aunt and uncle, if not your parents."

Edie nodded easily. Alvin just shrugged. I wasn't sure whether he'd be an asset or a liability; Alvin himself probably didn't know yet, either.

But we had our team.

Chapter 7

BRENNAN PROVIDED US with a large silver van, one with enough seating to accommodate the rescued Wardens, plus Luis and the two children; I would ride the motorcycle, both as an outrider and scout, and to provide more space in the main vehicle. He came up with supplies for us as well—sealed boxes of water with straws, energy bars, medical supplies, ropes, carabiners, lightweight tools, and other necessities. "Radios won't work," he told us as we inventoried the supplies. "If you need reinforcements, we probably wouldn't be able to reach you anyway. Get as many as you can out of there and bring them in, but watch yourselves. The Djinn are busy, but they're never too busy to come looking for trouble." He was distracted by another Warden, who arrived with a sheaf of papers in a trembling hand and disaster written on his face. "Dammit. Get going while you still can. There's extra gas in the back of the van, in case the pumps are out. Good luck."

That was it. Brennan had no time or energy for fond farewells, which left Isabel and Esmeralda. Es, predictably, just shrugged off our good-bye and went back to playing a handheld game that someone had left abandoned. We figured little in her universe.

Isabel was angry.

"You're taking them," she said, looking at Alvin and Edie, who were packing up the supplies into sturdy canvas bags. "Not me."

"*Mija*, we need a Weather Warden to make sure we can breathe on the way down," Luis said. "I probably don't have enough power to keep a tunnel open the whole way. Too easy for us to get trapped without an air supply, otherwise."

"But I can help you!"

"How?" He stared at her kindly, but steadily, until she looked down. "Isabel, I love you, and I trust you, but you're still learning fine control of what you do. You're powerful, no question of that, but Fire's a tricky thing."

"I'm better at it than you!"

"Yes, you are," he agreed. "You definitely are. But that doesn't mean you're as good as you need to be, right?" Isabel took a breath, but didn't try to argue the point. "Fire isn't as useful where we're going. Yeah, you're a strong Earth Warden, I'll grant you that, but so am I. So is Cassiel. We needed to choose someone who has something we lack, and that's Weather."

"That's stupid."

"It's strategy, bug." He tapped her gently on the nose and kissed her forehead. "I'm sorry, but you're better off here for now. Brennan will make sure you stay safe, and if you want to help out, you can. Just be careful, okay? And do not leave the building. No matter what Es tells you."

"Sitting right here," Esmeralda said without looking up from the beeps and boops of her game. "I'm not looking to leave right now. But if I decide to, you've got nothing to say about it, Warden."

"I know that," Luis said. "But if you take my niece with you when you do decide to leave, I'll find you, and we'll be having a nice, long talk about it."

"Wow, I can't wait to see how that turns out." She raised and lowered her shoulders in a fine, uncaring shrug. "See ya. Or not. Depends on if you die."

Her callousness wasn't unexpected, but it did have one side benefit; Isabel threw her arms around her uncle's neck and hugged him quickly. Then she turned to me and did the same. "Don't die," she said. "I'll hate you forever if you do. Come back safe."

I kissed her cheek and, like Luis, tapped her gently on the nose. "Promise," I said. "Get some rest." She looked tired and pale. She nodded and settled down in a heap on the floor. Someone—not Esmeralda, certainly—had fetched her pillows and blankets.

I didn't want to leave her, but I didn't know what else to say. Neither, from the look on her face, did Isabel; we'd left many things unresolved, but that was the nature of human life, I supposed.

As always, I avoided the elevators; there was grumbling from the two children, but I swung one of the two canvas bags on my shoulder, stiff-armed the door, and began the long descent without soliciting their opinions. Luis didn't bother to offer any; he just picked up the other bag and followed, leaving the children to decide on their own. When I glanced back from two floors below, I found them trudging down in our wake. They didn't look happy, but I hadn't expected that.

"Hey!" Alvin called down, as I rounded the corner for the twelfth floor. "What do you have against elevators anyway?"

"Claustrophobia," Luis said.

"It's not claustrophobia. I simply don't like leaving myself at the mercy of machines."

"Claustrophobia," Luis said again. "Cass, this might be an issue when it comes to tunnels; you know that."

"I'll be fine," I said. In truth, I hadn't thought of it, but he might possibly be right about his concerns. I wasn't comfortable in confined spaces, overall. "We have other things to worry about." Such as the children clattering after us on the stairs, one of whom had the power to absorb any attack we might throw at him. The only vulnerability a Void wielder might have would be physical, and when he worked with a partner—such as the Weather girl—she could keep us busy enough to make that type of assault problematic.

I was already thinking about how to defeat them in a fight. It probably did not bode well for our cooperative efforts.

At the bottom of the stairs, the door took us out into a large but deserted lobby area. It seemed undisturbed, but there were already signs of neglect; the polished marble floor was scuffed in places, and the large glass doors were smudged with handprints that no one had bothered to clean. It wouldn't take long for this place to show wear, I thought; if the Wardens or the human race survived the week, someone would need to take charge of sanitation and cleaning, unglamorous as that was.

It wasn't a concern I'd likely have to worry about. That seemed oddly cheering.

Outside, one of the Wardens had parked the promised silver van, and someone—almost certainly an Earth Warden—had arranged for the move of my Victory down from the roof. It leaned on its kickstand behind the van. I took a moment to take Rashid's sealed bottle out of my jacket, where I'd been keeping it safe, and rolled it into the blue jeans that were still in the backpack. It would remain better protected there, for now. I made sure the canvas bag fit securely, with both arms through the straps and the bag riding comfortably on my back. The weight was not as bad as I'd expected, balanced so, and I mounted the Victory with a sense of relief. Somehow, having the potential of movement, of escape, always made me feel less helpless, even if it was only an illusion.

Luis slammed the passenger doors and stood there with one foot up in the driver's side, looking at me. "You ready?" he asked. I nodded and started up the motorcycle. He held the stare for a few seconds longer, then smiled and kissed his fingers at me.

I couldn't help but smile in return. It was a foolish little gesture, but it warmed me.

Then he was in the truck, and we were rolling down the slight hill, away from the building.

Not surprisingly, it was cloudy; the day was chilly, but not cold. Not yet. It would be bone cold in the wind, but Brennan had helpfully thrown in an extra coat—too large for me, but the warmth would be most welcome. I accelerated as we hit the street, the freeway dead ahead.

We wouldn't be taking it.

The road out of Portland was clogged solid with cars, vans, trucks—anything with wheels that would roll had fled in the initial panic, and many had run dry of gas on the road. There wasn't enough equipment, time, or energy now to deal with removing the blockage; instead, the police had simply blocked off the freeway itself. I veered right instead, taking a side road, and checked the aetheric for guidance. The van eased in behind me, a silver ghost moving almost silently through the gray day. There were still vehicles on the road, but most people seemed to be staying inside, glued to whatever news agencies still broadcasted. Few wanted to leave the illusion of safety for whatever might be available elsewhere, until the illusion collapsed.

And then, of course, it would be too late, just as it had

been for so many in Portland and in Kansas and Missouri. Not everyone was dead there, it seemed, but those who were trapped were—according to the scattered news reports—rapidly devolving into chaos. It was spreading fast.

The road I located was a small, two-lane blacktop, but it was clear of any traffic, and I opened the throttle and flew. Misty rain began, but the jacket kept me warm and relatively dry. Behind me, the van turned on its lights. We were back in the tall, silent trees, and although the glow of Seattle was behind us, what lay in front seemed dark by contrast.

Wilderness, more dangerous than ever.

The mine where the Wardens had been trapped was geographically not far from the city, but the terrain was difficult; as we rose into the more mountainous areas, I slowed around curves, blind corners, and finally had to pull over as I saw the road that lay ahead. Luis parked behind me, and we stood together in silence, in the misty rain, staring.

"When the Djinn go full crazy, they commit," he said. The words were flippant, but his tone was not; there was no way to see this any other way than devastation. The forest was simply . . . gone, though fragments remained—the thick, splintered wrecks of trees, the tangled mess of branches and undergrowth ripped and thrown about like an uneven blanket. The road had disappeared under the mess. Part of it had burned, and smoke still rose in sullen wisps into the air.

It was eerily quiet. No birds called. No human voices, except ours, disturbed the silence. Except for the soft, almost subliminal hiss of the rain, it seemed lifeless.

"We need to clear the road," I said. There were tons of debris to be shifted. Even though the trees had been splintered and ripped apart, the shredded mass was unbelievably heavy, and it would be the work of giants to

clear enough of a path to allow the vehicles to pass—
assuming that the road beneath was still intact, which
was far from a given. I was beginning to calculate how
much power it would take when I felt a sudden warm,
dry breeze on the back of my neck.

I turned, and so did Luis.

Edie stood on the roof of the van, hands held out to
her sides, and around her, light seemed to physically
bend; it was as if she stood in full sunlight, while the rest
of us were in shade. When I used Oversight to layer the
aetheric into the real world, I saw the tremendous shad-
owy burst of power that rippled out of her, an aurora of
the darkest colors—storm black, corpse gray, vein blue.
It snapped together above us, a dizzying and complex
arrangement of polarities and elements, heat and cold
and brute-force power that almost ripped apart the sky
as it reformed the clouds.

The sullen neutrality boiled and turned into ugly darkness, edged with gray-green. The whole sky seemed to
turn on our axis, but no, those were the clouds, spinning
slowly and disorientingly over the wasteland.

The tornado came down in a white, whipping rope that
slammed into the field of debris. As it sucked up the
shredded remains of trees, leaves, and limbs, it grew wider
and darker, taking on the ominous appearance of a wall.

Edie's control of that wall was precise, and it stopped
its growth at the edges of the road. Luis and I had instinctively fallen back to the shelter of the van, and Alvin hadn't even left the vehicle, but above us Edie stood
firm and exalted, face upturned to the clouds. Her blond
hair writhed and rippled in the whipping winds, but the
pure force of the tornado was focused away from us. The
noise was astonishing, a roar that achieved an almost
human pitch, like a scream magnified into millions.

Beneath the tornado, the road cleared.

Edie lowered her gaze to the road, and the screaming, roaring destruction of the tornado obediently began to move at a leisurely pace, flinging off debris in all directions except ours. I saw shattered tree trunks hurled out in chunks that vanished into the far distance. Edie kept her full concentration on the tornado as it continued down the road.

"She can't keep it up," Luis said. He was clutching my arm in a painful grip now, and I could understand the impulse; the feeling of vulnerability in the face of what Edie had conjured was overwhelming. As a demonstration of raw power, it matched or exceeded anything I had ever seen—not just the power, but the fine control. "She's killing herself."

"No," I said softly. "She's *not.*" And that was, by far, more terrifying. He was right—Edie should have been draining herself at an awful pace, and putting her very life at risk. Instead, she was laughing, like the child she was, with joy. Her eyes had taken on an unnatural sheen that was—however impossibly—like that of a Djinn.

Whatever Pearl had done to these children, these survivors and thrivers in her training program . . . it had made them not as human as I had thought. They weren't merely Wardens with more power; they were defying the very laws that governed nature, and power itself. Djinn were built to do what Edie was doing; it was coded in their smallest components. Humans were built to survive here, in this world, and it was a very different thing.

Edie's tornado continued to sweep the road, back and forth, with precision and regularity, until the way was completely clear. Then she slowly closed her hands, and I felt the pressure above me collapse into overdriven chaos.

"Backlash!" Luis screamed, and tackled me to the ground just as that power erupted all around us in a hundred burning, stabbing lightning bolts, screaming down from the churning clouds. If a single bolt held the power of a nuclear device, this was the equivalent of the detonation of an entire nuclear arsenal.

And it lasted for almost a full minute before the energy spent itself back into the ground and the aetheric.

In the aftermath, my ears ringing from the splitting roar of thunder, I slowly raised my head. I was seeing afterimages of the lightning, even though I'd been face-down for most of it and had kept my eyes tightly closed. It had been like being trapped inside an open circuit, and my skin felt hot and fried.

The landscape looked, if possible, even more like something out of a nightmare. Instead of the debris lying in blankets, it was heaped into hills now, and the hills were on fire. Even the bare ground was blackened and smoking, and the surface of the road only twenty feet away seemed melted and sizzling.

Edie jumped down off the roof of the van and said, "That was cool, right? Did you see it? I've never seen lightning so close. It's whiter the closer you are to it. Did you know that? Only there was some dust in the air; some of it looked orange because of that." She was manic with excitement, I realized, utterly unconcerned for the damage that she had just done.

"You don't do things like that!" Luis came up yelling, fists clenched, and Edie took a step back from him. "Didn't anybody ever teach you how to balance your energy? How to ground it? What if there had been people around, or animals? How many would you have killed with that stunt?"

She looked shocked, then resentful and angry. A dangerous combination. I rose more slowly, and took Luis by the elbow to draw him backward.

He shook me off, still facing the girl. "Don't do it again, Edie. Tell me you understand what I'm saying."

"It doesn't matter," she said, and lifted her chin in defiance to glare. "Look at it; it's a wreck! The Djinn trashed it anyway, so what if it burns?"

"And if it spreads?" he shot back. "What then? What are you going to do to control it? Anything?" He was right. With the debris piled as it was now, full of drying, dead vegetation, it was already starting to burn with a vengeance. "Sparks travel, and they travel fast. A mile away and you're in virgin forest, full of life."

"Then I dump some water on it," Edie said. "Big freaking deal."

"That isn't enough. If the fire's hot enough, it just vaporizes your rain. What next?"

"I—" She was frowning now, and lost, so she quickly went on the attack. "It's not my problem! I was doing what you wanted. I was getting the stuff out of our way! That's what Fire Wardens are for, to fix these things!"

"That's not what Fire Wardens are for, to clean up your messes," Luis said. "It's not what Djinn are for, either. And if you wanted to get their attention, you've done it. That little display lit up the aetheric like the Fourth of July."

"So?" Edie challenged. "Let them come get me. I can take them."

"Who? The Djinn? How many, Edie? One, two, yeah, maybe, because you've got a hell of a lot of power. But you can't take five of them. Or ten. Or twenty. And the rest of us, we won't be so lucky."

"So?" she said again, and shrugged. "Not my fault you're lame. Why should I worry about you?"

"Don't," I said to Luis as he opened his mouth again. "You can't convince her. The best we can do is get on with things, quickly."

He didn't like it, and he definitely didn't like Edie's attitude, but he nodded. I could see the tensed muscles in his neck and shoulders, but all he did was pull open the door of the van. "Inside," he said. "Let's move."

Edie got in and took her seat next to the very silent boy. He hadn't done or said a thing the entire time, and that made me feel oddly more afraid of him than of Edie, with all her profligate waste of power.

Luis started the van, and I mounted my motorcycle. Without a word between us, I eased into the lead.

Driving through the burning piles of what had once been a vivid, living forest made for a sobering experience. The death of plants and animals left marks on the aetheric, just as those of humans did; the ghostly image of what this place had once been was worrying, and sad. I couldn't dwell on it for long; the road rapidly became more hazardous, as I dodged the occasional debris that hadn't been swept completely out of the way. This was made more difficult by the thick, drifting smoke. My eyes burned from the constant irritation, and my lungs seemed thick and congested as well. I began to cough, but I couldn't spare much attention from the trail ahead. The road had suffered damage from lightning strikes, and I weaved around the potholes, still smoking from their trauma, as well as the other things the tornado had left in its wake.

I slowed suddenly and stopped. Behind me, Luis hit the brakes fast, leaned out the window, and called, "What is it?"

There was a man lying in the road. He had on a thick blue jacket, blue jeans, hiking boots—typical covering for a day's trek out in the forest. There was a corona of thick blood on the road around him.

I put the bike on its kickstand and walked to him, then crouched to check his pulse.

He rolled over and smiled at me with shark-sharp teeth, Djinn eyes blazing a milky cold blue, and I knew in that instant that he was going to kill me. I'd fallen for an obvious trap. I hadn't checked the man in the aetheric, or I'd have seen this was only a shell, not a human with a true aura.

My own fault. It was a bitter thing to carry with me into the dark.

He snapped at me with that razor-edged grin, and without thinking, I lifted up my left forearm and slammed it into his jaws, forcing his head back. He gagged on it, chewing, but that arm wasn't flesh. It was metal, powered by Djinn engineering and my own Earth power.

It still felt pain, and I couldn't help the scream that forced its way out—but I didn't let him pull my arm free of his jaws. Better the metal suffer than my flesh.

"Cass!" Luis was shouting, and I heard him running to me. I'd get him killed, too, for nothing, for a simple lack of foresight....

And then the boy, Alvin, opened the passenger door and stepped out, and the Djinn who was on the verge of ripping my arm away stopped. All his attention was away from me and on the boy. I pulled my mangled forearm free and scrambled back, and the Djinn didn't bother to follow. He came to his feet in an unnaturally smooth, boneless motion.

Luis grabbed me and pulled me backward by the collar of my jacket, then yanked me up to my feet. "Get to the van!" he yelled. "I've got this!"

He didn't. Couldn't. And he must have been aware of that, but Luis was ever the hero. I would never be able to break him of that habit.

It didn't matter. The boy took a few calm, measured steps toward the Djinn, who was staring at him as if he couldn't quite comprehend what was facing him. "You should both get back in the van," Alvin said. "I don't know what this will do to you."

Luis seemed undecided, but I was not; I'd seen what Pearl's Void children could do, and the boy seemed genuinely concerned. Unlike Edie, he wasn't glorying in his power, or enjoying the confrontation; he seemed very grave, and very focused.

I pushed Luis back to the van, and climbed in with him. My motorcycle gleamed in the road between us and the confrontation that was slowly unfolding, but I had no desire to get out to move it. I loved the bike, but there was no use in dying for it. "We can't leave him out there alone," Luis said. "He's just a kid."

"No," I said softly. "Look." I grabbed Luis's hand, and took him just a little into the aetheric, where the ghost-forest still loomed around us. The Djinn was a blazing white fire there—unusual because Djinn normally weren't easily visible to humans on this plane, but he was channeling power directly from the Mother.

Facing him, the boy wasn't even there. What was there was a kind of howling emptiness, the exact opposite of a human aura; the boy didn't belong here, in this world. In this plane. There was something inside him that was very far from human.

I fell back into my body, and felt Luis jerk as he fell into his. He turned toward me, lips parted, eyes wider than I'd ever seen them. "What is that?"

"Him," I said, staring at Alvin. "Or what Pearl made out of him. He's still there, the boy, but there's something else in him. Something that isn't from any plane of existence I know."

"Demon," he said. The Wardens were familiar with demons, who could—and did—inhabit Djinn . . . or Wardens, if the conditions were right. But this wasn't a demon, either, not in any sense I could explain.

"More," I said. That was inadequate, but it didn't matter. I couldn't imagine what had happened to this child, but it must have been truly horrific. She'd taken him specifically to hollow out what made him human, and then fill that hole with something alien and totally, coldly uncaring about our world. I'd never understood that before, what she'd done to the Void children; it was even worse than the violation of the other children, like Isabel, who'd had their powers forced into early and violent bloom.

The boy was a walking bomb.

The Djinn had, perhaps wisely, decided not to attempt a physical assault; instead, he abandoned his human shell and rushed at the boy in a wave of power. A mundane human would have been killed instantly; a Warden would have lasted a little longer, but in the end, the Djinn was too powerful to fight effectively.

The power simply passed into the boy, and . . . vanished. Gone.

The Djinn shrieked and tried to pull himself back; he managed, at least partially, but as he tried to re-form into a visible body it was plain that what was left was mutilated and badly wounded.

And the boy hadn't so much as raised a hand.

"You should go," Alvin said to him. "I really don't want to hurt you. We just want to get by and save those people. Could you go?" He was astonishingly polite, but also completely unmoved by the torture he'd just inflicted. In his own way, he was dead, I realized. Merely better mannered than an average living person.

The Djinn snarled and attacked—not the boy, but me. I felt the hot, burning premonition of the assault an instant before the power erupted out of the ground below my feet and connected with a snap in the air above.

I was the conduit for the energy of the lightning bolt. And as I had no Weather Warden abilities, there was no chance I would have survived such an experience . . . except that Edie simply stopped it in midstrike, leaving only a *pop* of energy that exploded somewhere above, and a hissing sizzle of steam. In the time it had taken me to realize what was coming, the child had utterly destroyed the Djinn's attack, without moving from her seat in the van.

Alvin shook his head and said, "Okay, then." He sounded sad, but resigned, and in the next instant a complex net of something that I couldn't quite see, couldn't quite understand, emerged from the boy's slender body. It was like a living thing, something boneless and alien, but still anchored in his power and flesh . . . and it engulfed the wounded Djinn and simply ate him. No sound, no drama, no flashes or explosions. It was . . . easy.

I felt utterly, filthily sick, and grabbed for Luis. He seemed just as unsteady as I felt, but the two of us balanced each other. "God," he breathed, staring at the boy. "My God."

Alvin looked up and at us with a sudden, eerily predatory focus. He said nothing, but the two of us went still, instinctively. The thing that had emerged from him was slowly crawling back into his skin—a thing I could *almost* see, *almost* understand, though I didn't wish that. Not at all. "I won't hurt you," he told us blandly. "You're not enemies." I heard the unspoken *yet* hanging at the end of that sentence.

"How many Djinn can you handle like that?" Luis asked. He was struggling to sound offhand about it, as if he were merely interested and not terrified by the child's potential. Alvin shrugged.

"Three or four," he said. "It gets harder the more there are, of course. I get full."

I saw Luis's Adam's apple bob as he swallowed. He glanced at me, and I knew what he was thinking. I thought it—felt it—as well. "Full," I repeated with as little emphasis as I could manage. "You consume them."

"Of course," Alvin said. "I wouldn't let them go to waste. Not unless I can't help it."

He kept watching us with that eerily flat interest for another long moment, and then the last of the—shadows?—retreated back into him, and he was just a little boy again. Tired, and small for his age.

He trudged back to the van, opened the door, and climbed in next to Edie, who leaned out the window and said, "Can we go now, *please*?"

Luis said under his breath, "We can't. We can't do this."

"Do what?" I whispered back. "Use them to rescue trapped Wardens? Yes, we can. And will."

"We can't win when they turn on us."

I smiled grimly. "No," I agreed. "No, we can't."

And then I climbed back on my motorcycle and fired up the engine. When I looked back at him, Luis was still standing there, staring at me, but he shook his head in surrender and got back in the van.

And we drove down that smoky, lifeless, hellish road toward what I could only think of as the inevitable.

In about a quarter of a mile, the road curved and ended in a huge, tumbled mound of steel wreckage. It had once been some kind of structure, likely an administration building located near the mine shaft.

The only sign of the mine itself was an inset depression in the bare ground, curved like a bowl to a depth of almost twenty feet at its center. Featureless and silent.

I parked, and Luis pulled his vehicle in next to mine. As the engines died, the only sounds were the creaking of bent metal in the wind and the crackle of the fires burning sullenly around us. No birds crossed the silent, watching sky. *This is what the world will become,* I thought. *Wreckage and emptiness, with nothing left to feel, or remember, or mourn.*

Nothing but Pearl, staring into the dead cinders of her triumph, and smiling.

Luis and the two children got out of the van, and he grabbed the other canvas bag full of supplies. Mine was still secure against my back, but I opened it and checked the stoppered beer bottle that held our emergency option: Rashid. That, I rewrapped carefully and added it back to my bag.

"Right," Luis said, as I nodded my readiness. "Cassiel and I will open the tunnel. Edie, your job is—"

"I know what I'm supposed to do," she interrupted, looking annoyed. "I'm not *stupid*. I'm the one who keeps you breathing. And Alvin's the one who kills Djinn. Right?"

"Yes," I said, since Luis didn't seem to be inclined to answer at all. "We won't try to keep the tunnel open the entire length; we'd need to reinforce as we go, and there won't be time. We'll allow it to collapse behind us. We can open it again in stages as we come up."

"You hope," Edie said. "Maybe you won't be strong enough, and you trap us down there with you. What do we do then?"

"Die," I said blandly, and met her eyes. "What is your point?"

She raised her eyebrows just a fraction, and—unexpectedly—giggled. "None, I guess," she said. When she smiled, she looked like a lovely, adorable child, with a dimple denting her right cheek and light shining in her eyes. It was unfair, and I felt a surge of bitter anger at Pearl again. What might this child have been, if left to her own destiny? What might any of them have been? She'd taken the future of the next generation of Wardens and . . . twisted it. Corrupted it.

She'd left me no choices, and I hated her for that.

I closed my eyes for a second, and turned blindly toward Luis. My hand found his by instinct, and squeezed tightly. When I finally looked, I saw him frowning at me in concern. "You okay?" he asked. I nodded. I wasn't, because knowledge had come to me in a cold, furious burst, and illuminated everything, every hard, cutting corner of the road ahead. Even if by some miracle we survived all this, what future did these Warden children have ahead of them? The Wardens themselves had been destroyed and didn't even realize it yet because there was nothing to take up the fight after them.

Brennan had only seen the necessity of saving every possible Warden for the fight *now*. I was seeing that we needed every one of them for what would come after . . . when these superpowered Warden children might be left alive, disillusioned, and bitterly angry at the world. We couldn't only think about the immediate. The long-term outlook was just as grave.

I pulled in a breath and said, "Yes."

We focused our attention ahead and down, on the hole. "Opinions?" Luis asked. "We could pack the sides, or push the dirt up. What's best?"

"Up," I said, without really thinking. "Packing the sides will use more force. We need to conserve power."

He nodded, rolled his shoulders to loosen his muscles, and reached out his right hand. I held out my mangled left; part of the metal that served as skin for the artificial muscle-cables was ripped away, and two of the cables had sheared, leaving most of the hand useless and stiff, but it didn't matter, in terms of conveying and directing power.

Earth power rose up through Luis, thundered into me in a flow like a geyser, and out through both of us into the ground . . . and the ground exploded in a fountain of

loose dirt and rock that piled up to the sides, like a volcanic eruption of soil. We dug down twenty feet, and
then I nodded to Edie. "Help us down," I told her, and
before I could finish saying it, a dizzying combination of
winds had lifted us, stabilized us in an upright position,
and moved us over the hole. She could have dropped us,
and I thought it must have crossed her mind, but instead
she lowered the four of us with elaborate care slowly
until our feet touched the loose ground.

Even here, twenty feet down, I could see telltale scars
of the power that had raged above us; it seemed lifeless,
without any trace of living insect activity, although there
were plenty of dead, burned carapaces. Had there been
any still alive, I'd have used them to help us tunnel, but
the lack meant the soil was closer packed, less easy to
manipulate. Below that, another ten feet, lay granite, but
it had been pulverized into grains almost as fine as sand.

Luis and I continued to dig, moving the dirt up and
off to the sides at the top of the shaft. We broke through
dense glacial till material, and into an area of the mine
that had somehow survived almost intact as it angled
down. The beams and bracing had bent, but not broken,
and as we stepped out on the silty clay floor, Luis let the
tunnel begin to fill in behind us.

Almost immediately, the air began to feel thick; part
of it, I realized, was my own natural claustrophobia playing with my senses. I forced myself to breathe slowly and
deeply as we kept moving. The children seemed immune
to the feeling of burial; Luis produced a reassuringly
bright ball of fire to light our way, but it had the disturbing side effect of reducing the quality of the air still
more, until Edie began to reduce and recombine mole-
cules to release oxygen from the dirt around us. The
fresh air was almost overwhelming at first, but when
Luis murmured my name, I forced myself to refocus on

the task at hand. The intact mine tunnel ended in a jagged, sharp fall of stones—more dense till, a mix of finer and bulky gravel that had been ground down from mountains aeons ago by the immense power of glaciers. Below the clay lay more till, and then solid stone.

Luis and I pushed the rocks past us, tunneling in and down. It was hot work, and even with the constantly refreshed air I felt the pressure of the deep on me, the tight-pressing walls. The damp, cold feel of clay around me, the stink of it mixed with our sweat . . . It was just as well that the work before us took such power and concentration, because otherwise the fear that gnawed at my heels would have overtaken me completely. As it was, I did not dare to let go of Luis's hand. It was not entirely to strengthen the flow of power between us, and I thought he knew that; I could feel his concern through the link.

We had tunneled three quarters of the way down when, without warning, I began to feel oddly faint. My lungs were working harder to process the apparently sweet, cool air, and I found myself breathing faster. Thinking *why* this might be seemed more difficult as well, a slippery concept that flitted like fish through shimmering water. I had a headache, growing worse with every pulsebeat, and I felt sick to my stomach as well.

I was fumbling for water in my pack when Luis stumbled and fell to his knees. It surprised me so much that I dropped the bottle. When I reached for him, I found my hands too clumsy to help.

Everything seemed so *hard*.

"Stop it," I heard the Void child say. His voice sounded calm, but cold. "Edie, you've had your fun. We need them."

Edie, sitting cross-legged on the damp floor of the tunnel, gave him a disgusted look and shook her head.

"You know what, chipmunk? You're really no fun at all. Look at them. Aren't they funny like this?"

I couldn't think what was amusing about seeing us fall, scramble, grab on to each other, and try to rise back to our feet. My head pounded so, and no matter how many breaths I sucked in, it felt as if the walls were crushing me, suffocating me. No air . . . There was *no air*. . . .

"Stop it," Alvin said again. "It isn't funny."

She held up her thumb and forefinger, about an inch apart. "Oh, come on, it's a *little* bit. No? *Fine.*" She waved her hand, and suddenly the air that I was dragging in was full of sweet, cool, intensely real oxygen. I collapsed to my side, hyperventilating to enrich starving tissues, and heard Luis's lungs working at the same desperate speed. Now that my brain was clearing of its fog, I realized that we'd been suffocating.

"You," I gasped, and lifted my head to stare at Edie—who held up her hands in surrender, and shrugged.

"Nope," she said. "I didn't do it. You hit a pocket of methane. It's heavy; it displaces air from the ground up. You couldn't have known. It's odorless and colorless. Kills lots of people."

"She protected the two of us from it," Alvin said. "But she didn't protect you."

"Well, *we* were closer to the ground," Edie said. "I was getting around to you guys." Her smile was charming, and it had an edge of cruelty to it. "It's just a headache. You'll be fine. I wasn't going to let you *die* or anything."

No, she wouldn't have; she had a very definite understanding of her risks down here in the tunnels, and despite her mastery over air and water, she had no real chance of reaching the surface again without our help.

I slowed my breathing with deliberate control. My skin was slick with panic sweat, and although the temperature was cave-cool, I felt hot and trapped, and I was still suffering from the headache and a worrying tremble in my muscles. In a few seconds, I felt good enough to rise to my knees and pull Luis with me; he was still breathing too fast, and his dark eyes looked dazed—at least until they focused on Edie and her smile.

I held on to his shoulder as I felt his muscles go tense. "No," I said softly. "Don't waste your strength. We have to keep going." We were committed now, and there was no time for petty anger and vengeance. No room for a fight, either. I was waging enough of a battle to keep my instinctive, atavistic terror of this deep, closed space at bay.

He deliberately relaxed and nodded. His long, dark hair was sopping wet now, and stuck to his face and neck in sweaty points. "You okay?" he asked me, and put his hand on my chin, lifting it so I met his eyes. "No damage?"

"No," I said. There was the lingering headache, but it was subsiding. I wondered how far Edie would really have allowed it to go, without Alvin to control her. Too far, I suspected. It didn't take long for unconsciousness to set in, and brain damage, and death. She'd have been ... interested, I thought. Like a scientist with lab animals, or—perhaps more accurately—a serial murderer with a new victim. "No, I'm fine. Let's continue."

Luis rounded on Edie and said, in a deadly quiet voice, "You do that again, and I'll choke the living crap out of you with your own lungs. I mean it."

Her eyes widened, and suddenly she looked like the child she was. "I'm sorry!" she said. "Really, I'm sorry, I won't—I won't do it again. Please, don't hurt me." She shrank back, and Luis loomed over her like a dark, cruel shadow.

He snorted, shook his head, and relaxed. "Don't try to

play me, kid. You ain't got the skills. I'm not the Big Bad Wolf, here, and you're not Little Red. Save it for someone who doesn't know you're psycho."

He turned back to face the wall of debris in front of us, and began ripping it aside with vicious scoops of power—too much of it, expended too violently, but I understood the impulse. Because he'd looked away from her, he didn't see the change that came over Edie's face in that moment, the black glimmer in her eyes, the flat rage.

I watched her in case she acted on her temptations to hurt him. But in that instant, Alvin reached out and put his hand on Edie's shoulder.

She gasped and sat down, hard.

Alvin nodded at me, once, then folded himself into a calm cross-legged sitting position as Luis and I worked.

I wasn't sure, really, which of them I feared more. Edie, for her petulance and rages, was certainly the more volatile, but Alvin . . . Alvin had control, and no kind of real moral compass that I could determine. He was polite, and cold, and empty.

I almost preferred Edie's fury. It seemed more . . . honest.

Chapter 8

AN HOUR LATER, we'd moved so much earth and stone that Luis called a rest, and I sank gratefully down against the cool clay wall, gulping down sweat-warm mouthfuls of water until the plastic bottle was dry. "Eat," Luis told me, and pressed an energy bar into my hand. "Then have more water, but slowly. We're sweating it all out."

I nodded. I didn't feel hungry, but he was right—I needed to keep my energy levels high. The power he was channeling was burning through both of us, and despite the fact that we were literally grounded by—surrounded by—earth, the task was growing rapidly more difficult. As we drove deeper, the pressure on us, and the earth through which we moved, grew more dense. I felt filthy—my clothing clinging and heavy with sweat and caked mud, my skin smeared and as damp as if I'd just emerged from a salty ocean. And yet I was chilled, and grew more so the longer I rested. The damp, cool air made me feel every ache in my much-abused body.

I had time to examine the damage to my left arm, and

used a little power to smooth the jagged metal back over the broken cables. It would take time and concentration I didn't have now to fix everything—if I survived, which was far from a given just now. I did not favor our chances. Most of my arm was dead to sensation now, though the first two fingers and thumb could still curl, grip, and hold, and there were ghostly echoes of touch available from them. The Djinn had done damage to me, but it would have likely torn off a flesh limb. I'd been lucky.

"We've only got about another hundred feet," Luis told me. I nodded; I could also see the glow of the Wardens in Oversight, like fireflies trapped in a bottle. They were all alive, though some were prone on the ground—sleeping or unconscious. "Once we break through, we heal whoever needs it, rest, then start the trip back. We've been lucky so far. Maybe it'll hold out."

By lucky, he meant that the Earth herself didn't seem to have objected to our journey under her skin; it was a dangerous place for Earth Wardens, although it was equally powerful . . . a bit like Weather Wardens traveling by airplane. We were completely at the mercy of our element here, and never more than now, when the Earth herself was at least partially alert to the presence of Wardens pricking her skin. It would be a mere shiver for her to crush us here . . . or dispatch a wave of Djinn to destroy us.

I hoped she would not do that, because Alvin's abilities horrified me in ways that Edie's did not.

"I wish we knew what was going on out there," Luis said. "Orwell said they still had a few days to make port. Maybe they're making better time than expected." He was trying to be hopeful, but we both knew that what the Wardens could do now to control any Djinn-fueled disaster would be like spraying a fire extinguisher on a lava flow. "Seattle seemed to be holding its own." He didn't mention Portland.

I handed him another bottle of water, which he sipped in carefully controlled doses. I tried to emulate him, though I wanted to guzzle it as quickly as the first. My body seemed deeply starved for moisture. "We need a day off," I said, and that startled a low, bitter laugh from him. "Perhaps a vacation."

"Yeah," he agreed. "On a nice white sand beach, with the sun shining and a cool breeze blowing. Turquoise blue ocean. Maybe a couple of palm trees. Definitely some cold *cerveza*."

It sounded peaceful, I had to admit, though I had no real experience of the sort of thing he was speaking about; I'd seen photographs, and I could imagine it would seem relaxing. "Perhaps it would be a bit dull for us," I said. That got a less bitter chuckle.

"Girl, I'm definitely hoping for dull. Way too much adrenaline on this ride for me, you know?" He put his arm around me, and for a moment, at least, I felt as if I could breathe easily. Luis had that effect on me, though I don't think it was any sort of magic. Just . . . love.

Its own kind of magic, most likely.

We finished our water, made sure the children had finished theirs, and then began the sweaty, brutal work again. A hundred feet became fifty, then twenty, then ten.

And then we broke through into a cavernous space, dark and echoing, and heard a glad outcry from the other side. The first opening was small, but not too small for a dirty arm to be thrust through, to grab Luis's hand. The babble of words from the other side made it impossible to pick out anything in particular, so Luis pulled free, bent lower, and yelled, "Get back, all of you! Coming through!" He waited for another fifteen long seconds, then said, "Here goes!" and sent a last shockwave of power through the wall of tightly packed clay and till, and it crumbled in a shower and pulled into a pile behind the four of us. As the dust settled into a dull gray cloud, I was snatched into a desperate hug from a woman I didn't know; she quickly abandoned me to throw her arms around Luis, but I was instantly assaulted by yet another grateful Warden. There were too many of them, and all too grateful.

No one tried to hug Alvin, and those who dared approach Edie received a furious glare that warned them off. After the first rush of overwhelming glee, the Wardens began to sort themselves out into individuals for me. . . . The one with the most presence seemed to be the smallest, a middle-aged man with a barrel chest, dressed in the grubby remains of a quite nice business suit. The tie was long gone, but he'd kept the jacket, and his pale blue shirt remained relatively clean. "Thank you all," he said, and held up his hands for quiet. The chatter among the other Wardens died down, as if they had become used to following his lead; that surprised me, because there was a strong-faced older woman in the group who I'd have pegged as a natural leader at first glance. There were two other women, one thin and athletic, one much rounder, but taller. The other two men were as different as possible from each other; one was a sullen-looking young man in a battered T-shirt and mud-caked jeans, and the other was a silver-haired, dignified old gentleman in walking shorts and a brightly colored, squarishly cut shirt. "Thank you so much for coming for us. We were starting to think we'd been left for dead."

"Not at all," Luis said. "Believe me, you're needed up top. It's our job to get you back in the fight."

"It's still a fight?" The older man looked surprised. "I thought it'd be over by now."

"If it was over, they wouldn't be here to get us," the horse-faced woman said, and offered her hand to me. "I'm Salvia Owens." Under the coating of grime, her skin was a dark brown, and her eyes seemed to have a green tint to them in the glow of Luis's self-contained, floating light, which had brightened to show the group.

I shook and said, "Cassiel, and this is Luis."

"I'm Mel," the man in the business suit said. "That's Will, Carson, Naomi and Phyllis—Phyl, for short. And the kids . . . ?"

"Edie and Alvin," I said. "It's a long story, and we don't have time for it now."

"Why not?" Edie asked. "What were you going to say about us? That we're freaks? We are," she confided, looking straight at Mel. "I'm stronger than you are. Or you. Or you." She singled out the Weather Wardens in the group. Mel frowned a little, but he must have sensed that she wasn't lying, because he gave Luis and me an uneasy glance. "And don't even ask about Alvin. You don't want to know what he is. Better hope he doesn't show you." She held up her hand, palm out toward Alvin, and he smacked it, though not as if he was in any way exultant. Merely meeting her expectations of behavior.

There was something of me in him, I realized, something of a stranger trapped in a world he didn't understand, or truly fit inside. Sad. By any logic, that should have brought us closer together—we outcasts should stick together.

But not this time. What drove us was so very, very different.

"Is anyone here in need of medical help?" I asked the Wardens. They seemed grateful for the change of subject, but no one had significant injuries or problems. Remarkable, but they'd had access to clean, clear water; there was a large, still, dark pool in the middle of their cave. The Fire Wardens had kept clean-burning warmth available, and the Weather Wardens had scrubbed the air to keep it breathable.

Altogether, a successful isolation, though it couldn't have gone on forever. For one thing, they'd run out of food, and that was something neither Weather nor Fire could manufacture from stone and water. We shared energy bars all around—two per person—and explained what we'd be doing on the way back up—it was similar to how we'd descended, but theoretically, it would be easier, since the earth and rock had already been loosened. Theoretically.

Luis touched me on the shoulder, as I drained another bottle of water. "Cass," he said. "I know we probably ought to start back; there's no time to waste, but—"

"But we need to rest," I said, relieving him of the burden of confessing it. He hated to seem weak to me, or to anyone, but I could sense his exhaustion, and my own body was in no better condition. "I agree, but I think these people are ready to leave this place."

"Oh, we can wait," Mel said. "We need the food and time to get it in our systems anyway. No sense in starting this completely drained—believe me, I know how hard it is. Rest for a while." He moved off to another part of the cave and sat down to distribute the extra food we'd brought. They fell to it with enthusiasm.

Luis sank down next to me and stretched out with a soul-deep groan. "I don't think I've ever felt this bad," he said. "Though I keep saying that around you. How come what we do never involves beaches and suntan oil, anyway?"

I smiled. "Have you seen how pale my skin is?"

He cracked an eyelid and gave me an all-over assessment. "Oh, yeah. You're Snow White, *chica*. I always had a thing for that girl."

Edie and Alvin were huddled together, whispering; I didn't like that, but they weren't doing anything overtly dangerous or suspicious. "Luis," I said. "Get up."

"I just got down here!"

"Follow my lead."

He sighed. "Don't I always?"

I slipped the canvas bag containing extra supplies off my shoulders and retrieved Rashid's glass bottle from inside; I slipped it back inside my jacket and zipped it closed, holding it firmly in place. Edie and Alvin had stopped whispering, and they both looked up as I approached, with Luis only a step behind me.

"Are you hungry?" Edie broke apart an energy bar and passed the boy a piece.

"Not right now," I said. I moved fast, laying my hands on both their hands, and sent power racing through their nervous systems, triggering instant unconsciousness—at least, in theory. Alvin switched off like a light, his small body sliding to the side.

Edie didn't go down. My damaged hand had bled off some of the power, and as she batted it away, scrambled to her feet, and reached for power that would sear my flesh from brittle, baking bones, I saw my death in her eyes, saw it closely . . .

. . . And then she gasped in surprise, and her eyes closed, and she toppled. Luis, who'd brushed the back of her head with his palm, caught her and laid her carefully down next to Alvin.

Then he turned on me. "What the *fuck* are you doing?" he shouted. "God*damn*, Cass—"

"It had to be done," I said. "If you want to rest safely, they had to be under control. You know that. They're not hurt."

I said that last for the benefit of the other Wardens, who had jumped up in confusion and alarm. They didn't like it, but after a moment, one by one, they took their seats again.

I took out insulating blankets and wrapped Edie,

then Alvin. "They'll sleep," I said. "And so should we, Luis."

"Damn," he said again, and shook his head. "I just don't ever know what's in your head. I swear I don't."

"Am I wrong?"

"No," he said. He sounded discouraged about it. "Just—cold. I understand why you did it, but . . . damn."

That hurt, but I went back to the spot where we'd left our few belongings and stretched out on my side, pulling one of the thin blankets over my aching body. After a moment, Luis lowered himself down next to me and scooted close. His warm, strong body fitted itself against mine, and I was reminded, again, of the miracle that had happened between us . . . that despite my sharp, bitter barriers, he'd found a way inside, and allowed me to learn to trust. What hurt, I realized, was that I'd wanted him to approve of what I'd just done—and that wouldn't have been trust. It would have been blind obedience.

I snuggled back against him, and his breath ruffled my pale hair. His arms went around me, locking me in warmth and protection—me, who had never needed protection since the dawning of the world.

And I cherished it.

"I'm sorry," I said softly. "I disappointed you."

"No, you shocked me," he said. "You're not wrong, Cass. I guess I'd rather you were, but you're not." He kissed the back of my neck, waking shivers, and murmured, "Someday, when all this is done, we're going to rent some fancy hotel room with a great view and never leave the bed. Okay?"

"Yes," I said, and smiled as I closed my eyes. I could almost see it with him—the soft sunlight, the glittering ocean, the crisp pale sheets over his bronze skin. "I will hold you to that promise." I turned in his arms and kissed him, a slow and fevered press of our lips that throbbed with our pulsebeats. There was something about Luis that made me feel more alive, more *real* than I'd ever known. All the long eternity I had lived, and I had never understood why any Djinn would wish to seal themselves in flesh, live this strange and fleeting life with humans . . . but now, I couldn't imagine leaving it. There was something precious in it that had never been real to me, until him.

"Whoa, girl, let's not get this going," he said, but he was smiling as he kissed me again. "Thought we were supposed to rest."

"You are my rest," I said. It was a surprising thing to say, but it was true; I felt clenched muscles relax in his embrace, more than ever in sleep.

He said nothing, but he held me close, and in his warmth, in the silence filled with his breathing and heartbeat, I finally really rested.

It couldn't last, and didn't. Hours passed, and some part of me never failed to be aware; when Mel finally moved from his spot on the other side of the cavern and came toward us, I was instantly awake, sitting up and ready. The time had worked its healing, at least a little; Luis seemed to move more easily as he got to his feet, and the pulse of power between us felt strong and resilient.

"Time to go," he said. "Mel, get your folks together. Cass—" He looked at me, then at the two children still peacefully sleeping in their blankets. They looked innocent and vulnerable, but it would be a grave mistake to assume they were any such thing. "Cass, what are we going to do with them?"

"We leave them food and water and blankets," I said. "They'll survive."

It took him a few heartbeats to understand, and then I saw the weight come down on him, like the earth itself had descended. "Oh God," he said, and wiped his hand across his face. "You cannot be serious about this."

"It's the only way," I said. "We need to take them out of the fight, but I won't have the blood of children on our hands, Luis. I can't. If we leave them here, they're safely contained. There's no other place we can guarantee that, not up there, and we *cannot* give Pearl the chance of having them as allies. This is our only opportunity to take them from her without killing them. You know it."

"Jesus. I can't believe I'm agreeing to this, to just leave them here, all alone, but . . ."

"You can't!" The Warden Salvia said, and thrust herself out in front of the group of adults, staring at us with horror. "What are you *talking* about? You can't just leave children down here. I don't care how much food and water you give them—they're just *kids*! We have to take them with us!"

"You don't understand," I said. "They're not—"

"*You* don't understand," she said, and I felt the sharp prickle of Weather power coming to her call. "I'm not letting you do this. We're not. Right?" She sent a glare at Mel, the nominal leader of their group. He was still frowning, trying to understand what was going on, but he slowly nodded.

"No matter what you might think they are, they're kids," he said. "And you can't abandon them like this."

"I'm saving their lives," I said. "If you wish to start a fight here, then do so, but I warn you, I'm not inclined to lose." I lowered my chin, and felt the instincts boil up inside me—all the anger and trapped desperation that I'd kept so well under control during the endless trip down. "I came to rescue you, but if you want to be left with them, I will oblige you. You'll find that the view from within the tiger's cage, with the tiger inside, is not as innocent or charming."

Luis stepped in front of me. "This isn't a fight. Listen to me," he said. There was a quiet, controlled energy to him now, something that drew all their focus away from me. Unlike me, he invited their trust in a subtle application of Earth power that I couldn't possibly have matched; I could feel it surrounding him like a warm, soft cloud. "These aren't normal kids. I wish they were, believe me, but I saw them do things today that no adult Warden *would* have done, much less could have done."

"Even so . . ." Salvia began, but he cut her off—softly but firmly.

"They destroyed a Djinn today," he said. "Consumed him, like candy. You have no idea how dangerous they are, but we can't let them out of here. There's enough danger up there already."

He stopped there, and the silence spoke for itself. The other Wardens shifted and exchanged looks; even Salvia looked shaken.

"I'm not just leaving them here to die," Luis said. "We'll send help for them, but we have to get out before they wake up, because believe me, if we don't have a ton of barricade between us and Edie, she'll burn us all without a second thought."

That got them moving, though from the frown on Salvia's face, I thought she wasn't quite done with the issue yet; Luis and I joined hands and began forcing open the passage ahead. Behind us, we began to let the debris fall in a curtain, to block off the cave again.

Burying two children alive.

Mel turned toward us, eyes large and all pupil in the fire-lit darkness. "We can't just leave them alone," he said. "I'm sorry, but I can't do it."

Before I could stop him, he lunged through the falling rocks, and was gone.

"Dammit!" Luis spat, and tried to slow the flood of debris. I fought him. "Cass, let me get him out of there!"

"No," I said. "He made the choice. He knows the risks. Let him go. Maybe he's right. Maybe an adult should stay with them. Just not one of us. If Edie got her hands on an Earth Warden . . ."

Luis understood; he could imagine what she'd do. I felt the shudder move through his flesh. "Yeah," he said. "We have to keep going. You pulled the pin on that grenade. Focus on the fill behind us. I'll do the front."

From then on, it was pure concentration, effort, sweat, dirt, and pain, physical pain that drove everything else away, for a time. Moving so much earth was hard enough the first time; the burn was blowtorch-hot in my muscles now, aching in my head. The air was fresh, at least, and kept as cool as the Wardens could manage.

There was no room for claustrophobia, only focus. On effort.

I felt the roar of power explode behind us when Edie and Alvin woke; we'd tunneled a long way toward the surface, and there were metric tons of rock, dirt, and clay between us, but even so, I felt the temperature of the air ratchet up, trying to broil us alive. Edie's pique, expressed in fire. The Weather Wardens controlled it, looking shocked by the child's power. Salvia, at least, realized what might have happened had we given in to good impulses. She was the first to say what we all knew: "Mel's dead. They killed him."

"Burned him," one of the Fire Wardens said, shaken. Phyllis, I thought. "They burned him alive. All he wanted to do was help them."

Luis didn't say that he'd warned them.

We didn't say anything at all, just put our hands and heads back to the hard work of saving us. Luis and I were gasping for breath, sweating, trembling by the end of it; it was only the helping hands of the Wardens tearing their flesh and fingernails that broke through the last barriers. We were too weak.

And so it was that we were helpless, drained, and entirely off guard when the harsh glare of the sunlight through smoke resolved and showed us what stood before us.

"I've been kept waiting," Ashan, my Djinn brother, lord, and master, said. He stood facing us, flanked by others, a row of impenetrable and immortal force. He'd clothed himself in a human shell, a pale and perfect imitation of humanity down to suit and gleaming silk tie, but his eyes were a bright, unearthly swirl of colors that, taken together, made up white. "I don't like to be kept waiting, humans." He looked at the Djinn standing at his right and left, and nodded. "Take them."

There was a sound around us then, a kind of crystalline creaking, like frozen wind chimes, and everything seemed to grow darker. Even the Djinn seemed surprised. Ashan lifted his head, and whatever he saw on the aetheric made him gesture to the other Djinn in a blur.

But it was too late. I don't know what descended on them, and on us. I saw the Djinn grabbing for the Wardens, for Luis, and Ashan came for me, but something got between us. Something worse than Ashan.

Something that had me.

I tried to rise. Tried to fight.

Darkness took me down, fast and merciless, and the last thing I saw was Ashan and the Djinn retreating, and abandoning me to my fate.

They kept me in the darkness, and the worst of it was that I didn't know *why*. Why keep me alive? Why not kill me outright, as would have been best and safest?

But there was no doubt they wanted me alive. Suffering. Waiting.

I was aware of time passing, but there was nothing I could do except count the ticking seconds by the measured, rapid pace of my heartbeats. I was confined in a tiny space, but there was air flowing against my face. Whoever had me didn't wish me dead.

Not yet.

I had no illusions that miracle—or nightmare—would last forever, but it seemed to stretch to the breaking point. My mind was full of questions and fears. The Wardens we'd rescued . . . the children we'd abandoned.

And, always, Luis. I could no longer feel his presence, or the bond between us . . . yet I wasn't dying the slow, starving death of a Djinn cut off from the aetheric, either, so he *must* have been alive. That was all I could hold to for hope.

I was in a prison. A prison built to hold Djinn, indefinitely; it would do equally well to hold a Warden, no matter what their specialty. I could call no powers, not even a spark of light, and the tiny opening around me seemed to shrink, inch by inch, as my panic increased. I forced myself to breathe more and more slowly, focus on small sensations and details. The Djinn wouldn't understand human instincts, human frailty; if I panicked in this tomb, I would go mad before they noticed my lapse.

And then the pain began.

It started in small ways at first, a burning sensation on the outside of my left thigh, a pinch in my right upper arm . . . and then it grew worse. It wasn't burning, or pinching. It was something pressing into me, with exquisite slowness. Pushing, and pushing, and pushing, sharp points digging until they broke the skin and bored deeper.

Those were the first, and not the worst. The torture

came so very, very deliberately. There was nothing human about it, nothing driven by hate or fear or anger.... No, this was a cold, empty kind of pain, inflicted in a lifeless and distant way.

I couldn't keep calm. The pain ate away at my hard-fought reserve, sped up my breathing, brought back all the desperate panic that I'd striven to keep sealed away.

And it went on, and on, and on. The red-hot, invading pain. The whispering trickle of blood against my skin. My own ragged, too-fast breathing stirring the lank strands of my hair in the tiny spaces.

And then the screaming.

My voice wore raw soon, and my throat ached and bled from the effort. There was no more peace, no more logic, no more planning left inside me. Only the pain, the terror, the despair.

And then, from a vast distance, came the whisper of ... music.

It wasn't music as a human might hear it; this was the language of the Djinn, of tens of thousands of immortal voices raised together in a sound that held nothing but exaltation, beauty, harmony.

It was the sound of worship, and madness ... a divine, thoughtless madness that had no room for individual pain or pleasure, sadness or joy. It was my brothers and sisters, but they had ceased to be the individuals I'd once known.

They sang as they killed.

Death was moving across the face of the world, and I could feel it. Worse: I could *be* it. Some part of me knew the insane peace of surrendering will, conscience, logic, of becoming the Great Beast, and hungered to join it.

And then I heard Pearl's voice whispering to me. *Let go,* she said. *Let the music fill you, Cassiel. Let the earth take you as you change. I will make you into a creature of terror and beauty, a weapon for the new Mother's hand. I will make you my angel—not of mercy, but of death. Shining, cutting, crushing death, and you will be as beautiful as a knife. This is why I've spared you all this time, to serve me. Fight and die, or surrender and be reborn. Your choices, my sister.*

No. No, these could *not* be my only choices. It didn't matter whether I closed my eyes; I could see nothing, not even a glimmer of light, but now I deliberately squeezed them shut and brought up vibrant images in my mind: Luis, lying propped against pillows in bed, tracing his fingertips over my body, smiling. His skin gleamed like fine new bronze, and the indigo lick of flame tattoos on his arms had a sinuous grace and beauty that made me shiver. His eyes were a rich, dark cocoa, and his kisses held spice and sweetness and woke vast, unhurried needs inside me. His touch trailed heat, and his tongue woke fire.

I reached for him, and for an instant, just a single flash, I *saw him.* Not the image of him from our bed, not the smiling, lazy, sexual creature I'd imagined in that moment—no, this was a frightening vision of a hard, battered man, stained with smoke and blood, and his eyes were as dark as empty windows as he drew and shaped a fireball in his hands.

And I heard him, just a whisper. I might have imagined it, so quickly did it pass.

Luis said, *I'm coming.*

And then the singing madness rose inside me to a shattering pitch, and the needles piercing me drove deeper, and it was all darkness, solitude, loss. I was weightless, then falling into the darkness.

Alone.

Trapped.

Chapter 9

LIGHT.

It came in a white blaze that seared my skin, blasted my eyes even through the squeezed-closed lids, and I heard myself make a rusty, metallic sound of protest.

It was a single, thin crack in my prison, and I felt a tiny whisper of something so sweet and precious that I couldn't identify what it might be. Fresh air? *Hope?* Both seemed impossible to me now.

There was a sound that echoed even through the impenetrable walls pressed against me, and I felt a shudder go through the world, *my* world . . . and then, the tiny crack of light widened into a bar. The darkness shattered and left me bare.

I couldn't move. The weight that had trapped me in this tiny space was gone, but when I tried to lunge for the light, I couldn't get free. Moving woke screaming agony everywhere in my flesh and bones, and all I could do was open my eyes and stare in confusion at the blur of brightness in front of me.

There was a sudden, horrifyingly loud babble of

sound. Voices. I couldn't sort them out. It was all too real, too harsh, and no matter how bad the dark had been, at least it had been *constant*. . . .

I picked one voice from the noise. "Cass? Cassiel? . . . Damn you, *let me go*. I have to—"

"No!" said another voice. "Keep him back. He doesn't need to see this."

The first voice—I knew it, and I felt something resonating inside me, a kind of warmth, a glow that I hadn't even known was gone until it returned. Power, flowing into me. Making me live again.

I blinked. The haze before me resolved into the shape of a tall man, dressed in a stained flannel shirt, blue jeans, boots. His hair was long and untidy around his lean, angular face, and he was looking at me with an odd hesitancy.

"Cassiel," he said. It was half a whisper, and in a sudden move, he crouched down. I was lying on the ground, I realized. Above me was stone, and the light that had blinded me shone from a single flashlight he'd averted at an angle. "I'm going to get you out of there. You just stay still. Struggling will only hurt more."

I blinked and tried to speak, but the raw edges in my throat could only make an indistinct rough whisper. I tried to move my head, tilt it forward so I could look down at myself, but he was right; the effort woke sharp and screaming pain in my skull, neck, and shoulders.

"Where is Luis?" I managed to say. The man who crouched over me smiled a little, but his eyes looked tired and heartbroken.

"He's over there," he said. "First we have to deal with this, okay? He got us here. Now let me get you out. Stay strong."

I couldn't nod, but I blinked to let him know I understood.

Lewis Orwell, the most powerful Warden in the world, took a deep breath, lowered his head for a moment, and when he raised it, there was an aura of golden power that glimmered around him even here, on the human plane.

He bent forward and slid his large hands over my face, through my hair, around my head in a slow, sweeping motion.

It hurt. I stiffened with the snaps of agony, one after another, like tiny bones breaking.

His hands met at the back of my head, then moved down, cupping my neck, spreading out over my shoulders. Every gentle touch sent waves of agony through me, snaps of white-hot pain. He paused there for a moment. He was as close as I'd ever let any human get, his body all but pressed to mine, and Orwell's lips hovered very close to mine. His eyes were dark, very dark, and full of a power I didn't fully comprehend.

"Look down," he whispered.

I did.

I was encased in a coffin that had been fitted exactly to my body, one made of glittering pink crystal that shimmered in the artificial light.

And the coffin was alive, and it had grown into me. Needles of crystal, a whole forest of them, pierced and punctured my skin, some thin and just in the skin, some thicker and driving to muscle. Still others had drilled into bone.

They were flushed red with my blood.

"I have to break them," Lewis said, still very softly. "This thing is alive. It's fighting to keep you. It's feeding off you. I won't lie, this is going to hurt."

I could nod now. After a second's horror, edged with fear, I did.

"Hold on," he said, and jerked me violently forward. At the same time, I sensed a hammer blow of power coursing through him, through *me*, and all the crystals shattered at once in a mind-destroying white-hot wave of agony and fury and hunger and disappointment . . .

. . . And then I was lying limp on Lewis's chest, cradled in his arms. Screaming voicelessly, because the pain was *worse*, somehow, as if the crystals were still inside me, still drilling . . .

And they were.

The broken ends of the crystals were *moving*. Driving in.

Lewis wrapped his arms around me, and I felt another surge of power blast through me in a cresting wave that hit and shattered every one of the deadly fragments, until I was lying limp against him, covered in a coating of shining dust.

"Get Rocha, somebody," Orwell said. He let his arms fall free to hit the ground at his sides, and didn't move. I couldn't. My muscles felt loose and slack, unnaturally dead within my body. My bones felt as if they had been broken into dust as well . . . and then a strong pair of hands was pulling me up and into another embrace.

Luis.

The smell of him washed over me, familiar and strong—male sweat, damp earth, the spicy sweetness of peppers and chocolate. I saw the tattoos on his arms first, winding sinuously up his bronze skin, and finally I focused on his face.

"Luis," I whispered. It was all I could manage. He looked shaken and anguished, but he smiled and kissed me.

When he pulled back, there was blood on his face. Fresh red blood in a pattern of dots.

I raised my fingers to touch my face, and felt the holes left by the crystals, the wetness that seeped from them. My whole body wept red.

"Stay still," he told me. "Don't try to move. Just stay still."

It seemed like sound advice, and just this one time, I obeyed.

Two days in a Warden hospital in Seattle, while they pumped blood into my almost-drained body and carefully closed up every wound. The final count had been in the hundreds of punctures. Damage to my bones had been extensive, they told me, and I had several painful rehabilitation sessions with an Earth Warden to repair them.

No one explained to me what had happened until the afternoon of the second day, when Lewis Orwell dropped in and shut the door on a fluttering entourage of anxious Wardens with questions, alerts, and requests. He nodded to Luis, who was sitting at my side holding my right hand in both of his; Luis nodded back cautiously. "How's she doing?" Orwell asked. He had a pleasant, resonant voice, and like many Earth Wardens (except me) he seemed to exude a soothing, reassuring presence that everyone liked.

"I am fine," I answered before Luis could speak. "There's no need to keep me confined to this bed. The bones are healing."

"Note the present tense," Luis said. "You're not out of the woods, Cassiel."

"Of course not. We are in the Pacific Northwest."

"And . . . that was too literal. I meant—"

"I know what you meant," I said, "but I am fine. The healing will continue whether I am in the bed or out of it."

"She's right," Orwell said, and dragged a steel-backed

chair over to the other side of my bed, which he strad-
dled. He rested his chin on crossed arms and studied me
with clinical interest. "You're a fast healer. Comes from
the Djinn part of you, most likely." He fell silent, and I
wondered what he was thinking, or wanted me to say.

I stared back, unwilling to give the first ground.

"I expected you to be full of questions," he said.

"Did you?"

"Most people couldn't have come out of that sane,"
he told me. There was an interestingly tentative edge to
his voice now, as if he couldn't quite understand something he'd previously thought an open book. "But those
who did would want to know what happened to them.
They'd be demanding it. Unlike you."

I shrugged. It hurt; healing meant that the functions
were intact, but the residual pain would continue for a
while, like the fading ache of deep bruises. "You'll tell me
when you think you know," I said. "I could tell from the
discussion in the halls that no one understood very much."

He tilted his head a little to the side, as if trying to
consider me from a slightly different angle. "Hasn't *he*
told you?" Orwell glanced at Luis, who was sitting silently at my side. There was an odd dynamic between
these two men, something like a power struggle, but I
didn't understand why.

"He hasn't been forthcoming," I said. "He says he
doesn't remember what happened after we broke through
in the mine and found the Djinn standing at the top."

"And you?"

"Something came, something even the Djinn feared.
Ashan retreated, but they took the others with them. I
didn't see what it was that threatened them, but it took
me for its own. Then I remember waking up in the —
confinement." It hadn't been a prison. It had been a
coffin — no, worse. It had been a chrysalis, something

that would have transformed me into something else altogether. What, I didn't know, but I had come perilously close to finding out. "The other Wardens? Alive?"

"We found Rocha and the other five unconscious five miles from the mine entrance," Orwell said. "Rocha tells me they were going to be killed by the Djinn, so they went at it hard; one died of her injuries, but they were all pretty bad off when we found them. The first thing he wanted to do when he was on his feet was saddle up and go off looking for you."

"And you let him."

"No, I went with him. Good thing I did; you were buried in there deep, and there weren't a lot of traces to track. Between the two of us, we managed." He gave a modest shrug. "Then it was just a matter of digging you out."

Somehow, I doubted it was quite that simple. I thought back to the nightmare of coming into the light, of the crystals drilled into my flesh and bone. "What was it doing to me?"

"You don't know?" Orwell stared at me steadily for a long moment, then shrugged. "I'll be honest, I've never seen anything like it. Your flesh was turning crystalline, hard as diamonds. Your eyes—it had only just started, I can tell you that much. What you would have been at the end of it is anybody's guess, but it would have been . . ."

"Irresistible," Luis put in softly, and drew both our gazes. "Like the irresistible force. And beautiful, too. Scary beautiful."

It reminded me far too much of what Pearl had promised. I ached still in every cell; I was, I sensed, lucky that the process hadn't gone much further or I'd have never survived the reversal.

I forced myself to think beyond my own fears. "How long have you been here, Orwell? Where are the Wardens who went out to sea with you? The Djinn?"

"We docked in Miami four days ago," he said. "The Wardens are where they're needed. The Djinn . . ." He hesitated, and looked away. "They were taken as soon as we got out of the black corner. We lost them, one way or another."

"But they held," I said, and felt a burst of amazement that was almost pride. "The Wardens *held*. Against the Djinn."

"We're maintaining," Orwell agreed. He looked exhausted, I thought; leadership sat well on him, but it was a crushing load. "We're not winning. Look, I know from Brennan that you think dealing with Shinju is dealing with the devil, but trust me: Right now, I'll take the devil and all his pointy-headed minions as long as they do what I tell them. I *have* to, because our only other choice is obliteration." He let that sink in before he continued. "As best we can tell, the reason Rocha and the other Wardens who survived that mine are still alive is that Shinju brought her kids and fought on their side. They'd have been ground into hamburger, otherwise. As it was, the odds were way too close."

"Pearl—Shinju—is the one who sealed me in that prison," I told him. "I know it. I heard her voice."

"Maybe so, but I've got no energy right now for personal grudges," he said. "Revenge can wait until we've got bandwidth. For now, I need every soldier fighting our enemies, not each other."

I raised my eyebrows, and did not answer. Luis, on the other hand, did. "If she makes another move at Cassie, I'll find a way to kill that bitch. I mean it. I don't care what it costs." His grip on my hand was tight, too tight, but I understood, for the first time, his emotion. The hate and fear was a tight little ball inside him, bound with razor-edged guilt. "You saw her. You saw what it was doing to her."

Lewis Orwell inclined his head just a little, a silent acknowledgment, but he said, "Revenge can wait. And it will. Get me?"

"I get you," Luis said, though his tone and his expression were set hard. "What next?"

"I need her up and on her feet, and you both back in the field," Orwell said. "Things are moving fast now. Joanne's on her own, and she needs backup. I can't go. I'm sending you two."

"I can't leave Isabel—"

"Isabel's with me," Orwell interrupted. "Snake Girl, too. I need them, and I'm using them. All assets get deployed. Sorry, but that's just how it is. The kid's a soldier now, too."

He stood up and pushed the chair out of the way; Luis came to his feet, too, and released my hand. The stare between them looked far too confrontational for comfort, so I took a deep breath, bracing for the pain, and swung my legs over the edge of the bed on Luis's side. He grabbed for me instinctively as I pulled myself into a wavering, teeth-gritted-against-the-pain standing position, and I held on tight to his arm. It was sufficiently distracting to break the moment, and Lewis Orwell took advantage of it. He gave me a last, assessing look, nodded, and left the room, pursued by at least a dozen Wardens all pelting him with questions.

"Bastard," Luis said. "Son of a bitch has no feelings. I'm telling you—he's like a walking fucking iceberg, and he causes just about as much damage."

I allowed him to guide me back to a sitting position on the edge of the bed. It shocked me how fragile I still felt. I knew intellectually how damaged I'd been, but what still haunted me was the look on my partner's face when he'd seen me taken from that crystal prison. "Perhaps," I said. "But perhaps he can't afford feelings now.

He's right. If anything is to survive, we have to risk everything. Everyone. There are no safe places left."

He knew it, and he loathed that knowledge just as much as I did. "I need to protect her, Cass. I failed my brother. I failed his wife. I even failed *you*. I can't let her down, too." He put his arms around me. The care he took told me more about him than me; I might *feel* fragile, but he touched me like I was made of butterfly wings. As if I might shatter, like the crystal from which I'd emerged. "She's ours, and we can't let her down."

Ours. The child was, in many ways—not of our bodies, perhaps, but of Luis's blood, and through him, and his dead brother, mine as well. We owed her love, and safety. We'd always owed her that.

I put my hands on either side of Luis's face and held him still as I said, "We've already let her down. We let her down the instant that Pearl abducted her, and every day since we've been struggling to find meaning for her in that. But she's not ours. She's her own, always. And she wants to fight. She seeks it out, as I do. Step back, and let her be herself. It's the only way we cannot disappoint her now."

He tried to shake his head. I didn't allow it. We stared deep into each other's eyes. His were haunted, and I'm sure that mine held the shadows of the torture I'd endured.

My darkness won.

He pulled me into his arms, and this time, he used his strength; I lost my breath from the force of his embrace, but it was a good pain, a just and correct ache that came as much from my soul as my flesh. We stayed that way for a very long time, minutes long, before Luis pulled back and said, "You got a few things to make up to me, you know."

I blinked, thrown by his conversational swerve. "Why?"

"Not every guy has to take seeing his lover stripped

naked and lying on top of the head of the Wardens," he
said. "Even if you were covered in glitter and blood."

He was talking about my rebirth from the crystal coffin, when Orwell had pulled me out. Had I been naked?
It surprised me, but thinking back, modesty hadn't been
the largest concern I'd had. "You seem more worried by
the nakedness than the blood," I pointed out. He lifted
one shoulder in a half shrug.

"Yeah, well, we all bleed a lot around here," he said.
"But the naked part, that's supposed to be sort of private."

"You are very odd."

"You like that about me," he said, and kissed me.
Sweet and hot, spicy and smooth, he spiked my pulse
hard, and reminded me of the delights of physical bodies. I remembered the image of him that had come to me
there in the dark, in my deepest panic and pain . . . of his
bare skin, shimmering in the peaceful light. Of his fingers trailing over mine, waking fire.

In the end, it had been him who'd kept me alive at the
bottom of that dark, dark pit.

"Yes," I agreed softly, and licked my lips to savor his
taste again. "I like many things about you."

He groaned and stepped in closer, and my knees
parted until he was pressed against me in a hot, solid line
from chest to crotch. Beneath the thin cotton gown, I
was bare, and he knew it; I could feel the tension gathering inside him, coiling down deep, and his erection was
an obvious pressure against me. "Shit," he whispered,
and brushed my lips with his. "I wasn't exactly planning
on this. There's no privacy here, you know. And you're
not healed enough to—"

"I decide whether I'm healed enough," I said. The minor aches and pains had fallen away, driven back by the
adrenaline and sweet, anxious need that was forming in-

side me. "As for privacy, the door does lock. And we take our pleasures now, or risk never having them again. What would you want?"

He groaned and kissed me again, and I distinctly heard the metallic sound of the lock engaging on the door. Then the steel-framed chair that Orwell had used slid across the floor and slammed at an angle under the handle. "Just in case," he murmured, and I felt his fingers pulling at the ties on my hospital gown. "Mmmm, easy open. Very nice."

For answer, I used a tiny burst of Earth power to part the zipper of his jeans as I slid the leather of his belt out of the buckle. I paused then, suddenly struck by a new, odd thing: my left hand.

It was working.

I opened and closed my fist, watching the fingers bend, the hand itself curl; apart from the metallic shine to it, it felt and looked just as my right hand did. There was no sign of the damage that I'd suffered on the road from the Djinn attack.

"Did you . . . ?" I asked.

Luis shook his head. "Not me," he said. "I'm not that good. Orwell fixed you up. Said he needed you fully functional."

"Well," I said, and smiled as I eased his pants down, taking my time with the job. "I assure you, I *am* fully functional. And that's of benefit to you."

He gasped aloud as that metallic hand touched, stroked, played, and then he buried his head in the hollow of my neck to kiss, nibble, bite gently at areas that made me shiver and arch against him. "Hope the brakes are good on this bed," he said, and made me laugh. I hadn't thought I'd ever laugh again, but the vision of the two of us madly entwined on this bed as it rolled through the hallway, Wardens stopping to gawk . . . "Stop laughing," he scolded me, but I heard the tremble of it in his voice, too. "You're screwing up my concentration."

I made him gasp aloud, again, from what I was doing with *both* hands now. "Am I? Because it seems your concentration is quite . . . firm."

"Oh, now you're teasing?" His voice had turned ragged, dark around the edges, and I let him lift me up and back onto the bed. My gown drifted to the floor, and somehow the sheet joined it as he kicked off his jeans, stripped away his sleeveless shirt, and knelt in the open space between my legs. "I can tease, too. Payback."

He could, it seemed. The teasing involved hands, mouths, sweetly torturous control that made me bite my lips and beg him for release. When he finally gave in, when he was inside me, instinct and a desperate need took hold of me, and no matter how he tried to slow it down, I wasn't in the mood for leisurely lovemaking. Not this time. There was too much darkness to dispel, too much desperation, too little time left. He surrendered to me as much as I did to him, both of us lost in the fury and fire and urgency of it, and when he came he shuddered deep, holding me upright and close, and seeing the ecstasy take him triggered something wild in me as well, something that burst up from our joined bodies and spun us both crazily out of control, up into the highest reaches I'd ever climbed on the aetheric, and then drifted us down again like falling leaves to settle once again in our human, mortal, beautiful forms.

Luis collapsed against me, only just managing to hold his weight off at the last minute by resting it on his elbows. We were both covered in sweat, tasting it on each other's lips, and the glow between us lingered. Neither of us wanted to move, and it wasn't until the door rattled that he finally stopped kissing me in drowsy, gentle presses of lips, and sighed. The frustrated groan that followed came from the very depths of him, and I felt it resonating in my own body.

"Welcome back," he said, and laughed a little despairingly. "Now it's time to go. God, Cass. If I'd lost you ..."

I touched my lips to his in wordless reassurance. "You didn't," I said. "And you won't."

There was another impatient rattle at the door, and then a knock—tentative at first, then growing louder.

"We should probably—"

"Yes," I agreed, and kissed him again. "We should." Neither of us was in a hurry to answer the summons—and then, unexpectedly, the lock snapped back.

"Crap," Luis said.

There was an Earth Warden on the other side of that door; Luis's forethought in adding the bracing chair had paid off, because that stopped them from barging in—for a moment.

"Hand me my gown," I said.

He kissed me again, fast, and slid off to grab my gown, drape it over me, and then step into his underwear and jeans in a fast, expert motion. He was just zipping up when the chair clattered away from its locking position at the door, and it banged open.

Luis didn't pause. He picked up the sheet from the floor and put it back over me, winked, and turned to face the person standing in the doorway.

It was Isabel. Next to her, Esmeralda's human torso swayed on top of her snaky, muscular body. She crossed her arms over the tight, pink shirt she wore (embellished with the glittering words BITCH QUEEN) and looked down at Isabel, who had frozen, looking taken aback.

"See?" Esmeralda said. "Told you there was nothing wrong. They were just totally doing it."

Luis got his shirt from where it dangled at the end of

the bed and pulled it over his head. "Girls," he said in a
bland voice. "What's the emergency?" "Um . . ." Isabel's
cheeks were beet red, and she couldn't seem to look directly at either of us. "Nothing. It can wait. I just—I just
wanted to see how she was doing. When the door was
locked, I thought—"

"I told you," Esmeralda said in a bored voice, and
checked the finish on her fingernails. "Doing it."

"Shut *up*!" Isabel whispered fiercely. "God!"

"Thank you for coming to see me," I said, and was
very careful about where and how the sheet draped over
me. "I'm sorry the timing was . . . awkward. I'm much
better."

Esmeralda coughed and muttered something under
her breath; that earned a solid backhanded smack from
Iz, whose blush worsened, if that was possible. "Uh—
okay then, I—" Esmeralda was grinning at her now. "I
just—*shut up!*—I'll come back later." She turned and
left, head high, struggling to hold to her damaged dignity,
and Esmeralda broke into outright guffaws of laughter.

"Oh my *God*, did you see her face? The two of you
are so busted," she said. "Get a room. Somewhere else."

"Es," Luis said. "Beat it. I mean it. And lay off the kid.
She's six-going-on-fifteen."

Esmeralda stuck her tongue out at him—and showed
fangs at the same time—but she slithered off down the
hallway, petulantly knocking over a cart along the way.
Luis shook his head.

"I think we just scarred that kid for life," he said.
"She'll never look at us the same again."

"She knew we were lovers."

"There's a big difference between knowing and walking in on it," he said.

"So you regret it?"

He turned toward me, and his slow, intimate smile warmed me from within. "Not for a damn second," he said. "I wish we had a thousand hours just like it."

But we didn't, and hearing it aloud brought it home to both of us. The smiles and warmth faded. Luis cleared his throat, took a step toward the door, and said, "I'm going to go find out where he's sending us. You okay on your own to get cleaned up?"

"Yes," I said. As he shut the door, I threw back the sheet and gown and got out of bed. With the recession of all the complicated hormonal cocktails that had given me such a burst of . . . enthusiasm, I was left feeling weak, shaky, and even more bruised, though still oddly elated. The elation faded as I stood in the shower and scrubbed myself with the crisp-scented soap, and I was left feeling thoughtful instead. Lewis Orwell had seemed almost . . . resigned, I thought. Resigned to defeat, and willing to compromise at every step to postpone that defeat by another hour, another day. Rejecting Pearl was the right thing to do, but it meant hastening an inevitable death struggle.

And he, as all humans before him, would bargain to remain in play for as long as possible, in search of a miracle.

Pearl counted on that. Feasted on it.

But why hadn't she killed me? What could she want more than that? *I will make you a weapon,* she'd said. Always, she'd wanted me to join her—not as an equal, as a tool to be used.

I looked down at myself and saw the fading spots of countless injuries she'd inflicted on me with the cool, emotionless precision of a machine.

Ashan had been right all along. One day soon, it would come down to the two of us, facing each other over the heads of innocents . . . and I would have to make a choice that I, like Lewis Orwell, had been delaying in the face of the inevitable.

I finished in the bathroom, limped to the closet, and found fresh clothing—all new, still with the tags hanging on them. Either the Wardens had made arrangements, or Luis had gone shopping; either thought made me smile, because they had—whether through luck or skill— chosen soft, pastel colors, the kind that I most preferred. The pale pink leather jacket was buttery to the touch, as were the pants. Dressed, I felt much less fragile and helpless, though I was well aware how long it would take to recover fully.

Luis arrived a few moments later, as I was zipping up the calf-high boots. "Damn," he said, cocking his head. "You look scarily sexy. Look, are you sure you shouldn't be—"

"I was healthy enough to go to bed with you," I pointed out. "I should be well enough to get *out* of bed; it surely follows." He started to say something, then thought better of it and just shook his head. "Did you find where we are to meet Warden Baldwin?"

"That's a little problem. She's moving fast, and it's tough to guess where, and why; communication's been spotty at best. It looks as if she's heading toward our home base—into the Southwest. If we start in that direction, we'll be able to course-correct when she does."

"She must have fared well enough if she's still alive," I said. Luis shrugged.

"Well, she's got her powers back after whatever happened to them out at sea, but she lost one of the Wardens who was with her. Kevin, the kid. He's dead, killed by Djinn. All she's got now is one friend traveling with her, not even one with any powers, so she's totally on her own."

"*David* isn't with her?" I couldn't imagine a circumstance that would part him from her, in time of trouble. Not of his own accord.

"Yeah, well, that got complicated. As long as they both had no power, he could stick with her, but once she managed to get them both recharged and ready . . . Well, he's a Djinn, and not just any Djinn. A conduit to the Mother. He had to get the hell away from her, for obvious reasons."

David, once granted back his power, had been pulled into the mindless fury of the Mother. Of course. I didn't know why I'd thought that he, of all the Djinn, would be different—none of us could resist her.

That was part of why Ashan had exacted his complicated, painful, wonderful toll on me, to make me human. In a sense, he'd protected me, left me free to act on my own when he could not. I hated to give him the credit, but it seemed likely now that he'd foreseen much of what had passed, and might still come.

I used a hospital-provided hairbrush to tame my flyaway hair, just a little, and looked at myself in the mirror. I seemed ready. There was a slight rose-colored flush in my cheeks, a lingering glow, and my green eyes were clear and steady. The punctures were healed and fading.

We will do this, I told myself. *We must do this.* Joanne Baldwin held almost as much strength as Lewis Orwell; the Wardens needed her, desperately. Orwell himself had told me that indirectly; what they were fighting was not a war. Wars could be won.

We stood an excellent chance of not living another day.

And yet I looked . . . peaceful. Ready. *Alive.*

"Humans," I said aloud to the mirror, shook my head, and went to join Luis.

Chapter 10

WE DROVE THROUGH THE DAY, into the night, and saw the morning while still on the road. One benefit of being Earth Wardens: We had the ability to channel power to keep ourselves awake and alert, and although we'd need sleep eventually, it was simple enough to keep ourselves going on this journey. I rode my motorcycle, and Luis had appropriated a truck from a car lot; he'd found one that looked a great deal like his own, which made me raise an eyebrow and ask him how long it had taken to find *that*. He'd responded that if he was going to stand a damn good chance of dying in it, he wanted a truck that didn't embarrass him.

I couldn't argue with that. I was quite attached to the Victory.

We gave Portland a wide berth; the smoke of the dead city was a smear on the horizon, still burning. I kept my attention on the aetheric, watching for any signs of trouble ahead. The Djinn continued their relentless and unpredictable assaults; today, it seemed, they were focused on eradicating cities in Alaska and returning the entire state to wilderness.

There were few Wardens in Alaska. By midday, there were none. A night passed, and we kept moving.

We stopped, finally, as noon blazed in a cloudless sky; winter had lost its grip by the time we coasted to a halt in the small community of Farmington, New Mexico. Luis leaned out of the truck's window and said, "Time to stop for food. Once we get hooked up with Baldwin, there's no telling when we'll have time to eat again. That girl is even more of a trouble magnet than you are."

I shrugged, killed the Victory's engine, and dismounted as he climbed down from the truck. We were in the parking lot of a small restaurant that still flickered a red OPEN light in the window, although there was only one other vehicle parked there. The town had seemed deserted; there'd been almost no traffic on the roads, and we'd seen no one out on the streets on foot, either.

But this little restaurant seemed to be carrying on despite all of the evidence around it that perhaps it was time to take a day off.

A bell rang softly as we entered through the glass door, but that seemed to be the only sound, until I heard some metal clattering, and a woman rushed out from the back, wiping her hands on a towel. She was dressed in plain blue jeans and a checked shirt, and she had the look of a woman used to hard work and disappointment— but for all that, her smile was brave. "Welcome!" she said. "Things are a little strange out there today, but I'm still cooking. You folks grab yourselves a seat anywhere. I'd bring you menus, but really, it doesn't matter. I'll make you whatever you'd like."

Luis smiled at her and said, "How about a hamburger and a Coke?"

"Bread's a couple of days old, if you can stand that, but my produce comes out of the back garden, and it's still fresh," the cook said. "Best hamburgers in the Four Corners area, and that's a promise. You want cheese on that? And fries?"

"Sure. Cass?"

I ordered the same, which seemed to unreasonably delight the woman. She hustled off, and came back to deliver us drinks, frosty in mugs and fizzing with energy and sweetness. I sipped mine and watched as she hurried back to the kitchen. "Why is she so eager to serve us?" I asked. "Surely she knows how bad things are. And will become."

"Oh, she knows," Luis said. "Bet she doesn't even charge us anything. Sometimes people just like to feel . . . normal. Like everything's going to be okay. She likes to cook, and it makes her feel steadier. Gotta say, it makes me feel steadier, too. A little normal life in the middle of chaos—it's not a bad thing."

I didn't think so, either, but it alarmed me a little that in the midst of chaos humans clung so strongly to the lost normality of their lives. Her smile was bright and friendly, and she seemed so desperate to make us part of her circle of safety.

The food, when it came, was excellent; she brought a plate of her own and put it on a separate table. "Sorry," she said. "Proprietor's gotta eat, too. I won't bother you folks, and don't be afraid to ask for anything if you need it."

Luis scooted out a chair next to him. "Join us," he said. "I'm Luis. This is Cass."

"Pleased to meet you," she said. She was beaming as she picked up her glass and plate and sat down at our table. "You folks just passing through?" She laughed a little. "Stupid question. This ain't a time when people are settling down."

"Yeah, we're on our way somewhere," Luis said. "I guess this is your place?"

"Well, it is now," she said. "The man who owned it—he just ran away, left the place wide open. He told me I could have it if I wanted, so I figured I'd just keep it open for anybody who needed some food. Probably can't get much more in the way of supplies, but I'll use up what we got. No need for it to go to waste. I'm Betty, by the way."

"You from around here, Betty?"

She took a bite of her hamburger and shook her head as she chewed and swallowed. "Nope. I was what you might call on my own. Lost my house a couple of years back, been traveling hard ever since. I ended up here when our bus broke down, and then the driver couldn't get it fixed, so he went off to find help and never came back. Been here for about four days now, I guess. Seems like longer. Figured I might as well make the best of it."

"Well," Luis said, "you make one hell of a good burger. Glad you decided to fire up the grill for us."

"Ain't no big thing. I always wanted to open a restaurant someday," she said, and munched a French fry contemplatively before she asked, "You two trying to fix things?"

"Fix them, how exactly?" I asked.

"Don't know, but you two seem ... different. You're not running from something. You're running *to* it. And I don't think I've ever seen anybody quite like the two of you before."

"Well," Luis said, "Cass *is* extremely pale. It is kind of weird, even for a *gringa*."

Betty choked on her drink—iced tea, from the look of it. "Not what I meant," she said. "I seen them people on the TV, the ones who can do things. Magic and such. Strikes me you could be like that. I mean, I'm a good

Christian woman. I've always thought magic came from, you know, the devil, but—but maybe it don't, after all."

"If it helps, think of it as miracles," Luis said. "That's what I do. My cousin's a priest, one of my aunts is a nun, and my mom still drags me to mass every chance she gets. If I thought this power came out of a bad place, I wouldn't dare be using it."

It puzzled me, this apparently quite serious discussion of the obvious, but then I thought of Pearl. She was what this woman feared—evil masquerading as good for as long as might be convenient.

"I had a good feeling about you two right off," Betty said. "Might be a little wild-looking, but you've got good hearts. That's important."

The very unlikely Betty had something in her, too. Power, of a kind, though nothing that I recalled meeting before. It was a core of something I could only call a fierce, persistent *hope*. The kind that drove her, despite the hardships she'd endured, to make food for strangers and strive to provide a measure of comfort.

She was, I realized, *human*. Deeply, helplessly human, with all the faults and foibles, shining courage and power of that heritage. Unlike the Djinn, she had little control over what was to come; she likely didn't even expect to survive it. What she did, she did in the face of panic, terror, pain, and death.

She was *beautiful*. I caught my breath, staring at her, because it was as if my Djinn eyes had opened again, seen all the depth of her past and complex, intricate, unpredictable future. I had spent so much time with Wardens, who were at least somewhat like the Djinn; I thought I'd known humanity in its purest form.

But this woman—this one, hopeful woman—this *was* humanity, distilled and purified, and it humbled me.

I ate in silence while Luis and Betty chattered on—discussing pasts, comparing relatives, talking of nothing in particular, and certainly not the lives being lost, the cities burning, the horrific cost of what was to come. It might be called denial by some, but in that moment I thought it was the very strength that made humanity so successful . . . the ability to transcend reality, to create reality around them, even for a moment.

It was a gift the Djinn did not have, and until that moment, I had never imagined it to be so powerful.

"So," Betty said, when we had finished and there was nothing left on our plates but a few scraps and scrapes. "How do you folks feel about dessert? I've got some pies I made up fresh this morning, apple and chocolate. Even got some fresh whipped cream."

"Apple," Luis said, just as I said, "Chocolate." She looked from one of us to the other, and laughed.

"I'll have one of each," she said. "Might as well. Can't let it go to waste."

She stood up to go back to the kitchen, and stacked our empty plates; when Luis tried to help, she smacked the back of his hand in mock anger. I watched her go, and couldn't help but smile.

"I like that," Luis said. He was staring right at me. "Your smile. You're different when you do that."

"Am I?"

"Usually when you smile, it's to make a point, but that was just"—he shrugged—"human, I guess. And sweet. You're not often sweet, and it's nice."

I felt oddly uncomfortable with that, and shrugged, no longer smiling. "Perhaps it's in anticipation of the pie," I said.

"C'mon, you've gotta admit. Nice lady, overcoming the odds, making pies . . . Who doesn't love that?"

"Perhaps she killed the former proprietor and stuck his dismembered body in his own freezer," I shot back. "Not so heartwarming a story, then."

He threw a wadded-up napkin at me, and I was starting to smile again, perhaps with a wicked edge, when I heard plates crash, and Betty screamed.

I don't remember coming out of the chair, only the feel of the swinging door beneath my hand as I stiff-armed it open.

There was a Djinn in the kitchen. Tall, slender, human, and male in form; he had a long fall of blond hair and eyes that glowed an unearthly, livid white.

I didn't know him, and it didn't matter who he was, or had been; what he was now was rage and fury and pain given flesh.

And he was killing Betty.

His hand was locked around her throat. The broken fragments of the plates she had dropped were still bouncing and spinning across the floor, and time seemed to slow as I lunged forward. . . .

And the Djinn released Betty, spun away, and caught me instead.

She fell down, coughing and choking, but still breathing. He had never intended to kill her, I realized; she'd merely been a bell for him to ring to draw me to him. And that, I found, was all right. It was a choice I'd have gladly made.

Odd, how much I had changed.

Behind me, Luis shouted something that I failed to understand, but it didn't matter; the floor beneath the Djinn suddenly rose upward in a geyser of tile, broken concrete, dirt, shattered pipes, and slammed him into the ceiling. He lost his grip on me, and I tumbled back down the instant mound of debris to crash breathlessly into the steel casing of the ovens.

Luis headed toward me, but I pointed urgently at Betty. He changed course, grabbed her, and towed her backward, pushing her out the swinging door.

"Wait!" she yelled. "What are you doing?"

"Getting my damn pie," he said. "Stay down."

The Djinn hadn't been thrown off guard for long; he broke free of the pile of debris around him, but instantly met the flat side of a large skillet that Luis grabbed off the stove—still red-hot underneath, I realized. After he'd batted the Djinn across the face with it, Luis dropped the metal with a hiss of pain; the Djinn howled, evidently feeling the damage to its flesh as much as a human would have, but neither the crushed bones nor the badly burned skin bought us more than a few seconds.

Time enough for me to yank a natural gas connection loose from the wall. "Fire!" I shouted to Luis, who snapped his fingers.

The hissing gas line erupted in a blue-white jet of flame, engulfing the Djinn. It was a distraction, not a victory; we had little chance, it seemed, of destroying this one with the tools we had at hand. "Get Betty!" I yelled. "Get her out of here!" I was working hard to limit the natural tendency of the fire to eat its way back through the gas line, into a larger store; once that happened, the explosion would be spectacular, and there wouldn't be anything left of the restaurant. I had to buy time for Luis and the woman to get clear before that happened.

The Djinn was managing to extinguish itself, so I grabbed a bottle of cooking oil, ripped the cap off, and threw it in his direction. The plastic bottle was easy enough to melt in midflight, and the oil coated his skin and gave the fire fresh life all over him.

He was no longer amused.

I felt the coming blow, and the whole building rocked around me, as if it had suddenly been struck by a tornado, but the weather outside was calm and clear. The Djinn was breaking the restaurant apart—and in the kitchen area, sharp metal was everywhere, lying loose, or just lightly secured. A block on the counter holding a succession of cutting knives tipped over, and the knives slid free and rotated in the air, each finding and focusing in on me with their sharp points.

Half of them flew directly at me in a rush, and I had just enough time to fling out my hand and create a strong magnetic field on the front of the stove. The knives, and most of the other metal pulling free in the room, veered course and clanged against the stove's side in a near-unbreakable bond. The Djinn suddenly snuffed out all of the fire—even the flaming torch of the gas jet—and went very still. I felt the energy in the room change, as if something very large that had been casually swatting at me suddenly turned and focused its attention on me quite closely.

Another Djinn misted into existence next to the one who still smoldered with sparks in its blackened skin. Then another, and another.

I backed through the swinging doors, not daring to take my eyes off them. "Get in the truck," I called over my shoulder. "Take her with you. Start driving."

"Cass—"

"Do it!" I heard the front bell ring as they left, and the normality of that sound was made all the more wrenching by the three Djinn who simply misted right through the walls, walking toward me. I knew that I couldn't take on three Djinn; even with Luis, there was no possibility of surviving the experience.

Instead, I took in a deep breath and set *myself* on fire.

The effect was, indeed, spectacular; the flames bloomed along my sleeve, and I screamed in panic and made a show of trying to slap them out. In fact, I was spreading them over my jacket, then down my pants, until my whole body was coated in a writhing fury of orange fire. I screamed again, ran into a table, and fell to the floor, still burning. The floor around me began to sizzle and melt. Flames climbed up the wooden legs of the chair against which I lay.

I thrashed a bit, and then went still. The hiss of the burning floor and table was helpful in selling the illusion that my flesh was blackening and sizzling like meat on a grill, and after a few more seconds, the Djinn lost interest in me and misted away.

I let the fire go on for a few more seconds. It was as well I did, because the last Djinn to leave—the one I'd burned, who did in fact still trail smoke behind him—came back to watch for a moment. Not mistrust, I thought, so much as satisfaction.

When he was finally gone, I doused the flames, rolled up to my feet, and ran for my motorcycle. Luis's truck was long gone; I had done my best to focus the Djinn on me, not on him, so I was hopeful that he wouldn't be their target if he was fleeing. All I needed to do was fire up the Victory, and . . .

The Victory was a steaming, melted pile of scrap metal.

I stared at it, grim and *quite* disappointed, and with a muttered curse, moved down the street to another building, then another. It seemed that every vehicle in town had been destroyed, and I was still searching for something, *anything*, that could take me on the road when I heard, very distinctly, the blatting sounds of motorcycle engines, more than one, approaching down the deserted main street.

I ducked outside. A biker gang, at least twenty strong, was cruising through, checking out the prospects for food, fuel, or looting; they had the hard, grubby look of men and women who'd been on the road for days, and the hunted expressions of those who'd seen too much.

I stepped out into their way, and the first wave of bikes coasted to a stop just inches from my body.

Even idling, the Harleys were loud beasts. The one I immediately pegged as the leader was looking me over, frowning, and he finally said, "So, are you stupid, or just crazy?"

"Neither," I said. "I need a motorcycle."

Under normal circumstances that would have gotten a derisive laugh, but not this time. They had no more humor left, it seemed. I saw guns being drawn, including a sawed-off shotgun, which would have worried me if I hadn't already had considerable experience with firearms. I didn't blink, or look away from the leader's face.

"You need to get out of here and keep moving," I told him. "Stay away from towns. Try to live off the land, and conserve your fuel. Once it goes dry, there may not be more for a while. Things are going to get worse, not better."

"I'm still listening for a reason not to shoot you and get you out of our way," he said. "Got anything, blondie?"

In response, I deflated both tires on his bike. He yelped in surprise as the weight shifted, struggling to hold it upright. "I could destroy some of your bikes," I said quietly. "I could do that quite spectacularly, if I wished. They blow up so well. Or I could fuse the parts together. Or even fuse you *into* the metal, which I assure you would be very unpleasant, until you died of the experience. But I'm trying to be hospitable." I called a fireball and balanced it in a blazing hand-sized bonfire on my palm. "I need a vehicle. I'm sorry I have nothing to give you for it, but let's call it the spoils of war. If I'm still alive later, I'll buy a new one for the leader of the"—I checked the logo on the back of his weathered denim jacket—"Devil's Traitors."

To his credit, he didn't immediately back off, though his eyes had narrowed at the sight of the flame held so casually in my hand. "We're out of Albuquerque," he said. "You'd better make it a fucking awesome bike, lady." He looked toward the back of the pack, and pointed. "Take Pointer's ride. Pointer, double up with Gar, and don't bitch about it. We'll steal you another one down the road."

The tough-looking one-eyed man he indicated didn't seem pleased, but he did as instructed, leaving the Harley idling and leaning on its kickstand as he took his place on the other bike. I nodded thanks, and mounted up.

"Blondie," the biker said from the front of the pack. I released the kickstand. "If I see you again and you aren't wheeling in a brand-new shiny ride for Pointer, this ain't going to go well for you. Got me?"

I nodded. "Seems fair," I said. "I live in Albuquerque. I'll find you."

"Not if I find you first," he said, and let out the clutch. They picked up speed and left the streets in a swirl of dust and trash.

I hit the throttle, and went in pursuit of Luis.

He'd stopped on the side of the road twenty miles away, at another roadhouse; this one was deserted and locked, but he'd opened it up, and Betty was inspecting the establishment with enthusiasm. He eyed my new Harley with raised eyebrows. "Bike trouble?" he asked.

"Don't ask." I was annoyed at the way the Harley rode; the bars were too far forward and low, and it would take time to customize it properly. I missed the Victory. "She'll be all right here. We have to go. I'm not entirely sure the Djinn will leave us be, although I did a good imitation of gruesomely dying for their benefit."

"Would have paid to see that one," he said, and then shook his head, all humor falling away. "No, actually, I wouldn't. Let's never put on that particular show, okay?"

"I agree," I said. "Let's not."

Tracking Joanne was exhausting, and we dodged trouble over and over again; there were more Djinn now, and more active. The few humans we ran into seemed more interested in fleeing than fighting, which was lucky; it meant less destruction left in our wake.

But it took too long to match our course to Joanne's finally stationary position.

I released the throttle on the roaring Harley and coasted to a halt as we topped the last rise. We'd gotten an update from Lewis Orwell to meet Joanne Baldwin at a government contractor's secured installation in the Texas panhandle near Amarillo, and it was close, very close—though the smoke rising up into the clear blue sky didn't bode well for the installation's fate. Luis's truck stopped next to me, and he rolled down the window.

"Madre," Luis murmured, as we looked down at the true scale of the destruction in front of us. The buildings that had—presumably—once existed had been leveled into rubble. The secure fencing at the perimeter of the facility lay in twists and tatters, and near the center of the large debris field lay an enormous pit from which black smoke and dust still drifted. "What the hell was this place?"

There was a sign—damaged and ripped partway down the center, but still readable. "Some kind of research and construction facility," I said. "Nuclear weapons."

"Perfect," Luis said grimly. "My day wasn't sucking hard enough; I get to fry my balls off, too. Feel that? Radiation's off the scale."

"It can be dealt with," I said. "She's down there. In the pit. Buried, I think."

"Sure, because that'll be easy, given our great history with that kind of thing. Plus radiation."

"And there are Djinn down there, as well," I said, concentrating harder. The residual boiling energies of the fight made a confusing smear of livid color on the aetheric, but I could still see the flitting, telltale motions that betrayed the presence of my former brothers and sisters. "She's battling them."

He said nothing to that, just rolled up the window. I took it to mean we were cleared to go, so I gave the Harley its head and picked up speed as it roared down the hill. Luis's truck raced behind me. I pulled up at the fence and parked the bike, while he bounced his truck off the road and into the dirt, heading for a section of fence that had been completely shredded away in the blast. The torn edges of metal glistened like diamond as he rocketed past; he hit the brakes and slewed the truck to a stop near the edge of the still-burning pit.

"That might have been unnecessarily risky," I told him, walking over. He flashed me a grin.

"You know me, *chica*. I live for drama. So. We do this fast. Tunnel down, get her out. The sooner we're away from here, the better. Countermeasures for the radiation are going to take a hell of a lot of power we can't afford to spend."

I nodded and joined him at the crumbling edge. He held out his hand, and I took it, but Luis didn't immediately start the process of moving earth toward Joanne. He took in a deep breath, and looked at me.

"Cass," he said. "If we don't get through this—well, you know. But do your best to get through it, okay? I'm not ready for endings just yet."

I nodded. If he felt he had to say it, he assessed our chances to be even worse than they'd been so far, and that was poor indeed. I could feel it all around us—the fury was thick in the air, choking and hot as the smoke. The Earth wanted Joanne dead, and if we wanted to join the fight, she'd gladly take us, too.

I suppose we could have turned away, but Lewis's instructions had been specific: Find Joanne, and keep her safe. She was needed, badly needed, in this fight.

Currently, she looked as if she needed the help very, very badly.

We already had practice at tunneling, but this was a shallower goal than when we'd rescued the trapped Wardens outside of Seattle; this was more of a ramp than a shaft. I helped channel Luis's power with finer control, slicing through the first layers of dirt, stone, metal, and rubble and flinging them up and out of the way. Once the packed earth beneath was visible, the process became more of a brute-force exercise, carving an opening down at a sharp angle. It took a surprisingly short time, considering, but then the ground had already been shaken loose by the battle that had occurred here before our arrival—which must have been spectacular.

We were still only halfway down our makeshift ramp when I felt something *break* on the aetheric, something massive and immensely powerful ... a Djinn. That had been the death of a Djinn—no, I realized, not the death ... the *emptying* of a Djinn, and the burst of incredibly violent energy around the body of a Warden.

Around Joanne Baldwin.

No Warden could drain a Djinn, but a Djinn could go beyond his limits; it commonly occurred when one tried to violate the will of the Mother, or one of the laws that could not be broken without cost.

Like denying death.

Someone had just saved Joanne's life . . . and now the bright star that had been a Djinn was going out, its brilliance twisting in on itself, turning black and inverted and hungry.

I was seeing—and feeling—the birth of an Ifrit. It was what happened to Djinn who drained themselves past the point of no return, and now—like me—could exist only by consuming the power of others. I subsisted on the power of Wardens, but Ifrits didn't prey on humans; there was not enough power to sustain them.

They preyed on other Djinn, and when they did, they battened on in a mindless fury, to the death.

"Faster," I breathed. Already, the Ifrit—whoever it had once been—had secured on a victim and was ripping the immortal's life away in bloody, unspooling strips. The chaos intensified in that narrow battlefield below us.

"Yeah, enough nice engineering," he said, and just punched through the rest of the way, shoving aside concrete, rebar, fractured steel, earth, *anything* that was in our way. He dashed ahead and scrambled over the last few enormous chunks of concrete; below us was a mostly intact, though pitted and cracked, floor. I followed his example, and saw a hellish nightmare of smoke, flame, the residual aetheric glow of radiation . . . and Djinn. There were several facing us, though they'd momentarily paused.

Joanne Baldwin was a few feet away, though for a shocked second I didn't recognize her. She was filthy, tattered, and underneath the grime and streaks of blood, she had the tender-pink skin of someone very recently healed. Luis didn't allow it to give him pause at all, remarkably enough.

"Sorry we're late," he said, and jumped down the rest of the way, flexing his knees as he landed. His smile was sheer, raw nerve, though there was a hint of terror in the shine of his eyes. "*Madre*, you don't go halfway when you blow shit up, do you? There's enough rads burning in here to barbecue lead. We can't stay here long."

Joanne seemed both shocked and relieved to see us. She said something I couldn't hear over the sudden roar of a Djinn's attack; the Djinn was quickly countered by a blur that was moving in Joanne's defense. I was distracted by that, and focused in only as Luis said, with remarkable calm, "...moving fast. Hey, Cass, you remember Joanne?"

It was a foolish question; no one, having met the Weather Warden, ever forgot her. Whether such memories were favorable was another thing entirely, and we had far more to worry about than the niceties.

All I could do was nod, and she returned it shakily. To say that she'd looked better would be something of an understatement; I was amazed the woman was still standing.

I looked at the Djinn arrayed against us, and felt a tremor of memory; I'd faced some of these same ones as we'd emerged from another tunnel, in Seattle. Ashan's closest allies. "They're under the Mother's control," I said, which was probably unnecessary, given the near-insane pale shine in their eyes. "They won't stop coming for you. They know you hurt her in what you did here." And Baldwin had, indeed, scarred the Mother deeply this time with the raw, bleeding radiation—another wound on a maddened and angry beast already snarling with fury.

"I know that," Joanne shot back. "It was kind of the plan. Here. Rocha, take this. Try to bind one of them."

Luis gave her a puzzled look. "Try to *what*? What the hell are you talking about?" He wasn't following only because he was too busy calculating our chances; I, however, realized immediately what she was saying.

Bind.

She'd been binding the Djinn into bottles—and there, coming out of the shadows, misting into human form, was one of them.

David, the leader of the New Djinn. His human shell had skin that held a subtle bronzed metallic shine to it, and his eyes were the bright, unsettling color of melting copper. Beautiful, and eerie, and at the moment, full of fury directed at those who were coming for his lover. No—his *wife*. David, the Djinn, had bound himself permanently to a human, a bond as strong as any bottle in terms of vows . . . though now, I realized, he was bound a second time, into a glass prison that helped insulate him from the irresistible siren call of the Mother.

He nodded to me, as one equal to another. In my bad old days as a Djinn, I would have found it gallingly presumptuous; even the highest of the New Djinn was no match for the lowest of the True Djinn, or that had been my fixed and constant opinion then. Now my horizons had . . . expanded. David was a burning brand of power, steady and pure, and his origins mattered little. . . . If anything, the humanity from which he'd been born gave him more substance to me now. He had lived as I did now; he understood and cherished the pull of the world, the flesh, the strange and quiet beauty of a human life.

He loved Joanne. It was as much a part of him as the flesh that clothed him, or the blazing light in his smile. Something, perhaps, to aspire to be—something like David.

I had no more time to think on it. Two Djinn came for us in the same instant; the reaction from both Joanne and David was almost instantaneous, the stuff of pure, natural communion between the two of them. David might have been the most powerful of the New Djinn, but those he was facing were to be feared regardless, and there were too many of them. He met two of them head-on and was slammed back against debris, momentarily out of the fight—but Joanne didn't pause. Didn't even slow as she strode forward.

Weather Wardens had a power uniquely suited to battling Djinn, at least those unwise enough to maintain a form that wasn't completely founded in flesh . . . and most of the True Djinn rarely bothered with flesh and bone and blood. They preferred to establish themselves in a less corporeal form, and it left them vulnerable to the one thing that Weather Wardens commanded above all others: wind.

She raised a tearing, howling storm in the debris-choked cave. She was sensible enough to raise a shield to keep the worst of it from us, but the Djinn quickly realized their disadvantage. Some took flesh. Others stubbornly tried to battle her on their own terms—a less-than-winning proposition.

And one of those who had gone to hard, brutal, angry flesh headed straight for me, eyes glowing, head lowered, teeth bared to rip and chew.

Baldwin had pressed an uncapped glass bottle into Luis's hands, but he clearly was still struggling to process her instructions while simultaneously assessing the dangers coming at us on all sides. There was no time to explain. I grabbed it from him and shouted the incantation that sealed a Djinn into a prison of glass and hatred. "Be thou bound to my service! Be thou bound to my service! Be thou bound to my service—"

As fast as I said it, the Djinn was faster, roaring up on me in a flash of smeared light, and his fist made contact with my chest just as the second syllable of the last word left my lips.

I was incredibly lucky. It would have shattered my rib cage into powder, had that blow landed at full strength, but he was already dissolving into mist as it hit, shrieking his anger and frustration in an eerily metallic wail.

I had just imprisoned one of my own people, and he wasn't the first I'd subjected to this indignity. I did not have time to feel the guilt of it, not even a second, though I caught my breath on a gasp even as I corked the bottle and tossed it to Luis, then grabbed another empty container from the case that was lying on the rocks in front of us. I picked out another Djinn and repeated the incantation, faster this time, and she blew apart into smoke and dust before she was able to land a blow on me.

The third bottle, though, was already occupied, as I found out when I yanked out the cork and felt the tingling shiver of power speed through me. A Djinn came howling from her prison, and the hissing tentacles of mist solidified into a tall, dark-skinned woman with glossy hair in tiny braids, and a ferocious grin. Her eyes were as golden as a hunting cat's, and she tilted her head forward, tiny beads swinging and clacking at the ends of her braids, as she considered me, her new master. The grin was just as predatory as her eyes. Her name was Rahel, and she commanded respect throughout all of the hierarchy of the Djinn, because many thought she was utterly insane. She did enjoy making life difficult for anyone she encountered—human and Djinn alike.

I thought for a moment she'd target *me* for that chaotic instinct, but then she gave an ear-piercing yell of bloody joy and threw herself into the fray against those coming for us. *Interesting,* I thought. Not to mention perilous, trying to keep that one caged. I went on to the next bottle—fortunately, empty. We had cut the odds by half, and the Djinn who were fighting for us were more than capable now of keeping them from menacing our fragile human forms.

That was a very good thing, because although Joanne

was still standing, she wouldn't be for long. I could see the shock setting in on her—given the blood soaking her clothing and smearing her skin, no one could fail to be weak, even if the injuries had been healed. I was expending energy as well in the binding of the Djinn; I'd never realized what a drain it was, but each required an effort of will and power, and I was rapidly growing weary.

Luis was staying alert for any other threats, but when only one maddened enemy was left, he took the bottle from my hand and did the binding spell, slotted the bottle back into the padded box, searched my pockets for the other bottles as well to store them safely away.

And for the first time, it was eerily quiet in this hot, dust-shrouded ruin where fires still burned. The bound Djinn went still, waiting for instructions, and instead of looking to me, who technically held their bottles and their wills, they were watching Joanne.

She fell on her knees to the ground, as if driven there by the pressure. It looked more like a collapse of relief than one of weakness, but David went to her side immediately. She was safe, with him.

"What did we just do?" Luis asked. He sounded shaken. "Fuck."

"We did what we had to do to survive," I replied. Unlike the Weather Warden, I felt no relief; I was shaken indeed by what I'd done, and what the price would be for it. I was a Djinn, one of them, and I had just raped their will. There would be no forgiveness for that. I saw it in their eyes. I forced myself to forget that, and focus on more immediate issues. "We won't survive long if we don't leave this place. The radiation is too high even for Earth Wardens to stay here much longer." It was a constant burn now against my skin. A human, unprotected, would have been fatally compromised in minutes.

David gathered up Joanne in his arms; she made

some halfhearted protest, and he some response, but I saw the utter relief on her face, as if some endless pain had finally stopped hurting when she was in his embrace. They'd been parted for a time, I realized, and what I was looking at was not just love as humans knew it, but something stronger. Two halves of a whole, being mated.

The faithful, constant love of the Djinn was, I had always believed, unique in the world. I hadn't known that humans were capable of such things, until I saw how well the two of them fit together.

"Don't ever do anything this stupid again," David said to her as I picked up the box of bottles and led the way back over the scattered concrete blocks and up into the tunnel. I heard her scratchy, half-amused laugh.

"If I had a nickel for every time somebody said that . . ."

He dropped his voice to a low tone, too low for me to overhear, not that I wished to do so. It would be private, and serious, and I had enough of that to carry all on my own, along with the bottles. The box wasn't heavy, but it was unwieldy, and Luis took one side of it as we started the uphill journey.

"Second verse, same as the first," he said, panting with effort; we had packed the tunnel's earth as much as possible, but it was still uneven footing, and easy to slip. An angle that had seemed expeditious and simple coming down was less so when climbing out. "New rule: We don't do tunnels again. Sound good?"

"Excellent," I agreed, and meant it. I realized that I'd left the Djinn standing down there at the bottom, waiting for orders. "Should I put them back in the bottles? All of them?"

"Not all," Luis said. "You don't have David's bottle, anyway. I'm pretty sure Joanne does. I'd leave at least one out, in case we need the help."

"Which?"

He shrugged. "Rahel," he said. "She's always been friendlier to humans than most."

"Not to me," I said, thinking of her evil grin and the shine of those eyes. But I muttered under my breath, "Back in the bottles, all of you. Except Rahel." I was relatively new at enslaving Djinn, and it felt deeply wrong to do it, but a surge of power raced through me, and I felt it echoing in those I'd bound. They evaporated into mist, contained by the glass, and I stoppered the bottles quickly before we resumed our climb.

Rahel, in fine Djinn style, elected to leap the distance and wait for us up on the surface, while we toiled every brutal inch of the way. Once we'd achieved the sunlight, Luis braced himself on a toppled wall and crouched down, head lowered. Sweat dripped from the point of his chain until he wiped his face with his equally sweaty bare arm. "Damn. Next time remind me to angle my tunnels better."

"You were in a hurry," I said, and patted my pockets again to make sure I had put all of the bottles in the box. Luis added a last one just as David strode out of the tunnel and set Joanne up on her feet. He held her until he was sure she was steady.

"Anything to add?" I asked. Joanne nodded and pulled a few from the torn pockets of her jacket as well—all except one, which she considered, and then kept.

It wasn't David's. It was corked. When I gave her a questioning look, she said, "It's Venna. I can't risk her getting out again. She's—" Joanne shuddered a little, and David moved closer again, offering silent support. "She saved my life. And she's paying the price."

"Ifrit," I whispered. *Venna*. I'd mourn my sister when I could, but the love I'd borne her didn't extend to the twisted, blackened, starveling creature that existed now in that bottle. Ifrits could be killed, but it was a difficult matter, and one I had no desire to attempt in my current human condition. Of course, that human condition also protected me from her, but even so. Venna had been one of the best of us, of all of the Djinn; it pained me deeply that she'd become so lost. Ifrits couldn't be healed, not unless they destroyed someone more powerful than themselves, and even then the chances weren't good of success.

The only Djinn greater than Venna—and this was arguable—was Ashan.

I became aware of a burning thirst, and shrugged off the pack that I'd been carrying—it wasn't large, but some things I'd learned were necessities, including bottles of water. I had four. I took three and passed two to Luis and Joanne, then leaned against a wall to gulp down mine. The water was warm, but it washed the taste of dirt and death from my mouth, and relieved some of the budding headache I'd begun to nurse.

"We need to get moving," Luis said to me. "Radiation's still high up here, plus this place is going to get real damn busy, real soon. Might be chaos out there, but they're still not going to ignore an honest-to-God terrorist attack on a nuclear facility. Not if there's any government still standing."

"I'm not a terrorist," Joanne said, pausing in her quest to drain her entire bottle in one gulp. She looked pale beneath the drying blood. "I have clearances. Sort of."

"Yeah, well, you entered under false pretenses, blew up the place, and there's radiation all over the county, so I kind of think you're a terrorist by definition," he replied. "And because we came to get you, we're a terrorist cell, I guess. Great. Always wanted to be on some kind of no-fly list, although after today I guess that covers everybody in the world. Won't be too many planes getting off the ground these days. Too easy for the Djinn to take them out."

Joanne finished the rest of her water. I hoped she wouldn't make herself ill with it; she'd drained it too quickly. I wasn't so concerned for her as I was for my own fastidiousness; human bodily functions, including vomiting, were still very distasteful to me. "Who else is coming our way?" she asked.

"Not sure. Cops, fire, every federal agency still operating? Maybe the military. This wasn't some small-time target, you know. It's going to get a lot of attention, as much as circumstances allow."

"So I suppose we should . . . ?"

"Seal up the tunnel, contain the radiation, and get the hell out of Dodge? Yeah. That'd be a good plan." Luis— who also had finished his water too quickly—tossed his empty plastic bottle down into the tunnel, where it rolled into darkness.

"Bad recycler," Joanne said, but tossed her empty in as well.

"Jo, you brought down the whole fucking complex and cracked open a few nukes. I don't think a couple of biodegradable water bottles really count at this point."

He rose to his feet, and I rose with him, as if we'd been pulled by the same string. Our hands fit together as if it was the most natural thing in the world, and for a moment I remembered David cradling Joanne in his arms, and smiled. There were partnerships, and partnerships, and what I felt for Luis. . . .

It was not the time to analyze what I felt, and I shook my head to clear it as Luis began to call power.

Collapsing a tunnel was far, far easier than building one, or keeping it open; a little application of force, and the smooth, even structure began to come apart . . . in streams of dirt at first, and then, as the surface tension holding the earth together broke, an avalanche of soil and rock. Luis pressed down on the wrecked room where we'd found Joanne, and the last remaining roof supports collapsed, burying it in a roaring thump.

Dust erupted out of the mouth of the tunnel, gray and cloudy, turning darker as the collapse raced up toward us.

Then the entire pit sank down another ten feet, and silence fell.

"If we had time, I'd recommend covering this whole place in concrete," he said. "The radiation's contained, and I accelerated the decay, but it's going to take a while to cool off. . . . Damn—here they come." Luis turned slightly toward the horizon, and I heard the far-off wail of sirens. "Right. Time to go. Who needs a ride?"

Joanne—who'd taken my last bottle of water and somewhat wastefully used it to rinse herself relatively clean—shook her head. She was busy plucking the bottles *out* of the padded case where I'd put them, and wrapping them in a dense wad of material, which she then stuffed into my nearly empty backpack and handed to me. "You're the official keeper of the Djinn. Try not to fall on that," she said. "That would be bad."

I took the pack and adjusted the straps on my shoulders to let it ride comfortably. "What was wrong with the box?"

"One thing about carrying boxes—you tend to drop them in a fight," she said. "Wearing them is a much better option." She studied me for a few seconds. "You don't look happy about it."

I hated that she'd made me responsible for my tethered, imprisoned brothers and sisters, *hated* it, but I couldn't articulate the reasons. Nor would I, to her. "We need to go. The Djinn will be back on us soon, and we don't need more entanglements with humans." I knew, better than she did, that the rest of the Djinn would make us a priority now—we weren't merely annoying Wardens to be squashed; we were annoying Wardens with prisoners who knew that the accords between Djinn and Wardens were back in place and that it was *possible* to enslave the Djinn again. That was knowledge they would very much want to destroy at its source before the rest of the Wardens began to try to act on it.

Joanne was asking where we wanted to go. Luis said, "It's all pretty much apocalyptic at this point, so take your pick. I'd suggest heading to Sedona. That's where Orwell was taking the rest of the Wardens, if they didn't get held up on the way. It's a fairly good, protected place."

We headed for the vehicles, and Luis stopped dead as he stared at his truck. "Damn," he said, and kicked the front tire. It was sitting in mud—mud that stank of oils and mechanical fluids. "I must have busted a line. This thing ain't going anywhere." He could fix it, given time; Earth wardens were gifted at that kind of repair, but the sirens were keening close now.

"Then you're with me," I said, and pulled him with me toward the motorcycle. He let loose a string of Spanish obscenities under his breath.

"I ain't riding bitch," he said.

"Then you're walking," I said, "because it's my bike." I was not concerned for his macho sensibilities, and after a furious look at the now-visible flashing lights on the horizon, he climbed on behind me. I smiled—since he couldn't see the flash of teeth now—and gunned the Harley in a sand-spouting roar.

Joanne and David had their own transportation, a solid-looking car that seemed capable of good speed when required. Oddly, there was *already* someone in the car that was parked a short distance away, covered with the inevitable blurring curtain of dust ... and that was the car that Joanne and David entered, in the backseat. No sooner did the door close behind them than the car spun tires and headed for the road. "Who's driving the car?" I asked Luis. He shrugged.

"Knowing her? Satan."

I let out the clutch and followed. A few moments later, power shimmered the air, and I felt something passing over us like a hot gust of wind. "Veil!" Luis shouted in my ear. "We're hidden, so don't expect anybody to get out of the way for you from now on!"

I gunned the engine and passed the Mustang, slowing down to take a look at the driver, purely out of personal curiosity. He was a Djinn—or at least, that was my first and vivid impression, but then I had to wonder, because there was something not quite ... right. The *form* of a Djinn, but when I checked in Oversight I saw no sign of a Djinn presence inhabiting that form. It was like a lifeless robot—the kind of hollowed-out shell that Mother Earth was using to deliver her plagues, but this one showed no such signs of infection.

Merely ... emptiness.

As I was staring, the creature turned its head and met my gaze. Not vacant, after all. It was definitely being— piloted, I supposed, was the only word for it.

The Djinn's lips moved, and I shouldn't have been able to hear the words, but they came through clearly. "Don't you worry about it," said a clear, Southern-accented feminine voice. "He's not connected to the Mother. He's connected to me."

"And who are you?"

"Whitney," she said. "Djinn conduit for the younger side of the family. Pleased to meet you, Cassiel. I've heard all about you."

I'd heard little to nothing of her, but there wasn't time for chat. I just nodded, accelerated, and pulled smoothly into the lead.

We stood to make good time, I thought. It would not be too comfortable for Luis on the backseat of the bike, but he had a high padded back support, at least. He wasn't holding on to me, because that would have put his face in range of my loose, whipping hair, and the backpack I wore prevented closer contact in any case; it would be tiring for him to keep adjusting his balance and keep his alertness up for any emergencies.

As for me, I knew I'd enjoy the ride, no matter how dangerous it might become.

I checked the gas. We had an almost full tank; the Mustang that Joanne and David used would burn through fuel much faster; but then again, with a Djinn driver they wouldn't need to stop to refuel. *Neither do I,* I realized with a start. While as a Warden I could extend the life of the fuel, I couldn't necessarily *create* it . . . but a Djinn could, and I now had one uncorked, and ready for my call.

Rahel wouldn't be *at all* pleased with being put on such mundane duties, but that was hardly my concern now; I'd be dealing with the revenge of my fellows for a human lifetime, if I didn't manage to recapture my Djinn status . . . or, of course, for much longer, if I did. Now didn't seem to be the time to worry about it.

We negotiated roadblocks, both police and military, several times as sunset blazed red and faded to purple, then blue, then black. The desert night was chilly as we raced onward, following the Mustang . . . which seemed to be heading in the right direction, at least. The vibration of the engine beneath me soothed and invigorated me, although Luis seemed to doze behind me as he rested his head against the padding of my backpack.

Just when I'd begun to feel complacent, Rahel appeared in front of me, cross-legged, her back to the road. Floating mid-air, easily keeping pace three feet from the front tire of the Harley as it bit the asphalt in a blur. She was wearing a particularly objectionable color of lime green, something that made me think of the radiation we'd left behind us and cleared off our persons and equipment. Perhaps it had all been drawn to her clothing.

"Sistah," she said. "Or should I call you *mistress*, Cassiel?"

"As you like," I said. I didn't raise my voice; I could whisper and she'd have no difficulty hearing me, despite the engine noise and wind. "You do enjoy showing off, don't you?"

"Utterly," Rahel said, and laughed. "You should try it sometime. Being Djinn doesn't mean you have to lack a sense of drama. Or humor." The wind blew her thin braids into a clacking, twisting, eerily snakelike mass around her head, and in perhaps conscious mockery of popular culture's idea of a proper Djinn, she'd crossed her arms. I half expected her to give a nod and a wink, but the sharp amusement in her smile faded, leaving something more serious. "I have a message for you."

"From whom?"

"From your big, bad boss man," she said. "Ashan. He's still a bastard."

"Why would he speak to *you*?" I didn't mean it in a dismissive way, but it sounded so as I spoke it; I meant only that Ashan was a True Djinn, a *conduit*, and the True Djinn had little interest in, or interaction with, the New Djinn unless forced. The idea that he would seek out Rahel, speak to her, seemed . . . highly unusual.

"Perhaps because with the end of us all imminent, our family squabbles mean little these days," Rahel said coolly. "It cost him a great deal to regain enough control, even for a moment, to summon me and speak. You might at least have the courtesy to listen to what he felt was so important."

I nodded stiffly. It wasn't that I was unwilling to hear her, more that I was dreading what the words would be — and the trouble that they'd bring with them.

I expected her to simply recite the message, but as Rahel had pointed out, she did not lack a sense of drama. Her eyes flashed through with a sudden gleam of color . . . a faded teal blue, then a moonlit steel. Ashan's colors. And Ashan's voice issuing from her mouth, in an eerie puppetry. "The time is coming for you, Cassiel," he said, and that *was* Ashan, looking out from the shell of Rahel's form. Ashan's cold, certain voice, speaking to me from beyond time, from another place altogether. "Your little vacation from duty is almost over. Face your fears *now*. Face yourself. See what I know to be true about you . . . that you are not one of them, and never will be. If you value the continued existence of the Djinn, you will act. Soon. Unless you've grown too weak with your love of humanity."

He smiled, and it was not a pleasant expression, or a kind one. It woke rage in me, and fear, and a desire to throttle him blue, not that in his case it would make much impression on him at all.

And then, with just as much speed as he'd appeared, Ashan was gone, and Rahel was back in her own form, cocking an eyebrow at my expression. "I see you didn't care for what he had to say," she said. "How surprising. And you're usually so good-natured."

"Silence," I snapped. "Go do something useful."

"Not unless you have a highly specific order for me." She stretched herself out sinuously on thin air, propped up on one elbow, and yawned, showing pointed catlike teeth. Her eyes slitted vertically, and the pupils glowed an unnatural green in the Harley's headlights. Her skin had a warm matte glow to it, and in her own way she was as beautiful as anything I'd ever seen.

I wanted to rip her to pieces, and she knew it, and it amused her deeply. Anything I ordered her to do, she'd pick it apart, pull it to pieces, bend it all out of meaning and to her own benefit—and she'd waste my time, endlessly, in definitions.

"Please yourself, then," I said, and gritted my teeth as she rolled over to float on her back.

Then she began to sing obnoxiously cheerful popular songs to the burning stars and rising, orange-stained moon.

It was a *very* long ride.

Chapter 11

DAWN WAS STILL A HINT on the horizon when we began to pass signs that led not to Sedona, but Las Vegas; a course correction that mattered little to me, since there were also Wardens in that city, and people to defend from attacks. It surprised me that the Djinn had failed to discover us during the night, until Luis woke up with a raw, startled cry and surprised me into a wobble that I quickly got back under control. Losing control of a motorcycle at this speed was a very poor idea.

Rahel had stopped singing some time back, and vanished. I hadn't thought much of it, except that her boredom had finally outweighed my torment, but now Luis leaned forward and said in a raw voice, "The Fire Oracle's been turned loose. He's burning cities. I saw it. I can *feel* it."

He said it quickly, but with utter certainty, and I twisted to look over my shoulder. His face was set, his eyes shadowed, and I had no doubt he meant what he'd just said. "How is that possible?" I asked. "Oracles don't leave their positions, except the Air Oracle, who isn't confined. . . ."

"I'm telling you that he's walking, and burning. The destruction—" Luis looked ill and shaken. "I saw it. I was dreaming, but it was real. I know it was real. I saw—people—Cass, it's happening. It's really happening. She's going to kill us all."

He'd known that from the beginning, but something—some instinct for self-preservation and sanity—had withheld that knowledge from him on a gut level. Now he knew, with all the certainty that I'd always carried.

There were tears in his eyes, I could see them in the reflected light of the dashboard in front of me. "We're not going to win," he said. "We can't win, Cassie. We can fight all we want, but—"

I don't know if he would have gone on, or could have, but there was a *sound* from the Mustang behind us—a harsh metallic grinding sound as its engine seized and suddenly died. We were topping a hill, and below us the city of Las Vegas shimmered in a sea of light. The area seemed eerily normal, oddly quiet. I wondered if people were still gambling in the casinos. It seemed likely. People sought comfort in the oddest things.

I let off the throttle to fall back to the now-coasting car . . . and then the same thing happened to the bike's motor. A rattle, a cough, and then nothing.

I coasted it to a stop at the side of the road.

"Tell me we ran out of gas," Luis said.

"No," I replied. "It's not a mechanical problem. Get ready. Something's coming for us."

We had just gotten off the motorcycle when the Mustang's doors opened, and Joanne and David joined us; the Djinn in the driver's seat didn't move. He simply sat like a lifeless mannequin—as I supposed he was, unless Whitney decided it was necessary to move him. Each of them had canvas bags in the backseat of the car; Joanne dragged hers out and unzipped it. She pulled out a shotgun, loaded it with neat efficiency, and tossed it toward David, who fielded it effortlessly.

"I didn't think you needed weapons," I said to him. He looked up and gave me a fleeting smile.

"That depends on what's coming," he said. "And I never turn down an advantage. Not these days."

Joanne was loading the semiautomatic pistol when I felt something stirring around us, a surge of Earth power that made me draw in a sharp breath of warning—but it was already too late.

Joanne must have had an instant's warning, because she fell backward as a truly enormous eagle dropped out of the darkness overhead and extended its claws to rake her face. Light blazed out from a lantern that appeared in David's hand, and I saw the eagle beat its wings and correct it course to strike at her again. She rolled out of the way. David tracked it with the shotgun, but didn't fire.

I stepped in, focused all my attention, all of Luis's tethered power, on the eagle, and called it to me. It was a wild creature, and there was no malice in it, only fear and hunger twisted by the will of another out there in the darkness. It did not deserve to be used this way; the bird was a thing of terrible beauty, and I would not have it hurt.

It glided toward me, but at the last moment the power out there in the desert ripped at its mind, forced it to see me as a dangerous enemy, and the eagle shrieked out its rage and aborted its landing to rake claws across my chest. It caught leather instead of flesh, and sliced it cleanly apart as it wheeled and fled . . .

. . . Toward a sky full of hunting birds, all coming together in an unnatural mixed-breed flock to circle overhead.

Luis turned his attention not up, but out. "We've got more trouble," he said.

"More birds?" Joanne asked as she climbed to her feet and dusted herself off. "Jesus, I used to like them."

I shook my head. "Not just birds. What's coming is far more than that. They will catch us. We have to run now. No time for the vehicles."

Joanne raised the pistol she'd held on to. "We're armed."

I felt myself grin, humorlessly. "Humans and guns. Do you have enough bullets for every living thing that survives in the desert? We *have* to run. We have no choice."

"We can't make it all the way into Vegas," David said. "They're coming fast, and in waves. There's some kind of motel down the hill. We can make it there and hold them off."

"Maybe you can, but I damn sure can't run fast enough," Luis said. He sounded worried. "Cass—"

"I know," I said. "The car can coast down. I can handle the motorcycle."

"Those birds are going to dive on you."

"Perhaps, but I'm not leaving the motorcycle." I shrugged. "I like it."

He gave me a look that said I was insane—as perhaps I was—and got into the car with Joanne and David. Whatever Djinn force was animating the vehicle gave it a push, and the Mustang picked up rolling speed as the grade steepened. I had a more difficult time of it, balancing the motorcycle without the forward thrust, but I managed. We glided in a hiss of tires down the winding hill, and above us birds screamed. I heard the constant beat of wings. I kept a vigilant watch on them, waiting for an attack, but curiously, none came.

Not yet.

I'd expected the refuge David mentioned to be easily

visible, but I was surprised.... It was dark against the hills, and it loomed up suddenly, with an unsettlingly barren aspect to it. The building was large, multi-story, and utterly deserted, with a smoke-blackened plaster exterior; and there had been a halfhearted attempt to board up a few of the broken windows, but it was clear that no one was interested in the place any longer. I supposed that at the edge of the end of the world, securing an abandoned hotel in hopes of later renovation might not have been anyone's largest priority.

It would have been better to continue, but ahead I saw the Mustang was slowing ... and then, with a greasy gray puff of smoke, one tire blew out, and then another. It hobbled on for a few dozen more feet, loose rubber flapping loudly, and then there was a surge of power through the aetheric, and the tires reinflated. The Djinn, repairing the damage.

Then the tires blew out again—all four this time, and more decisively.

The car drifted to a stop, metal grinding noisily on asphalt as the rubber shredded away, macerated between stone and steel.

Luis got out of the car, as did the lithe form of David; I watched them move the limp form of what had been the Djinn driver out of the way, and Joanne took his place behind the wheel. Odd that it would take both a Djinn *and* a Warden to push a car; David ought to have been able to move it with a thought, even without tires easing the process.

Instead, they seemed to be working very hard at pushing the bumper of the car. It went only a few feet, and then Luis stumbled, and ...

... And the car's wheels sank into the road, as if into heavy mud. Luis was also trapped. David pulled him out, but not without difficulty.

I abandoned the bike, which was too heavy to maneuver without power, and ran for Joanne's side of the car, which was already sunken too deeply for her to open the door. I reached in the window and grabbed her. Pulling her out and carrying her was no easy matter; she was tall and not excessively thin, and the road was attempting to suck me down with all its might. I focused all my earth-derived powers to try to hold it back, and managed—just barely—to stumble my way through the black muck and make it to the harder gravel on the roadway.

Something was *very* wrong here.

I tried automatically to shift my vision into the aetheric spectrums, and suddenly felt claustrophobic, not free . . . because it was as if night had fallen there on the aetheric plane, where there was not, had never been, true darkness. I saw David stumble and fall, and I understood why; no Djinn could function with that crippling shock. Even human as I was now, I felt the impact of it, the horror. It was utterly, completely *wrong*.

I knew something cruel and terrible was happening, something potentially fatal for us all, and the fear sharpened as I heard David whisper to Joanne, "Kill him."

Luis was the only other male present, and he held up both hands in surrender as Joanne looked at him with dark, almost feral eyes. "He's not talking about me! I'm not doing it!"

I realized it in the same moment that Joanne did. "The Djinn who was driving your car," I said.

"He wasn't a Djinn," she said. "He was just a shell. Burned out. No will of his own . . . an avatar . . ."

"Not anymore," I said. "Something's filled him. Something *else*."

"Who, the devil?" Rocha asked. "'Cause this doesn't feel so great, and I can't see a thing on the aetheric. Cass?"

"Nothing," I said. "Careful. I hear wings."

We had only that single second before the eagle attacked again—not me this time, but Luis. He raised his right arm instinctively to protect his eyes, and I saw the claws sink in and rip free in bloody sprays. It clawed the arm aside, and snapped for his eyes.

I lunged for it. The aetheric might have gone blind, but there was still power in the earth around us, and I poured it into the feathered, strong body of the bird as I touched it and drew it close to my chest. "Hush," I whispered to it, and stroked its beautiful, glossy feathers as sleep took hold. "Hush, I won't hurt you, child of the skies." I pulled off the backpack and put it aside. My leather jacket, even shredded down the front, made an effective restraint when I stripped it off and tied the sleeves around the sleeping bird; it wouldn't keep him trapped long once he woke, but it seemed safer for him than leaving him unprotected and limp. I put him down carefully and said, "We need shelter. There were more on the way. . . ." I paused, because my motorcycle, which I'd carefully parked off the road, tipped over with a sudden crash, and began sinking into the softened asphalt. I couldn't completely abandon it, poor thing, any more than I could the eagle; I grabbed the handlebar and levered it back upright, slimed with melted road tar, and wheeled it out into the dense sand. It was likely no better, but at least it wouldn't suffer the indignity of Joanne's Mustang, which was now being crushed, consumed and destroyed somewhere beneath that simmering tarry surface.

I pulled the straps of the backpack on over my sleeveless pale pink tank top. The weight of the bottles was surprisingly light, but then again, they were empty of contents. Just full of power.

"Get everybody in the hotel!" Luis called to me. He

was helping Joanne guide David toward the derelict building, and I ran after them, well aware that the night was full of danger, and how vulnerable we were running blind in the aetheric as well as the shadows of reality.

By the time I joined them, David had single-handedly ripped the boards from the front doors, snapped the lock, and levered open the entrance. Luis and Joanne were already inside the lobby, and David nodded for me to follow them. He sealed up the doors with a crash as he stepped in. It wasn't merely locked; he'd woven the wood itself together into one solid structure.

The lobby reeked of smoke, mold, and the uneasily lingering ghosts of sweat, sex, and desperation. Never one of the showplaces of the town, the materials had been drab and cheap to begin with; destruction had rendered it oddly antique, though I was certain it could not be more than a few years old. Black colonies of mold swarmed the walls and spilled in clumps on the carpeting, and I was doubting sincerely that this was any place to stage our defense, save that it was the only shelter we could reach. It was too large, too porous—even with Djinn at our disposal.

"I think I lost money here once," Luis said. "Didn't really look all that much better then. I'll bet the drinks were stronger, though."

"Oh, you *know* they took the liquor with them when they left." Joanne sighed. "Liquor and cash. And frankly, a big-screen plasma isn't going to be much good to us in the current circumstances. Not even with free HBO."

She sounded cheerful, but with a bright edge of mania; Joanne, like the rest of us, had been pushed too close to the edge, and was all too aware of the drop looming below. Still, she was smiling. I was far from sure that I had the same grace within me. I worried that we'd not get out of here alive. I worried what Isabel was doing, and who had charge of her—and I prayed it wasn't Shinju or Esmeralda. I worried about . . . everyone.

Including Luis. He was holding together, but there were only so many shocks any of us could take before coming apart, however temporarily. He seemed stolid, but I remembered the ashen certainty I'd seen in him of the fate of humanity. How long before he, too, would lose faith?

Joanne led the way across the destruction and into a back room, which was less affected by smoke, mold, and general neglect; it had a small kitchenette, tables, couches, and bathroom areas beyond. A room for the staff, not guests; the furnishings here were even cheaper and more utilitarian than outside.

Luxurious, under the current circumstances, though I could imagine staff members grumbling about its Spartan pleasures.

As Luis and I helped David—still shaken and blinded by the disruption of the aetheric, as a human would be by a sudden loss of gravity—into a chair, Joanne turned to additional defenses. She called up power and began to melt the metal edges of the door and frame into a sturdy, permanent seal; it took a while and some fine concentration to create a solid barrier. Joanne finally let out a heavy sigh, rubbed her forehead, and must have realized that she was still holding a pistol in a tight, white-knuckled grip. "Probably not going to do much good anyway," she said, when she saw me watching.

"Maybe not," I agreed. "But we can ill afford to reject any line of defense."

She nodded and stuck it in the waistband of her pants, and I made way for her as she came to David's side. She took his hand, and his fixed stare slowly focused on her face. I turned away to give them privacy, and saw someone standing in the shadows.

Gold eyes gleaming.

Rahel, who must have been listening to Joanne and David's exchange, because she said softly, "David was right about the aetheric." Joanne responded instantly, summoning a handful of fire as she spun to face the potential threat, then held it at the sight of the Djinn. "I was following. I hit . . . something. I had to take physical form to get this far, and I don't think I can reach much of my power. It's as if we're in . . ."

"In a black corner," David finished, when she hesitated. "But only at half the strength of a natural-developing one. It feels artificial. Imposed."

I had never experienced one in physical form, and on the aetheric black corners—which occurred naturally, but with utmost rarity—were easy to see and easier to avoid, unless they formed around you. If this was how it felt at half strength, I never wanted to be trapped in one at full power; when I reached for the aetheric, I felt as if I was suffocating on darkness, and although I *could* reach my power, it felt muffled, tenuous, vulnerable. It would be worse for the full Djinn, of course. Much worse.

Rahel was eating candy as she contemplated our situation, and it made me feel unexpectedly quite hungry. As if she sensed it, Rahel scooped more snacks from the guts of the machine she'd cracked open, and tossed them to us in turn. I received some sort of chocolate-covered cookie. It was unexpectedly crispy beneath the sweet coating, and there was a lingering kiss of caramel. It was a taste, I decided, that I could have come to love.

A pity that what I was eating would likely be the last candy the human race would ever produce.

Rahel and Joanne were talking, but it was more banter than substantive conversation, I thought—unimportant. Rahel would not be so casual if there was any chance of our enemies striking at us immediately, which meant we could delay our inevitable deaths by at least a bit more. Then again, the Djinn were badly handicapped just now; they depended on the aetheric as their primary reality, with this world as unreal to them as that realm was to humans. It was possible she was . . . overconfident.

"Perhaps you should keep watch," I said, raising my voice over their repartee; both stopped and gave me a look, but then Joanne nodded.

"Rahel, that's your job," she said. "You see anything, *anything,* that looks suspicious, you tell Cassiel or Luis. Let David rest. And don't give me any of that wily Djinn crap, either. You know how serious this is."

Rahel said, "It doesn't get more serious, I believe. So yes, I will indulge you, sistah. But where are you going?"

"We've got bathrooms," Joanne said. "Hell, we might even have running water, if there's a miracle the size of China. I'm going to take advantage."

As Joanne walked away, heading for the back area, Rahel moved the blinds on a small strip of window that looked out on the lobby and froze in that position, as if she could stand forever.

No doubt she could.

"Let me see your arm," I said, turning to Luis. He seemed surprised, and looked down at it with a frown. His right was a bloody mess; the wounds still bled, but the eagle's claws hadn't reached any significant blood vessels, at least. The shredded tissues looked bad.

"Damn." He sank down on the tan couch, and his laugh rang hollow. "Kinda forgot about that. Thanks for reminding me." I sat next to him and examined the wound, then put my hands on either side of it. "Hey, if you're going to seal it, try to keep the tat intact. Took days to get that inked."

I gave him a flash of a look, then turned my attention to the problem at hand. There was muscle, nerve, and tissue damage—a surprising lot of it, given the fast and glancing nature of the attack. Birds had real power in them, and this one more than most. I began weaving together the muscles; nerves were trickier, requiring fine control that was difficult with the heavy, dark pressure on the aetheric. Closing the skin was, by contrast, a simple matter.

"Huh," he said, looking down at what I'd done after I wiped the blood away. "Not bad. Gives the tat some character with the scars. Here. Rest." He raised the arm—carefully, as it was likely still aching from the accelerated healing—and settled it on the back of the couch, and I removed my backpack and leaned in and against him. We both needed showers, but I could hear water running from the back; evidently, the owners of this place hadn't shut off all of the utilities before the fog of chaos had descended. That would be Joanne, I would bet; she had been the worst off, in terms of needing a wash. I didn't mind the way Luis smelled, though; his body smelled sharply male, vibrantly alive in ways that I would not have thought I could appreciate. I breathed him in deeply, and pressed closer. Now that the adrenaline of the ride was passing, even though I *knew* we were still under threat, I felt the drag of exhaustion pulling at me, trying to close my eyes. Here, in his arms, I felt safe. Illusion though it was, it was powerful.

And it lasted until Rahel suddenly swiveled her head sharply, at an utterly inhuman angle, to stare toward the showers. David came to his feet in a fluid and boneless motion, and I felt it, too, a power moving through the air around us, something hot and feral and *living*.

And aware of us.

David turned to Luis and me, and pointed. His eyes were blazing gold. "Stay here!" he ordered us, and he vanished in a blur, heading toward the showers.

"I don't take your orders," I said, and stood up; it was

entirely possible that Joanne needed more help than David, in his currently weakened state, could offer.

Rahel flashed across the distance between us, and before I could blink, was standing in my way with one taloned hand extended to me.

The pointed, razor-sharp ends of her nails were embedded, ever so shallowly, in my skin, just over my heart. "You *should* take his orders," she said, and narrowed her eyes as she smiled. "David's remarkably good at what he does when it comes to her safety, and he's far better suited to deal with this. So you just stay still like a good little human, Cassiel."

I drew in breath to order her away, and she casually reached out her other hand to lay a slender finger across my lips.

My voice locked in my throat. She took the finger away to waggle it mockingly in my face. "Ah, ah, ah," she said. "No cheating and ordering me to let you pass, *mistress*. I've been at this game a lot longer than you. If I don't want to do something, you can't make me. You're not human enough to surprise me. You're Djinn at heart, and I know how you think."

Luis stood up. I expected him to come to my defense, but instead he walked over to the chair where David had been sitting. Rahel glanced at him, then back to me. As long as I had her bottle, what he did was of little consequence to her . . .

. . . Until he picked up the shotgun David had dropped beside the chair, racked the slide, and pointed it directly at Rahel's head. "How about me?" he asked her. "Do I surprise you? Let her go. *Now.*"

Before Rahel could respond—either to attack him, or release me, and I knew they were equal weight in her at that moment—there was the explosive crack of a gunshot from the other room, and it was as if that single shot had cracked a black glass jar that had been pressing down over all of us. The thick pressure shattered, though the release carried with it a stinging whip crack of power that woke a red pain behind my eyes. Rahel staggered, and then her eyes widened. She released me instantly, pulled her claws back, and turned toward the bathroom as if my interference no longer mattered at all.

Joanne came out of the bathroom, wrapped in a towel, hair wet and pressed in dripping strings around her face. Her expression was blank, but there was a terrible distance in her eyes as David led her along with a hand on her arm. He eased her down in the chair.

She was still holding a pistol in her hand. He took it from her and placed it aside, then brushed his fingertips over her forehead, trailing them down across her face, her parted lips.

She slipped into a deep, gentle sleep. David sat back on his heels with a sigh and looked at the three of us. He focused on the shotgun, then Luis's face, and Luis cleared his throat and raised the shotgun to rest against his shoulder in a safe carry position.

"What happened?" Luis asked.

"The avatar, the empty one," David said. "Whoever is after us, they were using it to source the aetheric block around us. It—came after Jo. We had to be sure it wouldn't happen again."

"So you killed it," Rahel said. I couldn't tell, from the way she said it, whether that was praise or blame.

Perhaps David didn't know, either. He shook his head and settled against the wall, tense and fluid, eyes pennybright. "Not me," he said. "Watch the lobby. They'll be coming soon enough, now that they know they can't cut us off from the aetheric any longer. You two should rest while you can." That last was directed at Luis and me.

"The avatar," I said. "It was an empty shell?"

"It was a Djinn once," he said. "You know him. Go and look."

I stared at him for a moment, frowning, and then nodded. I walked past Luis, who was now sitting again on the couch; he started to rise to go with me, but I gestured for him to stay.

This I needed to do for myself.

The body of the avatar lay limp on the wet floor tiles. Its eyes were open, but entirely dead black now. It was just flesh, real down to the circulatory system, and blood ran sluggishly down the tile crevices toward the drain, but it was leakage, not true bleeding. One had to be alive to bleed.

I crouched down, staring at his face. It seemed familiar, and I took each of the features individually, trying to place him. Djinn could, and did, change appearance, but for some reason once we settled on a human form, we didn't often shift out of it and into another. It became part of our self-image, I supposed. My memory was long, but human faces had never formed much of a meaning for me. . . .

And then I knew.

He was one of my brothers, a True Djinn.

The memory came back to me, shockingly painful. His name was Xarus, and unlike me, he'd always been fascinated by humans. He'd walked in human flesh often, formed friendships, attachments. I'd always thought him peculiar, and weak.

Years ago, he'd been pulled apart on the aetheric—a natural accident, one of the few that could claim the life and soul of a Djinn. Had he not been trying to save others, *humans*, he could have saved himself, but he made the choice to destroy his immortal existence for the sake of a handful of fragile, temporary creatures.

And I had hated him for that. I'd hated the memory

of him still more when I'd discovered that his flesh shell still lived and breathed. Jonathan, then the leader of the Djinn, had decreed that the flesh of Xarus, the avatar, be spared. I hadn't known why, but perhaps Jonathan had known something. He often did, annoyingly. He'd had a gift for foresight that had bettered anyone's, even Ashan's.

Why, *now*, did I feel Xarus's loss at last, seeing his lifeless body reduced to meat? Why did it *matter*?

I put my hand on his cheek. It felt like human flesh. It *was* human flesh, Xarus's flesh, crafted like mine from the deepest instincts, the desires none of us ever acknowledged to be mortal, to know what their brief and bright lives were like . . .

It was the last of something that had been born immortal, and now it was gone.

I sat in the dark silence, with his blood crawling slowly toward the drain, and I grieved in ways that I never had, for one of my own lost. I'd felt anger before; I'd felt betrayal, and sometimes, loss.

But never emptiness. Never the raw knowledge of *caring* in the way that humans cared for each other, and missed each other.

And the ironic thing was that he'd been gone for almost a thousand years, and I'd never really liked him in the first place.

When I returned to the outer room, Luis was asleep. So was Joanne. David and I said nothing to each other, but he knew, and in a way, that eased my pain a little; I had more in common with him than I'd ever fully realized. More in common with all of them.

David was right. I needed to rest.

I couldn't sleep.

Instead of resting, although I was tired, I found myself pacing in the narrow confines of the common room as Luis and Joanne sprawled and dreamed on the couches. There was something nagging at me, something beyond my grief and worry, or even the anticipation of a fight to come. There was something we had missed. *Were* missing. It ticked in the back of my mind like a bomb, and as the humans slept, as David and Rahel kept a silent and vigilant watch, I struggled to understand what it was that bothered me so much....

Joanne woke, and David moved to speak with her in a low voice. She was upset; bad dreams, perhaps. I paid no attention. I admired her survival skills, but not her emotional instability.

"We should go," I said to Rahel, who was still silent and vigilant at her post. Unlike a human, she didn't feel the need to fidget, shift, relax, or even look away—the Djinn version of a motion sensor. "There's no need to linger here now. We can defend ourselves adequately, if pressed, now that we can reach the aetheric."

"Can we?" She smiled a cynical little smile, and lifted her shoulders in a tiny shrug. "Look at her in Oversight and tell me what you think then."

By *her* she meant, presumably, Joanne. I leaned against the wall next to Rahel and shifted my eyes into the aetheric spectrum, and saw what she had seen... what David must have seen as well. Joanne was not an especially powerful Earth Warden, able to fight the effects of radiation as part of her natural gifts; Weather Wardens had no such protections, and she'd taken the very worst of the beating down in that pit.

She was saturated with it, cells cooking and dying from the inside out, as if she'd been trapped in an invisible microwave.

"If she and her child are to live," Rahel said, "then David needs time to heal her. It won't be easy, and it's beyond the capacity of Earth Wardens. So we stay. She has to rest." This time, just for a split second, her eyes veered from their focus to rest on me, a flash of gold and warmth. "And you, mistress, ought to rest as well. You're not as strong as you believe."

I settled into a chair then, unwillingly. *I don't need rest,* I thought, but as soon as I released my iron hold on my body, it begged to disagree with aches blooming in every muscle. David's whispering in the Djinn language was a soothing litany meant for Joanne, but it lulled me as well, into an exhausted tumble into the dark.

At the last second, what Rahel had said struck me, rather forcefully. *If she and her child are to live . . .*

Joanne Baldwin was pregnant, and it *must* have been David's child—the child of a Djinn. And somehow, I hadn't seen it.

I turned my gaze on her in Oversight, and yes, there it was, the clear though subtle signs of life stirring inside her—curiously, not Djinn life, but something more tethered to the human world. David's child, but human in form and power.

Joanne and David had something more to fight for, it seemed, than just the world in general. The way that Luis—and yes, me—found strength in our love for Isabel.

David saw me watching them, and looked up. I smiled, just a little, and he returned it. "You think I'm mad, don't you?" he asked.

I shrugged. "Perhaps," I said. "And perhaps I'm not mad enough. But I believe that I'm learning."

Waking up came with a surge of adrenaline and terror, and I didn't know why. It was utterly silent. Nothing had changed in the room, except that David had fallen silent. I opened my eyes and saw Rahel at the window, looking out, and in the next second I saw her take a step back and allow the blinds to fall closed.

She turned to David, who looked up. They both nodded.

"Wake him," Rahel said to me, and pointed to Luis, who was blissfully snoring on the couch. "We need everyone now."

I shook Luis awake and endured his muttering about the lack of coffee, and we were joining hands to assess the situation on the aetheric when the first attack came.

Something wild and *very* angry slammed headlong into the sealed door. I was surprised that the cheap barrier held; it flexed against the impact, and a thin crack formed down the middle. "Brace it," I said, and Luis nodded, throwing our combined Earth power into the wood to stiffen it to a packed-steel density. Another, stronger power overlaid ours.

Joanne was awake and on her feet now, and despite the sudden emergency, she looked almost herself again — tall, strong, confident, with a smile curving her full lips and a light in her eyes. She loved battle almost as much as I did, I thought. That was . . . unique, in a Warden. "Time to get down to business," she said. "Let's do this."

Rahel evidently did not think our combined talents were enough, as she pushed a massive piece of furniture against it. "It will not hold," she said. "We should leave now, quickly. Is there a back door?"

"There's company waiting for us there as well," David said. "We're surrounded."

"Did you not think to warn us of that?" I snapped. "I *told* you we should have run last night!"

"It wasn't an option," David replied flatly. "We can get out of this. It's just going to take a little creativity."

Whatever was on the other side of the door hit with such violence that the barrier, even strengthened by three Wardens and a Djinn, bowed inward, almost rip-ping free of the wall in which it was anchored.

"What the hell is out there?" Luis blurted. Rahel seemed to find the question amusing.

"I don't think it would do your sanity any good to know. We must go up, not out. Nothing waiting out there strikes me as good at climbing, but they are *very* good at battering holes in things."

It was David who ripped an opening in the roof above; the hotel's guest room tower was seven stories tall, but at this end, the building was a simple one-story affair. Only fifteen feet, straight up.

David, of course, merely flexed his legs and easily made the jump upward. I grabbed my backpack and made sure it was securely against me, then began to think about how the rest of us were to get up to safety.

"Damn," Luis said. "Forgot my jet pack. Knew I should have packed that." I made a cradle of fingers and leaned down. He raised his eyebrows. "You're kidding, right?"

"Do I seem to be?"

"Hardly ever, *chica*," he said. He put his booted foot in my cupped hands, and I pulled Earth power to satu-rate my muscles as I lifted him, straight up. It hurt, that particular enrichment of the very limited capabilities of my human body; I felt the shriek burn its way out of my mouth without my consent, but the effort worked. I threw him high enough that David could grab his arm and lift him onto the surface of the roof.

But I also knew I wouldn't be able to do that for my-self. Not effectively. Which left . . .

Rahel.

I hardly heard David ordering her to bring me; it was unnecessary that he do so, because after all, I held her bottle. I could have done it just as easily. Only I knew that doing so would open up a million subtle avenues of resistance to her, as irresistible to her as catnip, even now. It was a risk not worth taking, as the door protecting us continued to steadily break under the mindless, violent assault.

"Sistah," Rahel said. I stared back at her, watching that shark's smile on her face. There was hate in it, and I understood it very well. I'd always had nothing but contempt for the New Djinn; I'd treated them as not just second class, but *other*—a mongrel breed of human and Djinn, unworthy.

And she hated me for that, and for enslaving her and so many others, even if it had to be done to save them. No doubt she had other grudges; we all did, we immortals with our endlessly long memories. I had few friends even among the True Djinn, and none among her kind.

Joanne asked, perhaps jokingly, if she had to make it an order for Rahel to save me ... and Rahel almost laughed, knowing as well as I did that an order from Joanne carried even less weight than one from me. "No need," Rahel replied. "And no time. I'll cleanse myself of her contamination later."

Before I could respond, she had seized me, and jumped, and in almost the same motion, pushed me away. I landed on the roof, disoriented and off balance, and tumbled. I felt the crashing impact of the backpack hitting the hard surface and rolled back to my feet, rage a comforting warmth inside me, and spun to face her again as the cold desert breeze stirred my hair.

Rahel grinned, and made a little *come on* gesture. *Her* bottle had not been smashed, though others certainly had been.

No time for settling our scores now, or even for taking stock of what we'd just lost. Joanne, Weather Warden and in firm command of the winds, levitated easily up through the hole, while Rahel, at David's terse order, began repairing the rip through which we'd come. Below, the sound of destruction was increasing. Whatever was below, it was *angry*.

I ventured to the edge of the roof and looked down. Luis joined me, took one look, and quickly stepped back. "Okay, I don't really want to ask, but . . . what the hell is that?"

"It's a chimera, a forced merger of several animal forms. Bear, mountain lion, scorpion." I said it easily enough; identification was automatic, and he could have done it as well, if he'd been able to overcome his instinctive nausea and horror at what we were seeing. As a human, it was disconcerting enough, but as an Earth Warden, feeling the utter vileness of what had been done . . . That was what drove him back, sent him reeling and gagging.

And it was what I was fighting, silently, as well.

There were at least four of the chimera in view now; one had a bear's head clumsily balanced atop a mountain lion's strong, sinuous body, but there were extra, armored legs erupting from the lion's sides, and a segmented tail with a vicious stinger curving out from the back and overhead. Nauseating and fierce, and mad.

"This isn't the Mother," Joanne said. She was standing with me, looking over, holding her long, dark hair back as the breeze batted at us. She was pale and grim, but not as revolted as Luis was, or I felt. "It can't be her doing this."

And it wasn't. I'd worried at that last night, paced, tried to shake sense out of what the avatar had been doing . . . and now, finally, it clicked together. *This* was what the avatar had been doing, under the cover of darkness, shielded from the eyes of the Djinn and even from the Mother. No, not the avatar; the avatar was only a flesh puppet, a conduit for another's power. And I knew now, looking at these things, who had wielded that power.

"It's Pearl," I said. "She's after me."

Joanne laughed humorlessly. "Wow. It's all about you, isn't it?"

"This time, I believe it is—"

"Watch it," she warned, and pulled me a step back. There were wolves circling below, too, weaving around the chimeras; they were leaping up, trying to make the jump to where we were. So far, they were unable to do so, but there was no reason to encourage them.

"Yeah, that's not the worst. Heads up," Luis said, and pointed up. I moved my head back, and saw a black circle of birds above us, wheeling in the warming air. The first rays of dawn gilded their wings with gold. "We need a shield, *now*!" He'd sensed something that I'd missed, but I saw it now . . . the birds shifted, no longer circling, but dropping.

Heading straight for us. I reached out and diverted some of the birds, but it was difficult; they were maddened, like the chimera below, driven beyond their own instincts by the torment that Pearl had inflicted on them. Death would be, for them, merciful.

But I couldn't destroy them. Birds were, for me, the most beautiful of nature's creatures . . . free and fierce. I felt Joanne raise a shield of hardened air above us, and flinched as the first of the birds hit. She'd tried to make it less apt to be fatal, but Pearl's attack drove them mercilessly into the barrier, waves of them, snapping their fragile bones, painting the sky with their blood.

Tears welled in my eyes at the sight. This was for my benefit, mine alone; Pearl knew me, and she knew what would hurt me. These creatures were dying for no better purpose than to anger me.

The mesmerizing horror of the suicidal assault had distracted us from the other issues, but luckily David and Rahel had been on guard; now I heard the rip of metal and saw David throwing a large metal dish toward the edge of the roof, where one of the chimeras had clawed its way up. It knocked that one over, but the next one's venomous stinger tail was already visible in another corner.

"Great," Luis said, resigned. "They climb. Yeah, of course they do, because it'd be too fucking *easy* if they'd stay on the ground." He readied a fireball in his hands, the burning plasma lighting up his face from below and making dark hollows of his eyes. He wasn't the only one turning to fire; Joanne also had pulled on that power, and as I glanced her way I saw her throw with a strong pitcher's follow-through.

Her fireball exploded against the chimera as it landed on the roof and roared at us in an eerie mix of bear and lion . . . and then shrieked in a high, chittering voice as the fireball set it aflame. Joanne threw an airburst against it, blowing it in a burning arc off the corner of the roof, screaming all the way.

The screaming continued, and I knew without looking that the other creatures had attacked it. Pearl's nature was nothing if not savage.

"More are coming," Rahel said. "I suggest you plan an escape." She didn't seem her normally remote self just now; it seemed the situation was dire enough that she actually *cared*. That was . . . alarming. Escape seemed a remote possibility. We had no car now, and my motorcycle—providing it had survived the night—wouldn't be any defense against the kind of creatures Pearl had at her disposal; she was summoning more birds for another suicidal strike, and the chimeras out there could easily rip us apart. I had no idea how fast they could run, and I wasn't tempted to find out.

There were three humans at risk, counting me; the two Djinn were in no danger. They could escape into the aetheric at any time. But not with us. Neither Rahel nor David had the particular, peculiar skill of keeping a human alive while moving through that realm, or they'd have already begun removing us to safety.

If they had to evacuate us another way, it would take time.

"We need to release another Djinn," I said, and took off my pack. I pulled out the padding and carefully unrolled it, layer after layer. The first six bottles had shattered, and three more were cracked and useless—a cracked bottle could not hold a Djinn. There had been ten bottles, and only the two that had been wrapped in the center were still intact.

And open. David's, and Rahel's. I felt an icy chill, because those Djinn who'd been imprisoned were now free—free to turn on us, to seek revenge against us. But at the moment, at least, it seemed the Mother had gathered back her children to her side. There was no guarantee at all that she wouldn't send them at us again soon, but for now, all that mattered was that they were no longer an asset to us. Only a potential, and deadly, liability.

I checked the last bottle, the one we'd separated out so carefully—Venna's bottle. It, at least, was intact, but she'd be of no help at all to us as an Ifrit, a twisted and blackened shadow of a Djinn. Releasing her meant only that Rahel and David would be damaged, or killed, as she blindly sought to replace her lost power with theirs. She'd cause chaos, but nothing more.

Joanne, without comment, took it from me and put it in her pocket.

I'd failed, utterly failed, in what Joanne had entrusted me to do—carry the captive Djinn safely to the Wardens. I felt a burst of hot fury at Rahel, but she'd done nothing except what came naturally to a Djinn; she'd struck out at her captor. It was an almost irresistible urge for her.

Joanne took a deep breath and said, "Rahel, take Rocha. David, take Cassiel. Get them out of here. Take them all the way to Vegas if you have to. David, you can come back for me. I can hold out here until you return."

It was a surprisingly logical choice, because Baldwin had all three powers at her disposal—Earth, Fire, and Weather—while Luis and I had only two, and Fire was his weaker gift. More than that, Joanne had been tested in battle many times, and Luis and I were relatively new at the combat aspect of fighting the forces of nature in this particular way.

But I worried. I didn't fancy even Joanne's chances against Pearl, here where she so clearly had taken the time to prepare her battlefield, build her soldiers, and was intent on not just killing, but devouring.

David was staring intensely at his lover, his wife, the mother of his future child, which I supposed he also knew. "Don't die," he said flatly. "Promise me."

It seemed a cold sort of good-bye, but only in words; what passed in looks between them was much different. They kissed, and whispered together for a few seconds, and then before I was quite ready, David turned toward me. There was a blind anger in him—not toward me in particular, but directed at the situation, at the necessity that tore him away from the woman he loved *now*, of all moments.

Before I could change my mind, his burning-hot arms had fastened around me, and the building, the chimera, Joanne, all of it was falling away beneath my feet in a shocking burst of acceleration that drove the blood down in my body, sending me into a weakened, gray-haze state for a few breaths until I was able to get my bearings again. David, with me as his helpless passenger, blurred through the cloud of birds, startling them out of formation, and the air grew icy around us before he steadied himself and thought to extend some heat—and breathable air—around me.

We were thousands of feet in the air, moving fast in the frozen blue. He'd gone high to avoid the creatures Pearl had sent for us, but now he began his descent in a steep, hurtling arc that whipped my clothes and hair into a frenzy around my skin.

"She'll call you back if she needs you!" I shouted.

"She'll call," he said. "But she doesn't hold my bottle. You do." David didn't need to raise his voice to be heard over the howl of the wind.

It was in my backpack. Physical location didn't matter—if I hadn't touched it, he'd have remained under Joanne's dominion, but I *had* put my fingers on it, and that had transferred control of him to me. I should have left the bottle with her, I realized, but in the heat of the moment I hadn't thought of it, and perhaps Joanne hadn't, either. "I won't hold you back," I promised him. "I'll send you to her."

"It might already be too late for that."

He was right, and the guilt of it gnawed at me. I forced certainty into my voice. "She'll be all right," I said. Thin white clouds appeared below us, and we punched through them with vicious speed, heading for a world that enlarged terrifyingly fast.

He didn't look at me. The lines of his jaw were tight as cables beneath his coppery skin. "No, she won't," he said. "She's never *all right.* But she'll survive until I can come back for her. Now don't talk to me. I don't want to know you're here."

I shut my eyes against the buffeting wind, the disorienting world through which we fell.

We hurtled toward the ground in a heart-stopping rush, and I watched the city of Las Vegas resolve beneath our feet with grim fascination. As a Djinn this would have been entertaining, but now, with flesh to tear and bone to shatter, it was simply terrifying. The city was spread out over a vast grid, but it seemed oddly lifeless at this height, buildings like tiny boxes, defiantly green lawns, blue dots of swimming pool water behind them. As we approached, the houses still had a structured sameness, but the center of the city, where we were descending, exploded into chaos—curved, asymmetrical structures with wildly extravagant grounds, pools, lawns, fountains.

Las Vegas was schizophrenic and beautiful, glowing even at the end of the world with its own false luster and very real power.

We came down in front of a vast glass pyramid, guarded by a sphinx that had never seen the sands of Egypt. David slowed at the very last moment and cushioned our landing, but even so, I felt the impact rattle all the way up my spine.

We hadn't been expected, but we were definitely awaited, and before I could draw breath, I felt the muzzle of a gun pressing against the back of my head. "Freeze," said a shaking voice. "In the name of the Wardens."

I turned around, took hold of the barrel of his gun, and fused it into a crushed ball. He was a boy, hardly much older than Isabel in her new teenaged body, and although I raised my hand to hit, I lowered it again, slowly.

"Stand down," said a firm voice behind the two of us, and I turned to see Lewis Orwell coming toward us. He looked—battered. Infinitely tired, unshaven, limping, but on his feet and leading a contingent of at least four powerful Wardens behind him.

And Shinju. *Pearl.* She looked perfectly composed, with that lovely smile fully in place.

"I'm going back for Jo," David said.

"You're not going anywhere," Lewis snapped, "until I get an update."

"She's in trouble."

"Always is. So talk fast."

David's eyes flared dark red, a color so violent that it made me take a precautionary step back. "I have to go. Now."

Lewis, for answer, took a bottle from his pocket. An open bottle. And incanted, quickly, the threefold charm of binding. *Be thou bound to my service.*

David laughed, a metallic sound with a bitter, biting edge of despair. "Too late," he said, and slapped the bottle out of Lewis's hand to shatter fifty feet away on the pavement. He grabbed Lewis's neck in one hand, and for a moment there was naked fury between the two of them, something so fierce that it was almost blinding. *"I'm going."*

"Wait," I said involuntarily, and David froze. "David, don't hurt him. Let him go." He did, releasing his grip almost instantly, and now it was Lewis whose eyes brightened, and focused on me.

"He's bottled," Lewis said. "And you have it."

I'd made a deadly mistake in trying to save Lewis's life; I'd betrayed a secret I didn't know would be an issue. David gave a wordless shout of fury, and I screamed back, "Go!" Before the word was fully off my lips, he exploded into shadows and was gone.

But it didn't matter.

"It's in her bag," Shinju said sweetly. "She'd keep it from you if she could."

I backed up as Lewis came toward me, but three Wardens were behind me now, and Shinju, and the straps holding my backpack simply . . . disintegrated. Shinju caught the falling bag and held it out with a formal bow to Lewis.

"What are you *doing*?" I demanded, as he unzipped the bag and took out bottles—the ones for David and Rahel. "Lewis, you *can't*."

He glanced up at me, and I saw all the humanity had been crushed out of him. There was only weariness and the weight of the world. "I can't do anything else," he said. "We need them." He held up one of the bottles and said, with an eerie calm, "David, come back here. Now."

David misted out of the chill morning air, and he'd never looked more Djinn than he did in that moment, all metallic luster and burning eyes, and a rage to turn the world to cinders. "Don't," he said. "She needs me. *She needs me now.* Let me go to her!"

"I can't," Orwell said. There was sadness in it, and infinite regret, but there wasn't any room for negotiation, either. "I'm sorry, David. Get back in the bottle. Now."

David screamed, and the sound ripped through me like a saw blade, bloody and torturous, but he misted out. The scream lasted longer than his ghostly image, and then he was just . . . gone.

Orwell capped the bottle and put it in the pocket of his jeans. "And this one?" he asked me. "Who belongs to it?"

"What did you just *do*?" I blurted, appalled. "She'll *die* out there without rescue!" And Lewis, of all people, would not sacrifice Joanne's life. At least, the Lewis that I'd known before.

I didn't really know the man who faced me now, looking so . . . different. It was, I thought, the losses he'd taken in battle, and something else. Something more in-

sidious. Pearl, or Shinju as they knew her here, wormed
her way into his trust, into all them. She'd convinced him
of many things that I wouldn't like, I sensed now.

Lewis didn't answer me directly; he only held up the
other bottle. "Tell me which Djinn belongs to this."

"How did you know I even *had* the bottles? Did *she*
tell you?" I jerked my chin at Shinju, who regarded me
with utter, maddening gentleness. "Lewis, you *cannot* listen to her!"

He didn't answer that, either. I almost didn't know
him in that moment; he looked exhausted and bruised,
but the real change was in his eyes. Suffering, those eyes.
And full of self-loathing.

"Please, Lewis. You *must* send him back to her. She
needs him."

"I can't do that. Get inside the building. It's not safe
out here." He looked up. Another Djinn was hurtling
out of the sky, a black and lime green blur that resolved
in an instant into Rahel, and in her arms . . . Luis, looking windblown and disoriented. She let him go, and he
lurched to grab hold of a handy fake-sandstone pillar.

Rahel glanced from Orwell to me, eyebrows raised.
"Am I interrupting something private?"

"Yes." Lewis was seething now, on the wire-thin edge
of control. "I assume this bottle is hers, then."

"Yes," I said. "It's Rahel's."

"Back in the bottle, Rahel. Now."

She sent me a furious glare; I supposed she expected
me to lie, but it wouldn't have done any good. I'd added
a few more years of torment on to my already lengthy
sentence, once she got free of my control.

And this time, I most likely deserved it.

Luis had steadied himself, and he was watching us,
frowning, standing with his weight balanced for attack

or defense. "What the hell is going on?" he asked. "Why didn't you send her back for Joanne? Is David going?"

"Ask Orwell," I said. "Lewis, what are you *doing*? You can't leave her out there alone. If Shinju's told you that she'll be all right, she's lying—"

"Shinju is inside," he said. "With us. And that's where I need you, too, inside. I can't risk a single one of the Djinn out there, not now; it's the endgame. We're losing cities, *whole cities*, and we can't keep it together much longer. We've already lost so many. David is one of the most powerful we could ever have on our side. I absolutely can't let him go." No wonder his eyes were so haunted, his face so pale and lined. He was managing the end of the human race, and it was burning him alive; his very passion was destroying him.

If it was grave enough that he could abandon *Joanne*, whom I knew he loved more than any of us . . . then it was the last death throes of the Wardens.

This was Shinju, I thought again. Pearl, taking her revenge in small, cruel ways. Abandoning Joanne hurt Lewis, and it would destroy David; it would hurt all the Wardens, in great or small ways.

I shouldn't have left her there alone. I should never have agreed to it.

Chapter 12

LAS VEGAS SEEMED shockingly normal. Inside the hotel, lights burned; slot machines rang, buzzed, and whirred. Dead-eyed humans sat and gambled away their last wealth, expecting no tomorrow. I supposed that at the end of the world, perhaps people would take their pleasures where they could, though I didn't see what joy could come of winning a game of chance now.

The very definition of a Pyrrhic victory. You win only to burn.

I thought about that scream that David had uttered; I didn't seem to be able to unhear that kind of pain and anguish, fury and horror. It echoed unpleasantly inside my head, driving out everything else, and I thought, *I have to get him back. Open the bottle and let him find her.*

I thought that up to the moment when Lewis opened a door and walked me inside the last refuge of the Wardens.

The smell of sweat, desperation, and despair was thick in the room. There was little noise; it was as hushed and quiet as a church, or a funeral. At one time, this would have been an expensive retreat for the ridiculously wealthy, a playpen for the spoiled, but now all of the elegance had been stripped and shoved away, and the room was a morgue, hospital, surgery, and battleground all at once. There was a space in one corner for Wardens to work, and currently there were six standing together, hands linked. As I watched, one collapsed. A black-coated staff member of the hotel silently picked her up and carried her to a cot, woke another Warden, and led him groggily to take the empty place in the circle.

In Oversight, this room was awash in reds and blacks, bloody with it.

And around us, hemming us in, was a descending white fury.

There was another room, the door left partially open; I glanced at it as we walked past, and saw ...

Isabel.

"Ibby!" I cried, and ran toward her. She was sitting cross-legged on the floor, but scrambled up to hug me when I hurtled toward her. Luis was right with me, hugging the child, kissing her.

She'd grown still more—no longer the slender early teen, she'd now matured to an age that had to be ringing the bell of adulthood. Seventeen, eighteen years of growth, perhaps, but the smile was still the unfettered joy of a child, and the relief of one.

"Mama," she blurted, and then took in a sharp, steadying breath. She shook her long, dark hair back and composed herself with an obvious effort. "I mean, hello, Cassiel. Uncle Luis."

"Shut up, *mija*," he said, and hugged her again. He kissed her on the forehead. "How did you get here?"

"I came with everybody out of Seattle," she said. "We were evac-ed out by helicopter, except for the Weather Wardens; they had to go in a truck. Es went with them.

She said it was exciting." The color was high in her cheeks, but she was trying very hard to seem composed. "You two look tired. But you're okay, right?"

"Yeah, we're okay," Luis said, and smiled.

"I'm so glad," said a new voice, and I turned. So did Luis, and his smile vanished. So did his good mood, and mine, because Pearl's human form stood there, cool and composed, smiling at us. I hadn't noticed in the stress of the moments before, but she'd affected a Japanese kimono, and put her dark hair up in a complicated style; of all those I'd seen in this place, she was the first to look rested and content. "Please, be welcome here with us." The *us* was significant, because she was talking about Isabel. And, I saw, Esmeralda, who was asleep in a piled tangle of coils nearby.

And beyond her was a room full of Pearl's children. Eerily quiet children, mostly awake and focused on things that weren't there—working on the aetheric, I assumed. Performing their altruistic duty to help mankind . . . until Pearl decided that was no longer necessary, of course. As soon it wouldn't be.

There were almost a hundred of them here, dressed in plain white shirts and pants, like a uniform. Isabel, I realized, was also in white. Even Esmeralda wore a soft white T-shirt on her human half instead of her usual flashy choices.

Pearl's kimono was a softly patterned white, with embossed flowers and dragons.

"Interesting," I said, holding her dark gaze. "White's the color for funerals in Japan."

"I know," she said. "I'm in mourning for all those we've lost. I'm surprised that you are not . . . but then, Cassiel, you were never what one would term the sentimental sort. You finally came to join the battle."

"Oh, I've been fighting," I said. "And I don't forget

who I'm *really* fighting, either. That was your doing, out there in the desert."

She cocked her head slightly, but her utterly polite and blank expression never shifted. "It's good to be aware of one's purpose," she said blandly. "Though I thought the Djinn had a different path for you than this. You could have become something so ... different. So powerful."

I had a suffocating flashback to being sealed in that airless tight crystal coffin, pierced by slow, pitiless needles. Changing, as she intended, to something *different.* Something *powerful.*

Something that she would control. Her angel of death, stalking the world.

"That's not going to happen," I said, and she bowed her head, just a tiny inclination.

"As you say." It was amusement, not agreement. "You are welcome to stay here with us."

"No. Isabel," I said, "get Esmeralda. We're joining the Wardens."

"I can't," Isabel said. It wasn't a rebellion, it was a statement. "I'm sorry, Cassie, but I can't do that. The Wardens aren't where I need to be. Es, either. They don't understand us, and they don't know what we can do. We're better here, where we can really use our powers to help."

There was the faintest shadow of a smile on Pearl's lips. Delicate, like the shadows of flowers and dragons on her robe. "The children know that I'll care for them," she said. "As I always have."

"*Care* for them," I repeated. The rage that I kept banked inside, that had driven me to survive despite all the challenges arrayed against me, against Ashan's edict and the Wardens' distrust, against the Mother herself— that rage warmed me now. Sustained me. I did not let it drive me, however. I knew that was what she wanted.

"Oh, you *care* for them. I've seen the wreckage of the children you no longer wanted, could no longer use. You keep those you can put to work, and once they're dry, you'll discard them. And none of them will outlive your rebirth, will they?"

But that, I knew, was a lie. Of all the children that Pearl had abducted, or coerced, or whose parents she'd persuaded to entrust them to her—of all these elite children gathered here with her in this room—she'd keep Isabel to the last breath, purely because I loved her.

Isabel was my punishment. Solely, completely, mine.

"It's my choice," Iz insisted. "Cassie, please understand—this is how I want to help. By being here. With her. I want you to respect what I choose to do."

Luis hadn't spoken, but he was staring at his niece with an expression that told me how heartbroken he was. "You can't want this, Iz," he said softly. "If you do, you're forgetting everything you learned. She *took you*, baby. She did things to you that hurt you. She made you—she made you believe that Cass was your enemy, that I was dead. Don't you see that? She's not your friend. She's our enemy."

"She's *your* enemy," Iz said. She looked just as grave, just as sad. "I'm sorry, Tío. I wish I could make you understand, but she made me what I need to be right now, and I need to be here. Please believe me. Please."

"They'll never understand, Isabel," Pearl said. She sounded so soft, so compassionate, and no one could see what she really was inside: a murderer, bent on extinction, bloody and complete. Someone who could only lust after death on an ever-grander scale. "They'll always try to stand in your way. But it's up to you. If you want to go with them, I wish you well."

She didn't mean it, of course; she'd never allow Isabel out of her control now, but Iz didn't know that, couldn't know it. To her, it sounded like pure generosity of spirit.

There was nothing I could say that wouldn't reinforce that impression and drive Isabel further into the arms of my enemy.

I felt a presence behind me, and looked back to see that Lewis Orwell was standing there. He nodded politely to Pearl, equal to equal. "Thank you for maintaining the perimeter," he said. "It's much-needed relief."

"I am happy to assist," she said. "Cassiel seems to think that these children are here against their wishes. Would you please reassure her, Warden?"

He glanced at me, at Luis, and said, "I've spoken to as many of them as I can. They all say they're fine. None of them have parents here with us." Meaning, I supposed, that this was a room full of orphans, with no one to come for them. No one to battle Pearl for their hearts and minds. And what else would they say? They'd all been twisted into her creatures. They had no voices of their own.

"If that's so, not all of their parents died out there fighting the good fight," I said. "Some were killed by— what do you call it?—*friendly fire.*"

"Maybe," Orwell said. "But that's a moot point now. If we survive, we can sort it all out then." He didn't seem to hold out any real hope for that, and he was most likely right. "I need the two of you on duty, right now. Come with me."

"Not without Isabel," Luis said.

Isabel disagreed. She crossed her arms and sat down on the floor, unmistakably daring us to drag her off against her will. Luis looked down at her, shaken and angry. When he grabbed for her, I intercepted his hand and shook my head. "Leave her," I said. "You must. This isn't over."

"Damn *straight* it isn't over," he said, and glared at

Pearl. "I'm coming for you, bitch. You are *not* getting that girl. Believe it."

Her gaze brushed mine, and I heard Pearl's mocking voice in my mind. *And you, Cassiel? No empty threats from you, even as I hold your child in my hands? While I hold her very soul?*

I smiled slowly, and said aloud, "No empty ones."

I pushed Luis out ahead of me, following the most powerful Warden on earth to our assigned battle stations.

I should have known that Joanne wasn't that easy to kill—even for Pearl.

Luis and I were remotely laying thick blocks of power at the base of a newly emerging volcano in Los Angeles. It was brute-force work, no delicacy to it; we were well beyond that kind of control now, after many exhausting hours.

We'd just finished the last layers of protection for the embattled city, and dropped out of the aetheric back into our bodies, when the shout rang out through the hushed, startled room.

"Cassiel! Luis!"

Joanne Baldwin—bloodied, sweaty, dirty, furious— was standing in the doorway. A stillness fell over the room, a sense of dull surprise; there might have been happiness, if anyone had still had the energy for it.

She ignored everyone except us.

Joanne scrambled over cots, prone bodies, and thumped down to land flat-footed facing us, weight distributed for a fight. She looked wild and almost Djinn-bright in her fury. "Where is he?" she demanded, and I saw glimmers of fire around her hands, evidence she was just barely clinging to her controls. "David was with you! Where is he, damn you? *What did you do to him?* You had his bottle!"

I think she would have burned me out of sheer terror and frustration, but Lewis Orwell—who'd been lying down on a bunk not far away—rose and came toward her. She had no chance to even speak his name before he put his arms around her, not so much to comfort her as hold her back. She pushed him away, but I saw her freeze, taking in what I'd seen hours ago—the state of the man, the sadness, the exhaustion.

"Where is he?" she asked, but in a much shakier, more vulnerable voice. "God, please—"

He took her arm and led her away. Breaking the news to her, I thought, in private—that he'd taken David, that he'd imprisoned him, that he'd made the decision to leave her to die while he'd used David ruthlessly here instead, to shore up defenses, defend the helpless masses dying out there in the greater world.

I'd felt ill even witnessing the trapped fury in Joanne's lover; he'd done as commanded, mostly because even he couldn't deny the necessity of it, but he had never stopped hating Lewis for it.

Together they had trapped and imprisoned almost a hundred Djinn, and those bottles sat locked in a case on the far wall of the Wardens' room. The only bottle that wasn't there was Venna's, the one that Lewis himself still kept.

And now Lewis was going to have to explain all of that to Joanne. That ought to be an interesting conversation . . . and one likely to lead to violence.

The door closed after them. The small meeting space inside didn't seem like a place to be having the kind of confrontation that was likely between two Wardens of that level of power, but then again, I supposed that having it here in the middle of innocent potential victims might have been worse.

"Hey," Luis said. He shook his loose black hair away from his face, grabbed a bottle of water from a cooler sitting nearby, and pitched it underhand to me. I cracked the top and drained several gulps, closing my eyes at the simple ecstasy of fulfilling a basic need. "While they're occupied, we need to talk."

"About . . . ?"

"You know what." He jerked his chin at the second, still larger room, where Pearl kept her children segregated from the Wardens. Where Isabel was. "This is coming to a head, and she's going to strike. We need to be ready when that happens, and I don't know what your plan is."

I'd been working on one, but it was depressingly likely that it, too, would fail. Still, he was right; we had to try. "Make your way over toward the door," I said. "We'll need a diversion."

"What kind?"

"Any kind, so long as it pulls the Wardens away from that wall." I glanced where I meant, and he saw the locked case with its mismatched bottles neatly lined up there. "I need only about fifteen seconds."

"You're not serious."

"Very."

"Cassiel . . ."

"Fifteen seconds," I said. "Please."

He finished off his bottled water, grabbed a cheese sandwich from a tray, and took a bite as he considered, frowning. Then he swallowed and said, "You're damn lucky I love you, you know that?"

Oh, I knew. And he knew I knew, so there was nothing to be said to that.

Luis rose and walked toward the far door, eating his

sandwich. I took his empty bottle, and mine, and walked in the opposite direction, vaguely in the direction of the large industrial trash can that occupied the corner. The Fire Warden guarding the case watched me with too much interest. Apparently, I did not imitate casual behavior well.

"Move away," she said to me. I raised my eyebrows.

"Why?"

Fire formed around her fingers. "Let's just say that I'm asking nicely. This time."

There was a shout from behind me, and a sudden smell of acrid smoke. A pillow on an unoccupied bed burst into flame, then another. The Fire Warden acted instinctively, focusing her attention on the immediate threat; while she did, I stepped up beside her and pressed my palm to the back of her head. *Sleep,* I whispered in her mind, and put her out before she could put her power to bear against me; it had to be fast, because Fire Wardens had the best reactions of anyone in responding to threats.

I caught her on the way down and eased her onto an empty bunk. From the outside, it simply looked as if she — like many other Wardens — had collapsed from exhaustion.

And my partner was frantically and obviously extinguishing the fires he'd started. "Sorry, sorry," he was saying. "Got it under control, no problem. Must be more tired than I'd thought. . . . Damn, sorry. Fire's sort of new for me. . . ."

I backed up against the case.

My discarded backpack was still lying nearby, all its contents dumped out; I grabbed it and dragged it over, and held it in my right hand, still facing away from the glass case. I used my left to reach behind me, and melted the glass in a neat, round hole through which I retrieved two bottles; it was a simple matter of misdirection, to slide them inside, shift slightly over, expand the hole, and grab two more. Then two more. When I had emptied a shelf, I sealed the glass seamlessly behind me and stepped away.

No one was watching me. The Fire Warden I'd put to sleep began to snore lightly.

And from the meeting room into which Joanne and Lewis had disappeared came shouting that penetrated even the world-class soundproofing installed in this wealthy little enclave. I draped my backpack casually over one shoulder by the handle, and picked up one of the piled cheese sandwiches as I watched Luis slowly weave his way around the Wardens, who regarded him with varying degrees of disgust or suspicion, back to me.

He ate another sandwich as I ate mine, and mumbled between bites, "Hope it was worth it."

"It was," I said. "She's getting ready. I can feel it."

"Pearl, or the Mother?"

"Both," I said absently. "The Mother has sensed our interference, pinpointed our location; she'll send everything she can against us to smash us. And that is what Pearl is waiting for." I nodded toward the half-open door into the room where Pearl was hiding like a hunting spider, lying in wait with her apprentices for the right moment to strike. I could see a portion of Isabel, sitting cross-legged and in a relaxed pose of concentration. There had been too many children awake in there, focused on tasks. It wasn't merely energy being expended to keep this place safe. It was . . . readiness. Watchfulness.

I had to get Isabel away from her before it was too late.

I just had no idea how.

The end came fast and without any warning.

First, the conference room door suddenly burst open, and instead of just Joanne and Lewis who'd gone in there, four came out: Lewis, Joanne, David, and *Venna*. David looked almost as hard and angry as the last time I'd seen him, when Lewis had confined him to the bottle. I was surprised Lewis had survived releasing him . . . but the real surprise had to be Venna, who should *not* have looked so like herself. I was still processing that startling information when I felt a brush of air, and suddenly Venna was standing next to me.

In mortal form, she looked like a small, innocent child, with straight golden hair held back from her face by a simple cloth band. She wore a blue and white dress, neat and proper, very like the illustrations I had seen in the children's book *Alice in Wonderland*.

It occurred to me a single second later that she shouldn't—*couldn't*—have looked that way; she'd been sealed into the bottle as an Ifrit, twisted and blackened, unable to heal. A skeleton of her former self.

If Venna had been restored, a Djinn of greater power had been killed to provide that miracle . . . and there was only one Djinn that it could be.

The magnitude of it stunned me.

"Hello, Cassiel," she said to me, but she was looking off into the distance, in a stare that made it clear she was watching the aetheric. "I'm so glad you are predictable."

"I—what?" That was baffling, until she tugged the backpack off my arm. "*You*. But I don't understand—"

"Conduits sometimes have the gift of foresight," she said. "It's a curse, really. You can't do anything yourself. You can only try to get others to do it for you. I never realized how bothersome that might be until now." She suddenly turned her bright blue gaze on me, and the power behind it was astonishing. Venna had always been incredibly old, incredibly strong, but this was . . . different.

"Conduit," I repeated, and closed my eyes briefly, even in the midst of all the chaos. "Ashan's gone."

She inclined her head. "Yes. Ashan is dead. I killed him. I may kill someone else, too. I'm not sure I'm entirely stable quite yet." She was very calm about it, eerily so. "But I probably won't kill you, since you're not really Djinn. I'm going to try to not get hungry unless it's really necessary." In a sudden, startling move, she grabbed my backpack from me, with its load of sealed bottles. "I'll be needing that. I can do this faster than you can."

She flashed from me to another Warden, then another, then another. She gave out all the bottles I'd collected, dropped the backpack, and turned to face Joanne, Lewis, and David. "It's done," she said, and looked up suddenly. "And it's here."

She was right.

A burst of energy hit Las Vegas like a bomb, buckling the floor under us, crashing cots and glass and people into one another, onto the floor, while above us chandeliers swayed, flailed, broke loose, and fell like glass bombs. The walls rippled and leaned, and the entire room twisted as the earth's torment vibrated up in waves.

The Earth Wardens were on it in seconds, controlling the furious shaking, but it was only the beginning of the end of us. Fires broke out in the walls, where the wiring ran, and took hold in unnatural white blazes that ate through drywall, wood, and steel alike. Luis squeezed my hand in silent apology, and ran to help control the flames that threatened to spill out over the injured who lay moaning on the still-moving floor. One of the Weather Wardens shouted a warning—something about wind shears bringing down high-rises, simply bending them until they broke.

Chaos.

And in the midst of it, I felt Pearl finally make her move.

It came in the form of a surgical lightning strike that blackened a ten-foot circle of space at the end of the room and left slag, dripping metal, and burned flesh behind.

The cabinet where the Djinn bottles had been, and all of the bottles I'd left behind, had just been vaporized.

The Warden I'd left sleeping nearby woke up, screaming in a high, thin, agonized voice, but it didn't last; her entire bottom half had burned to bones, and there was nothing I or anyone else could do to save her. There was an immediate reaction in the room as more Wardens responded, putting out the lingering flames, rushing to more wounded. They were attributing it to the Mother, and indeed, she *was* attacking us now, fiercely. . . . There were Djinn materializing in the room, and we had seconds to live, if that.

Pearl had just removed the Wardens' final, desperate defense, as those Djinn were set free who could have been used to fight on the side of failing humanity. All, it seemed, except the few that I'd managed to rescue, who were in the bottles in my backpack that Venna had distributed.

I thumbed the cap off the one she had left me. "Out of the bottle!" I shouted. "Now!"

In answer, I got a blur of wild, thrashing color, and then Rahel formed out of it with a world-shaking shout of fury that rattled the broken glass around us. She whirled, black braids flying, to focus those alien, cold eyes on me. Her hands were clawed, and ready to pull out my intestines.

"You can take your vengeance later," I told her. "For now, *help us!*"

She didn't have to do it. For a frozen, terrible second, I thought she'd simply choose to go on with her killing plan, take her last satisfaction where it came . . . but then she bared her sharpened teeth and said, "This will be a later conversation." She flashed over to a falling wall and held it up, dragging fallen Wardens away from it with the other hand. Her grin was awful and wonderful at once. "It's happening, Cassiel. Joanne and Lewis and David have gone to the Mother. They've left you all to distract her. Did you know you were so disposable?"

I couldn't believe her, but it was true, I realized; Lewis was gone. So were Joanne and David. I didn't know when they'd left us, and the aetheric was a horrible vibrating confusion of fury, light, power. The chaos spread through all the levels of the world.

Go, I wished them silently, and let the anger leave me in a rush. *We all have our fates. Go to yours, and I will go to mine.*

But mine wasn't quite done with me yet, no matter what Rahel thought.

I felt the surge of energy as the Wardens uncorked their bottles. From one of them I saw emerge a flash of indigo, of silver, and then Rashid—friend, enemy, New Djinn—was standing quite naked and elegant beside me, skin the color of the dark blue sky, eyes like moons. He said, "I'm devastated that you didn't keep me for yourself, Cassiel," but then he went just as still and quiet as the others. I recognized most of them, True Djinn and the newer, human-born ones; they were all powerful, and all dangerous in their own rights.

"Scaravelli's down!" someone shouted. "Orwell's gone! Who's next in chain of command?"

"Get Shinju!" someone else yelled, and that made me thrust myself forward, more out of dread than anger.

"No," I said. "Not her." I took in a deep breath and nodded to Luis, who raised his eyebrows, but turned to the scared and confused Wardens and began barking out quick, simple orders. Fix this; hold that; do this.... Tasks to keep them moving and focused. We couldn't afford the chaos. Chaos would feed Pearl even more.

I felt Pearl's power stirring beyond the wall, and remembered that she had a plan of her own — one that did not include the Djinn. She and her Void children had the power to devastate these last few Djinn who were under our control; she'd hunt those who'd gone wild at her leisure, but these were tethered for the slaughter.

"You!" I barked, and pointed at the woman who'd been handed Rashid's bottle. "Give him back!"

"Back?" she said, mystified, and shook her head. "I'm not giving—"

I hit her with a neat blow to the chin. It hurt like punching the edge of a knife, but I think it hurt her more; she staggered, and the Djinn bottle slipped out of her hands and bounced harmlessly on an unmade cot.

I got to it first, closed my hands on it, and Rashid said, in a voice full of plummy satisfaction, "If you wanted me so badly, you should have asked, love."

I couldn't answer him, or even look at him directly. What I was about to do was full of pain. "I've fought for you, Rashid," I said. "Now I expect you to fight for me."

"It wasn't much of a fight," he said, "but I'll do what you wish. Mistress." He leered at me, and bowed a little.

"Put on pants," I said, "and be ready at my command."

He seemed disappointed that it was my first order, but he nodded, and in the next blink his naked loins were covered in tight-fitting black leather ... so tight they might as well have been a second skin. Well, he had technically obeyed. I let it go.

"Here we go," Luis breathed, and grabbed my hand to draw me up a level to the aetheric. There was a storm forming there, and in the human world, one huge enough to swallow entire countries. It was coming into existence now, all around us, and on the aetheric the pearl gray skies had turned rotten black, bloody red, with flashes of unclean greens and yellows like suppurating wounds.

The Djinn vanished, heading out to do battle with our destruction . . . all except Rashid, whom I kept tethered to me with a pulse of will. As I watched on the aetheric, the Djinn formed a circle around the city, and a network of brilliant, complex light wove through them.

The storm hit that barrier, erupted in angry waves, sparks, flares . . . but stopped. For now. I could sense the intense power flowing from the Wardens to the Djinn, outlays that human bodies weren't meant to take; even then, the storm on the aetheric was stronger, far stronger, and already it was beginning to rip at the Djinn's wall, sending pieces flying away into the dark.

"It's not going to hold," Rashid said. He sounded muted now, shaken for all his traditional remote mockery. "You have less than a day, probably only hours. There are billions at risk now. Once the Djinn fall, there's nothing to stop it from devouring everyone."

"Get Orwell back here!" someone screamed, and Luis let go of me and dropped back into his body, striding across the littered and chaotic room to grab the Warden who was starting to panic. "They *ran*, they *ran and left us*. We have to get them back—we're all going to die here!"

The artificial discipline of the Wardens turned to panic as if a thin sheet of ice had cracked, plunging us all into freezing waters. The Wardens channeling for the Djinn were locked in place; they, at least, were not panicking, but the others—it was leaping from one human to another, this knowledge of their own destruction, and the cries and wailing took on an eerie, crazy edge.

Luis jumped up on an antique table that had been shoved against the wall, took an exquisite crystal vase from the top of it, and shattered it. Loudly. "Shut up!" he roared. It was a shockingly loud voice, and forced silence down on the room, in subsiding whimpers and gasps.

"Orwell and Baldwin don't *run*. They're doing something, something that might save everybody. That's the only damn reason they'd leave, and you know that. You're *Wardens*; you're not in fucking kindergarten. Wherever they went, they're fighting, and *you're* going to fight. The Djinn are buying time for you. Now stop screaming and start thinking!" He pointed at people, three in quick succession. "You, you, and you. Fire, Weather, Earth. Form a team. Start pulling power and strengthening the wall that the Djinn put up. The rest of you, split off in triads and start working. If you're not working, you're going to have my boot up your ass. Do you understand me?"

You might have heard a rose petal drop, so quiet were they, and then one of the Wardens at whom he'd pointed took in a breath and clapped another on the shoulder. "Right," she said. "Back to work. Alan? Join us?" The third Warden moved slowly to join them, joining hands.

The rest of the Wardens glanced at each other. Exhausted they were, and terrified, but he'd shocked them enough to remind them of duty, and there was a good deal of shame in the way they nodded to one another. One young man stuck his hand in the air. "Earth," he said.

"Earth Wardens, follow his example," Luis said. "Hold up your hands. Fire, Weather, find your partners. Hurry up." He jumped down, landing with a heavy thump of boots on carpet, and put up his own hand. Our eyes met, and he shook his head. "No, Cass. Not you. You said Pearl was on the move. It's time to stop her. I can't—I can't do it with you. If they see me take off, it's all going to come apart. I'm sorry, but . . . this is where our paths part. When we— When this is done, I'll see you again." He smiled, but there was an ending in his eyes, a quiet resignation and grief. "I love you."

"I love you," I said to him, and kissed him one last,

sweet time. I traced the warm skin of his face, the rough-
ness of his emerging beard, and stepped away. "I don't
want to leave you."

"You can't always get what you want," he said. "The
great philosopher Mick Jagger said that. Go, babe. I got
this."

I blinked away a blur of tears, turned, and ran for the
half-open doorway that led to Pearl's children.

The door slammed shut in my face. I hit it, extending
Earth power ahead of me, but the door held, bouncing
me back. "Rashid!" I yelled, and despite how the Djinn
felt about the practice of slavery, despite all of the games
and the carefully worded, treacherous game they played,
he didn't wait for my command. He hit the door in a
dark blue rush, and it splintered, vaporized for three
quarters of its width. Only the hinges remained, clinging
to a glossy strip of wood as they flapped wildly.

Inside, Pearl stood at the center of a circle of children,
all dressed in white. They were silent, eerily so, not one
of them shuffling or fidgeting, and Pearl's face was turned
toward the ceiling, and her smile was broad, peaceful,
triumphant.

"Now," she whispered. "Now go and take your right-
ful places. She's vulnerable, never more than *now.*"

The circle of children turned in their places, facing
out now instead of in, and next to me Rashid shifted
uneasily. "Cassiel—" The children were advancing now,
walking toward the door, toward me, and the foremost
in that ring were boys and girls who radiated that special
kind of darkness. Whatever inhabited them, it was akin
to a demon, and it did not belong here, in this world.
There were young ones, no older than five or six; there
were older children, as old as twelve or thirteen. Not one
of them deserved the fate that had come on them; they'd
been abducted, converted, abused, deceived, tortured,

and mutilated. Not one of them deserved anything from me but rescue, help, love, kindness.

But this was war.

"Cassiel," Rashid said, and a warning was plain in his voice. "They're coming for you. For the Wardens and the Djinn outside. You have to stop them."

"I know," I said.

"You have to *kill* them. They'll destroy me."

She'd sent the Void children first, because Rashid still presented a significant threat, and she wanted him gone, destroyed, unmade. The howling darkness contained inside them had grown, and I wasn't sure there was anything of the original souls left now; I wasn't sure they were anything but shells for a virus, burned-out avatars as Xarus had been.

Pearl had used Xarus to strike at us, out there in the desert; the artificial black corner had been her creation, a display of sheer, raw power. She'd created the chimera as well. Mother Earth wouldn't have been so cruel, so perverse.

"Cassiel!"

"Back in the bottle," I said to Rashid, half absently. The first Void child was only a few feet away. Rashid vanished, and I stoppered the bottle, pushing the cork in tightly and slipping it into the pocket of my pants. I looked past the children, to Pearl.

She had lowered her gaze to meet mine.

"This doesn't have to involve them," I told her. "It's between us. It always has been."

"Not anymore," my sister said, in that silky, soft voice I had once loved, and now hated so much. "My grudge isn't against you, Cassiel. It hasn't been for some time. You're a small, insignificant bug, and I don't care about you, other than to want you removed from my path. It's the Mother who's my enemy. And she's vulnerable. It's *my* time now. All you need do is stand aside, and I'll let you live a while longer. That's all you want, isn't it? That's all any humans want. To delay the inevitable."

It dawned on me, late and hard, that I couldn't see Isabel in the approaching waves of children. She'd matured; she was stronger, faster, taller than any of the rest, but she wasn't there. "What did you do with her?" I asked. It came out in a cold, clear tone, one that almost shimmered in the air with menace. "Where is Isabel?"

Pearl pointed, and I followed her motion, turning slightly . . . and saw a body embedded in the plaster of the wall. Isabel's face was a mask, mouth frozen open in a scream.

One hand still remained free in the open air, and it trembled, finger twisting as if trying to claw at the prison.

I had a nightmare visitation of being sealed in that coffin of earth, of the crystals boring into my bones.

"She thought she could make me trust her again," Pearl said. "She failed. I'll keep her for later; you didn't want to be my angel of death, Cassiel, but she . . . she will make a beautiful killer, I think."

I screamed, and with no thought for anything else — not even the hands of the children reaching out for me — I drew a pure bolt of Earth power up from the ground below, blasting through concrete, steel, wood.

I blew out the wall in which Isabel was trapped.

She collapsed in a broken heap of debris, coated with pulverized drywall, but I saw her moving just a little. I saw her dust-pale hair stir as she breathed.

The first Void child touched me, and his small, cold hand closed around my wrist.

Something dark crossed over into me, a small thing, a tiny pinpoint of darkness that moved through my flesh like a burrowing insect, relentlessly seeking out the deepest, hottest flame of my power. Another chubby hand touched me, dark against my pale flesh, and I felt it again, a tiny invasion of something cold, so cold.

I remembered the needles piercing my flesh, driving inward with smooth, unflinching whispers.

"You're going to breed the future, Cassiel," Pearl said. "A chrysalis for a great power, a *new* power. You're the first of the new angels. My dark angels. But first, you have to accept the gift that they're giving you."

More hands on me now. I had to fight. *Had to.* Rashid was right. I had no choice: I had to kill them or lose myself, horribly. Already, the tiny pinpoints of darkness were starting to draw together inside me, clumping, reproducing. Spreading.

My light was still burning, my power still strong, but I couldn't turn it inward, against this; I couldn't fight an enemy already inside me. Earth Wardens were the worst at self-healing, and she'd struck me at my most vulnerable point . . . not just in my body, but in my mind.

I couldn't fight these children. I couldn't hurt them.

The others were flooding around me now. They were heading out into the room with the Wardens, who'd been lulled into thinking that Pearl and her followers were helping, were safe. They'd hardly have time to realize that they'd been betrayed before these children, with their wildly enhanced powers, attacked them. Luis had inadvertently helped that along, by focusing the Wardens on the problem at hand rather than what might be coming for them on their blind side.

I was the only one watching their back now. Their last line of defense . . . and I had just lost the war for them, unless I acted now. *Now.*

But I couldn't look into the faces of these children and destroy them, no matter what logic might say.

Isabel was moving. She pulled herself to her hands and knees, and slowly raised her head. Beneath that caked, tangled mop of hair, her face was a mask of white dust, splattered with drops of shockingly red blood. She did not look human. The fury on her face, in the tight, coiled movements, all these came from some other place, a wound that Pearl had inflicted long ago that had never fully healed.

"You let Cassie *go*!" she spat at Pearl. Isabel climbed to her feet, and balls of wickedly twisting fire formed around her hands where they hung at her sides. "You let her go *now*!"

"Peace, little one," Pearl said, and gave her a fond smile. "Don't presume you can speak to me as if you matter."

"You did this to us, to all of us," she said. Her voice was raw and rough, almost a growl in the back of her throat. "You made us what we are."

"I made you great," Pearl said. "I would have made you a queen in this world, if you hadn't been so weak and foolish. But I will allow you to take Cassiel's place at my side, if you wish it. The transformation will hurt, of course, just like all the other changes I made to you to help you become what you are."

"Yeah," Isabel said. "Thanks for the encouragement. It's going to help a lot when I do *this*."

She flung her arms wide, and I felt a surge of power blast out of the core of the planet, *and* down from the aetheric, mixing and mingling in a pure white plasmatic burst that glowed eerily from Isabel's eyes, mouth, even her fingertips. Humans couldn't pull power directly from the aetheric, not as Djinn could . . . but Isabel was different. Pearl had *made* her different, just as she had the Void children, and the other Warden children she'd warped.

Isabel slammed her palms together in a wide, swinging circle, and the power rang out of her in thick, white, glassy waves across the floor, cracking concrete, shattering steel, dropping the entire center section out of the room and down into a dark, cavernous sinkhole.

"No!" I screamed at her, but she wasn't listening. The children who'd been caught in that section had fallen, tipping and sliding as the floor collapsed, and now they tumbled, along with the floor, into the unknown darkness.

I couldn't kill these children, but Isabel had been one of them. Children have no sentimentality for their own, not as adults do, and she didn't hesitate.

Pearl stayed where she was, hovering with her bare feet exactly where the floor had been. She hadn't so much as flinched. I'd seen the rings of power part and flow around her like water around a stone. For the first time, she was showing her true power—and that made her vulnerable as well.

The void inside me was growing fast now, shooting out dark tendrils. There were fewer children fanning out past me to attack the Wardens than there might have been, because of Isabel's actions, but still enough to kill what was left of the people—and Djinn—on the other side of that door. It was up to me to stop it.

I sent a fierce pulse of energy back through the hands of the children touching me, and one by one they slumped, unconscious. One slid over the ragged, broken edge of the floor into the abyss below, but I didn't have time to save him, didn't have any time at all.

"Isabel!" I shouted. "Stop the children out there!"

She headed past me for the door, lithe and quick, and as Pearl stretched out a hand toward her, I got in the way. What hit me felt deceptively light at first, like a shower of water, but almost immediately it began to burn through my clothing, and open raw bloody holes in my skin. Acid. I coughed and gagged on the burning smell of it. A

Weather Warden might have been able to wash it away, but as an Earth Warden all I could do was slowly change the composition of the acid into an inert form, and that took time.

The wounds it left me with were impossible to heal, and I had no time left, because lightning sizzled now from Pearl's fingers. I twisted in midair to avoid the strike; it blew apart an antique sofa pushed against the wall, and part of the wall behind it. A burning masterpiece of art slipped off its hook and toppled to the carpet, and I rolled forward and for the first time, touched Pearl's body, in the flesh.

It was cold. Ice cold. And where my fingers gripped, I saw white creeping into my skin, turning it the pallid consistency of rubber.

I pulled, but my hand had gone numb, and slid harmlessly off her skin. It felt . . . dead. Wholly and completely dead.

My metallic left hand was still functioning. I grabbed the bottle out of my pocket and flipped the cork free with my thumb. "Rashid!" I shouted. "Take the children away from here! All of them you can! *Now!*"

"I can't touch the blackened ones," he said, but it was in passing; he was already moving, and he grabbed a boy who was lunging for me with a knife in his hand. The child was only seven or eight years old, and burning hot from the unnatural forces of powers inside him; as Rashid pulled him back, the boy simply made the blade of the knife lengthen. The steel leaped across the open space between us, and the needle-thin tip stabbed an inch into my chest before Rashid could snap it and yank it free. He gave me a wordless look of alarm before he grabbed the fighting boy, then an armload of others, and with a single word of power left them limp and sleeping.

It would take time for him to get them all.

I heard Isabel out in the other room yelling at the Wardens. "Don't let them touch you! Kill them if you have to!"

"But they're just *kids*!" someone protested, and then the chaos intensified out there. The Void children could kill with a touch, pull away energy in a roaring flood. Where that energy went was a mystery; it seemed to tumble through them and off into the dark. They were no more than child-sized holes punched in the world.

Isabel was right. They had to be stopped by any means necessary.

And so did I, now.

I could feel that heavy pull inside me, like a black hole forming in the pit of my stomach. The drain was small at first, but it was growing, throwing its spiral arms wider and wider with each increasingly fast spin. I had moments left, if that, before I became as empty and as dangerous as these children.

Or worse. *Chrysalis*, Pearl had called me. A vessel for something else. Something greater.

Her dark angel.

No. That was not my fate. I was not going to watch this world burn, and everything fail, and see Pearl rise as the new Mother. I was not going to stand at her side, her creature, to pollute and torture and destroy what remained in the ashes.

I would not preside over the death of the human race.

Rashid had taken away many of Pearl's children, but he couldn't approach the ones armed with Void powers; they were the most dangerous, by far. He misted into view beside me, and dropped a small canvas bag at my feet. It was unzipped, and in it, I could see what looked like a rifle. He grabbed the weapon and tossed it to me; I caught it, surprised, and said, "I can't shoot them!"

"Darts," he said. "From the zoo. An entire bag." He

gave me a scary, wild smile, and winked, and I felt the same surge of hope and exhilaration as I put the stock of the gun to my shoulder, sighted, and pulled the trigger on the nearest Void child.

The dart took her in the shoulder, and she gasped in surprise and whirled around, face blank with shock ... and then just blank, as the drug raced through her system. She stumbled, lost her balance, and fell.

Isabel ducked back in the door and saw me. "I can't stop them!" she shouted.

I tossed the rifle, and the bag, to her. "Now you can," I said. "Go! Stay with Luis! I can handle this here!"

She knew I was lying, she must have, but in this last, desperate moment, she also knew that we had no real choices left. She hesitated one more second, staring into my eyes, and blurted, "I love you, Mom."

Then she was gone, and I pulled in a deep, trembling breath. There were tears in my eyes. *Tears.*

"You really love this human child?" Rashid asked me, as if it were a normal day and we were in casual conversation. As if the world weren't coming apart around us.

"Yes," I said softly. "Yes, I do. She's my daughter, in every way that matters."

Rashid shrugged. "And you used to be so ... fierce."

"I still am." I swallowed hard, and tasted darkness. "Rashid, the Void children touched me."

He looked sharply at me, eyes flaring bright silver. "You're infected?" He took a step back. "Give someone else the bottle. You can't keep me now. You know that. Your sickness will spread to me."

"Don't worry, I have other plans for you," I said. And I did; a plan had formulated itself somewhere deep inside me, and it was suddenly and brilliantly illuminated like a landing strip in the dark. "I'll set you free at the proper moment."

"Do it now!"

"I can't," I said . . . and then a pale pair of arms locked around me from behind, and pulled me backward with irresistible, bone-breaking force.

Pearl.

I tried to summon power and break free, but where she touched me numbness spread—a creeping cold that mirrored the darkness from the Void children that had infected me. My skin, already pale, turned a dead blue-white as infection spread like frost. I couldn't feel the bottle in my fingers, and as much as I tried to hang on to it, I couldn't.

Rashid cried out, but he couldn't help, couldn't come close to Pearl. And like all trapped Djinn, he couldn't directly touch the bottle.

It hit the floor, rolled toward the edge of the abyss, and was just tipping over the edge when he summoned a gust of wind that blew it the opposite direction, in a skitter over broken stone to relative safety . . .

. . . Until there was a flash of green coils untangling and dropping from overhead on an exposed beam, and Esmeralda reached down and scooped up the bottle.

I had been looking for her. Counting on her, in fact.

"Isabel," I whispered. I could only just draw the breath to speak, and when I did, my breath misted on the air. "Give it to Isabel. Hurry."

She laughed, dangling her human half upside down, fangs extended and glistening with venom. "Hell with you," she said. "I am *done* with all of you people. I used to be good, really good. But you treat me like everybody else does, like a freak. Not anymore, *chica.*" She waggled the bottle in front of me as she righted her body in a sinuous twist of coils. "He's mine now. Mine. Don't think just because I don't have Warden powers anymore that I've forgotten how to order around a Djinn. Rashid's my gorgeous personal insurance policy to get the hell out of this in one piece."

Pearl laughed, and that laughter crept inside me, too, heavy as fog. I couldn't hold my head up now. I felt like a flesh-doll, limp in her grip. "Poor Cassiel," she said, and I felt her cool lips graze my ear. "Can you feel it? The Mother is listening. She is listening to *humans* now. Unguarded, open, vulnerable. It's time for you to *choose*. Die with the Djinn and the Wardens, or live with me. Esmeralda's already made her choice."

Esmeralda dropped down out of the rafters with a heavy, meaty thump, and slithered closer, head tilted to one side, watching Pearl curiously.

"I'm not on anybody's side," she said. "Damn sure not on yours. I've seen what you do to kids. I never had many limits, but whatever mine were, you blew right past them."

"So you want to be my enemy," Pearl said. "That's an unfortunate choice."

Esmeralda shrugged. "I don't want to be anybody's enemy. I just want to be on the side that wins, that's all. There never was a place in the old world for me. Maybe there'll be one in yours."

I couldn't speak. I could just barely find the strength to draw in one raw, aching, freezing breath after another. Outside, the battle between the Wardens and Pearl's children had gone almost quiet; I wondered, with a growing dread, if Isabel was all right. And Luis.

"Es," I whispered. The dark inside me was starting to hurt as it grew stronger; it was pulling things from me, important things. Memories. Identity. Strength. "Don't. She will not win."

Esmeralda nodded past me, toward the abyss Rashid had punched into the center of the room—the hole through which had fallen so many children. "Oh, it looks like she will," she said. "Sorry, Cass, but I never was much of a martyr."

I slowly, painfully turned my head, and saw that the children, alive, intact, aware, were floating in midair. Rising up out of the dark, completely unharmed.

"Did you really think I'd let the Djinn do something so cruel as to slaughter all these innocent lives?" Pearl asked. "I saved you from yourself, Cassiel. The Wardens are finished, and humanity with them. I'm what comes next. And now, so are you, my sweet, cold sister."

Cold, so cold. The pain inside was excruciating now, a black fire I couldn't control or fight. The power I pulled from Luis was spinning away from me into that void, eaten by something ... something that was reaching *through*.

Something that was trying to clamber its sharp-edged way inside me, as her power froze and shattered every bit of strength and power left in me.

The children were forming into a tightly bound cluster around us, all facing outward ... so many young Wardens, so powerful, and all their power was directed inward, channeled together into a pure white shell around them as they floated in the air over the darkness. A milky, glassine skin that sealed them all inside, together.

And it began to kill them.

The power being produced was so vivid, so unnatural, that I could sense their small bodies failing under the strain. It didn't matter to Pearl. Nothing mattered now, except her goal, almost in her reach.

The Void children remaining in the bubble *imploded* ... their darkness exploded out of them, destroying their fragile shells, and flooded together like spilled mercury, spread in a sinuous curve along half of the dome.

It formed a liquid design, the blaze of power, and the absence of it.

Black and white.

Yin and yang.

The opposing forces of the universe.

"*Stop,*" I whispered. I grieved for the children who had just . . . disappeared, but that battle had been lost a long time ago; Pearl had chosen them, hollowed them out, made them avatars and vessels. The other children, the ones on the white side of the dome . . . those still had souls, minds, personalities. They could still be saved, if only I could stop this, *soon.*

But I was losing everything. It was bleeding, slipping, turning dark. Everything, dark.

Then I heard a whisper, and it rose up out of the remnants of the light inside me, out of the very roots of the earth. Not a word, but a feeling, an intuition. It was the breath and life and voice of the Mother, speaking to humans, brushing over us.

Life. Pure, untainted life, a power so pure and intense that it brought sharp tears to my eyes. It didn't warm me, but it promised me warmth, life, escape from despair. . . .

And then I felt Pearl gather to strike. In this moment, when the Mother was finally, gently opening herself to humans, allowing just the merest suggestion of contact with them, she was vulnerable through them.

I had to act. *Had to.*

But all I could manage was one last, dying burst of power—just enough to shock Pearl a little, break me free of her grip, and send me tumbling forward in a heap. I hit the glittering wall of power that had formed around her and the children head on, with stunning force.

It didn't yield.

Pearl looked down at me, remote and cold, and her

eyes were the lightless empty of the Void. "You reject what I offer, Cassiel. You offend me."

"Good," I said. It came out raw and bloody, but satisfying. "Kill me, then. If you can."

She walked down a set of invisible steps, as her children parted for her—some of them had already collapsed, their white light guttering out, and the rest were burning like candles in a furnace. All their power was flowing into Pearl, I realized; it was in the unearthly pale glow of her skin. She had embodied it, and the darkness.

If she completed this last, cruel act, she would be more powerful than anything else in this world.

I couldn't break this shell, or the cycle of power that was feeding back on itself inside it. I couldn't save myself, or the children. I couldn't do anything except kneel there, cold and empty, as Pearl glided toward me.

But I could do one simple thing, after all.

I could duck.

The power that lanced out of her erupted in a pure white bolt, heading straight for me; if it touched me, it would burn me to cinders.

But it didn't touch me. I let myself fall backward, anchored by my knees, and Pearl's strike hissed and burned the air an inch above my chest.

It bored straight through her own shell of power, lanced out into the room, slammed into the back wall, and kept going.

And I rolled out through the burned opening of the shell as it began to knit itself closed, sealing Pearl and the children in.

I barely made it over the closing threshold before it irised shut.

The black-and-white sphere containing Pearl and her followers began to rotate now, slowly at first, but growing in speed and strength.

I collapsed gasping on the broken stone floor, and wondered if I had enough strength to battle Esmeralda, who was the only living thing in the room left now outside of the sphere . . . but as I rolled myself over on my back and looked at her, I realized that I needn't have worried.

Esmeralda had felt it, too, that whispering touch of the Mother. Her eyes had gone wide and very dark, and they were filled with blind tears. She was still clutching Rashid's bottle in one shaking hand, but I didn't think she even realized she still had it.

She didn't see me at all.

"She forgives me for what I did," Es said. "I feel it. *I feel it.* I can—I can change—"

And she did, drawing in a deep breath; the thick, muscular coils began to shift, contract, drawing together in a smooth, tapering glide . . . and Esmeralda was *standing.* She looked down at her long, smooth legs, slender feet, and cried out—grief, joy, shock all boiling together. The white shirt she was wearing reached almost to her knees now, and it left her looking younger than before, a child playing at dress-up. I wondered how many years it had been since she'd been herself, been truly and completely *human.*

Just in time to lose everything again.

She blinked and looked down at me. "You don't look so good, lady," she said. "I've seen dead things on beaches with better color."

"Esmeralda," I whispered. "Get out. Go. Find Isabel."

"She doesn't need to find me," Isabel said from the doorway. "I'm right here, Mom." She was still covered in plaster dust, smeared and dirty, but she was alive. And behind her was Luis, bloody but still upright. He ignored Esmeralda, ignored the spinning sphere hovering in the middle of the room, and limped to me.

"We're okay out there now," he said. "Lots of sleeping kids. Djinn are holding the power bubble over us." He collapsed down on the floor next to me, and pulled me into his arms. "God, you're cold, Cass."

I couldn't tell him I was dying, but it was true; the darkness that I'd been infected with was eating away, steadily and quietly killing me. It was a kind of virus, I decided; as it fed on me, it reproduced. Soon, I'd be a vessel for it, like Pearl's Void children.

And then I'd be unacceptably dangerous.

I'd failed on every level. Luis, Isabel, even Esmeralda . . . *they* had succeeded. But I hadn't stopped Pearl. I hadn't even slowed her. All my power, all my history, and it had come to this.

To nothing.

Ashan was dead now; whatever plan he'd foreseen for me, it had been false, or it had died along with him. My failure would cancel out all of the great victories won by my friends, my family, by *humanity*, because I had not been strong enough, fast enough, Djinn enough.

I was doing worse than killing humanity. I was killing the Mother herself, through my failure.

But I could do one last thing right.

I could stop my transformation into the dark angel that Pearl wanted me to become.

I pulled free of Luis and touched his face very gently. "I love you," I said. It was a good-bye, and he knew it; I saw the shock ripple through him, and the awful resignation in the rigidity of his muscles. "I'm sorry."

"Don't do this," he said. "Whatever you're thinking, don't."

"Mom?" Isabel took a halting step toward us, then stopped. "Mom, what are you doing?"

"What I have to do." I said it gently but firmly. "We always knew it would come to an ending, didn't we?"

She shook her head. "No. I don't believe in endings. I'm not going to let you—"

Her eyes rolled back in her head, and she collapsed back into Luis's arms. He'd given her just a touch, a gentle push into the darkness, and now he held her gently in his arms and kissed her forehead. He wasn't looking at me any longer. "She's going to win, then," he said. "You can't stop her."

The room was lurid with the cream-and-black of the sphere, now spinning fast, whipping between black and white so fast that it blurred into a smear of gray. The power in the room was like needles in my skin, a burning, stinging rush.

"No," I said. "I can't." She was, I sensed, almost there, almost ready to unleash all that power into the heart of the world.

Almost ready to kill the very soul of our Mother.

And here, at the end, filled with a growing darkness, I felt an unexpected sense of . . . peace. Of quiet inside me, and in that silence, I heard a voice speak.

Make the choice.

Ashan's voice, an echo of his imperious tone. He might be gone from the world, but he was still demanding things of me.

I opened my eyes and said, "Esmeralda. I need your help."

Chapter 13

"I CAN'T DO THIS," Es said. She was scared—very scared, in fact, uncertain in her newfound humanity. "I don't know how anymore."

"You can," I told her. The darkness inside me was reaching critical stages. Only a moment had passed—a moment that had been taken up by the difficult task of getting Luis to withdraw, with Isabel, to a safe distance, because I couldn't guarantee what would happen next. "Your venom killed a Djinn. It'll certainly kill me. And I need to destroy this body, Esmeralda. I can't leave it, otherwise."

"But I just got *out* of being a snake," she said. "What if I can't shift back again?"

"You will," I promised her, and took her hands in mine. "Or it won't matter."

"Wow, you are such a cheerleader."

I smiled. "It's been interesting knowing you, Esmeralda."

"Likewise." She sighed, shook her head, and reached for the Warden powers she'd been so long denied.

And she shifted back into Snake Girl.

When she opened her eyes, they were reptilian, vertically slitted, veined with red and gold . . . and then she opened her mouth, unhinged her jaw, and the sharp, gleaming daggers of fangs descended and locked in place as she struck in a blur.

Esmeralda's fangs sank into my neck and shoulder, piercing skin, muscle, bone. Her venom burned like acid as she injected it.

I heard Luis shout—a wordless denial, a rejection of what I was doing, but he didn't try to stop it. He understood that it wasn't possible now.

I'm so sorry, I thought. The venom was fast, and fatal, and I felt my blood thicken in my veins. Two beats of my heart. Three. *I have loved you all, in my own way. And you are worthy of more than I can give.*

My heart tripped, faltered, and gave one last spasmodic pulse before going utterly, finally, completely still.

It hurt. Death hurt.

Ah, I heard a warm, gentle voice say. *You've chosen. That is good. You have been missed.*

It might have been the Mother, or my imagination, or the ghost of Ashan in my dying, fragile human mind.

Equally, it might have been the still, quiet voice of God echoing within me.

I exploded like a star out of my body, shed it like a burst chrysalis, and I wasn't blackened by the Void. I wasn't Pearl's creature.

I was *Cassiel,* immortal, born of lava and stars, and the Void choked and fell in on itself inside the shell I'd cast off. I was on the aetheric plane now, looking down with the remote interest of a scientist observing laboratory mice. It was hard to believe that the flesh cooling on the floor had encased me, only a few seconds before;

shedding humanity had been astonishingly easy, for all that I'd agonized over it.

The freedom, the power, the *life* was all around me now, coursing like blood, pulsing, intoxicating. Humanity struggled and sweated on the ground, but Djinn rode the currents of the world like eagles. So easy to forget them. To allow it all to slide away in the clean, healing stream.

You have only a moment now. The whisper came in cold, perfect clarity to me, a disturbance of light and shadow, pulse and ebb. It was not a voice, but on the aetheric, it could make itself understood.

The body slithered free of Esmeralda's coils to fall lifelessly on the cracked concrete. Dead, my mortal flesh looked pallid, blue-white, my green eyes shallow as glass. My lips were parted, as if I had something to tell the world, but that secret would never be uttered.

Esmeralda shrank back into her human form, shivering and fragile, and wiped my blood from her mouth with trembling hands. "I didn't want to," she murmured, and sank down on her knees next to me. "I didn't want to do that. *Why did you make me do that?*"

Luis carried Isabel back over. She was stirring now, murmuring drowsily in his arms; he put her gently on the ground and took up my failed human body instead, rocking it gently back and forth in the pulsing, inhuman light of Pearl's sphere . . .

. . . Which flared into a sudden, glaring, blinding burst, and exploded into starlight and suns, a universe being born and instantly dying, and out of it walked . . .

. . . A goddess.

In the human world, she was a glowing, brilliant creature, gilded in darkness; Luis shielded his eyes and tried to squint between his fingers to see her as she walked toward them, my misfit human family.

He let my body slip back to the ground, and stood up to face her.

Pearl was a vortex of energy here on the aetheric, drawing in currents and creating a lazily spinning wheel on which I drifted. She was opening a portal here, one that stretched through every level of the world, all the way down to the dark, hidden heart of the Mother herself.

As she was walking toward Luis, terrifying and majestic as the storm she had created, he didn't flinch. Didn't hesitate.

He attacked.

I felt the violence from where I stood, such a distant and remote observer; he called fire from the liquid center of the earth, focused its power through the lens of his own soul, and threw it on her like a burning blanket.

It simply slid away and left her untouched. She didn't so much as falter in her steady progress toward him.

Well? said a calm, quiet voice, echoing through the aetheric. *Are you just going to let him die for nothing? Or are you going to do what Ashan asked of you in the beginning?*

Venna? I whispered. I felt the echo through the world, here and not here. Her presence spread everywhere . . . but it was tainted, twisted, not entirely as it should have been. It was turning fragile and thin with every pulse of power.

I can't stay with you long, she responded. *I'm too damaged, but until there is a new conduit I will have to serve; Ashan chose me, even though I didn't want the responsibility. He knew what must be done, long ago. You must finish it, now, before it's too late. The Mother's heart is opened. She is listening. She is vulnerable. It's up to you to protect her now.*

I felt the aetheric . . . stop. The entire world, all of its levels and planes and complicated, clockwork parts, *stopped*. All the Djinn, all the Wardens, all the humans. Animals. Plants. Insects.

Everything living *stopped*, caught in a moment of utter, shining awareness as the Mother opened her eyes and looked on it with full, conscious intent. It was beautiful, and terrifying. Angels would hide their faces under that merciless, merciful gaze; humans went silent and still. I was aware that even Pearl, with her merciless progress toward my family, had halted, just for a moment.

I could see the Mother's consciousness flowing into the brilliant vessel of her Earth Oracle, not so far away from where my old physical body lay broken. She was distilling herself into one form, so that she could hear and speak to the representative of the human race. To Lewis Orwell.

While in that form, she was as vulnerable as she would ever be.

Pearl's shining, slick form appeared now on the aetheric, and was echoed on all the levels above and below. She was ripping through reality, heading for the Mother, and when she reached her . . .

. . . She would kill her.

Now, Venna whispered. *It must be now. I can't . . .* She, too, was losing power. The Djinn were failing, as the aetheric ripped apart in a disrupted chaos around Pearl; she was damaging the link between the Mother and her children, obscuring the flow of power.

They would die soon. So would I—I was now Djinn, one of them, and I could feel my own connection to the lifeblood of the planet beginning to choke off, dry up. A Djinn couldn't last for long without it. Humans could last longer, but they'd go mad, and they wouldn't even understand why they were ripping each other to pieces.

Storms would rage, before an unnatural silence fell. Everything, everything, would fail.

Ashan had known it would come to this, and he'd known that I could make the choice. By teaching me about them, about humans, by making me *become* one, he'd connected me in ways that I'd never have been able to know in my original, uncorrupted form.

The seeds of humanity remained within me, even now. I'd never be rid of them ... and I didn't want to be rid of them. Luis was within me, and Isabel. Manny and Angela. The brave Wardens dying; the courage of humans who had no reason to risk themselves for others.

Infinite beauty and tragedy. Humanity was flawed, and angry, and cruel; it was beautiful, and creative, and kind. It had spread over every corner of the world, and where it tread, things were never the same. The aetheric was scarred by them, and yet it was also made richer and deeper by what they felt, loved, made.

No other species had ever done these things, *created* these things.

And they were worth saving. All of it, worth saving.

You have to do it. Venna's last, faint whisper, a prayer from the soul of the dying Djinn as Pearl used the cutting, burning power of the human race, all their fear and hatred, lensed through the children she'd made so diamond-hard, to strike at the beating, living heart of the world.

And she was right. Ashan was right. I had been wrong, always.

I was Djinn. I was ancient, and ruthless, and powerful, and even now, with the world darkening around me, with the aetheric beginning to shatter and crumble into dust, I had one great and singular talent. I could kill better than any other being who had ever existed, throughout creation.

And now, I had to use that skill. Pearl's power came from humanity, from the souls of all of those packed into this busy world—six billion and more, each holding a spark, a connection, that when connected was a source of astonishing power. Only Pearl had ever tapped into it.

And now that source had to be cut off.

I gathered them up. *Every* human life, *every* boy or girl drawing their first, fragile breath, *every* old man and woman drawing their last. *Every* heart, *every* soul, no matter how good, no matter how evil.

Every Warden, as well.

I could hold them all in my hands, all the billions of precious, fragile lives. All the stories and histories and potentials.

And I could end them.

I felt Pearl turn her startled attention toward me as I rose on bright, burning wings, with all of humanity held in my hands.

You can't, she said, her words written in crystal on the aetheric as it began to burn. *You love them too much now.*

I did love them; I honestly did. Ashan had given me that gift, though whether he'd meant it as a gift or a curse was a mystery. He'd wanted me to learn something; I had, but I wasn't sure if it was the same lesson he'd meant.

But what I learned gave me the strength, the compassion, to do what had to be done.

I killed them.

Every heart, stopped.

Every breath, taken.

Every scrap of life, drawn into my own aetheric form, saved and protected.

No Djinn was made for this, not even me; I was a killer, not a protector, but I couldn't let the tiny sparks of their souls go out. Their bodies fell. . . . Luis, collapsing on the floor, entirely gone. Isabel. Esmeralda. Beyond, a roomful of Wardens snuffed out on a single breath. Cities full of bodies falling. Countries. Continents.

Not one single human breathed on earth, for the space of a full minute.

And Pearl's power supply failed.

She didn't realize what had happened for a wild second; she cast about for energy, failed to find it, and was immediately forced to break off her attack; the energy she'd siphoned from those doomed children had been meant to fuel a war, not her own life, but she no longer had a choice. Every second that passed ripped more away from her, because without that connection through humanity, she had nothing.

She *was* nothing.

The Mother was safe now, and the aetheric began to stabilize, though vast pieces of it had been burnt black; it would take years, maybe centuries, to heal the damage that had been done in only moments.

Pearl hung on, grimly, pouring power into her own existence, but it was like pouring water into a hurricane. She couldn't hold.

I watched as pieces of her ripped away, flying into the Void she'd created; she was no longer a glossy, freshly born goddess, but a crippled and blackened *thing* that fought to back away from the blackest, most starless void.

She ripped at the aetheric, trying to find something, anything to hold herself in life, but there was nothing for her now, no human to clutch and drain.

Death came for her in a silent rush, but she was not quite finished yet; Pearl sensed my presence hovering near her on the aetheric, and she turned on me, howling her defiance.

Grappling with me, on the edge of the Void.

We fell together toward the end of all things, and I felt her last, hot burst of triumph. *I made you kill them,* she said, and it was like all the evil in the world shrieking its last, hot breath into me. *I made you fall.*

I'm not falling, I told her, and came free with a sudden, flashing beat of silver wings that broke her into tiny flakes of ash and smoke, screams and despair.

She was a nightmare that humanity had dreamed, and now she disappeared into the Void.

I beat my wings and fought my way back up, away from the black pull of death, to the last whispers of light at the very top of the world.

The Void closed.

Pearl was gone with it.

The Djinn were silent now, amid the countless human dead, staring up at me. I had just murdered an entire race. The Mother was safe, but the agony of what I'd done would echo forever. Nothing would be the same. Nothing would be saved, not of the race that I'd come to love and cherish. Their cities and histories would fall into ruin, into silence, into dust. Not even their whispers would remain.

Unless I righted the balance.

I couldn't do it alone, and wordlessly, I sent out a call.

I felt them coming to me, on the aetheric—all my brothers and sisters, True Djinn and New, powerless and powerful. Some were bound in nets of glowing thread—those enslaved to bottles. Some were free, and wild with power.

One drifted close to me, and I recognized the tense, restless boil of blue-black energy within the netted cage that bound him. *Save yourself,* Rashid said. *Don't do this.*

But it had been Ashan's plan all along, and I was, finally, at peace with it. Ashan was gone, but the conduit remained.... Venna, though frail and broken, stood ready, and I reached out to her on one side, and to the caged, brilliant coppery flare that was David on the other. Together, they were halves of a whole, a key to the heart of the Mother.

Down in the human world, only a moment had passed. Long enough.

I let go of all that I had drawn in, all that I'd taken from those lifeless human forms. All the energy. All the breaths. All the heartbeats. But there is no perfect transfer of energy; there is always loss, both going and coming.

I'd known from the beginning that not all those I'd taken could, or would, come back. I had no control of that, or choice. Some hearts restarted. Some breaths were taken. For many, the seconds that had just passed went unnoticed, except as a nightmare.

I gave everything I had to make them live. Everything. Every last drop of power and energy that made me what I was, flowing out through Venna and David. When I had no more, I let go.

I had done what I'd been fated to do, and I was content with that. My light was going out of the world.

And then ... something touched me. Something huge, gentle, kind ... and wise. Not the Mother. Something beyond, as great in proportion to her as humans were to the tiniest insects.

I had been touched by something divine, and as the last of the Djinn Cassiel passed away ...

... My consciousness flowed back into flesh that I'd left behind.

Outcast, again, but this time, by my own choice.

Unfortunately for me, that meant that I had fallen back into a body that wasn't just drained of life, but *dying*. I had one breath left, maybe two, and a single heartbeat left before Esmeralda's very effective venom destroyed it beyond all repair.

"No!"

That was Isabel's raw scream in my ears.

My eyes were still open, but now I blinked away a film and focused on the girl's sweaty, white-streaked face. She was shaking and gasping, but she put her hands on my chest and drove healing power into me, warm and rich and golden, a flood of peace that quickly turned toxic as it battled the intense venom Esmeralda had injected. The damage was grave, and Isabel fought for me, fought so hard that the pain that came with it was something I could only accept, and embrace. My blood burned. My nerves fried under the stress. Organs pulsed and wept poison. Muscles ripped and re-formed. Bone knitted.

But even so, she couldn't save me. Not alone. But she wasn't alone, because she had a bottle in her hand, and the cork was lying discarded six feet away, and Rashid was kneeling beside us now, indigo face sharp and intense, eyes like burning glass as he cleaned the toxins from my blood and flesh, wiping it away as it burned its way out of my skin and through clothing.

It hurt, living. It hurt so much. And again, it wasn't enough. Rashid couldn't save me. Isabel couldn't save me.

And that was all right. I hadn't intended to survive, although it would have been good to see Luis one more time. Pearl had been right. I belonged with her, in the dark.

I was still fighting, weakly, to survive when the world shattered around us, and re-formed, as the Mother found her perfect match—a conduit of power who held the awareness of a Djinn and the compassion of humanity.

The human Lewis Orwell had died in her arms, and her intense love had transformed him in her embrace into something astonishing, bright, perfect. . . .

A Djinn. A brand-new Djinn.

Welcome, brother, I whispered to him on the aetheric, and the new creature that had once been Lewis stepped out of the mists and into the world for the first time, and brushed his fingers lightly over my brow.

"You do get yourself into trouble," he said, and his smile was all human, all Lewis. "There. That's fixed, Cass. Try not to break this body quite so much. It's all you've got left."

He faded out again in a white flutter of power—gone and not gone, not ever gone. He was the new gravity, the center of the Djinn world. Venna hadn't been able to hold for long, and David, I knew, had never wished to be a conduit; now neither of them had to bear that burden. It was Lewis, only Lewis, and no one had ever been better suited.

I drew in a deep, slow, lovely breath, and Rashid sat back on his heels, staring after the newly made Djinn. "Well," he said. "That's something you don't see every day." He looked down at me, and his smile was sad, and fierce, and a little angry. "I once asked you for your first-born. Do you remember that?"

I did, though I didn't feel the need to speak. He could see it in my eyes.

"I'll be back when it's time to fulfill that bargain. As much as your human loves you, I don't expect it will be very long."

He misted away before I could tell him that I'd kill him before he took a child of mine. That would, it seemed, be an argument for another day.

Isabel threw herself across me, still shaking, and I hugged her back, hard. I smoothed her hair, just as I had when she was such a small child, and she said, "Cassie, please stay. Please."

"I will," I whispered, and my eyes filled with human,

burning, perfect tears. "I will." There was something odd about my left arm and hand. I raised it and stared at it, not realizing for a moment what it was . . . and then I felt the pulse of blood in my fingers, and laughed out loud.

Whether it was a gift of the Mother, or something Lewis had left me, my metal arm was gone. . . . It was, in fact, a melted heap of bronze on the floor next to me.

My arm was flesh. Perfect, and unmarked.

I looked beyond my arm, and saw Luis holding Esmeralda in his arms. He looked up at me and shook his head.

She hadn't made it back. One of the many I'd taken, and lost.

My burden. My great and terrible guilt I would carry for the rest of my human days.

He gently lowered her to the floor and walked over to me. One effortless pull got me to my feet and into his arms, pressed hot against his body as he held me close, so close. He sighed and rested his head against mine for a moment before finding my lips with his in a bright, burning kiss.

"Something's different," he said.

Well, yes. The storm outside was breaking apart now; the black was fading on the aetheric, replaced by a still, soft pearl gray shot through with glittering, translucent colors. Everything was different. *Everything*.

But he wasn't talking about all that. He was talking about me, and as I considered it, I realized that I was no longer bound to him. No longer drawing life and power out of him.

I had it inside me, a fierce and glowing tide that stretched invisible roots down into the earth.

I was alive. I was a Warden, a real and genuine Warden, with power of my own.

"Yes," I said aloud. Even my voice felt different in my

mouth—stronger, more assured. *My* voice. *My* body. *My* life, to live and lose. The clock of the world was ticking in me, and it felt ... astonishingly good. "I'm human."

And he smiled a little, one side endearingly just a tiny bit higher than the other, and kissed me again, very softly. "You've always been human," he said. "You're just really, really committed to it now."

"And to you," I said. I put my arm around Isabel and pulled her close. "To you both."

And to the world that we faced now, damaged and hurting, but hopeful.

Ready to be reborn.

Unbroken.

TRACK LIST

I'm pleased to offer you an excellent soundtrack for this last installment of the Outcast Season series; I think these songs and artists offered some real insight and excitement to the story, and I hope you enjoy them, too. Please remember that these musicians deserve your financial support, and buy their music.

"All American Nightmare"	Hinder
"Hurricanes and Suns"	Tokio Hotel
"Here Comes the End"	The Raveonettes
"Fight the Power, Pts. 1 and 2"	The Isley Brothers
"Gone"	Jessica Riddle
"The Fire"	Rev Theory
"Rolling in the Deep"	ADELE
"Set Fire to the Rain"	ADELE
"Secret"	Missy Higgins
"Scare Me to Death"	Joe Henry
"Pins & Needles"	Opshop
"We Cry"	The Script
"Fall for Anything"	The Script
"Rusty Halo"	The Script
"Walk Away"	The Script
"Dead Man Walking"	The Script
"Medicate"	AFI
"Rise Above 1 (feat. Bono and The Edge)	Reeve Carney
"Keep the Streets Empty for Me"	Fever Ray
"Diables"	Cirque du Soleil
"You Did (Bomp Shooby Dooby Bomp)"	Chuck Prophet
"Living in a Dream"	Finger Eleven

RACHEL CAINE

THE OUTCAST SEASON NOVELS

Undone

Once she was Cassiel, a Djinn of limitless power. Now, she has been reshaped in human flesh as punishment for defying her master—and must live among the Weather Wardens, whose power she must tap into regularly or she will die. And as she copes with the emotions and frailties of her human condition, a malevolent entity threatens her new existence...

Unknown

Living among mortals, Cassiel has developed a reluctant affection for them—especially for Warden Luis Rocha. As the mystery deepens around the kidnapping of innocent Warden children, Cassiel and Luis are the only ones who can investigate both the human and djinn realms. But the trail will lead them to a traitor who may be more powerful than they can handle.

Unseen

After Cassiel and Luis Rocha rescue an adept child from a maniacal Djinn, they realize that the girl is already manifesting an incredible amount of power—and her kidnapping was not an isolated incident. This Djinn is capturing children all over the world and indoctrinating them so she can use their strength. If Cassiel cannot stop her, all of humanity may be destroyed.

Available wherever books are sold or at penguin.com